THE HIGHLAND RAVEN

BOOK #5

A RESISTANCE GIRL NOVEL

HANNAH BYRON

ISBN eBook: 978-90-832156-5-5
ISBN Paperback: 978-90-832156-4-8
Book Cover Design by Ebooklaunch
Editor: Michele Chiappetta of Two Bird Author Services
Website: Hannah Byron

"The wound is the place where the Light enters you."

~ Rumi ~

1

ALL THE RAIN IN THE WORLD

Alnor Castle, Scotland, January 1938

Brittle, raw sleet pelted the leaded windows of the library in the east wing of Alnor Castle. The twists of storm and deluge caused the delicate, colored glass to creak in its leaden panels, shooting an icy draft along the floorboards of the spacious, book-filled room. Three open fires that roared like the devil still could not produce a favorable temperature in the high-ceilinged Victorian chamber.

Even though it was merely three o'clock in the afternoon, the lamps had been lit above the reading table to keep the gloomy weather out. The art déco lampshades with their zigzags in ruby red and sapphire blue cast a flirtatious shimmer on the oak table below but provided little light. Still, fire and lamps established a veneer of coziness.

The rainstorm shielded the normally stunning view of Loch Fyne with its emerald water, arched shoreline and the Arrochar Alps across the loch. None of the familiar sights were visible today, but even if they had been, it would've made no difference to nineteen-year-old Lady Sable Montgomery, who was sitting at the table.

Huddled deep into her mink coat, both for warmth and comfort, she had almost completely disappeared.

Two slender fingers with tapered coral nails were clasping a gold-inlaid fountain pen. Prominently at the top of the cream sheet of paper, Sable had jotted in strong letters.

Herr Von Henkell.

Her pen hovered over these three words and with an angry scratch, the 'Herr' was crossed out.

Shifting in her chair, she tried to stifle the uncontrolled clattering of her teeth, while wild shudders shook her thin frame. Because of the tearing discomfort in her abdomen, she kept crossing and uncrossing her legs. The delicate jaw, half-covered under a mass of silken black hair, was clenched, but her cornflower-blue eyes were dry, even though red-rimmed.

She paused for a moment. Hesitated, steadying her hand. Then the words jumped from her Parker of their own accord criss-cross over the pad, like an illustration of poorly drawn grasses, showing neither rhyme nor reason.

Dreckig.

I hate you all.

No right.

Swine.

Burn in Hell

Dirty Paws.

It was MY ba...

She ripped the page from the writing block and crumpled it into a ball that landed with a precise arc into the fire. Sable got up from the table with such animosity that the antique chair toppled on its back. She dealt it another kick as she marched to the fogged-up window.

"No!" she hissed, pressing her heated forehead against the cool glass. "You'll not force me into submission. Not now. Not ever. I detest the lot of you, and it's me that soon will be gone while you all rot in hell!"

But how? Sable felt the dry palms of panic tighten around her neck. How was she, at nineteen, going to break free from here?

Without her allowance? Not even her charming features and fashionable dowry would help her out of this pickle. A fallen woman!

Even relying on Freddie Frinton-Smith, her oldest and best friend, who—before the Sable scandal—would've done everything for her, couldn't be counted on. Marrying Freddie had once seemed an option that had crossed Sable's mind in her darkest hours, but who would want to wed a girl like her now? Maybe only because his father's estate was facing extinction and the Montgomery money would be like lavish water on a withering plant. Sable the trophy?

"No!" she repeated firmly. "I'm not marrying Freddo; I'm not marrying anyone. I'll stay at Alnor until Dadaigh comes home. He'll supply me the money. He'll have to. Then I'll leave for good."

"No man will marry you after this, Sable Montgomery. And don't you come crawling back to me! I did everything you can ask from a mother to get you sorted." Sable cocked her head, her voice affected and high-pitched, mimicking her mother. Oh, that stab-in-the-back she-devil. That was all her mother was. Spilling her entire arsenal of sick tricks on her daughter.

As if the evil spirit came to descend on her, Sable heard that high-pitched voice coming in the corridor toward her, apparently in the company of that sneaky maid servant.

"Nellie, I told you *so* not to let Sable escape from her room! I cannot monitor the wench in this outback part of Alnor. It's way too spooky here. Why did you let her go?"

Sable leaped from her place at the window and resolutely bolted the library door, on which her mother started banging seconds later.

"Sable, for God's sake, what are you doing here? Let me in! Let me in!" The doorknob rattled, followed by more banging.

Sable held her breath, not moving one muscle. Her ears on high alert, her pupils wide. She said nothing while the banging went on. Then some swearwords and something that sounded like a slap. A yelp from Nellie.

"Sable, open the damn door! You're not your father hiding in here as a coward."

The anger in her mother's voice rang through her shaking body, but the heavy oak door between her and her fuming parent gave some sort of security.

Be still; she'll go away. Her party is starting at five! She'll need all her time to doll herself up for her Germans.

The banging subsided, and the voice changed to a throaty pleading, "Sable, dear, you're unwell. Let your mother in. She'll look after you!"

Not in a thousand years! I want Dadaigh!

When that tactic didn't work, the threatening came back. "You make sure you're at the dinner table at eight, dressed and acting normal. Or I'll tell the steward, Donald Stacey, to break down this wretched door."

Sable stayed still as a cat in a gutter, but the fear was gone. She'd won. For now. With a lot more grumbling and swearing, her mother's voice disappeared into the castle's bowels.

After the initial breath of relief, the fear crept back in. Her mother would return, of that Sable was sure, and she wouldn't accept a locked door twice. This temporary withdrawal had more to do with Misty Fletcher's waiting sequin evening dress than with the acceptance of her daughter's victory.

I need a plan. And I need it fast.

Sauntering back to the window, Sable peered outside but the first dusk was now mingling with the rain, and she could only see the vague contours of the holly bushes just outside the window. Frowning, she drew a heart with her index finger on the damp glass, a smaller heart inside. *Isabe...* Then hastily wiped it out with her palm.

"No!"

This wasn't just a 'no' to her mother. This third 'no' she exclaimed to herself was a loud and clear 'no' to her past, to this life, to Alnor and its ghosts.

Turning her back to the window and leaning against the windowsill, Sable scanned her father's library in the dying light of the winter afternoon. Apart from the crackling of the fire and the sleet that beat the windows like popping corn in a pan, the room was quiet, far away from the bustle of the grand kitchen and the dining room where preparations for her mother's cocktail party would be in full swing.

If Sable strained her ears, she could hear the vague scraping of chairs over the age-old parquet floor and the distant strumming of instruments of some jazzy ensemble that was Misty Fletcher's latest craze. Flown in all the way from London's West End just to amuse her and her cronies. The bill, no doubt, sent to her ex-husband, the Baron of Alnor.

Sable rejoiced in the silence that reigned in this wing of her father's castle and now fully understood why he fled to this room as often as he could. Hushed in a deep silence, the place felt as she'd strayed into Sleeping Beauty's realm, where all the inhabitants were comatose.

"If only," she grimaced, "if only I had the power to make them sleep eternally. All of them. In the entire castle and beyond. That would be their due punishment."

Her father's bookcases ran along three walls, many of the volumes dating back to the 18th century, thick brown leather volumes silently collecting dust and must as they filled the cases from floor to ceiling. In between the bookcases, the sad deer heads with dead eyes spread their antlers to the stucco ceiling. This was so Dadaigh.

"As dead to the life I once lived as if the Styx rolled between it and me." She recited Edward Bulwer-Lytton, her father's favorite author. How he would wander this room reading Bulwer aloud. She hadn't understood him then. Still didn't. Her aloof, evasive Dadaigh. How had they both got so entangled in Misty Fletcher's claws? The dead deer had no answer. Nobody had.

But now that Dadaigh had fled to his London house, or perhaps even to the Continent, nobody entered this book haven anymore, apart from perhaps the occasional housemaid with a quick sweep of her duster here and there. Though every corner breathed Earl Archibald Montgomery, 6th Baron of Alnor, his permanent absence even added to the bottled-up silence.

Then how on earth had she, Sable, landed here? She'd sought solace after the cold hard hospital, after the heart-breaking separation between her and her ba... *No, not that!* She'd sought solace in her father's spirit here in his treasured bibliotheca, the cornerstone of his ancestors' literary collection.

He'd been so proud of this rich inheritance. Once upon a time. High-brow Dadaigh, who—if he didn't have to play the social part of diplomat—lived for books and hunting parties. *But where was he now?*

Dadaigh. Talcum, tweed, and tobacco. She could smell his scent to this day. Her small hand in his, lying side by side on a knoll of grass, stalking the gigantic stag Dadaigh called Christopher. The same deer that now stared down at her from between Bulwer's drab volumes with heavy-lidded dead eyes.

Poor Christopher, poor Dadaigh, poor Sable.

They seemed all three to be bobbing together in Charon's boat on the Styx River, sailing straight into the underworld. But then Sable shook herself from her morbid thoughts and clenched her fists.

Even her father had let her down, knowing darn well he shouldn't have left his vulnerable daughter in the care of that selfish, heartless woman. Knowing she would be ruined by her, just like flapper girl Misty Fletcher had ruined him twenty years earlier. Still that niggling doubt. Could he have saved her from her mother's machinations? Would he if he'd known the truth of what was happening at Alnor?

No!

Nobody cared for Sable, not even Dadaigh.

From one moment to the next, the library suffocated her.

"SABLE, PLEASE OPEN THE DOOR."

Nellie's docile voice sounded from the other side of the bolted door. Not more than a whisper. Then a soft knock and again, "Sable?"

Her hackles were raised. Though the door was locked, she spied around her, ready to slip behind the velvet curtains and pretend she wasn't there.

She would not open the door. It certainly was a trap! But her body failed her, as transfixed and frozen as her mind, she walked to the door and with dead fingers unbolted it. God only knew why.

"Oh, there you are. What on earth are you doing in here, my dear? It's freezing and your mother is asking for you." Nellie, silver strands in her once frisky, blond hair, her small eyes fluttering both guilty and innocent, looked up at the young lady, nervously rubbing the palms of her hands on her navy, silk skirt.

Sable stared at the maid, hard, not moving one muscle while the blue eyes flashed. *How dare you! Dash it! You know my mother was here a few minutes ago!*

The wimpy maid, one of her mother's latest useless additions, cast her colorless eyes to the floor. "Will you come, Lady Sable? It would cause so much less trouble."

A cynical snigger escaped Sable's mouth. *Causing less trouble.* The phrase alone. She could picture her mother uttering the honey-coated words to her maid. *Tell her that.* Or...? Always threatening everyone around her with those stony eyes that glittered like hard gemstones while the voluptuous, painted mouth curled in an endearing smile. Sable knew no one as cloak-and-dagger as her mother.

"No! I want my tea here. I actually want a bed made up here in the library for tonight. Tell Butler Simms to bring the foldable bed down, along with my bedding. You can bring my nightwear. And don't you dare send the steward here, as mother suggested."

The light-gray eyes flashed quickly up before going down to the carpet again at the sight of the coral-tapered finger pointing at her like a loaded gun.

"You can't, Lady Sable, it's unheard-of." The maid's voice was a nervy whisper.

"What happened in this damned place is what's unheard-of, Nellie. Now, do as you're told. I'm waiting for my father to return."

"Yes, Ma'am. At what time would you like your tea, Ma'am?"

Irritated by the maid's 'ma'am-ing,' Sable sneered. "Now! And make sure no one disturbs me here until I've spoken with my father."

"But Lord Archibald might be held up in London. It may be days before he returns." The guilt in the maid's voice made Sable cringe, and she felt the blood rise to the roots of her hair. She breathed in and out, trying to calm herself. Nellie had only been sent here to smooth ruffled feathers and would likely be sent packing by the whimsical Lady of the house if she failed in her mission to get a grip on the obstinate daughter. The maid looked so miserable on her spot on the Persian carpet that Sable strode over to the table, grabbed her pen, and scribbled across the pad.

"Mother, it is my express will to stay in the library until Father returns. Nellie is not to blame. I don't want to see you *or anyone else! Sable."*

Tearing the sheet from the pad, she folded it in four and handed it to the help, who was already shrinking away. "You don't deserve this favor from me, Nellie, but I hope it'll cover your spineless back."

"Thank you, Ma'am."

"Out!" The coral fingertip flashed once again in the maid's direction. Nellie backed out in a hurry, her soft-soled shoes soundless as a burglar's.

Sable turned to the window, her shoulders sagging, a tremendous sadness enveloping her soul. Jamming her fists in the pockets of the mink coat, she stood, realizing she'd always been alone but never so much as now. The hole in her body was larger than life. Her womb was a scar that burned over the curse.

She felt beaten, backstabbed, bastardized.

2

FREDDO

Sleep came in fits but gave no respite. Sable didn't know if lying awake on the uncomfortable bed with the slats pressing into her back was better than the brief intervals of unconsciousness. She'd promised herself no more crying, but in the night, in that unfamiliar library with the wind howling around the west corner of the Scottish highland castle, the memories pressed upon her as grain is crushed by millstones.

She'd long lain awake hoping to hear the familiar screeching of the Rolls Royce's tires on the gravel, a sign Dadaigh had answered her cry for help. Being able to pick up his arrival had been Sable's other reason to choose this outpost of the castle, but after midnight the reality was all too clear—he hadn't come for her.

A dozen outrageous plans flitted through Sable's restless mind, from a tour through the outback of Australia, to studying art in New York. Anything to get away from England and Scotland, from Mother and Von Henkell. But Sable cared little for adventure trips and even less for creating art. She knew it was naïve, but she'd never considered her future in any serious way.

Well, it isn't easy to know what you crave when you're dragged from one boarding school to the next, spending your holidays with parents whose only engagement is being at each other's throats and not being endowed with any special skills yourself, she realized, not without self-deprecation.

High time to change. But what did she want to do? In all honesty, she didn't want to do anything. If there had been a Sleeping Beauty pill that took her out of this world until everything was nice and normal again, she'd gobble it up without a second thought.

As the gray morning brought a fresh dose of sleet and shallow light, Sable finally fell asleep—the dreamless, deep state of oblivion she'd begged for. When she woke, it was in a confused, blurry state, her eyes still closed when there was a rap on the door.

"Dadaigh?"

"No, it's me, Freddo. Can I come in? Are you decent? Why's the door locked?"

"Freddo? What are you doing here at this ghastly hour? And who told you I'm here?" Sable shot up, wildly grabbing around her on the bedclothes to locate her dressing gown she'd spread out over herself for warmth. Inwardly, she rejoiced to hear her friend's voice.

"Ghastly hour, Sab? It's eleven o'clock. Have you been partying again?"

"No, I haven't." She quickly rushed out of bed to unbolt the door. Then she installed herself on the uncomfortable bed, stuffed some cushions behind her back. While rubbing the long black locks from her sleepy eyes, she announced, "You may come in now."

The first thing she noticed was his backside, as he kicked open the door with his shoe. On turning around, he grinned widely as he displayed the breakfast tray he was carrying.

"Hello, Sunshine!"

His smile, the slick black hair, the glance in the blue eyes under smooth brows. As always when she saw Freddie after a while, it struck Sable how close she was to him despite their very different lifestyles. Freddie, a free student at Oxford; she, the imprisoned Cinderella at Alnor. Growing up as neighboring children, their lives had been so entwined that Freddie felt almost like a brother, a kindred soul.

Sable frowned, deciding not to give in to the familiarity but to look disturbed by his unannounced appearance.

"What *are* you doing here?"

But Freddie was undisturbed, placing the tray on the table with the same broad smile and coming toward her, plopping down on the bed as if it was the most normal situation in the world to find his childhood friend asleep in the middle of the morning in one of the dampest and most uninhabitable places of Alnor Castle.

"Does it matter? I'm here! I'm here for you. Coffee, tea, a freshly baked bun?"

His good humor and infectious laugh worked to perk her up. The shimmer of a smile lingered on her lips.

"All right, Freddo, maybe I am a little pleased to see another human who isn't around just to rip out my soul. Make it a coffee, to wake up."

"That bad, huh?" The blue gaze rested on her, serious for a moment; then Freddie slipped off the bed and darted to the table.

"You must tell me, Sab, why on earth you're hunkering down in this backwater of the barony. You're getting way too eccentric before even hitting twenty."

Sable watched the slim back, the almost graceful movements as he raised the silver coffeepot and poured the black liquid into the gold-rimmed cup, then buttered a bun for her with his little pinky raised. Too graceful for a man.

The gossip about his Oxford student time, more revolving around fellow students than girls, had reached her ears. Could it be true? Did she need to marry Freddie Frinton-Smith, not just to redeem herself but also to save him from himself?

Sable bit her tongue. She wanted so much to confide in him what her mother had done to her, why she'd been sent away and where to, but could she...? Someone needed to know and if that couldn't be Dadaigh, why not Freddie?

As if he'd guessed her musings, Freddie said in a low voice, "You think you're in a pickle, Sable Montgomery? Well, here's another example of terrible trouble in perfect paradise."

Momentarily forgetting her own misery, she said in a worried voice, "What's wrong, Freddo? You know you can tell me anything. You're the only one who knows about my dire doldrums." Making up alliterations had been a fun game since Sable was in pinafores and Freddie—three years older—in plus fours.

Handing her the cup and saucer and placing the buttered bun in her lap, he sat down, staring at the sleet-covered windows with the look of a punished dog. He seemed to search for words, suppressing deep-seated emotions. Sable wasn't sure what she felt or what was going on as she studied his profile. Was this their call? Should they...?

With a sudden spasm, Freddie raised himself from the pit of his obvious despair to face Sable.

"Is horrible Henkell still here?"

The name sent an involuntary spasm through Sable's body. Reflexively, she put a protective hand over her belly, then stopped herself and frowned. Her brain momentarily could not follow this new train of thought while she was preparing herself to hear what was troubling her friend.

To distract herself from her confusion, her white teeth bit into the bun like nobody's business. With her mouth full, she spat out, "How should I know? I've set up camp here after returning from the clinic. Haven't seen a soul. And what does it matter? Or do you want to kill him for me?" A sarcastic smile flashed in his direction.

Freddie certainly wasn't himself today, as he now took time mincing over her proposition as if it was a real possibility. After a while, he spoke in a clipped voice. "I would, Sab, if that would solve the problem. This specimen is even more detestable than the rest and I hate Germans more by the day. I'd just hoped Von Henkell would've shown the decency to return to his post in London. I think his Benz was on the drive, though. Can't even keep his dirty paws off your Ma."

"Don't worry about Mother," Sable snapped, lighting a cigarette. "She won't let anyone's paws, dirty or clean, touch her unless she wants to." And with a sigh, she added, "Alas, not a skill I seem to have inherited from her."

Freddie ignored her last remark. "I don't know what's wrong with these Germans. Never cared much for the Krauts anyway, but since Hitler is whipping them into a frenzy, all hell has broken loose. I was in Frankfurt with David only last week and..." He stopped abruptly, rubbed a weary hand over his forehead, then added in an overly chirpy voice, "More coffee, perhaps?"

"For Pete's sake, Freddo, what's bothering you? You hop from one topic to the other like a restless robin."

Uncertain eyes scanned her face and Sable saw how raw he felt. He looked exactly like the little lost boy he'd been at age ten when his new fishing tackle, a birthday present from his beloved grandfather, was swallowed by the wild current of River Clyde and he stood watching it swirling downstream. That look, lost and guilt-ridden at the same time. "A soul a tad too sensitive for this world," her father would say.

"All right." Freddie surrendered. "I truly came here for you, motored up all the way from Oxford in that draughty two-seater of mine to see how you were doing, Sab, but I am not entirely altruistic. Not doing well myself."

A new silence, followed by a sigh.

"Dad's found out about David and me." A quick glance in Sable's direction, pleading understanding. "So far, it's all been just for fun, a bit of old-boys-together play, but with David... it's different. Serious. Real."

Sable listened intently, her heart swelling with pride that he finally confided in her, though she'd no idea what he was talking about. How could two men be serious about each other? In what way? It sounded like something from a novel. Freddie continued in a morose tone.

"Dad's furious. Fumes he'll disinherit me unless I get engaged to a suitable debutante or—for that matter—any marriageable girl. This year. Or it's game over." Hurt blue eyes sought her help and Sable felt her stomach squeeze tight, a wave of wooziness. *He was asking her without saying so much.* He *was.*

Was she destined to marry Freddie, after all?

"But ... but ..." she stammered, "we don't love each other in that way, Freddo. We're buddies, odd creatures that don't fit in with the rest."

"I know." The voice was almost inaudible. "But you're in a dead spot as well, so maybe we can help each other out."

"It's not that it hasn't been on my mind, Freddo. I just think it wouldn't be fair to either of us."

"Well, we are odd creatures, as you said yourself. We don't need to live like husband and wife. I'd never claim you or tell you what to do or not to do."

"Like a marriage of convenience?"

"Yes, something like that, though I'd totally understand if you wouldn't want to be associated with a man who prefers his own sex."

Sable thought about this for a moment, had to admit the idea of a male couple didn't really appeal to her, but Freddo was Freddo. If this David made him happy, who was she to stand in his way?

She shrugged. "It's all rather sudden. I was thinking of going abroad. Just cut out the past year and start somewhere afresh. Only haven't got an inkling where to go, or what I want to do."

"We could go to Italy, Sab. Live there for a while, though I'm itching to join the RAF and become a pilot. I'd like to throw some bombs on Hitler's Eagle's Nest near Berchtesgaden."

This last remark made Sable burst out in laughter, a high, tingling sound that gurgled up from her throat. "You, a fighter pilot? I still remember you saying the best human action is lying on the soft sofa, listening to Duke Ellington, while snuggling the round bottom of a Johnnie Walker Black Label whisky glass in your hand."

Freddie jumped up from the bed and started pacing the room on his long, slender legs, a deep line furrowing the black eyebrows.

"For once, I'm serious, Sab. Frankfurt and that mess you landed in with that gory Von Henkell have changed me. Your nemesis might be promoted to German ambassador to the United Kingdom while Hitler continues to stir up hate for men like me and David. We're what he calls Untermenschen. Can you believe it? Not just Jews but people from all walks of life, artists, invalids, Romas. The world's turning insane right before our eyes, and we have to nip it in the bud before it's too late."

Freddie's political fervor made him even speak in unbeautified sentences for a change, while he pushed the black mane from his eyes and kept pacing, a cigarette dangling from his well-formed mouth. Sable followed his movements with her eyes in a mixture of adoration and incredulity. Freddy *had* changed, and she wanted to be part of that change. Part of him, part of his excitement for a noble cause, any cause but her own. Freddie's spirit seemed somewhat lifted as he continued.

"If we go through with this wedding thing, I'll see that you're taken care of in a place where you want to be, but after that I will join my university air squadron at RAF Abingdon in Oxfordshire."

Sable waved her arms, spraying a fountain of gray ash from her cigarette over the bedclothes. "All right, all right. Let me process all this for a minute, please. What does David say about your flying craze?"

"We'll go together. He wants what I want. Now get up, Sab, I've got a plan and I think we could pull it off."

"Tell me first." Sable felt wonderfully re-energized by their conversation, seeing a way out of the cold and uninhabitable library where she had barricaded herself, but the plans for their unorthodox wedding were still completely shadowy to her.

"How about we go to Glasgow to escape the parish priests and have our runaway wedding today?"

"Glasgow?" Sable looked shocked. The idea of an 'irregular marriage' without her parents was an end-of-the-line scheme, even to her freethinking mind.

"Why not? We can do it today if we want. Glasgow's about one hundred miles from here. If you get your lazy bum out of bed now and we hop into my two-seater, we'll arrive before two o'clock. Plenty of time to tie the knot."

Sable looked doubtful. "And then? What do we do then?"

"Hang around, get drunk." Freddie's laughter lacked cheer.

"I haven't got a dress."

"Don't be silly, Sab. You've got at least one hundred dresses in your upstairs cupboard."

"I'm not leaving the library." She stiffened, unwilling to move.

"Then ring the bell and ask that weasel of a maid of yours to bring your stuff here. We don't have to tell her what for."

Sable liked the idea of Freddie taking charge, and her mind worked fast. Nellie could pack her a suitcase. She'd tell her she was going to stay with the Frinton-Smiths for a week. There would be no red flags about that. And they could slip out the back door and avoid the main entrance. But then additional problems popped up.

"What if my father comes back for me? I haven't got a dime on me."

"We'll phone your dad as soon as we're married. Don't worry. I still have my allowance. We can live on that for at least a couple of weeks. Until our families get used to the idea, we're a decent married couple." Another cheerless laugh. "Now, is it a yes or a no, my dear? I thought you'd jump at a new Freddo-Sab flimflam like a greedy girl."

Sable was aware of the seriousness underneath the banter, and it was ultimately the agonized merriness—her own exact feeling—that made her cry out. "All right, make me Mrs. Frinton-Smith if you must. I'm quite done with being a Montgomery."

HALF AN HOUR later they were racing down Alnor Avenue in Freddie's Green Morris 8, the beige soft-top rattling, the wind howling, and her white-leather suitcase strapped on top of the trunk with a piece of rope. Cold and warm in the same breath, Sable felt terrified and exhilarated; too ruffled to utter a single word, but hoping she was finally taking life into her own hands.

One last glance at the Gothic towers of Alnor Castle, gray, grim and stony-hearted; the hated black Mercedes in the drive, gleaming in the late morning sun. She could still smell the warm leather of the back seat. It made her retch. She could still hear the shrill voice of her mother from the top steps. "Come back, you ungrateful wench! Come back!" It made her shudder.

Letting herself sway by the moves of the Morris on the curvy highland roads, Sable was sure as her present pain that it would take a long time before she'd set eyes on the place of her youth again.

3

HEADING FOR THE WEDDING BELLS

"Hand me your hip flask, Freddo!"

Before he could even react, Sable had her hand in his coat pocket, rumbling for the metal whiskey container she knew the son of the whiskey distiller always carried with him. The jerk on his coat was so sudden that the car swerved, with Freddie almost losing control over the wheel.

"Hell, Sab, are you mad?"

The Morris narrowly avoided a signpost, while two wheels came off the frosty ground and rotated noisily in the air. With a firm pull on the steering wheel, he got the car squarely back onto the road. It slipped, protested, but then continued at high speed.

Sable shrugged, unperturbed by the near accident, screwing off the lid and taking a big swig. The yellow-brown liquid burned in her throat, then all the way down her gullet, making her want to spit it out immediately. She swallowed hard, her eyes pricking with tears. *Rats!* Frinton-Smith whiskey sure was a force to reckon with, even if old Frinton had lost all his money in the 1929 crash and the brand was now owned by some American billionaire.

"Potent stuff," she piped, taking another swig, feeling it go down with a little more ease. A cigarette balanced the heat in her throat.

"Now be careful with that precious gold," Freddie warned. "Make sure you keep some for me." Sable handed him the flask. He downed most of its contents with a practised slurp.

"Damn shame!" he hiccupped, tucking the flask back in his gabardine coat. He didn't specify what he was referring to, the lessening content of the liquor, or losing the family firm.

With her stomach warm and a content fuzziness enveloping her, Sable huddled deeper into her mink coat. The lack of night's rest and the monotonous purring of the old Morris soon made her doze off, but she'd hardly nodded off when she awoke again with a spasm, an involuntary gasp escaping from her.

Stop it!

Eyes opened wide, she fixed her stare on the winding road with the glassy black water of Loch Lomond on their left and the snow-capped Beinn Chaorach lurking like a dark shadow over her right shoulder. It was the best of both worlds, nestled between highlands and lowlands. This was real, and the past was gone.

Sable's breaths slowly returned to normal, as she fought hard to shake off the memory of hands groping under her silk vest, nausea, pain, and the disappearance of a white bonnet. A shudder strong as the wings of thunder rippled through her entire body, like a loose cannon unless... unless she could have another drink.

It was all her own fault. She was to blame for it from shoddy beginning to sad end. She'd let it happen. And now she'd have to live with her self-hate.

So far, Freddie seemed unaware of her inner turmoil, whistling "Happy Days Are Here Again" under his breath. Sable studied her friend's profile, the long lock of raven hair that covered this side of his forehead, the squinting blue eyes with the long lashes, a fine nose, lips that often curled in a smile like now.

Was this to be her husband? And what would *he* expect from her between the sheets? He'd said so much as not wanting her in that way, and she hoped it was true. She wasn't ready for intimacy, hands on her body. How would she tell him?

Freddie stopped whistling.

"We'll be fine, Sab. Don't worry. We're two lost souls, but we're going to turn this damn life into a carnival. Our own carnival."

He had picked up on her despair.

"You always know how to cheer me up, Freddo."

She sat a little straighter and looked ahead through the windscreen splashed with dead flies and bugs. A sudden longing for Glasgow gripped her, and the car couldn't go fast enough. All she yearned for was leaving this miserable period behind her, never go back there again.

She and Freddie had never fallen out. They trusted and respected each other... It was love. Life without Freddie was unimaginable, even if they didn't see each other for months. And he was the only one, except for her mother and limp-wristed Nellie, who knew what had happened to her. Not the details, but the gist of it. Freddie was her linchpin in this damnable life. All would be right in the end.

Though her pretty pink dress wasn't white and missing the traditional veil, Nellie had, despite grumbling, done her long hair up in a fashionable roll on her neck—just like the movie star Olivia de Havilland. She hoped she looked as ravishing as her idol. Instead of a veil, she'd don her head with a black fedora. That would scream freedom.

But then an additional problem doomed up.

"We don't have rings."

For a moment Freddie looked thoughtful, the laugh evaporating, but then he pulled his family signet ring from his pinky and tossed it in her lap.

"See if this fits you. It'll do for now. I'll snap up a diamond ring for you as soon as Father rolls over and my allowance is secure."

Sable turned the gold ring around in her fingers. It was sturdy, square, solid. A male ring with the three wheat stalks engraved in gold in the blue seal. It fitted her ring finger perfectly.

"I can't! It would be an offense to your family." She pulled it off, but Freddie wouldn't take it back.

"Only a temporary transition, Sab."

"But what about you?" She glanced at her ringless fingers. In her haste she'd forgotten all about jewelry.

"It's not that important for a man, is it?" His sideways glance at her was insecure, as if she knew the rituals of a municipal wedding better than him. It was her turn to reassure him.

"No, it isn't. I'm sure the city clerk, or whatever he's called, will give us permission to go out and buy a ring after he's wed us."

When Glasgow finally came into sight, it began snowing heavily, with a sudden drop in temperature to a scant five degrees Fahrenheit. The wind also picked up as the Morris protested inside and outside; the wind having almost free rein through the creaks in the linen hood.

Squinting through the snowflakes that clung to the window, Sable could discern the steep tower of Glasgow University in the distance. But as the front window steamed up with their breaths, the view became poorer and poorer. Freddie kept wiping the front shield with his palm but to no avail.

"I've got to pull over for a bit," he had to admit. "I'm afraid we'll veer off the road if I press on."

"Look, we're lucky. There's an inn." Sable cheered, pointing to the outside light swinging in the snowstorm with the painted shield underneath flapping left and right. "It's called The Lamb."

Freddie cautiously steered the shuddering Morris into the drive and turned off the engine. He let out a sigh of relief.

"I could do with a bite and a sip of that." Pointing his thumb to the whiskey sign with three wheat stalks and FS in curly letters, his face a grimace. The family emblem was the only reminder of the famous whiskey brand that once had been his future.

There were no other cars in the driveway. For a moment Sable feared the establishment might be closed.

"What now?"

The idea of sitting out the storm in freezing conditions, while the hours that the town hall would still be open diminished, wasn't at all appealing. With a dry-sounding, "Let's try," Freddie opened the car door. The wind immediately slammed it shut again.

"Holy Moly, that's one ghastly gale." He tried again, more firmly holding onto the doorhandle and this time slipped out. Slithering around the car on his fashionable brogues, he opened Sable's door and helped her out. The snowdrift instantly powdered her black coat.

"You look like a cheetah." Freddie managed a lopsided grin but as he gave Sable his arm, she felt his spirits were as low as hers.

"Some food will do us good. And a fire to thaw out."

To her relief, the inn door, a heavy, glass-paneled double-entry with a lamb's head on each side, gave way, and they found themselves in one of the darkest public places she'd ever laid eyes on. She sensed something fresh in the air that put her on edge. Almost ready to turn on her heels and face the cold again, she felt Freddie grip her arm more firmly.

"Give it a shot, Sab." His voice was a strange whisper in the deserted saloon.

"But it's empty. Maybe it's closed, or even abandoned?"

Two small lamps were lit over a long counter, but the tables were unlit. There was a smell of stale, old beer and long-cooked sausages. The sand on the floor crunched under her stylish boots. Sable wrinkled her nose, not accustomed to working-class guesthouses like this.

Just as she wanted to convince Freddie to leave the dismal tavern while they still could, a wiry woman with a high widow's peak and shrewd dark eyes came through a backdoor, drying her hands on her stained apron. Freddie took the lead.

"Good day, Ma'am. Are you at all open? Do you serve meals?" The mousy-haired woman in her drab dress glanced at the classy couple with an unwelcoming look, as if they were disturbing her day-to-day chores and had no business being there.

"We got stranded in the snowstorm and the door was open." Sable smiled at the woman in the friendliest way she could muster. Now the place was at least inhabited by one human. She might as well give it a whirl. From the woman's countenance, it was impossible to say if she was a maid or the innkeeper's wife.

Without further confirmation of The Lamb's opening hours, or a word of welcome, the mousy woman pointed to a table in one alcove by the front window.

"I've only got some ale stew left." The sloven woman had a high-pitched voice, shrill as a train whistle, clearly not one inclined to chit-chat with customers. She wiped the not-very-clean table with an even dirtier cloth, while Sable and Freddie sat down opposite each other.

Sable's stomach turned. She hated ale stew with a vengeance and didn't dare to look at her companion. As children, they jokingly called it 'ale chew' as often the traditional dish wasn't as tender as it was supposed to be.

"That will do just fine." Freddie beamed at their host, ignoring the kick of Sable's foot in his shin under the table. The woman gave a curt nod and disappeared into the shadows. A hinged door flapped twice.

They were left alone in the dusky dinner room, with a jumble of chairs and tables and a grimy red-plush carpet on the floor, worn with wear. The counter, once an imposing mahogany bar that ran along the largest part of the room, was dented and in need of a polish. It exuded a strong smell of old beer and liquor.

"Not looking forward to our prenuptial meal," Sable grumbled as Freddie offered her a cigarette. She inhaled deeply, then let a stream of gray smoke curl from her nostrils. At least the cigarette tasted good.

"She didn't even offer us a drink. This is a weird place. Wonder if it's haunted?" Exhaling the smoke, she dove deeper into her mink coat, not daring to take it off.

Freddie chuckled. "Wanna go down that road, Sab?" He was referring to the ghost stories they used to make up as children, lying side by side on the Persian rug in the Frenton- Smith summer villa on Skye.

"Better not," Sable answered drily. "We've got more urgent business, I think."

"Like what? I don't think we have a care in the world. We'll be out of Scotland in no time, happily hopping on our honeymoon."

The snowstorm only increased, decking the corners of the brown-glazed windows with a thickening pack of snow. It looked like the end of the day though it was still the beginning of the afternoon. The driveway disappeared under the snow, and the green Morris was topped with a white hat.

Sable's heart sank. It was already hard to keep up a cheerful countenance and the dismal weather shrank her world to misery again.

"If we ever make it to the wedding registrar today, how on earth are we going to find witnesses? We'll need people to sign with us, don't we?"

At that moment the hinged door flapped again, and the wiry woman reappeared with two steaming plates. Freddie refrained from answering Sable's new roadblock.

"Ah," he uttered with the same beaming smile he kept specially for their host, rubbing his fine hands together, causing his signet ring to sparkle in the dim light. "That smells good."

Sable ignored the wink he gave her. Noisily but without a comment, the woman placed the plates on the brown table.

"Drinks?"

"Two double whiskeys. Make it FS. No ice."

"Aye." She made her way back to the counter.

Sable stared down at her plate. It looked as drab as the inn's brown interior and turned her stomach into a twist. The cold and hungry part of her said "eat;" her mood said, "no way." She would wait for the whiskey to wash it down. Freddie had fewer qualms. Tucking his napkin in his expensive chemise with those elegant fingers, he picked up his fork and dove in. He even managed a "hmmm."

The whiskey in her empty stomach hurt, but in a good way, and Sable managed a couple of bites. The stew was "chew" but not too much. The woman had again disappeared through the door at the back. Silence reigned in the dining room, except for the scraping of forks and the putting down of glasses.

Two bright lights shone through the snowed-in windows. Sable peered outside. Another car. More stranded travelers.

"Seems like we're getting company." Any diversion from the silence and feeling of gloom was welcome.

"Big car," Freddie observed, as he chewed ostentatiously on a piece of beef. "Head lights are far apart. My guess is it's a Bentley." He swallowed, downed the last of his whiskey and longingly directed his gaze at the empty counter. Sable sat up straighter. Unknown visitors would cheer up the dreary place.

Car doors slammed, voices in the air, crunching soles in the snow. The door swung open and let in a flurry of snow and a cold draft.

They stared at each other. It seemed like minutes.

"Sable?"

"Father?"

A flood of relief and panic fought in Sable's chest. She rose slowly, the once-white, now-gray napkin dropping to the floor. *Dadaigh!* He stood tall and forlorn in the middle of the room, his chauffeur Elrod at a polite distance behind him.

Earl Archibald Montgomery should have been an imposing man because of his height and healthy countenance, but his eyes, gray and soft as a bird, revealed his introverted self more accurately.

At this moment he looked like he wanted to bolt out of the room, back into the leather upholstery of his Rolls Royce. Archibald Montgomery hated unannounced assemblies, certainly when high emotions were expected to explode.

Sable had crossed the distance between them, her own blue eyes so like her mother's, looking up at him with begging eyes. *Embrace me, Dadaigh. Help me through this.* But the earl's arms hung stiffly by his sides, while he gazed down on his daughter as if he didn't completely recognize her. Yet, there was also an embarrassed tenderness in his expression, even mingled with sadness. But no words escaped his pressed lips.

"Dadaigh." It wasn't more than a sniffle. Sable let her head hang, unable to meet his eyes any longer. But she couldn't help herself. Throwing herself at him, she clasped her arms around his rigid body, sobbing against his chest.

Slowly, slowly, he answered her embrace, but it remained awkward.

"Now, now, dearest, such a public display of emotion isn't proper."

At that moment the hinged doors flapped open, and the sloven lady came to see who the new guests were. Sable quickly withdrew from her father's weary hold. Still sniffling, she wiped her nose on her sleeve. Freddie was at her side, proffering her his white handkerchief that smelled of Dior Homme. With glistening eyes, she thanked him. He took her hand and escorted her back to the chair at the window.

Earl Montgomery snapped back in his diplomat-in-control attitude, conversing with the inn lady about having a meal. When emotions weren't needed, he was a man of the world.

"Ye want to sit with the young ones?" She'd obviously gleaned an intimate relationship between them.

"Of course, if that's not inconvenient to you?"

Studied Dad, diplomatic Dad, distant Dad, Sable thought as some part of her spirited self surfaced. The woman started pushing chairs and tables around. She really seemed to run the place completely on her own.

"Whisky for everyone," Freddie chimed in, his clear-blue-water eyes still on Sable. She smiled back at him gratefully. He cared for her, looked after her needs. Feeling how little she was getting from her father, she started looking forward to being Freddie's wi...

Oh no! Her father would never consent to his daughter getting married to an impoverished whiskey dealer, certainly not if he found out their true reason.

So, he'd better not now.

For the time being, however, the Earl seemed more interested in being out of the storm himself and getting the worried-looking Elrod and himself some food and liquor. Sable was aware of Freddie's constant gaze on her, but she averted his questioning eyes, fiddling with her napkin.

The start of a personal conversation about her well-being or her plans wouldn't stem from her father; she knew that much. He hadn't even inquired what they were doing here near Glasgow in the middle of a snowstorm. Why on earth he always avoided asking her anything was beyond her.

She knew that underneath the thick veneer of diplomacy and standoffishness her father loved her dearly, but he was such a recluse, forever awkward in the presence of the two feisty females in his household. Always on the qui vive, lest there would be another burst of drama he was supposed to handle but couldn't. He might have good reason this time.

The snowstorm was finally dying down. A furtive glance at her watch told Sable it was close to three 'o'clock. If she and Freddie wanted to go ahead with their plan, they'd have to leave instantly. Maybe they could just pay and walk off, but the whole reason her father was back in Scotland was because she'd summoned him. The tight squeeze Sable felt herself in made her blurt out,

"Dadaigh, can you lend me some money?"

"Money?" He dabbed the corners of his ash-blond moustache and looked stricken. He'd clearly expected something unusual coming from her mouth but not a request for money. Sable knew that to him she now sounded just like her mother. And she bit her lip, hated the hurt look on his face.

"I want to go abroad," she added softly. "That's why Freddie and I are here. We were on our way to London. I'd hoped to catch you there, you know, when you didn't come to Alnor." Now that she'd started talking, she couldn't stop anymore.

"Both Freddie and I need to snap out of our current situation. And *his* father"—a furtive look went in Freddie's direction—"sort of cut off his allowance. We just want to go to the Continent. Travel around a bit, nothing fancy or wild. And you know, Dadaigh, that Freddie will look after me."

She deftly steered around the topic of marriage. Her brain worked fast. If her father lent them money, they could stay the night over and marry tomorrow. Even stay in this dreadful place.

"The Continent?"

Sable's clever eyes discerned the slight shift in her father's tone. A sliver of hope. She could read him like a book. He longed for this situation - whatever it was - to be over and done with no more words spilled on it, but something was holding him back. Obviously, to win himself some time, the earl directed his arrows at Freddie.

"Don't you have studies to attend to at Oxford, young man?"

"I'm taking the semester off, sir."

Freddie, who liked the Earl and the way he said "young man," looked at Sable's father with affection. Dadaigh, strange and withdrawn as he was, had always shown a particular fondness for Freddie. Sable had often secretly wondered if he would have loved to have had Freddie for a son. They shared that I-best-cover-up-this-sensitivity and whip-smartness type of personality that was rather rare in the male species.

Her father asked no further, drank his whiskey, glanced at his pocket watch, then observed in a professor-like tone, "The Continent is a rat's nest at the moment. I'm not an advocate of young people traveling around there."

"But Italy, Dadaigh?" Sable was hopeful he'd agree to her sniffing up some architecture and refinement, as many of his contemporaries thought proper for their children.

"Certainly not Italy, my dear. As instable as it can be with Benito Mussolini in power."

That seemed the end of the discussion, with the money issue still unsolved. Elrod, who doubled as butler to the London house and as the Earl's personal driver, cleared his throat. The always glum-looking, elderly butler probably considered it time for his employer to move on. But what was her father's plan?

Making use of the shift in energy, Sable asked casually, "Are you continuing to Alnor Castle, Dadaigh?"

The familiar confused, almost helpless expression clouded her father's fair face. He twisted the end of his long mustache, a clear sign he was in a pickle when asked about his former residence. He'd come to Scotland for his daughter, not to come into the orbit of his estranged, former wife.

"Let's all go down to London instead!" Sable exclaimed in a cheery voice. Now it was Freddie who kicked *her* under the table. She ignored his hint, suddenly seeing a much better option.

They would find a way around this together. Money was more important than marriage—not just to her, but also to Freddie. And Dadaigh had deep pockets. Living with him in London might be superior to rushing into a hasty marriage. They could still travel but be free as birds.

"I have to go to Alnor. There's business I've to attend to with Stacey, the steward." Her father's voice had taken on a defeated tone.

Sable's heart sank. No invitation to protect her. Maybe he hadn't even come for her but only traveled north to take care of his estate. A smoldering fury shone in her blue gaze as she spat out, "But what about me, Dadaigh? Do you ever think about me?"

Her father inched back in this chair, clearly shocked at her vehement accusation.

"But, my dear, the business will take me only two days. I'll lodge at The Four Horses. You could come wi—" He stopped half-sentence, querying not his daughter's but Freddie's face for an answer.

Freddie pasted a neutral look on his fine-boned face, well accustomed to the Montgomerys' head-scratching discomfort in solving family issues.

Sable's attention was not on Freddie, though, but on her father. She shook her dark head in dismay. So, he wasn't even staying at his own house, driven out of his property by his money-grubbing, domineering ex-wife and her German crowd. What kind of a father was he? Though she knew this weakness in him, Sable was temporarily too baffled to voice another cutting remark. Everything was up in the air now. Where'd she'd go and with whom? And she longed so much to be her own boss, to be liberated from these failing individuals. She was rapidly turning into one herself.

Her father's silence was shamefaced and sheepish. But somewhere, from the depths of his impotence, he regained control over himself. His voice was slow and croaky in short, uncertain sentences.

"You both stay at the house in Cavendish Square. I'll lend you money for the trip. I'll get my business done, then come down myself. I'll talk to Frederik Frinton-Smith. Do nothing foolish."

He seemed exhausted after these utterances, up till now his most personal ones, twisting the long mustache with even more fervor than before.

"Thanks, Dadaigh. That sounds like a good plan. Let's do that, Freddo." Sable sank back in her chair a little more relaxed.

Her father pressed some ten-pound notes in her hand. The feeling of the white notes in her palm, her first real own money, was exhilarating. Sable felt blissed out, ready to spend it all in one go. Which she might.

For her the family meal was over, and everybody seemed to have come to the same conclusion.

What remained was a quick peck on her father's cheek before they left the grubby inn to continue their journeys in opposite directions. To Sable, it felt as if there had hardly been a reunion. It was water off a duck's back.

～

WITH FREDDIE again at the wheel and Sable in the passenger seat, the Morris slowly maneuvered southward. Long spells of silence filled the boxed-in space while the car crawled forward like a lethargic spider.

The road had mysteriously disappeared under a thick pack of snow and was only traceable because of the car tracks before them. Sable knew Freddie to be an experienced driver, who'd toured the continent in this same small old car, even as far up as the North Cape, so she presumed herself to be in safe hands. The glow of money in her pocket made her exultant. Nothing could break her now.

"Stay over in Glasgow?" Freddie's voice sounded less enthusiastic, clearly unsure what route Sable would decide on, now that she was her own woman. Marriage or no marriage?

"Yes, let's spend the night in Glasgow and then continue to London tomorrow morning. Wait till my father's back. I'm sure he'll be able to wring some money out of *your* dad for you. Once a diplomat ... that sort of thing."

"Hmm..."

"Not good enough?" Through the half-dark she peered at her companion, trying to read his expression.

He didn't reply and Sable sank back in the upholstery, for the first time in a very long time feeling a fuzzy sense of relaxation.

"Of course, I'll share my money with you," she mumbled as she closed her eyes.

4

A NEW BOYFRIEND?

London, 1 February 1938

innie was pinning the last thick tress of raven-black hair on top of Sable's head, then fastened the sapphire necklace around her slender neck.

"You look stunning, Miss Sable. Truly a lady." Her maid's plain Cockney voice shook Sable from the intense scrutiny of her own person in the oval mirror. The woman behind her was looking down on her with a righteous pride of her own, as if she was single-handedly responsible for creating Starlet Sable.

Knowing her father had appointed the London maid to look after Sable in the large house on Cavendish Square, she tried to be civil with her but actually found her rather bossy.

Born and bred within hearing distance of the church bells of St. Mary-le-Bow, Cheapside, in the City of London, Minnie was Sable's opposite in many aspects—raw, real, with broad hips and piercing coal eyes. At twenty-five there was little in life a secret to Minnie Middlewater. It was as if she looked right through Sable's thin veneer of control on life.

The color of the five large sapphire stones in the heavy platinum setting mirrored the blue in Sable's eyes, and she was temporarily mesmerized by their light. Sable loved the playfulness of light, her artistic side as she called it.

Still with her eyes on the flicker of blue against her creamy skin, she pulled on long white gloves and adjusted the press studs at her elbows. Her low-cut, strappy gown of forest-green silk that fell just over her knees, newly purchased from Lanvin but with the Hollywood glamor stamp, caressed her body like a nebulous night.

Minnie arranged the brushes and powders while Sable sat perfectly still on the stool in front of the dressing table, still staring at herself. Was she truly only nineteen? It felt more like fifty, even if she had to agree with Minnie that she looked drop-dead gorgeous right now.

Lighting a cigarette and inhaling the smoke, she held the diamond-studded cigarette holder deftly between her white satin fingers, while the curling smoke surrounded her and made her look even more mysterious. Tonight, she would strike. It would be her party, her game.

Obviously getting uncomfortable with her mistress's silent and still posture, Minnie tried again to engage her in conversation.

"Anything else you need, Miss, pe'haps a stola, or would you prefe' your fur cape?"

Sable swung around on her stool, facing the fidgeting maid. She was keenly aware of failing at muzzling both Minnie and butler Elrod into submission, despite her outbursts of discontent, even fury. Both servants treated her with feigned respect.

There was a strained politeness in particular between the two young women. Sable couldn't help disliking Minnie, whose favorite saying was, *I don't suffe' fools gladly*. Was she a fool in her maid's eyes? Well, she wouldn't go down without a fight.

"The fur will do. You can ask Elrod to order the taxi. Five more minutes, and I'll be ready."

"Do you want me to wait up for you, Miss Sable?"

"No, no need. I can get out of this dress myself." And with a mischievous smile she added, "Or I'll have a willing slave to do it for me."

Minnie's busy hands stopped in mid-air, ready to reprimand the younger girl for her brazenness. Then she swallowed distinctly, pursed her lips but said no more.

Sable knew her father had given the staff express instructions she was not to go out alone at night. The West End was not a place for underage ladies of good breeding to be traipsing around on their own, but there was no holding her back.

The Earl's daughter did what she wanted and when she wanted since returning to London, from what now in hushed tones was referred to as "the young Miss's misfortune up north." Despite the distant grumble of the servants, Sable went where her whimsical mind led her, frequenting jazz clubs, bottle parties, queer clubs, and dining clubs in the bohemian area of Soho.

It had been Freddie, of course, who'd first introduced Sable to the queer clubs, and now they were her favorites. She felt freer, less followed around by predatory males. Plus, these boys— because they were more like chattering boys than men—were so much more fun. One could drink and dance with them all night, and they would lift her on the table and clap their hands as she danced.

But tonight was going to be special. The blood flowed a little faster through her veins. If everything worked to plan, she'd be out of here soon. Egbert had agreed to meet her.

"Your taxi, Miss."

Sable had to curb herself from skipping down the stone steps of her father's house like a girl of ten. Giddiness was the best feeling, that tightrope of danger and delight.

"Shim Sham Club, Wardour Street."

As soon as she sat in the back of the Austin taxi, nicknamed High Lot, Sable pulled off her gloves and slipped a huge sapphire ring that matched her earrings and necklace around her finger. Why she still went through the charade of pretending to go to an upper-class ball instead of a shady nightclub, when she was sure her small household knew, was beyond her. Maybe she still needed some pretense for her own sake.

Since she'd been in London, Sable felt finally free, finally happy among artists, artists' models, writers, Blacks, queers and Jews. But the restlessness had continued. There was an entire world out there. Staying too long in one place was incredibly boring—even if she was making many new friends and collected even more admirers.

Freddie had soon gone back to Oxford, and David, after his father had gingerly reinstated his allowance. They hadn't touched again on their wild plans for an elopement marriage, easing back into their familiar, I-know-you-and-you-know-me friendship.

"I'll motor down on the weekend, and we'll turn London higgledy-piggledy," Freddie had promised, kissing her cheek, clearly in a hurry to be reunited with his genuine love.

"Do bring David. I want to meet him!" Sable had called after him, waving from the front door of 6 Cavendish Square. But after three weekends there was still no sight of Freddie, nor of her father.

"Your father has been called away for urgent business in Bucharest," butler Elrod had announced at breakfast. *All the better,* Sable thought. *I don't need anyone's eyes on me right now.*

The taxi swirled around Oxford Circus and dove into Oxford Street where late-night visitors were still window shopping at Marks & Spencer's or strolling down leisurely for an early performance at the London Palladium. *The World's Leading Variety Theatre,* it read in gilded letters.

Sable smiled, suddenly remembering how, as a girl of fourteen, she'd stood there with her father, mesmerized by the commotion that was going on at the entrance of the cream-white theatre. The theatre manager, George Black, in a pin-striped suit and slick combed hair, bowing like a folding knife.

"Alfred Hitchcock is filming his new thriller inside," her father had told her. Sable had no clue who Hitchcock was, but anything related to films and thus Hollywood had her instant attention.

"Can we have a look, Dadaigh? You know Mr. Black, don't you?"

"I guess we could, dear." Her father's gray eyes had gleamed with excitement as they crossed the road. Sable had ambled decorously by his side, already imagining herself on the big screen as Hitchcock's newest discovery: Starlet Sable.

It had been dark inside the amphitheatrical building except for the brightly lit stage, where two enormous lights on either side of the stage shone on a dark-haired man in a raincoat wearing a homburg. He was shouting in a bass voice at the music hall performer, "What are the thirty-nine steps?" The performer, dressed in bow tie and with pomaded hair, recited a list in a rapid jumble of words. Sable could feel her father tense next to her.

"They're filming John Buchan's novel," he whispered excitingly. "That's Richard Hannay."

"No, it's not. It's Robert Donat." Sable knew all the actors and actresses by name.

"Shush!" But she didn't need any shushing as her mouth fell open. The beautiful Madeleine Carroll, blonde wavy hair and woeful eyes, appeared from behind the curtains and walked up to Donat with swift, dainty steps.

"Ohhh..." was all Sable's throat produced. The way Carroll held her slender neck so graciously, cocked her head slightly to the side, batted her eyelashes at her co-actor. Sable was already practicing the actress's every move while her little hand was safely tucked in one of her father's hands.

"WE'RE HERE, MA'AM."

Sable was roughly awakened from her reminiscing by the taxi driver's announcement.

"I want to be an actress!" she blurted out, suddenly knowing what her true north was.

"Whatever, Miss. That'll be 3 bob."

Sable handed the stoic man his money with her mind still on the glorious career that lay ahead of her and left the car before he could open the door for her.

"An actress!" she repeated to herself, pulling her fur stola closer around her as a cold gust of wind whistled around Warbour Street. Shards of jazz music escaped from the doors of the Shim Sham Club as people hurriedly entered the establishment to escape the February cold.

Sable stood on the pavement in her stylish dancing heels, still contemplating her new destination. Out of nowhere, her mother's face flashed before her; magical Misty Fletcher, the most popular 1920s flapper girl, who'd been whispered to have lounged in the Prince of Wales's arms more than once before becoming the wife of the sixth Baron of Alnor.

Her fiery portrait hung over the fireplace in the Alnor dining room, come-to-bed, ice-blue eyes, a delicate oval face framed with a jet-black bob, gaily glancing at the painter over her bare shoulder.

Her daughter's shoulders slumped. Not the white screen then. She'd in no way become like her mother. Angrily, Sable pushed aside two Black men with hobo bags who stood waiting to go inside and strode into the club.

It was smoke-filled and dimly lit. A huge Black man with glistening pearls of sweat on his broad forehead and temples banged away on the piano at the far side of the bar. Shards of the music floated to her, mixed with the powerful smell of alcohol and cigarettes. High-pitched female voices tinkled over sonorous male basses, and waiters shouted with all their might to pass through the thronging crowd, carrying heavy trays filled with glasses and bottles high above their heads.

Sable took a deep breath, letting her eyes and ears adjust to the dusky cacophony. This was her world; this was what she lived for! Damn the future, damn her past.

"Sable, over here!"

A male voice blasted over the noise. A broad, friendly face, a lock of hair the color of Sahara sand over the wide white forehead, twinkling bluish eyes that had never known sorrow. Egbert van Eijck, the jet-set son of a Dutch shipyard owner, Sable's latest best friend and conquest.

Egbert jockeyed through the crowds, kissed her cheek and, grabbing her hand in his big paw, pulled her to the dancefloor. The
Dutchman was robust, rich, and reliable, characteristics that were all
too attractive to Sable. Amsterdam was her next destination; she was
sure of it.

Certainly, he would ask her to accompany him, most likely after
what she'd planned for him tonight. The thought that, though of a
different physique from Von Henkell, he resembled that blond, blue-
eyed Nordic race made her shudder inwardly. But copious amounts
of alcohol would help to quench all doubt.

"Where have you been?" Egbert yelled in her ear while pulling
her closer in his embrace. "I thought we were supposed to have
dinner at Quaglino's at eight p.m.?"

Sable let his strong arms envelop her as she nestled her cheek
against his massive chest, but she had no intention of answering his
half-irritated, half-concerned request. Men like Egbert were used to
having everything handed to them on a platter.

Well, not Sable. Being fickle and mysterious was the best course
to entrap a desirous male in her nets. If needed, she'd use her mother's example just to get what she wanted. Then, she'd return to
sincerity.

Drawing her even closer to him, Egbert clearly enjoyed the
suppleness of her youthful body against his, contenting himself with
the fact she'd finally arrived. Sable wasn't hungry. She never was
these days, and the constant questions about her meager appetite
had caused her to back out of dinner appointments whenever she
could. A truth she wasn't ready to share with her beau.

"I could do with a glass of champagne," she announced as she
pulled his head toward hers to be heard over Duke Ellington's *Prelude
to a Kiss*.

"Coming up!" he shouted back, letting his grip on her go, and
snapping his fingers in the ear of a passing waiter, who was clearly
heading in the opposite direction with a full tray. But no matter how
busy, waiters and doormen alike attended immediately to Van Eijck's

demands. The tray was left on a side table to serve their richest client at his wink. Another ideal in a man, Sable observed.

The ideal man, meanwhile, steered Sable to the small round tables that stood on an elevated platform around the club and pushed out a chair for her. He pulled his own chair close to hers so that their thighs met under the table. Sable could feel the powerful muscle of his upper leg demanding her attention. His arm went protectively around her shoulder.

Are we a couple now? Sable mused, not sure what that meant, but the knotty thought slipped from her mind again as the champagne arrived. A 1929 Veuve Clicquot, her favorite. Egbert was so thoughtful and never considered his wallet for her. She watched him as he oversaw the waiter's deft yet routine actions, pouring the sparkling golden liquid into tall flutes whose crystal cut danced in the electric lights, while the jazz band thumped away on their instruments and the audience clapped and cheered.

They clinked glasses and shouted "chin-chin." She drank greedily to rid herself of the awkwardness of his close maleness to her. But instead of shrinking back from his intimacy, Sable forced herself to inch even closer, gazing up at him with misty blue eyes that would mesmerize any mature male.

"Bill!"

Egbert's booming voice rang over the clamor as he drew out the name of the man he called to. A tall, rather wild-looking, red-haired hunk of a man in an aviation uniform spun around as he was passing their table. As he turned, Sable looked into the most intense azure-blue eyes she'd ever seen, a deep soulful cyan with a harsh metallic finish that stripped her of all her carefully built-up defenses like the sun burning through a cloud.

Sensing how she was revealed as her true self under the scrutiny of these eyes, despite her glazed state of half-drunkenness, the untrimmed Viking kept her in his vision while turning his attention to Egbert.

Sable struggled to protect herself from his scorching of her tough-girls-bad-luck attitude and somehow kept him at a distance from probing further into her soul, sitting straighter, sipping her champagne.

Her quick mind took in everything, the discrepancy of his pilot uniform—not RAF as far as she could discern—the strong, bearded face that was mainly attractive because of the intensity of his eyes under reddish brows, the proud mouth, and the glow of thick, deep auburn hair glistening in the nightclub's many electric lights.

Egbert had left Sable's side and risen to greet his "Bill" with extensive joviality. She picked up the distinct accent of her own highlands as the man replied. A Scotsman! She should have known! He breathed the North with every fiber of his being.

Egbert introduced her briefly, evidently keen to dive back into a conversation with this friend. Sable and Bill shook hands. His handshake was firm, and spoke of tolerating no excuses. At hearing her last name, one reddish brow went up, but he soon turned to Egbert again, ignoring her further. The firm press of his hand left a lingering vividness in her palm.

As tall as the new man but chubbier, Egbert now also turned his back on her and the two men became engaged in a lively conversation, which mainly comprised of yelling short sentences in each other's ears over the Shim Sham hubbub. Sable caught words like 'Lysander' and 'military' but couldn't make heads or tails of their interaction.

This Bill made her uncomfortable in an unknown, dubious way, but also fascinated her. Used to perking up whenever an attractive male person came into her orbit, this was unlike other times, unsettling in a thrilling way. It was as if she, too, came alive through his magnetic energy.

For a while Sable was amused by this meeting of clearly good friends, comparing the two men, and deciding 'her' Egbert, though less attractive, was kinder, with a jolly and easy-go-lucky appearance where the man in uniform was austere though regal. But when their ear shouting kept going on and on, she began to feel neglected. Topping up her glass herself — where was Egbert's care now? — with the last of the Veuve Clicquot, she let her eyes dance over the club and its occupants, dozing in half-drunkenness on an empty stomach.

The Metropolitan police might well describe Shim Sham as a "den of vice and iniquity;" to Sable it all looked tame scandal-wise. A group of four very black men had cleared the dancefloor and were entertaining the guests with a lively tap dance that got slightly wilder around the edges to the improvised jazz jam session under the leadership of the sweating man at the piano.

Girls in pearl strings and evening dresses clapped their slender white hands and giggled. Sable was so used to seeing all different ethnicities dancing and partying together that the color of someone's skin didn't matter at all to her. She smirked. If only her Dadaigh could see her now. He would be appalled beyond measure.

Yawning, she pulled Egbert's sleeve in irritation. He didn't react, still engaged in his intense, short-sentenced dialogue with the uniformed stranger.

"I've had enough!"

Getting up, she deliberately bumped into the pilot, mumbling a lip-deep, "Sorry." This action got her the desired male attention. Egbert instantly slipped a proprietary arm around her waist, making it impossible for her to move away from them.

"This is my special girl, Sable!" he yelled, as if they hadn't been introduced yet. The mystery man let his forceful gaze bear down on her for a spell. It made her feel as if she was but a mere irritable ant under his microscope.

Was there annoyance, even a hint of aggression in his eyes? Whatever it was, it resulted in the same puzzling uneasiness she'd felt the first time his eyes were on her. She reacted with irritation in return.

Men had no power over Sable Montgomery, not anymore. It was supposed to be the other way around from now on. So, she met his eyes with the same brute force, trying to make herself taller as she had to look up at him, pulling down the corners of her beautiful mouth in a scornful grimace.

"I'm going!" She shouted in Egbert's ear, trying to peel his paw from around her waist. All the time she was acutely aware of the

Scotsman's posture blocking her way to the exit, his two feet firmly planted on the floor, bearing his uniform as if he was already at the battlefield, ready to lay siege.

Egbert readjusted his arm around her, ignoring her call to leave.

"Wild Bill used to work as a pilot for my dad; now he works for me. Flies me around in my Ford Tri-Motor. Wherever my fancy takes me."

Wild Bill. What kind of name was that for a pilot? Sable staggered, suddenly frightfully tired. She'd been drinking too fast and eating too little. The entire nightclub spun before her eyes, and she needed Egbert's arm to steady her.

"I'm heading home," she slurred, losing interest in the club and the pilot, only longing for her soft bed and sleep. But now the Dutchman understood the hint and went into action.

"I'll take you home." With the same possessiveness, Egbert took a swift leave of his employee with a hearty "so long, Captain" to steer her toward the door and the cold but fresh evening air.

The Captain, aka Wild Bill, had already turned his back on them. The last Sable saw of him was his tall blue back disappearing into the dancing crowd.

Relieved to feel the upholstery of the taxi against her back and Egbert squarely next to her, no longer distracted by others, she closed her eyes and let her dark head rest on his shoulder.

"6 Cavendish Square."

There was nothing more she had to do. He would take control of everything.

Sable woke from a tapping on her arm.

"We're here, sweetheart. You need any help?" A kiss landed on her cheek, while she saw through squinting eyes how Egbert paid the driver. Could she walk? Her head was swimming and her legs felt like lead.

"I need ... I need you," she affirmed, half-serious, half-seductive.

"No problem, sweetheart." Egbert was already around the car and helped her out. She leaned heavily on him.

"Come in for a nightcap." She made it sound like a casual, almost business-like invitation, and before he could turn her down, added, "The staff's all gone to bed. I told them to."

"In that case..."

She saw Egbert's eyes lit up consumed with desire. He'd not expected her to be this easy. Well, she had another surprise for him.

MINUTES later he was in her bedroom, zipping open her green evening dress, his arms already around her, itching for the touch of her skin.

"Wait!" Sable stopped him, feeling increasingly dizzy and drunk, but realizing it was too late to back out of his amorous clutches now. As she'd been the one to put the signs on green, she now had to live with the consequences. *Let it be over soon, and then I'll ask him to take me with him!*

Egbert, clearly no other thought in his head but the soft silken girl in his arms, started dragging her limp body to the four-poster bed, half-dressed and half-senseless.

A sharp rap on the door.

"Miss Sable!"

Sable froze. Minnie. What was she doing up?

Another rap, another "Miss Sable!" This time even more urgent. Had she locked the door? Even Egbert sat up, stopped kissing her bare skin.

Minnie, hands on her broad hips, stood in the doorway, gasped, then looked dark as a storm at sea, mumbling, "Raspberry tart."

At the sight of the unwelcome maid, Sable's blood boiled. The impunity of the girl! Had she no manners at all? Yet another part of Sable rejoiced at the interruption, as if some sudden angel had saved her from a dire mistake. Rising up to some form of dignity, she implored the girl for an explanation.

"What is it, Minnie? I told you I could manage." But the room swayed, and Egbert inched away from her, straightening his tie, looking aghast.

Behind Minnie stood ... her father. His ashen face was tight and perplexed, the even grayer eyes going from his half-naked daughter to the bulky man in her bedroom.

Egbert tried.

"It's ... it's not what you think, sir. Sab ... your daughter was unwell, and I was..."

"Out, young man!"

And to Sable with more authority than she'd ever heard from her father, tinged with deep sorrow, he added,

"Have you not learned one thing at all from your ordeal, Sable? Not one thing? I forbid you to make the same mistake. I forbid it!"

So Dadaigh knew. *He knew, after all.*

THE EARL'S voice wasn't loud, not even angry, but very definite. His expression was obvious as daylight. There was not an inch of space for negotiations. Sable noticed how Egbert glanced at her lying like a sunken maiden ship on the bed, how he mumbled an apology and slipped past her thorny father, to disappear out of sight.

Sable bowed her head. Not ashamed of what she'd done, but disappointed in herself. Her father's eyes so clearly showed the pain she'd seen in them so many times before. To him, she was now cut from the same cloth as her mother. She'd lost his respect. And most likely his love.

5

PHONEY FREEDOM

The next afternoon, with a hangover headache and a stoic soul, Sable let butler Elrod drive her to Victoria Station in her father's Rolls Royce to catch the train ferry that would take her to the Continent. In the trunk were all her earthly possessions that would sustain her in her new life abroad. In her heart, there was ice and a germ of hope for a clear break and real freedom.

"Who cares?" she'd shouted, when her father had informed her he'd have her quartered in a place so far away from the opposite sex, she would have to cross half a country to meet a member of the male species. An All-girls' school in Switzerland.

As the Rolls rolled along Hyde Park, Sable suppressed a wave of nausea, cursing London, cursing her family, even cursing Egbert. He'd sneaked out like a slick fox in the night, leaving her to deal with whatever consequences she'd had to face on her own. If he'd been a proper gentleman, he'd have done more for her. At least, he could have sent her a farewell note at breakfast, but there had been nothing. There would be no Egbert Van Eijck from now on in her life. Sable was sure of it.

"Big deal!" she mumbled, a word that more than ever larded her vocabulary these days.

"What's that, Miss?" Elrod turned his bristly head, topped with his chauffeur cap, to his sulky passenger in the backseat.

"Nothing, Elrod. Mind your own business."

"All right, Miss."

"Shut up!"

Her future was blank to her; the school, apparently called Le Manoir on Lake Geneva, a nondescript institution. Of course, she'd been to girls' boarding schools before, even to a French-speaking one in Paris for a year. But being sealed off at school again? At nineteen? It was a hopeless waste of time and energy.

Sable didn't want to learn anything. She wanted to live wild and free. But how and where? Now she'd be stuck for months with a bunch of girls who most likely were only fillies, who still wore ribbons in their hair and giggled and gossiped about the other sex without ever having been near one. Argh.

Without even saying goodbye to Elrod, she followed the porter amidst the throngs of people to Victoria's International platform 2, where she'd take the night ferry, first to Dover and then across to Calais and ultimately to Gare du Nord in Paris. She knew the drill. It held no adventure for her. Everything was dull. London was dull. It was as well that she left the city behind.

Businessmen, soldiers in uniform, women pushing prams, they passed her in waves, seemingly all very determined to reach their destination through the shortest distance and in a minimum of time.

Almost in a dream state, Sable followed the porter who pushed along her two bulky valises and her hatbox. She couldn't comprehend the hurry of humans, their comradery, their tears at saying goodbye. Her heart was hard as the rocks of Dundee, her lips pursed, her brows knitted.

In order not to break, she kept her blue gaze fixed on her belongings, forcing herself to put one fashionable shoe before the other. Drained, deserted, disposed of.

When a couple, arm-in-arm on the way to a teary goodbye, bumped into her, she couldn't help lashing out.

"Pair of twats, can't you watch where you're walking?"

"Sorry, sorry, sorry!" The couple apologized, but it did nothing to improve her mood.

Stop the pity party, Sab, grin and bear?

It was as if she heard Freddie's voice and took strength from it as she boarded The Golden Arrow that would take her away from it all. Seeing that her luggage was tucked away safely, she pushed a handful of shillings into the noncommittal, deadpan-faced porter's eager palm and sat down, after closing all the striped curtains of her compartment.

"Shut the door behind you, Porter." Her voice was low and cutting.

Vaguely aware she was positioning herself as just another condescending upper cruster, she could not stop herself at this point. Little did she care what anyone thought of her right now. The porter, clearly used to his bad-tempered clientele, closed his fist around the coins and then shut the sliding-door with a brief nod, showing his pretense at respect.

If only I could stay in Paris for a while! Sable thought as she looked around what was to be her private space for the next thirteen hours. Sinking back in the plush upholstery of the first-class compartment, she considered what a prolonged stay in Paris could be like with no one to spy on her. She knew the city well, the fashionable areas, Place Pigalle, Montmartre, Quartier Latin. Would she blend in, find a place to call her own for a while?

The Earl may not be generous with his affection for her. He had —this time—been generous with his money. But Sable's thoughts yo-yoed from exhilaration to despair within seconds, as they always did, this time plummeting to an absolute low of defeatism. What to do in Paris, on her own? It wasn't as if she knew people there, and she was fed up thinking of having to talk up men again to have some company. Friendship with women was out of the question. Women were simply competitors.

Am I just weak? Has that German bastard undermined my willpower after all? Or is it something else? Sable closed her eyes, feeling she didn't want to open them again. There was nothing for her in this world that was really worth living for. Even Freddo, with his new lover and plans to destroy Hitler from his plane, had deserted her.

While The Golden Arrow rocked on the rails toward the Channel, sleep enveloped Sable as a temporary freedom cape. The sloping green hills of Kent were shrouded in darkness, dotted here and there with twinkling electric lights below and bright stars in the clear winter sky above. Croydon, Tonbridge, Ashford, they all flashed by as Sable's dark head lulled against the cushions, her hands clasped around the crocodile handles of her expensive handbag, her soul freely roaming the Highlands of her youth.

She slept, dreaming of a pair of blue eyes that beckoned her to another life, full of adventure and fun. A jive and a clear sky. Standing wide-legged in River Clyde, she was screaming with delight. A silver trout danced on her fishing rod through the mist of early morning. In the distance loomed the imposing peak of Beinn Chorranach, always the anchor that whispered the song of home.

He was there with her—whoever he was—and made her feel safe as Solomon's birds. Safe and loved. A mode of living she knew deep down that it *could* exist. But where? Where? Turning to face the blue-eyed mountaineer, she was disappointed on the dot. *He* had become Freddie, armed with his lopsided smile and effeminate gestures. Sable's heart withdrew inside herself again. She would never marry Freddie. That much was clear now.

Drowsy and sleep-drunk, she was rubbing the misfortunate dream from her subconscious as the train came to a screeching halt. Train doors opened noisily, people shuffled past in the corridor, voices called out. The train had arrived at Dover Marine Station, the last port of call in England.

Before Sable could sufficiently recover herself and wake up, an abrupt knock rapped on her carriage door. Dazzled, she sat upright in the dark, her mouth dry, loose locks of hair in her eyes. Searching for the light switch, she groped around in the dark without success. She would need the light from the corridor to orient herself.

"Yes!"

A beam of electric light flooded into her compartment as the door slid open. A young steward in a freshly ironed white uniform with a boyish, round face peered inside the dusky place doubtfully.

"You're okay, Miss?"

"Yes!"

She took advantage of the new visibility to switch on both the night lamp and her cut-and-dry supremacy.

"What is it you want?" Her interrogative looks and pretty face threw the young man off balance. He gazed down on her, clearing his throat, which made his Adam's apple move up and down above the starched white collar of his uniform, his white-gloved hands wringing together rather nervously.

"It is ... I mean, you are Lady Montgomery, are you not?"

"I am." She raised one dark eyebrow, enjoying the scene a little too much.

"The question was asked ... uh, Lady Montgomery, if you will dine alone here in your carriage, or rather be escorted to the Pullman Car Company, or ... or ..." He seemed to have run out of options as she wasn't helping him with an answer.

"Or? Do I have other options, steward?"

"Would you rather come on board? Mr Hancock ... uh, the ship's captain knows your father ... uh, Earl Montgomery. He takes this sea voyage all the time when he travels to the Continent and prefers to sail with the *Canterbury V*. So ... uh, Captain Hancock requested if you'd care to dine at his table in the messroom?"

The young shaver seemed unable to believe the flurry of his own words and took to wringing his hands again, staring down at his polished black shoes.

Sable's mood instantly improved. Being singled out was something she savored.

"Shut the door and don't go anywhere. Let me freshen up and slip into something more appropriate." The blush that spread over his already blotchy face dispersed the last cobwebs of her depression.

"Keep that door closed and guard it with your life while I undress."

The beardless cheeks turned crimson, but he did as he was told.

Now Sable took all the time in the world to dress up, enjoying every second of the situation. The result had to be stunning. And that took time.

"Excuse me ... uh, Lady Montgomery ... how much longer will it take? We're about to park in train on the ferry. We must disembark now, or ..." The steward's voice was frayed with nervousness.

Clad in a pale-blue satin evening dress, a single string of pearls and matching earrings, fashionable black heels and her dark hair tossed high on her head, Sable appeared in the door opening, an unlit cigarette casually placed between her red lips. The steward rushed toward her to give her a light. Casting his eyes down but not before taking a quick peek at her impressive beauty, the young man uttered timidly but with good sense.

"Uh ... Miss Montgomery, it's freezing out there. I think you'd better wrap yourself in something warm."

This considerate thought made Sable smile genuinely for the first time. Kindness always wormed itself under her shield of protection. Grabbing her fur and slinging it loosely around her shoulders with the cigarette still between her lips, she exhaled.

"What's your name, stew? I like you."

"Ronald, Miss ... Ronald McGuffey. At your service."

"Good, Ronald McGuffey. Now take me to your Captain Hancock. We can't keep your boss waiting much longer now, can we?"

After having been in the dark for hours and still battling fragility and a prolonged period of drunkenness, Sable blinked against the light of the chandeliers in the well-lit messroom of the *Canterbury*. An oval table was set in the middle of the dining room and despite the slight swaying of the ship, it was decked to the nines with a white damask cloth, white porcelain plates, silver cutlery, and crystal glasses. There was even an ornamental flower arrangement of red roses and white carnations in the middle.

A handful of men and women in evening dress were seated around the table, steeped in subdued conversation with their table partners, while an ensemble of two female violists and a male cellist dressed in white and black played Mozart's *Eine kleine Nachtmusik* in the background.

To Sable, it felt as if she'd stepped right back in time. When her parents still entertained together at Alnor Castle, the intimate soirees had exuded sophistication with genteel pleasantness. Sable, too young to take part, would watch the guests sit around the table from a slat in between the glass sliding doors that separated the two halves of Alnor's main dining room when there was a need for an informal dinner.

Before the loud Germans conquered Misty's head and heart. Before the sliding doors never closed again. Before Dadaigh was gone.

Sable took a deep breath, knowing how all heads would turn when she walked in. Savoring every second of that magnificent feeling. As if she mattered, as if her true beauty and poise were seen for what they really were.

A snow-haired, snow-bearded man with a weathered face in a black uniform—the personification of what a sea captain should look like—raised his straight posture from the head of the table where he'd been talking to an elderly lady in a black evening dress.

With both hands outstretched, hairy as if covered with white spider webs, the elderly captain closed the distance between them. Kind hazelnut eyes took her in from head to toe, appreciative and accepting, while a generous smile spread widely in between the white whiskers. Sable couldn't help but smile back at him. Captain Hancock was indeed the type of person her diplomat father would bestow with his trust.

"Lady Montgomery, what a pleasure! Your father couldn't stop praising you to the heavens and beyond. And now I understand why. Dear girl, you're picture-perfect in every respect. Please do me the honor of being my table companion tonight. Come and sit next to me. I can't wait to make your acquaintance."

He shook her hand with the same warmth that radiated from his whole being, and not waiting for her answer, led her to the empty seat next to his, while Sable felt all eyes burn on her with a new intensity.

For a moment she faltered, even had the thought of backing out of their glares and returning to the seclusion of her carriage. What tales had her father been telling about her to this man? Hopefully, they hadn't met up recently. But then again, the steward had said that her father always traveled on the *Canterbury* ... and he'd just returned from Romania.

Sable's head spun but outwardly she remained calm, sitting down straight-backed as the waiter tucked in her chair. She was her own girl now; she could do this. There was no reason to believe this was a trap of some sort.

The captain, his white-spider-web hand warm and encouraging over hers, pointed out the other guests at his table with the crooked finger of his other hand. The names and titles went over Sable's head, but she nodded with what she hoped was sufficient friendliness, meanwhile racking her brain for something intelligent to say.

She could flirt and she could party, but she wasn't good with chatting up old people, and this ensemble seemed ancient to her. Not one person her age, not one person just a tad bit out of the ordinary.

Clever Papa probably arranged this to give me a taste of what he expects me to become, Sable thought with a grain of admiration for her parent. She could appreciate ingenuity even if it was at her own expense. *Well, dear Dadaigh, I'll play my part for now. See how long it lasts.* Turning her attractive, youthful face to the Captain, she said in a honeyed voice but with a deliberate Scottish accent,

"The pleasure's all mine, Capt'n. I feel, though, that I'm at a grave disadvantage. Ye seem to know all about me but mah incorrigible father, Earl Archibald Montgomery, has refrained from givin' me any information about yer existence. Bad Dadaigh never talks to me of his travels, or the comp'ny he keeps."

During Sable's candy-coated, yet over-affected statement, the other conversations had fallen silent. This was an easy trick, and it almost bored her how easily people got caught in her actress net. She could be the center of attention everywhere, whether or not she wanted to.

The elderly black-clad lady on the captain's other side covertly rolled her eyes. *Where is this going? I certainly have to know!* Her watery sea-green eyes were fixed on the bold newcomer with a mixture of disdain and fascination. Mr Hancock, on the contrary, seemed to care not a bit for decorum and even less about her affectation and accent.

"Oh, but my dear girl, I dined with your Dadaigh only yesterday. He was on his way back from Romania if I understood him correctly. He told me he was so looking forward to spending some time with you in London. That's why I was utterly surprised to see your name on the passengers' list today. Pray tell me, what's the sudden change of plan?"

Could she say *"none of your bloody business"* to this amicable sailor whose gentle eyes danced inquiringly over her face? She managed only just to suppress the urge to make her fist land on the table so the lamb chops would land next to the guests' plates and wine glasses would topple over, staining the damask.

"Damn you." She gritted with jaws and fists clenched, not clear whether she was addressing her father or this good-natured, nosy skipper with his perpetual benevolence as an act of God hanging around him. Her smile was forced, the accent impeccably Scottish.

"Nothin' out of the ordinary, Sir. My father must have forgotten he'd banished me to a Swiss finishin' school before he went abroad."

That would settle the score, she hoped, as she saw the black-clad woman on the opposite side of her open her mouth in a shock that seemed to ripple down the table where more silver-haired foxes gasped and "*ooh-lal-laed.*" But she was clearly mistaken where the unperturbed sea captain was concerned.

"Oh yes, fathers are so forgetful. Only last week I forgot my eldest daughter's birthday—mind you, she's had over 35 of them already but the womenfolk, my wife and three daughters, kept nagging me about it for days."

There was no escaping this man's optimism, and Sable decided she'd had enough. One last glance around the table told her there were only bores and brownnosers here. Feigning a headache would be the sensible option to back out of this disastrous dinner, but she'd have to make sure food would be delivered to her carriage.

The unexpected had happened. Sable's appetite fully returned for the first time in weeks; she was starving, most likely because she'd not touched her usual quota of alcohol all day. Turning to the white-haired skipper with her sweetest smile, she forgot her acting accent in her haste.

"I'm suddenly not feeling well, Sir. So sorry about that. I have to lie down." She grabbed her forehead and pretended to be suddenly pained with severe aches.

"Of course, my dear girl. But what a great pity this is. You were the light at my table tonight. Not everyone has sea legs, I'm afraid."

Right, a sailor would certainly pin her sudden retreat on seasickness, even though the Channel was calm as a gliding moon that evening. Plastering another apologetic smile on her face, she rose from her chair, swaying without qualms on her legs. Capt. Hancock raced to help her and held her steady, then snapped his fingers.

"Steward, assist Lady Montgomery to her carriage." Ronald McGuffey hastened to take her arm, while she nodded a scatty goodbye to the astounded guests around the table. Before she was escorted away, Capt. Hancock fished a card from his breast pocket and pressed it into her hand.

"Here are my details, my dear girl. In case you ever need me. What I'll do for the father, I'll do for the daughter. Now be well and au revoir."

Mumbling a half-hearted, "Thank you, Sir," Sable stuffed the card in her purse and in two ticks forgot all about it.

With a rumbling stomach and steward McGuffey at her side, Sable left the messroom after having been present there less than fifteen minutes. She felt no remorse for having dressed up for nothing and being disappointed in the dinner party. For the first time in a long while, she yearned to be alone, to put her stockinged feet up and eat lamb chops with her hands with the grease sliding down her lower arms, gulp red wine from a bathroom glass and not give a flying duck what the world thought of her.

All Sable wanted was freedom—however phoney that freedom was—freedom from all the gobbledygook she'd taken as known but that had served her no purpose but getting more and more miserable. Her parents' egotism and betrayal, Freddie's abandonment, the emptiness of her London life. All she wanted now was the right to enjoy herself every day of her life from this day forward. This was *her* life, and she'd mold it into anything she wanted. Her time, her rules.

Bye, Britain. Bye, past!

6

AN ALL-GIRLS' SCHOOL

Two days later, Lausanne, Switzerland

Le Train Bleu ploughed with difficulty, huffing and puffing, through the snow-laden tracks toward Lausanne. After they had crossed the French border into Switzerland, the snow-fall further intensified. When finally, after the slow and arduous journey, Lake Geneva came into sight, it was a white sheet from shore to shore, still, shrouded, and serene.

Despite being used to snow-capped highland mountains and long winter months of ice and cold, Sable was pleasantly impressed by the more picturesque winter scene that the Swiss Alps provided. Not the rugged wildness of her home country.

It more resembled a tableau she'd once admired with Dadaigh on a visit to the Victoria and Albert Museum on Cromwell Road. The exhibition had been on 19th-century romantic painters, like Caspar David Friedrich and Johan Christian Dahl. The first and only time Sable had stood still long enough in front of a piece of art to appreciate it.

And here it was again. The painting coming to life in real time. As sweet-flowing as it was ungraspable. A no-human-foot-has-yet-trespassed-here fairy tale of pristine white. Reflecting what Freddie would frame "a chocolate-box-mood landscape," a soul-tearing Christmas card scenery, meant to evoke a vague yearning for religious mysticism.

A still, brown hare with ears erect sat in the middle of the field under a branch with red berries, each topped with its own mini-white hat, while in the distance a charming half-timbered chalet loomed, its extensive balcony overlooking the bare valley and the statue-like hare.

The passing, dreamlike scenery on the other side of the window evoked an abrupt, novel longing in Sable's cold chest, a recognition that there might be a sense of beauty existing outside of her, like the chorus of a love song, the lingering of a warm embrace. While she watched intently from her train window, she felt emotions well up in her heart, a struggling will to connect to life again, a fuller and more rewarding life than she'd led so far. The intensity of the emotion rattled her, and she killed it with an iron will.

Don't go there, Sable! You don't do deep.

Sable Montgomery didn't 'do' solemn and still; she didn't accept the sublimity of untamed, unspoiled nature. The very thought of that emotion—or any emotion—would rip open her heart. She wasn't ready for or wanting any of that.

Secretly, so that no other people in her compartment saw her action, she retrieved her handkerchief from her handbag and wiped her moist eyes. Then blew her nose. Yet she felt revived. As if the beauty outside had created a brief but clear insight into her own soul. It had some depth, after all. Not everything had been killed.

Soon the train rolled into Lausanne Central Station, and her long journey was over. Sable disembarked and looked around for help, but the station was busy, and all porters occupied. No one took notice of her, and she felt uneasy as her luggage was still piled up inside the train.

"Hello, *s'il vous plaît*, can you help me?" she called out to one porter who rushed past, afraid the train would leave with her belongings.

"Un moment, Mademoiselle!"

"I haven't got *un moment*, you oaf!" she shouted to his disappearing back.

"Mademoiselle Sable Montgomery?"

An Italian sing-song accent behind her made her turn on her heels. A short, stocky man in a chauffeur's uniform and black cap, which was covered in downy snowflakes, stood wide-legged on the platform, taking her in with a bemused, not very deferential expression.

"Yes? And you are?" She couldn't help the tinge of haughtiness but was also aware she'd better tone it down a bit as this man might be her last resort to get her luggage down from the train. As he knew her name, he must have been sent here to come to her aid.

"Je suis Le Manoir chauffeur. The name is Filippo Maltese. Monsieur Maltese to the students."

Again, that air of superiority Elrod would never show in such a pronounced manner. Sable dug in her heels. He was a mere Italian. *What had gone to his head?*

"Well, *Monsieur* Maltese." She stressed the 'mister' to show her disdain. "Would you be so kind as to collect my luggage from the train and carry it to the car?"

With his dark-brown eyes still on her, the chauffeur snapped his fingers, at which a porter in livery hastened to his side. He addressed him in Italian, which Sable only half understood.

The porter nodded and in polite French asked her to follow him inside the train so she could collect and carry her hatbox herself. Mortified but understanding Monsieur Maltese was not one to cross, Sable did as she was told.

As she sat in the back of the Black Renault watching the chauffeur's broad neck under his cap, she cursed softly. *I'll get you, just wait and see.* Then, looking out of the window over the snow-laden streets of Lausanne, the realization of a new life in a new country dawned on Sable. Nobody knew anything about her here—not her past, not her future. It was highly unlikely that her father had alluded to anything that had happened to his daughter in Scotland which would compromise his good name to the school director.

"I am free!" Sable exclaimed at the misted-up window. "Finally I'm free to do as I want."

"Any problem, Mademoiselle?" The Italian chauffeur threw her a suspicious look in the rear mirror. He clearly didn't understand English. Another bonus, Sable noted.

"Pas du tout, Monsieur Maltese. Happy as a bunny here."

He refrained from saying anything until they slowly crept along the elevated driveway that led to the school standing magnificently on the border of Lake Geneva. Filippo had to drive carefully as the road was slippery with snow and ice.

"Bienvenue à Le Manoir, Mademoiselle. We have arrived. Please be careful when you step out." Another look that said he thought little of her. Sable wrinkled her nose. Snooty man.

The view over Lake Geneva was wintery and beautiful but didn't have Sable's attention anymore. She gazed up at the school building as it appeared in between tall pine trees.

Nice, she decided, *but possibly terribly boring. Especially until spring.*

"I HAVE orders to take you to the school library," Monsieur Maltese announced. "You wait here for Madame Paul." No further explanation. He just disappeared. Quite a lukewarm reception after such a long journey, Sable thought. Her luggage was standing in the corner.

A rather skittish maid in a black dress and white apron came in to offer her tea but quickly slipped out again after leaving the tray on the table. No one came for what seemed a very long time. What a horrible reception.

The clock showed an hour had passed. Tired from traveling and unhappy about the less-than-enthusiastic welcome, Sable took to pacing the large space with its book-lined walls.

"The last place on earth I want to be trapped inside is a library," she told the books and tables as she passed them with an annoyed frown between her dark eyebrows.

"Lady Sable Montgomery, so sorry to have kept you waiting. An emergency with a student kept me occupied."

Sable turned on her heels to see a fashionable, middle-aged woman with a perfect figure and well-coiffed hair come toward her. Most remarkable were the woman's eyes, almost the same color as Sable's but with a much harder glint, as if ice had crashed on ice. But there was something in the woman's proud posture and almost metallic voice Sable recognized, could appreciate.

A steely resolve, a don't-try-to-fool-me attitude. Most women were too soft, lacked oomph, at least in Sable's opinion. Also being addressed with her titled name melted her earlier reserve.

A lukewarm, level hand shook hers. The touch was neither giving nor taking, pleasant nor unpleasant, but gave the impression of an unwritten pact being sealed between them. *Carefully*, Sable's intuition whispered to her. With Madame Paul, everyone would have to walk on tightropes.

"Please follow me to my office. It's just down the corridor."

Erect as a great pine and with lightly swaying hips because of elegant heels, the headmistress led the way. Following her, Sable adopted as if by instinct the same manner of walking. Here was an example of a strong femininity she'd gladly mimic. It also seemed wise to remain in the formidable schoolmarm's good books. At least for the first few weeks.

Seating herself in her large office chair behind a mahogany desk that could easily have made proud Napoleon's headquarters, Madame Paul's coral lacquered index finger pointed to the modest chair on the other side of the voluminous desk, never taking the all-seeing celestite eyes off her target.

Sable withstood the probing look; it lifted her spirit more than anything else had done in the past weeks and months. Female power! She'd underestimated and neglected its force but here it was, in all its glory, and she would benefit from it. Of that, she was sure.

"Time to introduce myself," the lacquered but perfectly accented voice began, "I am Madame Paul Vierret, Le Manoir's headmistress since 1930. The girls all call me Madame Paul. I—in my turn—call the girls Mademoiselle followed by their first name. This is also the way you are supposed to address each other during class. Outside class these formalities may slacken somewhat."

Sable nodded, giving the imposing matron her most sugary smile as she adopted the upper-class French manners she'd learned at the posh Lycée Molière in Paris. To be honest, she found the charade with the Mademoiselle-names rather cumbersome, but as they took each other's measure from opposite sides of the table, Sable concluded she'd give Madame Paul a fair try. A pact of convenience would work best for both.

As they exchanged some more niceties, the gauging of each other's personality never stopped.

"I've placed you in a room with another British girl, Anna Adams. Mademoiselle Anna is, let us say, a little less forthcoming than you, but I hope you'll have a positive influence on making her more communicative. I hope this arrangement is to your satisfaction. All the other important school rules and instructions will be given to you later today. Now, let me show you to your room."

Madame Paul rose, smoothing her navy-blue dress that breathed Paris fashion, and making a swift, rise-up movement with her manicured hand. The turning of her wrist made her diamond bracelet flash with a hard glint in the wintery sun that fell through the window.

Sable rose as bid but, in her turn, waved an impatient hand. This was a red flag that demanded setting a boundary.

"I will—of course—abide by school rules, Madame Paul, and I understand some girls prefer to share bedrooms, but I'd rather have a room of my own. I expect my father, Earl Montgomery, has already paid you lavishly for my tuition, but in case a private room means extra costs, please just send him the bill. He'll readily pay, I can guarantee you."

Sable cast her another sugary smile, while it remained quiet for a long thirty seconds. The clock on the mantlepiece chimed three. Outside the office, muffled treble voices could be heard passing by in the corridor. A dog barked somewhere outside. Madame Paul cleared her throat.

"I'm afraid you've misunderstood me, Mademoiselle Sable." The voice was lower, slightly less friendly. "In order for the girls to develop appropriate social skills and forge lasting friendships, we intentionally have two-person bedrooms. That's the *rule*." The word *rule* was given extra emphasis.

Meanwhile, the headmistress held the elaborate oak door open for Sable, ushering her outside. She thought fast. No way was she going to sleep in a room with another girl. She wanted to smuggle in drinks and smoke her cigarettes—habits no roommate would accept. She tried again, a lie that wasn't completely a lie.

"I suffer from insomnia. I take to pacing my bedroom for hours at night. I will keep the other girl awake."

"Mademoiselle Sable, just try it. If it doesn't work out, we'll cross that bridge when we come to it."

They entered a long corridor on the second floor with brown doors on either side. Madame Paul rapped on a door with number 7 on it and waited, but no answer came from within.

"Mademoiselle Anna must still be in her flower arrangement session," the schoolmarm remarked as she opened the unlocked door. "Come in!"

Sable entered a rather narrow bedroom with two single beds covered by blue and green quilts on either side. Heavy snowfall blocked the windows from any view, and Madame Paul flicked on the ceiling lamp to increase the already fading daylight, despite it being the middle of the afternoon.

The room was sparsely furnished and lacked all ambiance or coziness. It was sterile, stoic, and sensible. Apparently, Le Manoir wanted to radiate austerity and frugalness in no uncertain terms, which—as Sable saw it—was ridiculous, because as a finishing school it was supposed to breed big-mansion wives. Luxury and lavishness would be the very core of their supposed jobs as married wives to big-city bores.

If she'd had the courage, she would've walked straight out, but

Madame Paul—clearly sensing her budding rebellion—blocked the exit with her elegant self. Instead, Sable wrinkled her nose and sighed. She'd have to use all her powers of persuasion to be moved out of here as soon as possible and get at least such a Spartan place of her own. It wasn't luxury she craved; it was not being bothered by imbeciles.

There was no trace of the Anna girl except for a hairbrush that lay on one bed, a stack of novels on the bedside table, and a pair of slippers underneath the bed. The Brit girl clearly fitted the impersonal atmosphere of this Swiss house of correction. *Good for her!*

"This is Anna's bed and her drawer. The other side is yours. You share the en-suite bathroom."

Still blocking the exit as if fencing in an unruly filly, Madame Paul pointed here and there to show Sable the obvious. Then she turned in the door opening and snapped her fingers.

As a god in the machine, Filippo appeared with Sable's suitcases, squeezing past his boss who tucked in her invisible tummy. After dropping her belongings at her feet, the chauffeur left the room in a gallop, hardly taking the time to grant them both a slight, semi-polite bow.

"I'll give you a moment to freshen up, and then I'll ask Anna to come and collect you. We'll have tea together so I can introduce you to the other girls."

Despite herself, Sable felt the need to give it one more try, forcing the semblance of wet eyes. "I beseech you, Madame Paul, please let me have a room of my own."

"I think not, Mademoiselle Sable." The tone was vinegary, and she instantly understood why. Wrong tactic. This woman only understood power, not weakness. Sable could've pinched herself for her slow-wittedness and silently vowed she'd find another way.

Turning her back on the headmistress, she huffed. "I see. It'll do. For now."

After the stiff schoolmistress had turned on her heels, Sable ran to close the door with a firm snap and then footslogged back through the constricted space to sink down on what was to be her bed. She took to staring at Anna's stack of books without really seeing them. Her body was tired, screaming for a drink and a cigarette. She rumbled in her handbag to search for the tin whiskey flask Freddie had given her. Frinton-Smith whiskey. The taste was bittersweet. It was good. She got some pep after it settled her stomach.

After two futile attempts, she opened the half-frozen window, letting a gush of cold air and a flurry of snow land in the room. Still wrapped in her mink coat, she lit a cigarette, sending the gray plume of smoke into the white world outside. It almost froze in mid-air, mingling with the gray and white atmosphere.

She shivered, longing to lie down on the bed and send the smoke to the ceiling. It was out of the question on her first day here. She would certainly be detained if the smell of smoke hung heavily in the room. Anna didn't smoke, at least not here. Whether her temporary roommate would be dissatisfied with Sable's habits was the least of her concerns.

"Roommate!" Sable raved to the snow and cold, taking one final, deep drag. "I'll give her one night and then she'll be out of here. Or I'm in another room."

With an angry gesture she extinguished her cigarette and flushed the stub through the toilet. Then she finally lay down on the bed, flat on her back. With her hands folded over her tummy, she stared up at the whitewashed ceiling. Her mind was blank, her emotions dead, her abdomen still. The room seemed deathly quiet and motionless after two long travel days on the tracks.

She dozed off within seconds until from somewhere in the building's belly a subdued wave of voices erupted. Sable woke from her slumber, listened to the unfamiliar sounds, still groggy and craggy. Classes must have ended.

As the door opened, she turned on her side to watch the entrance of what was to be her one-night roommate. Anna slid inside, long dark-brown hair in a simple ponytail held together with a clip, a slightly built girl, not very tall. She was wearing dark-framed glasses on a straight, mildly freckled nose. Her eyes were chocolate brown with heavy black lashes around them. Her expression was placid, unreadable, with a firm mouth that would clearly only speak when needed. The creamy white skin with its dainty beauty spots and slightly pointed chin made her attractive in a peculiar, boyish way.

Yet there was something indistinctive about Anna, as if she could blend in anywhere and not be seen. A secretive, closed person. At first sight, not the worst roommate.

"I did not know there was anyone here," were her first words, English with an accent Sable couldn't place, something Slavic, certainly not upper-class English. *Was she Jewish?*

"Anna Adams!" The Delphic creature held out a slender white hand with the same sprinkle of freckles, no rings, no nail polish. Sable sat up, took the hand which also disclosed nothing in its elastic shake.

"Sable Montgomery." She thought of squeezing in "Lady" but refrained from doing so at the last moment. The girl puzzled her, made her hold back herself.

They clearly didn't know what else to say to each other. Anna went through the door that led to the bathroom and Sable heard water splash. A minute later she returned, the dark hair now loose, covering her thin shoulders. The glasses were gone. She looked younger, a tad more fragile but her voice was clipped, business-like.

"I'm going down for tea. Are you coming?" No intonation, no connection.

"Sure. Madame Paul told me you would show me the way."

"Did she?" Again, that toneless voice. "Are you ready to go down?" Anna hardly raised her sentences at the end, which made them sound not like questions, but rather facts.

She stared for a moment at Sable's unpacked suitcases and then at her crumpled travel outfit as she rose from the bed. Sable stretched, yawned. She would not make any excuses for her appearance.

"Yes. Why wouldn't I be?"

Anna's brown eyes rested on her.

"It's forbidden to smoke inside the school." A remark, no more, as if insubstantial but with a lingering warning.

After grabbing a warm cardigan, Anna left the room with Sable
having no other choice but to follow her. *What a haughty lot here*, she
thought angrily, *first that ill-bred chauffeur and now this urchin.* Her not
giving them a piece of her mind had more to do with her travel-
weariness than her character. These too-big-for-their-boots individuals had something coming for them. When she was rested.

The tea lasted endlessly and was a total bore. To top off Sable's
misery, it was stone-cold in the lavishly furnished but impersonal
afternoon room. She wished she'd dressed more warmly but would
not show it. Straight-backed in her thin merino traveling dress, it took
some effort to repress the shivering of her limbs. Her fingers were
almost too cold to hold the teacup's ear and the delicate cup landed
rather clumsily on its saucer, followed by a stern look from Madame
Paul.

The food was good, ham sandwiches and rich fruit cake, which
was oddly enough not served by staff but by the students. The girls
were all dressed in thick jumpers and warm cardigans, their legs
wrapped in woolen stockings. Had those Swiss no sense of heating
their premises, or were they just too frugal?

Glancing around the table, Sable gauged the other girls to see if
there were possibilities for a pact, specifically to teach that Anna a
lesson. Potential recruits were two Paris fashion-conscious girls introduced as Margarita and Blanche; then there were two stiff-looking
English girls, Julie and Bella, identical twins. They huddled together,
obviously a herky-jerky foursome without proper leadership. There
could be possibilities there, though they had scant glamour and
gumption.

The rest of the students comprised an odd assembly of eastern
European girls from the Balkans or even Russia. They hardly spoke
proper English, though their French was better than Sable's. She had
no interest in those girls.

Tomorrow she would make her first move. For today, she was just
too drained and sleep deprived. Tomorrow she would set about reor-
ganizing the power structures at her new all-girls' school.

7

THE GIRL BOSS

Summer 1938

S able had withdrawn to the washroom at the back of Le Manoir, where she could smoke her cigarette without being scolded and could relax in a precious moment to herself. She'd now been pigeonholed for six months at what was only a gormless place to her. A grim, lusterless winter had changed into an Alpine summer with a soft breeze from the lake and plenty of sunshine, with the occasional shower descending from the icy mountain air.

The irritating, cream-colored cows with their clanging bells could be heard at all hours in the meadows above the school. Another sign of the local half-wittedness according to Sable.

How long still? Her father had written, *Just a little longer*. Sable yearned to be twenty-one and do as she wished. Her mood was slipping below freezing point despite the sweet weather and the wonderful food.

Sometimes, when she tried hard, she could see how pretty her surroundings were, the sloping meadows dotted with what Monsieur Georges, their art teacher, called the jewels of the Alps—lilac asters, sun-yellow cowslips, vivid-blue gentians, and the famous white edel-weiss. She'd had to name and paint and dry these flowers until she was sure she'd hate wildflowers for the rest of her life.

With a somber frown bending her dark brows, she fixed her gaze on the white sails of the expensive yachts that slid by silently through the navy-blue water. Toward freedom, toward God-knew-where. Then she raised her eyes to the tall mountains on the other side of the lake that stood there as sturdy giants guarding their surroundings. She sighed, swinging her legs, enjoying her smoke.

It was odd to find herself here in Switzerland, a country that clung to its neutral status between aggressive powers with an almost religious fervor.

Le Manoir forbade all talk of politics and news, even if some girls burst out in tears during dinner, sobbing that their countries were threatened with annexation by Hitler's army.

Sable didn't know what to think of it all. Politics and Hitler were not her concern, but she had a longing to know what all the fuss was about. Why the agitation was held at bay by Madame Paul and her staff. What was there to hide from almost adult girls?

Yet politics seeped in at the seams no matter how much both country and Madame Paul tried to block out reality. Even to Sable, in her shut-out, kept-under-wraps state, it slowly became clear the Continent was fast spinning out of control.

Her thoughts, as they often did, turned to Freddie.

Freddie, dear stalk-legged Freddie with his unquenchable wish to be an athletic hero. If only he knew she was so unaware of the state of the world, he'd call her *dummy dumbbell* all over again, just as he had teased her when she didn't understand the 1929 stock market crash when she was ten and he thirteen.

With trepidation, she retrieved a white envelope from her pants' pocket and flattened the creases. Gray ash smudged Freddie's Oxford digs' address. It meant he was still studying, not pursuing his dream of becoming a fighter jet pilot. His letter had arrived in the mail that morning. The first one since she'd left England. She'd written him at least four times. With an angry frown, she tore open the envelope and scanned its interior. Freddie's distinct handwriting, a little curly and immaculate. A vague scent of Dior Homme wafted into her nose.

My dearest Sabbo,

I can almost see the frown chiseled on your forehead as you read this letter. And yes, I apologize for my tardiness. No excuse, just laziness and, you know, time-flies-and-that-kind-of-balderdash.

Anyway, I hope you're out of the woods and an accomplished matron by now. I think of you often and hypothesise what would've happened if we'd gotten married after all. Would we be traipsing around the globe together? Would you have been happier? Would we be happy together?

Pathetic questions, of course. We both know it was as well we pulled the plug. It wasn't destined to be. But I know you know me, and I know you. You can read between the lines of this aide-mémoire better than anyone else. No, things aren't good here. Oh, it's not the usual thing. Dad pays my allowance, and David and I are still you-know-what. It's the political situation that's making me melancholic.

On the one hand, Mosley and his fascist Blackshirts are far too dominantly marching through our English cities, and I sincerely fear for the direction our dear country is heading. On the other hand, this appeasement movement that Chamberlain is so stuck on to mollify Hitler and his henchman is also insufferable. We need action, a strong stand. But who can deliver that? My soapbox isn't attracting many listeners.

I know you probably see me as a worthless-rich-son-of-a-whiskey-magnate, but David has really changed me. He's so serious and studious. I greatly admire his determination and outlook on life. I want to leave the cynical party-going life behind me, but they won't let me join the RAF as a pilot yet. I've passed all the tests and exams but now am twiddling my thumbs. Hopefully next month!

Law doesn't hold my interest anymore, and joining Frenton-Smith Distillery is as far detached from my plans as can be. Sometimes, I feel myself wishing we were at war with Germany, and I could really do something of consequence.

Anyway, I realize I must sound terribly boring and lacking in fun to you. That was my main reason not to write. I felt I would disappoint you, too. We were just two lost souls, Sab, and I truly hope you've found a reason to live for. You so deserve it.

Another reason I didn't pick up the pen was because I was doubting if I should let you know, but horrible Henkell is now the German ambassador to the UK. There, it's said. It's criminal and makes me furious, but also in this respect my hands are tied. Please, don't let this news upset you, my dear Sabbo! I just wanted to make sure you got it from me and not find out this rotten luck once your finishing schooling is done.

Thanks so much for your letters. It sounds like there are no great shakes in Switzerland, not a sizzling shindig but passable. Loved your description of the schoolmarm and the silly schoolgirls. You're clearly the Girl Boss. You're a Boss in every respect, Sabbo, and I hope you feel proud of that.

Let me know when you're back on British soil and we can be reunited again.

YOUR DEVOTED FREDDO.

SABLE LIT another cigarette and stared at the transparent plume of smoke swirling upwards. His letter—though not very personal— touched her deeply. She so clearly saw Freddie before her, the dark mane, the blue eyes, her soul-twin brother, restless and always on the run, just like she was. It was what he didn't say in his letter, but she felt it, felt it so strongly, almost as if he was tied to her. *Give me a reason to live for. Give me a goal I can throw my force behind.*

And then his news about Von Henkell now being promoted to UK ambassador. It had been on the cards; she knew that all along. It was typical for Freddie to take her feelings into account, but frankly, she couldn't care less. That was the one thing being abroad had done for her. A clean break with the past. Von Henkell existed in another world, not hers. If she ever returned to London, it would only be as a passerby. Her London life was of no consequence to her anymore. She felt old, beyond her natural age.

The only thin thread connecting her to London was Dadaigh. But his sparse letters were as short and impersonal as the justice of God. She'd stopped caring for them. No word from her mother was good news. Parents were as much a nuisance as the silly girls here at Le Manoir.

God, life was senseless. It made her feel so powerless, so boiling mad! But there was nothing to vent her anger on other than to trample some Alpine flowers or pull a trick on one of the immature gooses. Another cigarette perhaps.

Sable returned to gazing at Freddie's letter in her left hand while in her right a burning cigarette quivered. The picture he had of her here, the picture she'd fed him in her letters... As if she was in a privileged situation at this wretched finishing school, with all Madame Paul's backing and a room of her own, girls who flocked to her side as soon as she showed her face, and a proper fear ingrained in those she didn't support.

But Sable knew better. She might have taken Anna's room and sent the girl packing to stay with that Dutch ballerina, blue-blooded Edda of some sorts, but it hadn't really been Sable's victory over Anna. Anna had presented Madame Paul with a fait accompli after one night with Sable. Her rich London uncle would withdraw his funding from the Swiss school and create a scandal in the papers. Anna had commanded her own room. Not Sable.

That was the actual story, though Madame Paul had said nothing of the sort. She kept her cards close to her chest. It was Anna who'd slipped a copy of her uncle's letter under Sable's door. No note attached, just the letter. Sable bit her lip.

Ever since that incident, she and Anna had been like chalk and cheese. Though the mousy Jew stayed out of her way, and shared the common pretense that Sable was the most popular girl at Le Manoir, Anna's loathing of her person was clear. And it hurt. Anna was the stronger in a cold, silent manner, passively but steadily undermining her position. The wench had no use for words or actions; her attitude said it all.

Sable took to pacing again, a habit that had only increased when she became overly restless. Although she ate well and could not get her hands on much alcohol, she grew thinner, a tawny strength, while the lines around her mouth, an early sign of what she would look like in old age, already were etched permanently on her face.

Extinguishing her cigarette and stuffing Freddie's letter back in her pocket, she made her way outside and walked around the corner of the brick school building, yearning for some admiration from her devotees. Anything to break this desperate feeling of isolation. Fake friendships built on Sable's pecking order. That's all it was. Fake, fake, fake.

Just before rounding the corner, she halted in her tracks and retraced her steps to take cover in the ivy that overgrew the brick wall. There was a new arrival. The tires of Filippo's black Renault came to a crunching halt on the gravel next to the stone steps that led to the school entrance. Sable saw how a tall girl, attractive and sophisticated, with a ribboned straw-hat on her blond hair, got out of the car.

If it hadn't been for her hesitant movements and her slightly hunched shoulders, the newcomer could've been an actress with the glamour and beauty of Hollywood. Sable saw how she lifted her face to take in the school, the profile so pure and regular. Then she turned her attention to Filippo, her face both kind and deferential, as he placed her suitcases at her feet.

"Another goody-two-shoes," Sable murmured to herself.

"What's going on?" Margarita, who'd slinked up to her, was peering over Sable's shoulder.

"Hush! A new victim," she whispered.

"The girl looks all right to me. Maybe she can be one of us," Margarita suggested, her round face reverently inclined toward her leader.

"Then she'll have to work for it. We could do the music trick tonight?"

Margarita smirked. "Perfect idea, Sable, as always."

An involuntary sigh escaped Sable's chest. She was so tired of the French girl's piping, idolizing tone. She could've strangled the round-breasted popsy there and then. How unbearable and silly could one be? But she needed Margarita and her clan just a little longer. Until she could escape the school. Damming in her irritation as best as she could, she whispered,

"Hush!"

Madame Paul came sailing down the steps and Sable looked forward to the first swipe the headmistress would take at the new girl. She was the perfect prey. Just too darn nice and naïve. Madame Paul didn't do nice; she only did nasty.

Both Sable and Margarita strained their ears to catch the conversation taking place in the courtyard.

"Mademoiselle Esther Weiss, welcome to Le Manoir."

"Possibly another Jew," Sable scowled, "but the Weiss girl certainly doesn't look like one."

"She's making the mistake of proffering her hand first," Margarita snickered behind her chubby hand.

They heard the headmistress gurgle a short "uh-uh." Madame Paul shook her tightly coiffed head with the light-brown coil decorating her nape. Sable was already mimicking her in that brawling voice while raising a tapered forefinger.

"Lesson one, Mademoiselle Esther. Wait until the older person extends his or her hand."

"Please stop, or I'll wet myself," Margarita begged, giggling so loud that Sable had to put her hand over the silly girl's mouth and almost choked her. Madame Paul looked in their direction. Just in time they ducked out of sight, with Margarita still wriggling under Sable's firm grip. When they peeked around the corner again, the headmistress and the new girl had disappeared inside.

Sable felt an unexpected surge of pity for the nice new girl. She'd looked like a washed-up cat, already being scolded for doing nothing wrong. How could it be so hard for the other girls to manage the Sphinx, as they secretly called the headmistress among themselves?

To Sable, she was like wax in her fingers. If ever there was a predictable, easy to charm individual, it was Madame Paul.

It had taken Sable one week to read her thoroughly and then become her favorite student. She'd managed that by learning her rules faster than the gin's grip on a wayfarer and by not being afraid of her. Madame Paul had no power over Sable Montgomery, none. *I'd make a great secret agent*, Sable had contemplated. *I learn the rules and can then bend them with no one noticing.*

"Let's find the others," she commanded. With Margarita on her heels, she went in search of her team: Julie, Bella, and Blanche.

"MADEMOISELLE SABLE, please collect the new student, Mademoiselle Esther, from room 6 and accompany her down to tea."

The celestite eyes that rested on her had that knowing look Sable already recognized. *Train the new one into submission.*

"Of course, Madame Paul. Right away." Though she wanted to loathe the woman, Sable couldn't suppress a feeling of pride. It simply felt too good to be singled out and trusted by someone. *A little longer*, she told herself, *then I'll make sure you hate me and send me away. Twenty-one, only a few months away, and I can go where I please.*

Sable hastened to meet the beautiful blonde who had stirred so many whispers among the girls in the past hour. *From a rich jeweller's family in Vienna. Blonde but a Jew. Already engaged.*

Before Sable could set out on her mission to accompany this new acquisition, Madame Paul, standing in the door opening of the etiquette class, added a final word.

"Girls, there's yet another student arriving today. Mademoiselle Océane Bell from the United States. I expect you to help both new students settle in; they will both be in room 6." Gaping mouths and glances were exchanged. Eager faces nodded in quick unison before it would end in another tirade by the schoolmistress about lax manners.

Somebody from another continent, as far away as America, sent an irrepressible ripple of excitement through the classroom. Even Sable felt something resembling a thrill. Maybe the girl was from New York and could tell her what it was like to live in the Big Apple.

The Russian teacher Monsieur Petrov, as always immaculately dressed in his three-piece suit, complete with upturned bowtie and lace pocket, clapped his perfumed hands in irritation at the distraction from his all-important etiquette lessons.

"*Allons-si, mes filles*! Attention back to diplomatic conversations when discussions at the dinner table turn too political."

Sable was given permission to leave Monsieur Petrov's class early to do her principal girl duties and followed Madame Paul into the corridor. Seconds later she tapped on the brown door, repressing a nervous tremor. Esther opened the door, an inviting look on her sweet face.

Eyes beautiful as precious sapphires locked with Sable's. The kindness and intelligence struck her as a cricket bat, and she knew she'd have to fight off liking this girl. Sable didn't do kindness. It was simply too treacherous.

"Yes?" A warm, welcoming smile curled the gorgeous mouth, making Sable clench her fists.

"I'll take you down to tea." She tried to make her voice sound harsh, but it came out hoarse.

"Okay, thank you. Let me grab my cardigan." The girl disappeared again into the room that looked orderly. A black-and-white photograph of her and a dashing-looking dark-haired man rested on the side table next to the bed.

"Sorry for my bad manners," the blonde apologized. "My name is Esther Weiss." She extended a white-gloved hand.

"*Lady* Sable Montgomery." It was terse, the stress on *lady*, which had the right effect. The turquoise eyes widened while Esther's sweet face nodded appreciatively. Sable turned her back on her and started marching down the corridor to the staircase. Esther hastened to keep up with her.

"How long have you been here, Mademoiselle Sable?"

Sable didn't answer. Conflicting thoughts on how to approach this

Esther phenomenon distracted her. She'd been here way too long. *Eight months, none of your business, whatsoever.* Sable simply kept marching at high speed until they arrived at the terrace.

On nice summer days, like today, tea was served outside under the parasols. Sable felt the eyes of her gang on her but kept a deadpan expression. For now, she wanted Esther to herself before she'd decide whether to feed her to the dogs or not.

There was something about this Austrian girl, a quality so pure and real, speaking of incredible strength under that sweet presence. Even Sable didn't want to squash it, though she knew she might have to, to keep in Madame Paul's good books. Pointing to one of the wicker chairs that stood around the set table, she growled, "You sit there."

Esther threw her a confused look, vexed, clearly not understanding the latent hostility. Sable turned away from her, biting her lip but walking over to her friends. *Sometimes being a favorite sucks,* she thought, *especially when you're serving the wrong master.* It wasn't the first time she realized Madame Paul might be the wrong master, but for now this was how the cards were dealt if she wanted to remain the headmistress's favorite student a little longer.

Glancing over her shoulder, she saw that Dutch Edda, who now was Anna's roommate, had taken the bewildered Esther under her wing. Edda was a category of her own, not mixing much with the others, not even being close to Anna. Practicing her ballet moves for hours if her recently broken ankle permitted it. She was a prima ballerina even if she didn't dance.

Sable felt neutral toward Edda, not having been much in touch with her, mostly staying out of her way. She hadn't harassed her. Hadn't needed to. It was an open secret at Le Manoir that Edda came from one of the oldest European aristocratic families and was most likely more titled than all of them together.

Madame Paul never burnt her fingers on aristocracy. Sable suspected that the headmistress came from simple origins herself and doted on titles. And Edda breathed just that. You didn't get near the girl without feeling you came close to royalty, straight as a ruler and majestic as the sun at noon.

After tea, that long-winding process of afternoon etiquette, was over and done with, it was time for the most boring topic on the Le Manoir schedule: ironing class. The only thing that cheered Sable up somewhat was that Esther had chosen her as a mentor for her first assignment, though inwardly, it made her smirk.

If there was anyone who had no clue about ironing, even a serviette, it was Sable Montgomery. But this would give her the opportunity to single out the newcomer and find out what made her tick. Sable had always wanted to be a blonde with green eyes, tall as Esther, and seemingly not have a worry in the world, with a man waiting for her to marry her and a future that was already laid in stone.

As soon as they had entered the laundry room, where the ironing boards and irons stood in a neat row like soldiers on parade, Sable sat herself in the windowsill, watching how Esther heated the iron and spit on it routinely to test its heat.

"I'm supposed to give you ironing instructions but by the looks of it, a chipper German girl like you knows more about ironing than me."

"I'm not German, I'm Austrian."

"Who cares?" Sable made an impatient movement with her manicured hand. From her cardigan pocket she retrieved a packet of Craven A and a silver lighter, then brought a tapered finger to her painted lips.

"Not a word! Understood? We're not allowed to smoke in and around Le Manoir. You do the ironing, I smoke. If you keep your mouth shut, you and I are on a good footing."

"Sure." Esther shrugged.

Sable wasn't happy that this novice didn't seem very taken by her. With a brooding frown, she watched as Esther's deft hands flattened and folded one embroidered pillowcase after the other. It seemed as if the heavy cast-iron iron weighed nothing in hands, which were apparently not just beautiful but also very strong.

Staring at Esther's industrious work, the blue eyes squinting through the smoke, Sable chose another strategy.

"To answer your initial question, Esther, I've been at Le Manoir way too long, ever since the beginning of winter. At first, it was kind of doable, certainly because it wasn't all sunshine and roses at home. My parents are entangled in an endlessly drawn-out divorce procedure."

She took another drag on her cigarette, the crease between her brows increasing, her eyes diverted from Esther and her busyness.

"My mother's a great fan of scandal, always has been. The new low was the-soon-to-be-ex-Countess-Montgomery being caught in the arms of a married admiral by a photographer of *The Daily Express*. Not the exposure my father wanted for his marriageable daughter with his blue blood in her veins. As if I care two fiddlesticks about marriage or being marriageable. I like men, like to have fun with them, but marriage? No thank you!"

Uttering a scornful laugh, she extinguished her cigarette on the windowsill and threw the stub out of the window. She already regretted sharing her secrets, though she hadn't touched on the most important reason for her presence in Switzerland. She'd acted so like her mother. Not that Egbert Van Eijck had been married and nothing had really happened between them, but still. Dadaigh was trying to steer her the other way. And the big, ugly secret that lay behind it all...

Anger returned to her like a boomerang. Why was she disclosing any of this to the Austrian petticoat? What was it about Esther that triggered her sensitivities? It was totally unnecessary to tell her anything about her private life, and it was so not done to shed any light on her dysfunctional family.

Still fuming at her indiscretion, she heard Esther produce a heart-felt, "I'm sorry." This only added fuel to Sable's frustration. Now she was thoroughly cornered, as if she'd been seeking the stranger's sympathy, even approval. Not a place she liked to be in. Was this silly school eroding her common sense? She certainly had stayed way too long. And kindness was her enemy.

Torn in two directions—open up or withdraw—she heard Esther ask in that soft, kind voice with the Germanic undertone, "So, what is it you don't like about Le Manoir, Sable?"

Sable took to her pacing, fists in her bright-colored summer cardigan pockets. When she reached Esther, who stood on the other side of the ironing board, she fixed her with her brilliant blue stare.

"Just what I told you. There are no men here to have fun with. At least not until the skiing season and we get those handsome instructors who aren't at least one-hundred years old like Monsieur Petrov and Monsieur Georges. I can't wait to be kidding around in the snow and feel the blood in my veins flow again. What about you? Do you like romping around in the snow?"

The provocation was deliberate, her path chosen. Sable enjoyed the look of shock in the prim virgin's face across from her. She'd shut herself like an oyster again, making sure Esther wouldn't come under her skin for a second time. Not even if she tried. Which was very unlikely now.

At that moment Mademoiselle Brunner, the spindly spinster who oversaw the household classes, entered the laundry room. Dark clothed, with a pristine white apron over her clothes, thin as a rake and with round glasses that perpetually slipped down the bridge of her narrow nose, the teacher looked from Sable to Esther and back, the short-sighted eyes on high alert.

By instinct Sable grabbed the last pillowcase out of Esther's hold and cried rather shrilly, "We're doing fine, just rounding off our business, Mademoiselle Brunner!"

Mademoiselle Brunner sniffed.

"Who's been smoking here?"

"No one," Sable lied. "I smelled it too. Must be one of the garden boys down behind the bushes."

The sticklike household teacher moused over to the open window to gaze down into the garden. Sable signaled to Esther not to betray her. But it was too late. Sable realized that this was Brunner's chance.

The prim tutor had lain in wait so long to pounce on her,

disliking her with a force that bordered on a personal vengeance. Well, the dislike was mutual, but so far Sable had felt protected by Madame Paul, who'd always taken her side when the laundry miss reported on Sable's sloppy household work. This time, as always, she counted on the headmistress's protection.

"Mademoiselle Sable, can you wait outside the door while I make Mademoiselle Esther's acquaintance?"

"Biensûr!"

See, there it was. Not a cloud in the sky. Sable slipped out of the door and back to the other girls.

"Bingo!" she cheered. "Let's play the music trick on Miss-Way-Too-Nice tonight."

8

ALL IS NOT AS IT SEEMS

"Come into my office, Mademoiselle Sable." Madame Paul's voice had that metallic ring that meant something was amiss.

"Blast," Sable murmured, realizing either Brunner or Esther must have sold her out after all. Probably Brunner. Esther was just too affable.

Sable smiled across the table in her own affable way, marshalling all the diplomacy her father had taught her to keep the headmistress on her side. But frankly, it was all just a bore, if not outright ridiculous. Why bother? She just wanted to go home. If only she had a home to go to.

Madame Paul's icy voice sliced through the air. "It was told that *you*, as Mademoiselle Esther's ironing mentor, have not given her the correct ironing instructions. By now, Mademoiselle Sable"—At this, the celestite eyes fixed her over the rim of the glasses on their pearl strings—"you should know how important it is to apply oneself to the task at hand. How will you ever be able to satisfy your future husband if you do not..."

Sable mentally shut her ears with her fingers while fighting hard not to spit the hoity-toity madam in the face. *Satisfy, husband, apply oneself?* It was just too gross for words.

All I want is to be free, to do as I want for a change. Not for a husband and not for you, Madame Sphinx!

While Sable fought her anger and despair, she made a vow to herself. Out of here as soon as possible, the right way, or the wrong way. It didn't matter anymore. She was done pleasing this frigid woman with her etiquette and hogwash. Why not get up now and just walk out of that door and never return? Who would stop her?

Lack of money would.

Sable sank back in her chair. Caged again.

"Mademoiselle Sable!"

The voice that called her name sent icy blood through her veins. Sable stared back hard at the woman opposite her, finally stripping her inwardly of all the former admiration she might have had for her at the beginning.

It had all been a trap. Like her entire life had been a trap set up by stuck-up, soulless creatures who were poles apart from her and had never known her or cared to know her. A small voice inside her whispered, "Just a little longer, Sable. Just a bit longer and you'll be free."

Sable swallowed her anger down hard, plastered the fake smile on her pretty face and squeezed her hands in her lap. She made a pretense of listening to the headmistress, who, as always, made sure she didn't spill the blood of her own teachers using her vast arsenal of circumspect diplomacy.

What was in it for her? If it was sloppiness she was convicted of, she would easily shake it off and blame it on Esther, but apparently it would not be that easy.

"It has also come to my attention that you have again"—Madame Paul halted here and the celestite eyes fixed Sable as a beetle in her chair—"*again* been smoking on the school premises."

What's the big deal? Sable thought angrily, but she knew smoking students was Madame Paul's red flag. For some obscure reason.

"I'm sorry. I won't do it again. I forgot." She hoped her mumbled apology would be enough to leave this oppressive office. It remained silent for a while.

"Last warning, Mademoiselle Sable. If you're found smoking again, you will be grounded for a week. No perks, no outings. Homework and early bed."

Sable's insides screamed the entire arsenal of the profanities she'd like to level on that haughty woman, but she just about managed not to let them slip out. *What was the big deal?* Instead, her face reddened, and the frown deepened. Humility bolstered Sable; it failed in its purpose to subjugate her. Fists clenched, she was relieved to hear the words, *"that will be all,"* which was the signal that permitted her to leave the hated office.

Back in her room, Sable paced the length of it for more than an hour, brainstorming all manners of escape but tossing them out one by one. If only Freddie had a place of his own and wasn't so entangled with David, she could stay with him. And what about Cavendish Square? Or take the last money she had and go to Rome?

Alnor Castle was out of the question. Mother was still holding the fort there with her odious German friends. No, there'd be no return to Alnor, no subjugating herself to Misty Fletcher and her entourage. As long as Dadaigh didn't take control back of their home, she would not show her face there. As if he ever would.

"It's high time I leave Le Manoir. This awful prison has quenched the last bit of soul I had left. But where to? Where to?"

AFTER DINNER, Sable kept a close watch on Esther. She was of two minds about her. Break all ties with her infatuated cronies and only try to befriend the Austrian? Or keep the power structures as they were and test the new one as discussed with Margarita?

When she saw Esther descend the stone steps to the lake, geared up in hat and gloves, she followed her at a close distance, a burning cigarette dangling from the corner of her red lips. As she was moving out of sight of the school entrance and Madame Paul's office at the

rear, she defied *the last warning before being grounded.* The more strin-
gent the threat, the more forceful the defiance.

It was an exquisite August evening with the sun, still warm as an
oven, sinking fast behind the slate-blue mountain ridge, creating a
dramatic splendor into the heavens with all the warm colors of the
painter's palette, bright yellow, burnt-orange, scarlet red, peachy-pink
and midnight purple. Gray slate from dispersing clouds drew
smudges across the color arrangement, while the dark side of the
mountain ripened into blackish green velvet.

Sable stood a moment in awe with a sudden yearning to be a
painter, or at least a photographer. This picture, this landscape, this
moment. Any self-respecting painter would have gotten out her paint
gear, easel, and brushes to mimic the evening spectacle. If only she
had that gift.

Feeling the pure, soft caress of the oncoming breeze on her
cheeks, she pushed back the long black mane from her forehead to
expose more of her face. With eyes closed and face turned upwards,
she tried to feel it all, to feel again. The sweet scent of lavender and
Bourbon roses, the soft lapping of the mini-waves on the shore, the
last rays of sunshine warming her marred body. This was life without
problems, life as it should be, when her heart wasn't racing on,
wanting something else, wanting something more.

Just this. Just the promise of a clear, starlit evening. Peace. No
movement.

Letting out a deep sigh, a mix of grief and relief, she opened her
eyes again. Then extinguished her cigarette with a routine swirl of
her sole. The frown was instantly back. Looking toward the lake, she
saw Esther was seated on a flat stone near the shoreline, her bare feet
in the cold water, staring out over the lake, her blond hair almost
completely shaded by the straw-hat.

Sable snapped out of her own introspection and started studying
her target. There was something forlorn about the girl, the way she
sat there in deep contemplation, seemingly not needing anyone from
her new surroundings but radiating an unspeakable loneliness. As if
no one and nothing could take away her pain.

It was then that it struck Sable that Esther was hiding a painful secret as well. She did not know what it was, but it for sure had to do with the people she'd left behind in Vienna. Jews and Hitler weren't a good combination, and had the Führer not occupied Austria in the spring?

But instead of feeling empathy for her, the story she made up about Esther longing for her family enraged Sable. Why would this girl mourn over loved ones she'd left behind? She *had* loved ones to mourn. It wasn't fair. Sable had no one. Not even... not even that which had been hers and what she couldn't name...

As happened so often under extreme stress, Sable's mood swung from tragic despair to wronged enragement. The fury that boiled in her chest had to be taken out on someone; someone had to be punished for it. But as she closed the distance between her and Esther, a vague remorse squirmed in that same chest. She swallowed the bile. Why would it be different this time? She'd had no scruples press-ganging the new girls so far. So why treat Esther differently and become the laughingstock among her titled gang?

"Hey, Esther! What are *you* doing here, sitting so sadly on your own?"

It sounded a tad too friendly. *No pussyfooting around it*, she scolded herself. Esther didn't react, as if she hadn't heard her. She just kept staring over the water with unseeing eyes, deep in a trance.

Sable sat down on another stone at a slight distance and lit another cigarette. *To hell with last warnings!* Inhaling deeply, she felt the familiar scouring pain spread throughout her lungs, almost pleasurable, certainly a comfort.

"I got *caught*."

Startled, Esther shook herself from her reverie and stared at Sable as if she'd tumbled from the sky. "What was that?"

"I was given a last warning."

"I'm sorry. What for?" Esther's smile was wry, her eyes still in another world.

"Smoking."

Now the green eyes looked puzzled as they went to the smoldering cigarette between Sable's smoke-yellow fingers.

"Doesn't seem to stop you."

"I can't. Smoking is the only joy I've got left in this world, now they've taken booze and boys from the menu."

"That sounds dramatic." Esther's voice was level; she was clearly not very impressed by Sable's lamentable life circumstances, neither pleased with the interruption.

Sable played with the sash of her belted dress while she smoked, winding and unwinding it around her index finger. Then cleared her throat.

"I don't blame you directly. But it is the *good* girls like you that ruin it for the rest of us."

Esther raised one eyebrow, still puzzled but not compliant. There it was again, that refusal-to-bend quality in the do-good damsel. It made Sable fence-straddle between being drawn to her and deeply angered. The confusion was genuine.

"Blame me? What have I done?" Esther's genuinely surprised, sweet voice made her inhale her cigarette even more forceful.

"Put me in a bad spot with Mademoiselle Brunner. That's what you've done."

Esther rose to her feet, clearly uncomfortable with the way the conversation was going, making clear she wanted to get away from Sable sourpuss. *She's probably been forewarned by Anna and Edda of my reputation*, Sable thought. She got to her feet as well, intent on making amends.

"I told you I don't blame you. Don't go yet. Do you by any chance play an instrument, Esther? Your hands look so musical." Sable didn't miss the glint of pleasure that sprung into the beautiful sea-green eyes.

"I do. I play the piano and I sing."

"Exactly what I need to be cheered up! I feel like dancing. To get rid of this spleen. I hope you can play dance tunes, not just boring Mozart?"

The pleased expression vanished from the kind face and turned to hurt and renewed suspicion. Mozart didn't equal boredom to Esther. Sable understood she'd have to lure her with another compliment.

"Oh, don't pay attention to me. I'm Neanderthalic when we talk music! What can you play, Esther, outside classical music? Any jazz, Benny Goodman perhaps? I'd love to hear *Sing, Sing, Sing* tonight?" Sable swung her hips, laughing with her red lips and bearing white teeth. Esther stood rather stiffly, then shrugged the slightly hunched shoulders.

"Is there a piano at Le Manoir? I haven't seen one."

"Of course, silly. There's a whole music room and even a theatre with a stage. We're supposed to act and sing and dance like the hussies Madame Paul looks down on with a vengeance. Come now!"

Sable let out a high-pitched laugh that sounded strange to her own ears. Was that her laughter? It had become fake like everything else. Shaking herself from her self-focus, she realised she hadn't convinced Esther of her scheme yet. The good-girl attitude was still sauced all over the Austrian's features. Time to turn up the pressure a notch and counteract objections raised.

"It's been a long day, and maybe my roommate, you know, the American girl, has arrived in the meantime."

"Oh, don't be a spoilsport, Weiss. Do you want to hang out with me and the popular girls, or do you rather prefer that cripple Van der Falck?"

"Don't say that!" Now Esther's voice was acrid as quick lime. "It's inappropriate to taunt the disabled. And by the way, Edda is far from disabled; she simply broke her ankle."

"All right, all right, Miss Faultless and Fix-up. I didn't know you'd already chosen sides and didn't want to be in my group of friends."

This was unexpectedly the right chord.

"Oh, but I want to be friends with you, Sable. Very much so!"

"Good. That was what I had hoped."

A tiny, genuine smile crept to the corners of Sable's mouth. For the very first time in her life, she was aware of seeing a glimpse of a different type of woman than she'd ever encountered. Not one who thrived on competition with her own sex or getting her way by scheming. It was a novel experience that such women existed. Her soul wanted to learn more, to get closer to a woman like Esther, but her ingrained defense mechanism threw her back into her old self.

Sable didn't do *good*—Sable distrusted, mistrusted, and mistreated. That was the tough cookie she wanted the world to see. But here was Esther standing squarely in the way of that world-wise version of herself. Sable wanted, craved that innocence, the real thing.

What now? she reprimanded herself. A girl like Esther would never be her friend. They were like Odette and Odile in *Swan Lake*. And she, Sable, would always be the black swan.

So, when Esther answered, "All right, one Benny Goodman song. After that, I'm off to my room," Sable knew the path she would walk.

Cheerfully, she replied, "Great! Now come quick before Madame Paul sees us. I know a safe route."

Grabbing Esther's hand, she didn't let go as they jogged up the stairs to the school's back entrance. Esther began protesting again, but Sable held her firmly in her grip.

"But you said..."

"Shh ... never mind. The girls are all waiting. It's a surprise." She felt the blonde girl's resistance wane as she trudged her along the back corridor until they came to one of Le Manoir's many brown doors with a copper plate that read *Music Room & Theatre*.

"Wait here for a moment, Esther." She opened the door to spy around in the music hall.

"Rightio, coast's clear!"

Ushering Esther in, she quickly closed the door behind them. Together they walked along the aisle of the large, dusky room that was only used for performances, graduation ceremonies, and the Christmas musical.

The deep-red velvet curtains in front of the windows were drawn and only several shady lamps were lit in a row along the outer walls. A grand piano stood close to the elevated stage that was also closed with burgundy draped curtains.

Sable whistled between her teeth and from the shades her gang emerged, giggling softly, and poking each other in the ribs.

"Is she doing it?" Margarita, the first in the picking order behind Sable, asked in her French-accented voice.

"Sure, she's doing it! Es is a fine girl. She's one of us."

Feeling Esther's initial hesitation about the illegality of their action re-emerge, she felt a need to reassure her. With resolute steps, Sable marched over to the grand piano and opened the lid. Ruffling through the sheet music that was stacked in a neat pile on top of the piano, she instantly transformed it into a mess with several sheets floating to the floor. Esther bent to pick them up. Sable hissed in a low voice, the adrenaline surging through her veins.

"Let them be, Es, the music teacher Monsieur Grimaldi will see to that. Now sit. Here it is."

Sable placed the music of her choice on the standard and backed away from Esther, who seated herself gingerly on the edge of the plush-upholstered piano stool. Sable sat down on the front row of seats with her quartet. They listened for a while to the superb, lively notes ringing up into the air.

Having played this trick on two newcomers before Esther, the code was clear. The culprits left as soon as their victim's fingertips touched the keys. It wouldn't be long before Madame Paul was notified by one of her staff that another dissident had slinked inside the theatre to bang on the piano.

Her gang was already getting up and moving away, but Sable was sitting as if frozen in her seat. This wasn't Benny Goodman, Esther was playing. It was much, much better. She was performing a piece from memory. And what a virtuoso she was. The tones rippled and rollicked through Sable's entire being. It tore at the very fabric of her soul, made her heart sing, yearn, explode, then break her open, tears streaming down her cheeks. It was ... Chopin's Ballade No 1. Dadaigh's favorite.

Sable was catapulted back to 1935 when her father had taken her to the Queen's Hall in Westminster to attend a Chopin concert by the London Philharmonic. It had been everything she's dreamed of—her new dress, the posh balcony seat with plush chairs, the tall glass of lemonade with a straw, the semi-dark, gold and burgundy auditorium, the wild waving conductor, the large orchestra, the rippling sounds, the deafening applause rising to her ears, almost as harmonious as the music itself. But most of all, it had been being with Dadaigh. Talcum, tweed and tobacco Dadaigh.

Margarita nudged her.

"We should go. The Sphinx will be here any minute."

Sable let herself be torn away, still straining her ears to hear the melodious, lovely sounds.

Almost as if walking in a dream, she let her girls take her to their secret hiding place behind the stairs. Just in time. Madame Paul sailed past them with a face that forecast thunder.

The girls around Sable muffled their giggles behind pudgy hands. Sable felt terrible and would have given her right hand that moment to undo what she'd done, but she was stuck behind the staircase, unable to move as she heard Madame Paul bang shut the piano lid while Esther screamed. Clearly, the lid had come down on her fingers.

With her own fingers in her ears, Sable scrambled to her feet and ran to her room. She threw herself on her bed and cried for the very first time in over a year. She cried and cried until her whole body was limp and her face swollen. She hated herself, hated Madame Paul, hated the world, hated everything, and everyone.

.

9

CAN YOU SEE ME NOW?

St Moritz, January 1939

Sable zipped up her magenta alpine jacket and pulled the warm fox collar tighter around her face, then gave her reflection a last glance in the mirror. She was pale, she was thin, and she didn't like the lines next to her mouth, but the red lipstick and heavy eye makeup made her presentable. Almost. She took a deep breath. Though things had been bad in the past months, at least she was now back in the mountains. Mountain life, even in winter, always gave her morale a boost. And it was her very last month at Le Manoir.

Like a prisoner in solitary confinement, she had grown sickly in the past year, but now she felt health and restoration approaching, just out of reach but soon to be hers.

Though most of the girls hated the cold and snow and knew not the first thing about skiing, Sable had grown up in tough exteriors and though not a pro on the long slats, she was well above the beginner's class.

How she loved the feel of the cold air blowing by as she raced down the slope, the sense of speed and movement, the whoosh of the skis, promising escape, and finally freedom. Sable was in her element.

But the very best of all was that she was in the company of men again. Also, the ski instructors were no ordinary men. They were tough and good-looking, real men. Just like commandos and rugby players, muscled and rock-solid. Precisely the type of men Sable couldn't resist.

It was the exact reason she told her reflection to look her absolute best. She couldn't just rely on wearing the most fashionable and expensive ski-outfit of all the girls. It was paramount that she conceal the traces of emotional destruction that were wearing her down and wearing down her beauty. The languish had been going on for way too long. High time to revive.

First there was Bernt, who was blond and tall as a Viking, but taciturn and non-approachable. Bernt was hands down the best-looking of the instructor team, and his unavailability made him doubly attractive. Sable did not let a moment pass to gain his attention, whether by sliding down into the snow next to him so he had to give her a hand to scramble to her feet, or by securing a place at his side during après-ski.

Gerhard, whom everyone called Gerry, was slighter built than Bernt with bronze-brown hair and eyes, adorned with a fashionable mustachio and a swashbuckler gait. Even after the lessons, he didn't take off his ski gear, most likely to make a splash on the finishing schoolgirls as he strutted around the ski resort as if he owned it.

Gerhard spoke a funny mixture of German, French and some English, but he mostly talked with his arms and the gestures in his face. He was comical, companionable, and carefree. All the girls loved him, but he only had eyes for Sable, and she meant to keep it that way.

There was only one chink in the armor and that was—as always —Esther Weiss. Esther proved to be a champion skier and in recent days had even assisted with the skiing classes for the less adept students. It secured her constant proximity to the instructors. Especially Bernt, who smiled even less than he talked, saved his best moods for Sable's rival.

Still standing in front of her mirror in her private ski lodge—all the other girls shared beds in the resort's dormitory—Sable bit her lip. She knew she was being unfair to Esther, who, even after she'd set her up in the music room, had only avoided her and never confronted her with her treason.

And Esther had found a great friend in that other stellar girl, the American Océane Bell. Esther and Océane had forged a friendship that piqued Sable. They seemed to need no one else and made sure they always had each other's back. Something Sable couldn't say was the case with her own gang, which had diminished anyway, as the twins, Julie and Bella, had finished the course and returned to England. Some minor cases hung on to her club, but it had withered.

The longing for friendship, some form of it, any form, had gnawed on Sable. After she'd decided not even to be Madame Paul's favorite, her already waning interest in the course deflated completely. Life had been dead lonely with no word from Freddie and the occasional two-line, noncommittal scribble from her father. Loneliness had become Sable's constant state.

At various moments, she'd been on the brink of apologizing to Esther, asking her forgiveness and forging a new bond with her and OC, as the medical student was called. But pride had prevented it, and now it was too late. She'd be gone in a couple of weeks and see none of the Le Manoir students ever again.

Still, she'd never pulled another prank on new arrivals, not because of Madame Paul's reprimand after she found out who was behind the music event, but because she felt ashamed of herself.

Time to shake herself from this rotten state of mind. She was in St. Moritz. She would enjoy herself. She would show she could be fun, too.

"Let's go," she told her reflection. They were expected for a last night at dinner with the group and the instructors. Hence, her effort to look extra nice. It was still the end of the afternoon as she was way too early, but she went downstairs anyway. If she was able to choose the first seat at the table, she could make sure she was positioned right next to Bernt. Just in case he chose Esther and Océane over her.

On stepping outside into the crisp snow-laden air on her dainty snow boots, Sable saw Esther and Océane sitting side by side on the boardwalk in front of the ski equipment storehouse. As customary Esther was still in her ski outfit with her skis standing next to her against the wall, ready to be called on duty by the instructors. Her blonde curls peeped out from under her red woolen cap, her gloved hands playing with the leather straps of the ski poles that lay in her lap.

Her breath could be seen pluming up into the chilly afternoon air as she laughed out loud at something Océane was telling her. Océane sat with her legs apart while she cleaned her skis, with that serious frown on her intelligent face. But then she laughed with Esther, a giggle so merry and carefree. Slightly built, dark-haired and petite, Océane was her friend's physical opposite, but they shared the same well-bred, coming-from-a-respectable-family background and values that Sable both loathed and envied. There seemed to be much to say for less blue blood and more common sense.

Both Bernt and Gerry were nearby on the small slope, teaching village children the art of skiing. Sable watched their graceful movements, their patient attempts to keep the children standing upright on their skis, their Swiss German voices shouting orders in their practised ways.

The scenery was serene, simple, unscarred. People who cared for each other sought each other's company, their chirpy, carefree voices carrying far into the thin mountain air, while Sable stood alone, quiet, shadowed. The echo of her isolation was as soundless as the plume of her breath freezing in mid-air.

It came as a flash. She didn't know from where, but all she knew was that she wanted to be part of them, of this peace, of this harmony. Without thinking it through, she entered the open barn from the other side and selected a pair of skis. Kicking off her fur-lined boots, she grabbed the first pair of ski shoes from the rack; they were way too big, but she didn't care.

What did it matter that she had no gloves or ski glasses? She just planted a ski helmet roguishly on her head. All frost, fear and foresight went by the wayside. Sable didn't even feel that the air was thick with the impending blizzard. Some part of her registered that what she was about to do was reckless and rash, but the longing to be seen, to be heard, and mostly to be admired, was stronger.

The sun was sinking at breakneck speed behind Piz Nair Mountain when Sable skied past Esther and Océane on the sideboard and then along the instructors on the small ski slope. They saw her, she was sure of it, and the thought gave her wings. Success at last.

To be seen. To be admired for her come-on courage.

There was a shout that sounded more like a warning than a championing, which Sable pooh-poohed with a wave of her ski pole. *Can you see me now?*

The icy air stung her cheeks, tore at her jacket, while her mane flared behind her like a black sheet under the wide helmet, her freezing fingers cramping around the leather straps of her poles as she flew at full force over the snow that was slippery from too many tracks, giddy with excitement and heedlessness. She'd show them. She didn't know what it was, but she'd show them.

This is suicide, a tiny voice in her head whispered, but she ignored it. *It's hubris*, another voice clamored with the first, giving her wings. She was one with the cold, with the wind, with the elements. She was finally one, not the fragmented, shattered human being she'd been for the past two years.

"This is for you, little one!" she cried aloud as she raced down the slope into the dark. Tears froze on her cheeks as she kept going down, down, down ... into oblivion.

The world was white around her, all darkness gone, the black pit at the bottom of her being dissolved. She could see the light, a warm globe of golden light that promised peace and healing from eternal pain. Finally.

10

THE ACCIDENT

T he world was a funny place. It kept losing its shape. It was black one moment and white the next. One moment there was oblivion, another moment there was pain. It stood still one moment and moved the next.

There was a strange sizzling sound in Sable's ear, and something pressed on her head, but her body young and free in a smock dress ran along the meadow. She was shrieking with laughter. There was sunshine, and happiness, and delicious tea cakes.

Ladies in summer dresses made of white Belgian lace and light straw hats on their well-coiffed heads were seated at tables shaded by canvas parasols, while the men in white played cricket and tennis.

The lawn around the gathering was immaculate and very green. A gramophone was playing Gershwin. The doors to Alnor Castle stood wide open and the clamor of male voices from the terrace wafted over the music. The air was filled with cigar smoke and luxury perfumes.

Sable was running around the tables in her smock dress with Cousin Geoffrey behind and Freddie up front. They were playing donkey cart.

"Sable, come here!" Dadaigh called. She saw how her father had detached himself from his friends on the terrace and was now standing next to her mother who was sitting at the largest table, his hand on her delicate shoulder. Panting for breath and with beads of sweat on her forehead, Sable galloped to her parents and came to a halt.

"Time for your present, my Bhobain, my little rascal. You're seven today!" Her tall, mustached father looking impressive and godlike, retrieved a wrapped parcel from behind his back. She stretched out her arms to receive it. Her birthday was such a magical day in the year. Dadaigh never forgot to make her feel special on this day.

"What is it, Dadaigh?" Her eyes were enormous, her voice a tremor of hope and anticipation.

But when she wanted to unwrap the parcel, a knife-like pain shot up her neck and through her skull. The pain was so acute that it blinded her. As she opened her mouth to scream for help, a strange voice rang in her ear.

"Mademoiselle Sable, can you hear me?"

A foreign accent and someone making dents in her head with warm fingers. She tasted blood, saw bright-lit stars.

Then the voice became her father's again but now she was grown, and he was imploring her to tell the truth. What truth? There was no truth, at least not one she remembered. She started crying; she'd done nothing wrong. Her father looked worried, then withdrew and was gone.

"Please, Dadaigh, come back. I did nothing wrong." But her soul knew her guilt.

Her father's voice was far away. "Your mother told me you..."

Sable gasped and shrieked. The pain in her head was more than flesh and blood could stand. She wanted to cry "help" and "Dadaigh, come back!" but no sound came. The strange voice that wasn't her father's came back to her. Somehow it had a soothing lull.

"I'm sorry I'm hurting you, Mademoiselle, but we have to make sure we take off this helmet before any further swelling. Bernt, give me more light."

Bernt? Was he the German? He was not called Bernt ... he was ... he was called Joachim.

Her father came back just in time, the soft dove-gray eyes taking her in, a sad and wondering expression on his face that had aged beyond recognition. He was so obviously disappointed in her.

Something heavy was lifted from her head and the pain eased a little, but it felt as if her head was twice in size now.

"I don't remember, Dadaigh. I think I never will. My mind is blank after I've approached it so many times. There's simply nothing there in my memory. I remember the back seat of the Mercedes, the smell of the leather, and that makes me nauseous every time. Then the black gap before the sickness..."

"She's throwing up," the German voice said. *"Quickly! We've got to get her to an ambulance."*

"What happened, Sable?"

"I don't know. I'll never know."

"She's come around."

Sable strained her ears. A woman's voice. Not her mother's. Was it a nurse? It had that same Germanic ring, and it sounded familiar and yet foreign. There was so much to think about and so little time. Who were all these people, and why were they pulling on her body? If only she could hide from all of them for a while and regain her strength. Be independent from the lot.

DESPITE THE PAIN that felt as if someone was scraping a small garden rake over her eyes, Sable blinked into a light shining in her face, too harsh and bright. She smacked her lips, which felt thick and caked with something that tasted like mud and had the texture of gravel. There was blood in her mouth, a disgusting iron tang. Though her heart thumped in her ears, blocking out most sound, she was aware of a lot of consternation around her.

She squinted; the bright light was gone but so was her focus. Then vaguely, as if trying to see under water, the face of a girl came into view, an oval shape framed with blond curls, her eyes big and ill-humored.

Something clicked in Sable's brain. She wasn't in Scotland; she was in Switzerland. The girl was Esther Weiss. Seconds later, another face, leaner and darker, appeared next to Esther's, and she recognized Océane, who was bending over her. Before she slipped into unconsciousness again, she felt a firm, yet gentle hand grabbing her pulse.

Seconds, minutes, hours later she opened her eyes again. They were still there. She wanted to say something, but her throat was blocked; no words came out. It was Océane who tried to comfort her.

"You've had an accident, but you'll be okay. We're just taking you to a doctor for a simple check-up. Can you tell us your name?"

"Sable." It sounded croaky as a raven in flight.

"How old are you?"

"Twenty."

"What month and year are we?"

"January 1939."

Océane put a hand on her sleeve.

"See, Sable? You'll be right as rain soon again. Esther and I are now saying goodbye to you. The doctor's arrived. Be well."

Sable tried to smile, utter a *thank you*. Briefly, Esther came into view one last time, that beautiful, all-forgiving smile lighting up her face, though there was a concerned look in the green eyes.

"Be well, Sable!"

"I'll write to you, Esther!"

It was a promise Sable knew she would keep. It all came back to her in a flash. She knew Esther had been coming for her after her stupid race down the slope, after she'd almost killed herself in that dark pit. She'd felt her warm presence there, heard her soothing words. *You'll be all right.* Esther had done that for her. After everything.

WHEN SABLE NEXT WOKE, it was pitch-black around her. She didn't have the foggiest idea where she was and how she had landed there. She blinked in the dark, trying to orient herself. Her entire head felt like a truck loaded with heavy stones. All four limbs ached as if someone had tried to pull them out of her body.

Her back was flat on a bed that was neither soft nor comfortable, with only a flimsy cushion under her head. No part of her body obeyed her brain's instruction to move, apart from her head, which she could turn a little to the left and right. A stinging pain in her upper arm made her touch it with the fingers of her other hand. A needle was stuck in it. She was on some sort of drip. A machine behind her suddenly started beeping.

A hospital? Was she in the hospital? And could someone turn off that awful sound? But nothing happened. No one came while she rolled out of the fog and remembered.

It wasn't so much the pain now. It wasn't even the memory of what she'd thought when she went downhill. This was different. This was as scary as scary gets. Swallowing, her throat dry, her eyes wanting to cry but remaining as dry as cork... She remembered, so clearly, as she was catapulted back in time.

Two years earlier, in another hospital with white walls and red blood. A terrible pain in her lower abdomen. A scar she didn't dare to touch or look at for fear she would die of grief. Her womb was so empty. Betrayed, battered, dishonored. The psychological pain was much bigger than all the physical pain in the world. Too big a pain for one small human. And she was so small, so insignificant.

What had happened? What had she done, and what had she tried to accomplish? Sable shuddered. Had she really wanted to end it all?

Lying in that silent hospital bed except for the beeping machine and the distant sound of two voices in the corridor, Sable tried very hard to recall. It seemed essential to know what she had tried to accomplish, but the hard pressure of thinking hurt her bruised head even more.

With the first existential question still unresolved, the next big thing popped up: what now? She couldn't return to Le Manoir—of that, Sable was sure. She'd crossed that bridge; Madame Paul wouldn't accept her bending of the rules any longer.

Had she deliberately thwarted her dreaded return to the finishing school? Who was she? What did she want? Why was her life always such a mess and who had messed up, if not she herself? Oh, the endless, impossible quizzing of her own mind. It was impossible to hold all the threads of her bouncing thoughts together.

But the strangest thing was that amid all the frantic brain activity,

Sable somehow felt at peace. As if, at least for now, the pain and the questions, the endless restlessness and the existential can of worms were an external part of her. As if that which had hit her head had finally struck home, thrown her back into the here and now where she would take small steps, tiny, tiny steps back to something real. Healing and real.

She wanted to heal. Wanted to glue the broken pieces of herself into one whole. Like a precious Greek vase that lay shattered on a marble floor but was now ready to be lovingly patched together again. As she lay there, still and contemplative, her thoughts drifted to something she'd seen after her fall, as if in a hallucination. It was dear to her, very dear and important. What was it?

Dadaigh! My Dadaigh.

A surge of intense longing swept through Sable. How she needed him now. How they had both abandoned each other, forgotten the bond, drifted apart. It hadn't only been Mother's fault. They were to blame themselves. She was to blame. Would he help her now, listen to her, sit down with her, and discuss a future for her?

"Dadaigh..." she whispered, "I need you. I need you to give me, to give us a second chance. Let me explain I really wasn't to blame. I'm not who you think I am. Please, Dadaigh."

At that moment, Sable knew she would return to London and make a final, desperate dash to capture, recapture her father's heart. To secure the bond they both needed. To end their mutual loneliness. It was up to her, solely up to her.

This thought, this longing would now be Sable's bedrock, and she knew it would give her the strength and the resolve to heal, to heal with a plan.

Finally.

11

BAD TIDINGS

"You're well enough to leave the hospital today, Mademoiselle Montgomery."

The French-speaking nurse with a narrow face and the clearest violet eyes, which never seemed to rest on anything for longer than a second, stood at the foot of Sable's bed. One glance went from the file in her hand to the patient in the bed, the next to her watch. Her free hand withdrew the white curtain from around the bed.

The next moment she was checking Sable's pulse and examining her head wound. The darting nurse nodded approvingly and added in her overly chirpy voice, "No reason to keep you in here anymore, Mademoiselle. I'll help you pack your belongings. We've rung Le Manoir, and the school's chauffeur has brought a small suitcase with your belongings so you can change and then he'll drive you back to the school."

Sable listened to the carer with little enthusiasm or energy. She'd been in St. Moritz hospital for two or three days, having lost track of time. Long, lonely days with an aching head and stretched-out hours of lying awake in between short, disturbing naps.

She tried without success to piece together what exactly had happened to her during the accident, but nobody in the hospital knew the details. Esther would know. She'd ask her when back at Le Manoir. If she dared and if she really wanted to know, of which she wasn't sure. The pit of that dark slope was a black page, even in Sable's bothersome book of life.

"Sit up, Mademoiselle. Time to get dressed. It's still snowing outside, so we'd better get you all warm and cozy for your trip to Lausanne."

The violet eyes took her in wonderingly. There were questions in the nurse's eyes that she did not mention aloud. Of course, she'd seen the scar on Sable's belly. She knew what it was, but it wasn't her place to ask.

Reluctantly, Sable swung her legs over the edge of the bed, feeling dizzy and befuddled. The last thing she was looking forward to was spending time in the car with that condescending Italian. She really could go without his ironic wrath, but she felt physically too weak to protest.

It was also unclear what would await her when she arrived at Le Manoir. She hoped to ring her father straightaway, pack her stuff, and travel back to London. *De suite*! Go home and stay home. Somehow, London felt more like home now because her father was there. It was a new feeling and one she cherished. She'd make it work between them, if it was the last thing she'd do right in this world.

To her surprise, Filippo Maltese was all smiling and helpful when she walked on feeble, unwilling legs toward the black Renault with the golden lettering. He wouldn't even let her carry her small handbag but hastened to the nurse who'd accompanied her and took everything out of her hands.

"How are you, Mademoiselle Sable? It was such a shock when we heard you'd been injured. I hope you're feeling much better now?"

Knowing his acid treatment of her before, Sable initially thought he was poking fun at her, but the look on his weathered face was sincere, and the way he held the door open for her and made sure she was comfortable on the backseat was a clear sign he was really concerned about her wellbeing.

"I'm fine, Monsieur Maltese." It sounded prim, and Sable cast down her eyes at the investigating look in the coffee-brown eyes. *No kindness, please. No pulling on my heartstrings.*

"Will you be okay like this, Mademoiselle? Or perhaps an extra rug? It's a freezing day, you know. I'll turn up the Renault's heater, but I need to check the back seat heating. It doesn't seem to work properly."

"No fuss, please. I'll be all right."

"Would you perhaps rather sit up front, Mademoiselle Sable? I know it's against the rules but in your delicate situ..."

"I told you, I'll be all right, Monsieur Maltese. Please, just drive."

"As you wish, but if you change your mind halfway, just tap on the back of my seat."

"I will." She turned her eyes upwards. He was certainly overdoing it. She wasn't an invalid.

Filippo had been right though. It kept snowing relentlessly and the temperature inside the car dropped to arctic conditions. It was so cold in the back seat that at some point, Sable couldn't feel her own feet anymore. She was shivering all over.

When she met the chauffeur's gaze in the rearview mirror, she tried not to let her teeth clatter. Her head ached, and she felt sick, trying not to throw up her meager breakfast of coffee and toast.

"Don't be a fool, Mademoiselle. You've played that part long enough, don't you think?"

She knew she had to give in, or she'd freeze to death. "All right!"

Filippo immediately stopped the car and helped her into the front seat, then drove off again. Silence reigned for a while inside the confined space, though it wasn't strained or uncomfortable. At some point the Italian started whistling a tune that sounded vaguely familiar to Sable. The words just didn't come to mind.

As if guessing her train of thought, Filippo clarified. "The Internationale. Socialist song. Any objections?"

It made her smile. What an odd question.

"I'm apolitical. I've heard the song, of course, but I don't attribute any meaning to it."

"Ah, you're wrong there, Mademoiselle. This is not a time to be apolitical. Neutrality will not save us from tyrants like Hitler, or Franco, or Mussolini."

Sable pondered this for a while.

"So, are you a socialist? Not in favor of your leader?"

"Worse," he grinned, his leathery face changing into a fine web of interconnected lines. "And, no, Benito is not my Il Duce, Mademoiselle. The man's a bully and a cold-blooded killer."

"I didn't say he wasn't," Sable said with a chuckle. She enjoyed the stocky Italian's ardor. It warmed her frozen bones and took her focus off her own aching head.

"I know nothing of the circumstances, but listening to you, it doesn't sound like you'll have an enjoyable time visiting your home country when you think like that. I mean, I don't think Mussolini is kindly disposed to people who don't adore him and put him on a pedestal."

The Italian sighed and, scratching the gray-peppered head under his cap, added in a sad tone, "You're right there, Mademoiselle. It's that bad I may never see the homeland again. Just because I'm a member of the wrong political party."

"Is Mussolini after you? Have you tried to assassinate him?" Sable sat up straighter, already imagining a heroic role for the chauffeur. He shook his sadness from him and took to grinning again.

"Don't give me any ideas."

"So, I don't suppose you're a Hitler supporter either?" Sable thought of Freddie and his hate of the Germans.

"Cut out of the same cloth." The Italian spat in his hand, a sure sign of his contempt.

"I guess I'll have to make my mind up about the situation sometime soon," Sable contemplated aloud. "It's not as if I like Germans, not at all."

A shiver ran down her spine. But all Germans? Become a socialist? Or, Heaven forbid, a communist? Her father would die in his chair if she announced anything of the sort.

"Ordinary Italians and ordinary Germans are not the problem," the chauffeur lectured. "It's the crazy leaders who whip them up into atrocities."

"So, how do you not get whipped up?"

"Common sense." Filippo paused a moment, then added, "And some knowledge of mass psychology, I suppose."

"Do you mean you have to be stronger to row against the tide?"

"Yes, and to think for yourself. Make up your own mind. That's what youngsters these days seem to find so hard. What is it, Mademoiselle, that *you* want out of this life?"

Sable huddled deeper into her mink coat and felt how she slowly thawed. Even the throbbing in her head was temporarily less on the forefront. The chat with the chauffeur perked her up, contrary to what she'd expected getting into the car. This talk was about real life, real things, real questions. She frowned.

"I think you're right, Mr. Maltese. I don't know. I suppose I'm one of these floundering youth you refer to."

"It's Filippo for you, Mademoiselle." He gave her a quick smile that once again crinkled his broad face into a myriad of fine lines, a warm, encouraging smile.

"Then you must call me Sable!"

"So, you no longer insist on being addressed as Lady Montgomery?" It was followed by a wink.

"No, I'll drop the Lady. I think this accident has actually done me more good than harm. I may still not know what I want to do with my life, but at least I'm going to patch up things with my father. It's high time."

"Family is a great place to start with the patching up, Sable. And I wish you luck. I've seen you from your arrival, I've seen your struggle to accommodate, and all the while I knew there was something special in you, but that you had first to find out you were your own worst enemy. I see great things for you in your future."

At this, Sable let out a hearty laugh. "Then you're the first person in my life to believe that, Filippo. But thanks anyway."

"What about your father? Doesn't he know?"

Sable shrugged. "Not sure. Maybe. I intend to find out."

"Well, I'm sure that one day—it may not be your happiest day—you will remember the words of that simple Italian chauffeur at your posh finishing school, and you'll be terribly proud of yourself." It was said with the same warm passion with which Filippo had spoken of his own beliefs.

Sable felt herself choke up. In a croaking voice, she whispered, "Do you really think that, Filippo?"

The coffee-brown eyes shot her a quick glance, intelligent eyes that held no irony or scorn anymore. "I never say my words idly, dear girl. See you at the battlefield!"

These words were cryptic, but Sable somehow understood their meaning. A new comradely silence fell between them. When she ultimately saw the tall school building rise up through the pine trees at the end of the stately driveway, she blurted before she knew the companionable bond would be disrupted by Madame Paul.

"Thank you, Filippo, you've done more for me than even my own parents have ever done for me. You've given me confidence and hope." Her voice was unsteady, her body felt weak, but her spirit was strong.

"Now you just watch out for Madame Paul, Missy, because she isn't in her element, and you know what that means."

"I'll be going home to London soon. I hope you'll drive me to the station?"

"I sure will!" He tapped his black cap. "I'll bring in your luggage. Now, you go inside before you catch a cold."

Madame Paul was waiting for her with her arms crossed over her chest. Her glasses, attached to their long string of pearls, balanced halfway down the bridge of her nose. The celestite eyes peering over the rims were even colder than the weather.

Sable had already assumed her position as favorite girl was over, but now knew for sure. Bringing herself and the skiing team in danger had been a bridge too far. Madame Paul could oversee and manage what happened in and around Le Manoir, but during the Winter skiing holidays she had to give up that authority. Anything that went wrong in St. Moritz counted as doubly faulty.

So what, Sable thought defiantly, *I want to be out of here, anyway. Let's just hope I can thank Esther and Océane. I don't care two fiddlesticks about the Sphinx or the other girls.*

"In my office!" Madame Paul made a movement with her hand, not even greeting her or asking after her health.

"All right, if you want to play it that way, go ahead," Sable mumbled.

As soon as they were seated opposite each other in the monstrous office, facing off as two bulls in a meadow, the headmistress embarked on her fumy rhetoric. "It's come to my atten—"

She was interrupted by the telephone. With unconcealed discontent, Madame Paul stared at the black machine as if the very power of her fixation would blaze up the set and make it disappear.

Sable couldn't hide a triumphant smile. With all her etiquette blah-blah, Madame Paul was so ill-equipped at handling out-of-control interruptions, certainly when she was just gaining speed to deliver one of her fiery sermons on girls-who-have-to-be-straightened-out-once-and-for-all.

To hide her smile, Sable bowed her head and fiddled with the sash of her belt as Madame Paul, steam almost coming out of her ears, picked up the receiver. Sable hoped it would be a lengthy and important call, or some sudden emergency, and she could escape to her room to pack.

So immersed in her thoughts of how it would be to leave the dreadful place, it took two tries from Madame Paul's side to pull Sable's mind back into the office and the here and now.

"I'm so sorry!" The headmistress's voice sounded grave.

Sable looked up, still half in her reminisces but on seeing the strange look on Madame Paul's face, cried out, "What is it? What's wrong?"

"It's your father. He's had a heart attack. He's in The London Hospital."

Without thinking what she was doing, Sable grabbed the receiver while Madame Paul struggled to keep it in her own hand. The telephone set sailed over the mahogany surface like a skater losing his balance.

"Let go!"

They both shouted at the same time. Sable struggled vehemently, though she knew students could never use Madame Paul's phone. She was stronger and more determined, so she won.

"What's going on? What's with my father?" she yelled into the receiver.

"It's Elrod here, Lady Sable. It's his Grace's heart, but he's stable now."

"I'm coming home straightaway!" she shrieked, feeling the blood drain from her face as her life fell to smithereens. Dadaigh tethering on the brink of death? Just when she'd decided to reunite with him. Nooooooo.

"I'm coming back home! Keep him alive!"

Throwing the receiver back into the astounded headmistress's hand, Sable leapt to her feet. She was the one giving the orders now.

"Ask Mr. Maltese to ready the Renault and get my luggage from upstairs. I'm off to the station."

"But, Mademoiselle Sable, we have busi—"

"I don't care anymore. I want to be with my father."

Without listening further, Sable stormed out of the office and, taking two stair steps at a time, ran to her room. Her head pounding, her vision blurred, she shoved everything in sight into her two suitcases, then clicked them shut and fell back on her bed, wide-eyed and sick to her stomach, embarking on a furious, confused prayer.

"Please, Dadaigh, don't die on me now. Not now. Not now! Please get better. Please, Dadaigh, not now."

Her breath calmed down; the pounding at her temples slowed. Sable took in the surrounding room with the slanted walls and Spartan furnishings, the window overlooking Lake Geneva, the brown bed, brown cupboard, brown door, brown curtains.

This had been her bedroom for the past year. Not a sanctuary, hardly a hiding place. It held nothing for her now and would hold nothing in the future. The entire experience at Le Manoir had been a wasted year of her life, time that could not again be recaptured in any form.

In her dazed state, she still held the vague notion she wanted to thank Esther and Océane, but when Filippo knocked on her door and her cases were hauled down and back into the Renault's boot, Sable gave up.

She glanced back one more time at the square school with its many red-awninged windows, the lake in winter livery, the sloping meadows white even so, the stern staircase to the entrance, in which Madame Paul stood looking stricken herself, waving a white lace handkerchief as Sable drove back through the driveway, she'd only entered an hour earlier.

"Change of plan, Sable?" Filippo's warm voice tore through her grief.

"My father had a heart attack. I must get to London as quickly as possible, Monsieur Maltese."

"Filippo for you, remember, Sable? And I'm so sorry to hear that. I hope your father will recover. I understand your relationship is complicated."

Count on the Italian to cut to the core. "No, yes, it is... it was, until I realized after my accident that I wanted to be closer to him. And now this."

"You'll have time with him, Sable. Don't fret." His words reassured her enough to sigh deeply and stop wringing her hands. Filippo had an odd wisdom around him. Maybe he was right. Hopefully.

"Now, for the timetable, dear girl. The afternoon train leaves in thirty minutes. You'll be in Paris early in the morning to catch the train ferry. Within twenty-four hours, you will be at your father's bedside."

"Thank you, Filippo. One more thing. Let Esther know I'll write to her. I owe my life to her, and I want to thank her properly. Didn't have the opportunity now."

"I will, Sable. And don't forget what I told you. I believe in big things for you. Once you've straightened out your life. And who knows, maybe one day, we'll meet on the battlefield."

She smiled. "I doubt it, Filippo, but it would be a swell day if it happened."

Waving goodbye to him standing in front of Lausanne station, she was taken by an emotion that was both joy and sadness. Even if she never saw the Le Manoir chauffeur again, she'd never forget him. Filippo Maltese had given her something precious and rare—self-confidence and a feeling of grandeur unrelated to title or position. He'd seen her, really seen her. She walked taller for it.

As she followed the porter carrying her suitcases into the busy railroad station and to *Le Train Bleu*, Sable knew she returned home a changed person. Whether it would stick would be for time to tell. Le Manoir had given her something after all.

A friend, an unlikely friend.

12

DADAIGH

Arriving in London at the end of January 1939, Sable's nerves were frazzled by the busyness of the big city around her and the long journey behind her. She'd drop off her luggage at the house in Cavendish Square and find out more about her father's state of health before going to the hospital. She felt apprehensive, and the strange lump in her belly worried at her like an ill foreboding. Her head was still hurting and in a spin.

"6 Cavendish Square," she instructed the taxi-driver, who, with a grumpy face and unfriendly growl, lifted her heavy suitcases into the trunk of his black Austin. *Heavens*, Sable thought, *welcome back to the general London mood where politeness is a rare commodity.*

But when he'd closed the trunk, the taxi driver, a towering giant wearing a veteran's cap from the Great War on his copper curls, took to staring her up and down with his Celtic-blue eyes.

"Is it Lord Montgomery's house you want, Miss? The Earl your father?"

When Sable nodded, the cabbie added with a sorrowful expression., "The Earl's in a bad way, isn't he? Read about it in the paper. So sorry, Miss. I'll hurry now."

The elderly taxi driver did indeed speed up the short distance from Victoria Station to Cavendish Square, swerving around the red double-decker buses and hundreds of cars and vehicles. Sable stared at the familiar sights without seeing much. She was mentally preparing for how she'd find her father and how she'd go about breaking down the barrier between them.

Maybe his illness would help her, make him more mellow, with more time on his hands to listen to her. If only they were given the time to heal, to enjoy doing things together as fathers and daughters did. It was her sole mission, and it had to succeed.

Elrod, even more bent and worried-looking, was already opening the stately front door while the taxi driver was still hoisting her luggage up the stone steps.

"Welcome home, Lady Sable, how good of you to come so soon. Your father can't wait to see you. He's been asking for you all day."

That seemed like a favorable sign. Sable's heart skipped a beat. "Thank you, Elrod. How is my father now?"

The look on the stern-faced butler, with his white side-whiskers and reddish face from too much port wine, wasn't very encouraging as he said in his rather fussy way, "Let me pay the cabbie first, Miss Sable, and then I'll serve you tea and tell you all about the Earl's health."

Sable, drained and bone-tired, sat down on the familiar mauve sofa in her father's sitting room, her hands folded in her lap, waiting for Elrod to bring her tea and give her the rundown on her father's condition. She looked around the room.

As always, it possessed her father's inner quiet. The Rococo clock on the mantelpiece ticked softly, almost as if not wanting to make a sound. Even the fire lit in the spacious fireplace crackled in a subdued way behind the screen. The thick velvet curtains and double-glazed windows muted the traffic sounds from outside. The thick carpet dampened the sound of footsteps. Dadaigh's house was so silent, extensive, empty, yet elegant.

Sable had never thought of her tall, solidly built father with the soft, introverted eyes, the continuous frown that said he didn't understand the life of emotions but was sharp as a tiger's tooth in diplomacy circles, as a pillar of silence. Yet he was. Maybe it had been the noise in herself and the ripples of noise her mother always created around them that had made it impossible to experience this silence.

It freaked her out. It gripped her throat. What if this silence was eternal? Dadaigh not here. Never here anymore. No, they had time. Filippo had said so. Sable took to her pacing, fists in her pockets, head a booming noise, interrupting the silence. She wanted, needed to understand this man who had created this silence. Who had created her. She was sure she'd always underestimated him.

Look at the way he'd decorated this house with taste and luxury after separating from her mother, not needing any guidance in the leading of his new bachelor's life. And yet. There was this gap. He'd let her down.

They'd let each other down. Maybe she was more like her father than her mother, running away from emotions that were felt too strongly. Well, she was here to make amends for that now.

Sable startled when Elrod came in with the tea tray, stopped her pacing, stared at him as if he was the devil himself. The owlish butler said apologetically, "Ah Miss, I didn't mean to give you a scare. I got some of your favorite lemon meringue pie. I believe Minnie made it yesterday."

Sable returned to the mauve sofa and sat down, trying to relax. After all, this was home. Her home.

"Oh, is Minnie still here?"

"Yes, she is. The young lass has been my right arm, helping to look after your father. After he returned from Romania and ever since you left for Switzerland, his Grace hasn't been himself anymore. We didn't know what ailed him, but he lost his appetite and went to the Embassy only if he couldn't get out of his commitments. So, Minnie tried to cheer him up with cooking his favorite foods, and I tried to interest him in the latest operas or nudged him to go to his Club, but he simply seemed to have lost interest in life."

Sable listened intently to the butler's account of her father's deterioration. She realized again that in her own hour of sickness, the message had been so clear to patch things up between them. Had there been a transmission of some sort through the air? No, only wackos believed in that.

"I want to see my father now. Is that possible?"

"But Miss Sable, you've only just returned after your long journey, and we understood you've been in hospital yourself. I can see you still have a head wound. Wouldn't you want to freshen up first and lay down for a while?"

"No time to lose, Elrod. Please take me to my father directly after tea."

"Of course, Miss, I'll get the Rolls ready. And I'll also ask Minnie to pack some pie for your father. Hopefully, he'll eat some of it. He's so fussy with the food in the hospital."

"Maybe, we can get him home soon, Elrod. I'll look after him together with you and Minnie."

The loyal butler gave her a long stare, then cast down his eyes and started collecting her tea things. "You've changed, Miss Sable. And not for the worse, if I may say so. So, the finishing school did you good?"

Sable laughed full out for the first time. "I'm afraid not, Elrod. It was a wretched place, so don't rejoice too soon. I can still raise hell. Now get me the car!"

He smiled his thin smile under his bristly gray mustache, the red veins popping to the surface. "I wouldn't expect otherwise, Milady."

13

A HEART-WRENCHING GOODBYE

The London Hospital, 25 January 1939

Sable slinked into the dimly lit hospital room with her heart aflutter and her hopes low. Elrod had refused to accompany her inside despite her ardent request not to let her go in alone. At the thought of having to see her strong father lying ill in a sickroom, Sable's legs felt as if they would buckle under her.

"I want you to have a moment with him on your own. He sees my old face every day. Go now."

With those words her father's loyal butler of forty years had pushed Sable through the white door of the private hospital suite. She'd never felt smaller or more forlorn in her life, but she shuffled to his bed with the white bedspread, the familiar beeps and buzzes she had heard next to her ears in recent days. Squeezed between her fingers, she held the paper bag with the lemon meringue pie.

Fighting the overpowering mixture of antiseptics, deodorizers, and sickness that forced itself up her nose, Sable tried to breathe through a dry throat, pushing back hot, burning tears. The thin curtain around the bed clung to her travel dress like an evil magnet. The sick man's room was shrouded in shadows despite the curtains at the windows being drawn. The atmosphere was hot and stifling like her father's steward's greenhouse in the summer.

Dad. Dadaigh. Father.

A white, tall forehead ... the sleek, gray hair combed back ... sunken, shaven cheeks and eyes closed in hollow sockets against a white pillow. Long slender fingers without rings, resting motionless on the white sheet. The hands looking paper-thin. So frail, a shadow in a shadowed room dressed in navy silk pyjamas that seemed two sizes too big.

Even more than his poor health, Sable was shaken by seeing her father dressed in nightwear. She'd never seen him in anything but a three-piece suit, even in summer.

Her father was asleep, monitored by the beeping equipment. Then there was a rustle in the corner, and Sable found out a nurse had been sitting there in the shadows. The white-aproned carer quickly leapt to her feet and, quiet as the hush of evening, came to stand next to her. In a whispered tone, she said,

"You must be the daughter. I'll give you a moment. I'll be next door if you need me. His Grace will probably awake soon. He sleeps so lightly." The nurse disappeared on her silent soles.

Sable inched closer to the still figure in the bed, biting her lip at how ill he looked. This man didn't resemble her father. Perhaps a ghost of the former Earl Archibald Montgomery, 6th Baron of Alnor, but not her robust, healthy Dadaigh. This was a sick man, a sinking man.

Sable couldn't stop herself. She dropped the bag on the bedside table and took to pacing the room. Fifteen steps one way, fifteen steps back. No matter how drained she was herself, she couldn't sit in a chair and stare at that twilight being in the bed. She couldn't.

"Sable?" He moved, opened his eyes.

"Dadaigh!" Sable was at his side in one sprint, taking the cold, thin hand in hers, pushing back stinging tears.

"Is it really you, my girl? I don't know where my glasses are."

"It's me all right, Dad, but you don't need your glasses. I'm here and I won't go away anymore."

He frowned, then smiled weakly. "Fine, my dear, but I want to see you. Can you fetch my glasses for me? Those nurses keep hiding them from me."

Sable longed to just hold his hand and perhaps kiss the sunken cheek, feeling that old distance of misunderstanding creeping up between them. With it came the irritation. Couldn't he just enjoy the fact she was here? Come all this way *for him*?

"Sure, Dadaigh, let me have a look. Or do you want Elrod to find them for you?" She started pulling open drawers and peeking inside them.

"No, not Elrod, he's hopeless as well. Have you found them already? I'm blind as a bat." Sable found the black-rimmed heavy glasses next to the bathroom mirror and handed them to her father. He planted them on his nose rather awkwardly.

"Would you like to sit up a little, Dadaigh? This looks like a bed that can be pulled up."

He peered at her through the misted-up glasses, and she looked back at him. They stared at each other, gray eyes into her blue ones, and for a moment there seemed to be a connection. But then she heard him say...

"What happened to your head? And why are you so thin? Didn't they feed you in Switzerland? I paid enough for that school to serve you beef and pork every day."

"Hush ... Dad." Sable put a finger to her mouth. "Don't get upset. I'm fine. Can I give you a hug now you can see it's really me?"

"A hug?" He looked out of sorts at the suggestion. "Are we getting soft in the head, my dear?" The remark stung like a hornet, and Sable backed away from her father. An icy ring of protection closed around her heart. Dadaigh would never change. Her plan would never work. But then she saw his eyes soften behind the misty glasses.

In a kind voice he mumbled, "I didn't mean that to sound unwelcoming. It's just that ... just that we were never the cuddly type, now were we?"

Sable raised her hands in despair. It was true, but things could change, couldn't they? As she sank into the chair next to his bed, a memory flooded back before her eyes. A flash as sudden and huge as a snow avalanche. Daddy throwing her in the air in a pink lace dress, time and time again as she squealed in delight and the shirt billowed around her like a balloon. Then he caught her in his brawny arms and kissed her gleaming, red cheeks. How old was she? Three, four?

The memory was so vivid—as if it was happening right there and then, her bruised head producing a lucidity that seemed almost otherworldly. A comfort, warm and welcome, washed over her. They'd been close as hand and glove once upon a time. Her Dadaigh and she.

A breath of relief escaped her body. She could pull this off; the love was there, somewhere deeply buried in both of them. They were father and daughter, just as they were meant to be.

Taking his withered hand, she said in a soft voice, "Dad, I was in a skiing accident. Nothing serious, just a concussion but when I was lying down, I remembered something. And now I just had another flash."

She hesitated, exchanging a quick glance with him before staring down at the wrinkled, blue-veined hand she held in her own soft, young one.

"It was my seventh birthday at Alnor. It was summer, and you had a present for me. Everything ... uh ... everything seemed fine, and we were happy. Really happy. Do you remember that day, Dadaigh?"

Now the tears came, first one, then two, and then an unstoppable stream down her cheeks. They fell on his hand. He unclasped his grip, raised his hand to her cheek, wiped away the tears.

"I remember, Sable. I do remember. Now please, don't cry. I cannot bear tears. You know that. Certainly not yours."

Sable looked up at her father, her eyes misty and sorrowful. The zephyr-like gaze rested on her with great compassion but the moment their eyes met, she saw him withdraw within himself again, putting on his neutral-ambassador look. Dad and emotions, they seemed each other's worst enemies these days.

Pointing to the box with tissues on his bedside table, he said in that even voice of his. "There now, dry your tears. Why would a happy memory upset you, my daughter? There is no reason for it."

"Oh, but there is plenty of reason!" She rebuked with passion, "Everything went downhill after that birthday, you and Mother separating and we not seeing each other apart from during holidays. Don't you know how much I missed you, Dad? Don't you know how awful it was to live with Mother?"

She clung to his hand that he tried to pull out of hers, the don't-go-there-I've-had-enough-drama expression on his gaunt face. But now the door to affection was ajar, at least in Sable's mind; she couldn't help herself anymore, the pent-up emotions rolling from her like a tidal storm, in which she clung to her father's heartstrings like a sinking sailor. *Forget Misty Fletcher, Dad! I'm not her!*

Her father shifted in the bed, his tired eyes searching his daughter's. "I honestly didn't know living with your mother was not what you wanted, Sable. Your mother insisted you'd stay with her, and I didn't think it my position to separate mother from daughter. It seemed more natural that she'd take care of your upbringing. And I was always travel—" He hesitated a moment, then added in his level voice, "I simply supplied all the funds needed. That was the deal."

Not with me! Sable thought furiously. It was unbearable. She shot up from her bedside chair and took to her pacing at a ferocious speed. Her hands were such tight fists, her nails made red marks in her palms.

"How can you say that, Father? When you know full well what Mother is like. She's not fit to bring up a child. Why did you leave me in her care? Why? It has had disastrous consequences. Look at me!"

As he laid his weary eyes on her, she saw something break in his inner resolve, a crack through which his pain showed, his impotence, his remorse. It was something. Something at last. But she wasn't ready for his side of the pain. It bore so heavily on her heart that she raced back to the bed and hid her head in the bedcovers, sobbing loudly. "Sorry, Dadaigh, I shouldn't have said that. I know you had to travel so much for work. And I know I was a troublesome child, but I wanted your attention so dearly, so dearly."

She felt his quivering hand on her hair, stroking it softly. *Please continue doing just that*, she inwardly prayed, yearning for his gentle touch, his gentle voice.

"There, there now. We've both been foolish, but we can try again, can't we, *mo Bhobain?*" *Mo Bhobain*, my little rascal. He hadn't called her that since God-knew-when. She'd even forgotten he used to call her that.

Sniffling in the bedclothes, his hand still on her sore head, Sable begged, "Please get better, Dadaigh. I want to tell you everything. Everything that really happened to me!" Feeling revived and revitalized as a fading plant after a petrichor rainstorm, she raised her teary face. Now her father stretched out his arms, and she slid into his embrace, weak and warm but without distance. It felt glorious. She was home. Loved, longed-for, not liable.

"Sounds like a plan, mo Bhobain. Now, tell me what Minnie has baked today to prime the pump of my degenerated appetite."

Father and daughter ate the pie until the last crumbs were done. It lay on Sable's tongue to tell him of her ordeal right there and then, to have it off her chest, to close the final distance between them, but she swallowed her words. Her father was livelier than she'd seen him so far and she was bone tired, from all the emotions, the travel, her unhealed wound.

"We'll talk more in the morning, Dadaigh, but now you must rest. I can't wait to make plans for you to come home. I will stay with you and look after you. For as long as you like. We have so much to catch up on."

"You'll get bored in no time, my doll. You're a fine young lady, but your caring capacities are slightly underdeveloped. I'll have a battalion of nurses to look after me and then there are Elrod and Minnie. You can pick up your old life and have some fun for as long as it lasts. I'm afraid this phoney war phase with Germany won't last very long and before we know it, we'll be entangled in actual combat, which will change everything, also for you. Mind you, I know what war's like."

He pulled the sleeve of his pyjamas up to his elbow and showed her a red blotch the size of a small pancake, frayed around the edges and misformed by scar tissue.

"1917. Verdun. Trench mortar." He pulled the sleeve down. "Mind you, I was the lucky devil. The one that got away. My entire battalion was killed that night."

Sable shuddered. Her dad had never talked about his past. Oh, she couldn't wait to hear his stories! And he was so wrong that she wanted to go partying again. She wanted only to be with him. Forever.

And maybe he was right. Freddie was also certain that Chamberlain's appeasement policy was just a stopgap. If they were to be at war, she needed to protect her frail dad more than ever.

"Don't say that I'll be bored in your company, Dadaigh! How can you even think that?" And with a wink she added, "Maybe all that table setting and napkin folding developed a sense of duty in me after all. Looking after you won't be a duty, and for once I'm very serious." She grabbed both her father's thin hands and kissed them.

"All right, mo Bhobain, I can't wait to be out of here and back home. And with you next to me, I'll for sure live another twenty years."

She kissed him on the sunken cheek; he pulled her close once again.

"Bye, Dadaigh, see you tomorrow."

"Bye, mo Bhobain. Now be a good girl!"

14

ALL THE PAIN IN THE WORLD

London, 26 January 1939

S able was lost. *She found herself in a maze of poky streets in a poor neighborhood of a large, anonymous city. She was late for her appointment, and she started running over the squalor that littered the streets. Soon the streets turned into only alleys, becoming narrower and narrower.*

Tall brick walls raised above her on both sides, way up into the gray sky that hung like a thick veil over the houses. The walls were moist, and big droplets fell onto her neck and her bare arms.

She desperately wanted to ask directions to the place where she was expected to go, but only two half-naked children were playing in a door opening, poking sticks in a puddle. They had uncombed hair and looked hungry. Just when she thought she couldn't go on any longer as the street was so narrow that she had to squeeze between the walls, she heard a voice calling her name...

Gasping for breath, she wildly sought in the dark for the light switch. It was three in the morning. Elrod was calling her, knocking on her bedroom door.

Dadaigh!

It wasn't a dream. The nightmare was real.

Three weeks later

Sable was too drunk to pick up the phone that kept ringing next to her ear with a persistency that made her push her pillow over her head. She still registered the irritating vibration but couldn't care less, turned her head away from it and fell back into oblivion.

Hours later, she woke from the sun glaring into her eyes, licking her cracked lips. Her throat and the cavity of her mouth felt like cottonmouth, dry as a clot of clay. Sickness and a severe headache, the aftermath of copious amounts of heavy liquor, made her whine.

On waking up more, she found she lay entangled in her evening dress that was wound around her middle like a misplaced religious habit. No undergarments, bare legs.

No!

At this new discovery she didn't want to wake up, open her eyes, face life, as shards of the evening before surfaced in her groggy brain.

Egbert!

Turning around in the four-poster bed, she glanced through her eyelashes and sighed with relief. He wasn't there. But her pounding head said something about her inviting him into her room and into her bed. Had something happened? She tried to remember and then gave up.

If so, what did it matter? Nothing mattered anymore.

Hoisting herself on one arm, she rang her bell. Then stared at the black crepe-de-chine dress that hung on the outside of her cupboard, just returned from the dry-cleaner's, and a wave of anguish washed over her again.

Daddy. Dadaigh was dead. He'd died on her. Just like that. The night she'd walked out of the hospital. They hadn't been given a second chance. They hadn't been given any chance at all.

Minnie poked her round head around the door, looking stricken and afraid. Sable vaguely realized she was giving the staff hell, who had their own grief, but she couldn't help it.

"You rang for me, Miss?" It was hardly polite, but Sable was beyond care.

"Bring me a coffee and a whiskey. And where for Heaven's sake are my cigarettes?"

"Don't you think you should 'ave brea'fast first, Miss?"

"No! Coffee, whiskey, cigarettes."

Minnie raised her eyebrows but said no more. She just dropped a new packet of Craven A on Sable's half-naked posture, together with a note. With a huffy voice that disclosed she had been crying, the maid added,

"I'll bring your requests in a minute. Please get dressed, Miss. You 'ave an appoin'ment with Mr Brown, your father's solicitah, at eleven o'clock."

Minnie stood gazing down on Sable for a moment with a look on her face that spoke volumes. That look clearly stated, *How on earth is this misfit able to run her father's estate? She can't even look after herself.*

After Minnie left, Sable flipped open the envelope. It took some time for her eyes to get into focus. It was a note from Egbert.

Dear Sable,

I'm very sorry for what you are going through. I just wanted to let you know I stayed with you last night, but I didn't take advantage of you. You were so far gone that I didn't dare to leave you alone, so I slept in one of your chairs. I'm sorry that the staff may have a very unfavorable opinion of me again.

I honestly think you need help. If you think a change of scenery may do you good, you're very welcome to accompany me to Amsterdam. I'll be leaving from Gatwick later this week. William Mitchell, my pilot—you may remember I introduced you—will fly my plane.

I'll check on you tonight. Please go easy on the liquor. Grief and alcohol aren't a good match.

Your friend, Egbert.

Sable flung the note on the floor and lit her first cigarette of the day. It tasted like sawdust, but it was a slight comfort. Tears pricked at the sides of her eyes.

"You dislike me, God, now don't you? Please, take good care of my Dadaigh. I don't deserve You, but he does."

Then she cried and smoked and drank the soothing liquor until, white-faced and with a dead heart, she made her way to become the owner of 6 Cavendish Square and all that was in it.

She was only twenty-one. Who would believe it? Like a wounded snake dragging its full length along the dusty track, she made her way to Mr Brown's office on Edgware Road. A broken heiress, only longing for oblivion all over again.

15

SABLE GOES TO WAR

London, 20 May 1940

Incessant rain battered the windows of 6 Cavendish Square, and even though the gauze curtains were drawn, the dismal weather entered the sitting room where Sable was rumbling through the papers in her father's desk. Her face was taut, her black hair bound tight in a ponytail and her face without makeup.

Ever since the death of her father, she'd taken to wearing black. And though it was over a year now since he had passed, she couldn't bring herself to consider wearing color. In her black slacks and jumper, thin as a rake and with the lines showing in her face, she was almost ethereally beautiful, constantly balancing between life and death. Slowly sipping a glass of water, she retrieved a piece of paper in her own handwriting and stared at it as if it had come from outer space.

It was a draft of the letter she'd written to Esther a month after her father's death. The handwriting was irregular, the tone haughty. She'd clearly been drunk and out of focus. No wonder Esther never replied. Sable's eyes flew over her own words.

· · ·

London, 1 March 1939

Dear Esther,

I never properly thanked you for saving my life in those bloody Alps, so that's why I'm writing you now. Especially after how I treated you, I didn't expect this from you. I'm trying to better my life, but it's difficult. I'm born trouble, my mother says, and she should know because after all, I'm her daughter. She's onto her fourth marriage next week and the husbands get worse as time progresses.

Anyway. I'm sure you're not interested in my story, which is quite bleak and unhappy despite the title and the looks. You're much better off, my dear. Your soul is as Weiss as your name, mine as black as mine.

I'm not a writer, as you can tell from this letter. I just wanted to let you know I adored you from the first day you stood there on Le Manoir gravel, straw hat, and all that loveliness. Gosh, girl, make something of your life and marry that dashing fellow of yours and be happy ever after. I'll root for you!

If you care to reply, you can use the Scottish address I'm adding. It's where my mother used to live, but it's owned by my Scottish father, my real Dad, not one of the stepdads. I'm currently in London but with all the rumors about war, I might move up north soon. Have no clue where my mother is right now. At least, she can't squander the castle in one of the Monte Carlo casinos anymore.

Yes, that's how bad it is but as we say here in rainy London, "Chin up, old girl!"

Take care, Esther. You were my favorite!

Sable Montgomery (without the Lady stuff!)

· · ·

SABLE CRUMPLED the letter and threw it in the wastepaper basket. Why had she not told Esther of her father's passing? She frowned. It had just been too painful, too raw. And all that talk of her mother? What had gotten into her? What a pathetic Sable spoke from these words, but the letter was sent, and no reply had come.

Sable lit another cigarette and took a gulp from her crystal glass. An old habit as she coughed up the unexpected water. Her thoughts were jumbled, but the trouble with her mother had been real and prominent. Tucking in her legs on the straight-backed chair, the glass balancing on one knee, the ashtray on the other, her blue eyes squinted.

It had been a week before she'd written this letter to Esther. A hat the size of a gigantic turquoise egg, a dress in the same chintz-colored material and impeccable high-heeled black pumps, a feather boa around the scraggy shoulders. Her mother had rung the bell of 6 Cavendish Square demanding entrance. Elrod had answered the door and called for Sable, who'd scrambled to the door just in time to stop her mother from pushing the elderly butler out of the way.

What had happened next still made Sable swallow hard and cling to her water glass as if it still held liquor. She'd positioned herself in the door opening, shivering with nerves but strong as steel. Identical blue eyes had locked horns.

"What do you want?" Her tone had just the right level of authority. Her mother's painted eyelashes had quivered for a moment.

"Well, Sable, honey, to come in, of course. I'm so sorry I couldn't be at the funeral, but I was held up in the Bahamas."

"Go jump in a lake, mother. You weren't invited and you know it."

The honeyed, pleading tone, a new nuance to her mother's voice, had continued.

"But darling, I wrote, didn't I? And I tried to come earlier. It's just … it's just that the admiral had left me on the island with no money. I had to borrow my way here. But here I am now!" The beaming smile on the bright-red lips was laid on with a trowel.

Aha, it's money you need, I should have known! Fury shot through Sable, who guarded the door like a gangbuster.

"Now let me in, dear. I can't be standing here on these steps forever. I want to tell you the big news. I'm going to get married to Graf Von Bissing, who know, you met hi—"

Sable shut the door on her mother with a bang, then locked and bolted it as if her life depended on it. Elrod, who was still standing in the hall, had tried to calm her as she fell to the floor in a blubbering mess.

"Don't open the door to that woman, don't open the door," she'd yammered while her mother kept ringing the bell. Minnie hastened with a glass of water and an aspirin to calm the sobbing Sable. For what seemed like hours, she'd only cried, "Don't open the door for her."

It was the last she'd heard or seen of her mother.

Sable took another sober sip and another drag on her cigarette. She stretched like a cat, shook the nasty memory from her. Her mother was gone. Esther was gone. Just as well.

While she continued sorting her father's papers, the telephone rang.

Expecting Elrod to pick it up, she didn't pay it attention but when it started ringing again and nothing happened, she put down glass and ashtray, then sauntered over to the black Bakelite set on the sideboard.

"Yes?"

"Sable, is that you? Thank God!"

"Freddie?"

"I'm downed in Belgium, Sable. We're in a bad way. The Germans are chasing us across the polders and ditches. With tanks and Junkers. Wave after wave. The noise is abominable. Fires and explosions everywhere. People falling dead by the roadside like matchsticks. Men, women, children. We've been walking for days now without water or food. I have no clue where we're heading."

Still with her head on her father's legacy, she didn't understand what was happening on the other side of the phone. It was Freddie all right, but the noise and the crackling line made it hard to hear, let alone grasp what was going on. A terrible fright squeezed her throat, but she piped up in spite of it.

"Oh my God, Freddie, but how did you end up in Belgium, of all places?" Before she could wedge in more questions, he continued in his short, staccato sentences on the other side as if he was an automaton. Sable pressed her ear to the receiver as hard as she could while her heart pounded in her chest. She could barely make out his words.

"We have no place to escape to. We'll soon end up as German mincemeat. Thousands of British soldiers. Belgian civilians too. All fleeing southward. Last we heard was, *Go to the French coast.* Dunkirk. David's injured. He's in awful shape. There are no medics. If this isn't the dark night of the soul, I don't know what is."

Despair over the possibility of losing another loved one made her head reel while she tried with all her might to get a hold both on herself and on the snippets of information she tried to glue together to a coherent whole. But it was impossible. She was weak in her knees, jumping as a skittered cat at the explosions she heard and the cries of agony in the distance. Tongue-tied and wide-eyed, she was too baffled to utter a word.

"Sab, are you there? Can you hear me?" Freddie was almost crying. She had to answer, cleared her blocked throat, and crowed out a response.

"Yes, yes, but please, Freddo, what's going on? What do you mean by being downed? And what's all that noise? You're giving me such a dreadful fright."

"Never mind the details, Sabbo. We're in dire straits. Can't find a quieter place to talk. Got to go again. I'm using some major's field phone. The battery is low. Can't get hold of my parents. That's why I phoned you. Get in touch with them if I don't come back. Pray for me, Sabbo dear. You are my best friend. I know I let you down."

Sable fought for answers. Fought to keep his voice going. *Don't die on me, Freddie!* Feverishly, she tried to think of what she'd heard on the BBC. Holland had fallen; the Germans were capturing Luxemburg and Belgium on their Blitzkrieg way to France. But why was

Freddie in Belgium? Had he joined the RAF after all? Were British troops on Belgian territory?

Not knowing what she was saying, she spoke without thinking, desperately hoping he'd stay on the phone a little longer. As if this telephone line was her lifeline.

"Of course, I'll contact your parents, Freddo. But please come back. Please don't die. I can't live without you. I'll see what I can do. Maybe I can do something, however small. I promise, I will. Please come ba..."

"I love you, my Sabbo. Pray for me! Got to go."

And with that, the connection was broken.

Aghast, Sable stared at the receiver in her hand as it signaled its indifferent *toot toot toot*. She trembled all over as she went on wobbly legs to the mauve sofa and sunk down on it. With a quivering hand, she lit a cigarette while her other hand grabbed for one of the whiskey tumblers she expected to have sunk in between the cushions. Then corrected herself and found her water glass. Her heart was booming like a trombone in her chest. She spilled the plain liquid on her blouse.

Death. Freddie. The two elements didn't click in her brain. Though he might roam around on other continents, they were two sides of one whole and the one side couldn't do without the other. Certainly not after losing Dadaigh. He was her only hope, her only close companion in the entire world.

There was a knock on the door. Elrod came in with the evening paper but stopped in his tracks when he saw her stricken face.

"What is it, Miss Sable? Have you seen a ghost?"

She tried to talk, but tears choked her throat. "It's Fr... Freddie Frinton-Smith."

Elrod looked puzzled, clearly thought his young mistress had landed in some fresh trouble.

"He's ... he's dying in Belgium, Elrod. He says he's downed or something, but ... I just had him on the phone, you see."

She was aware she wasn't making much sense, but to her surprise saw that Elrod's eyes lit up.

"Was Mr. Frinton-Smith with the British Expeditionary Forces? I did not know. Thought the young man was a student at Oxford. But it's all over the papers, Miss, the disaster with our forces in Belgium. Here, the Prime Minister has called it 'a colossal military disaster', saying 'the whole root and core and brain of the British Army' has been stranded at Dunkirk and seems about to perish or be captured.'" The butler tapped his finger with the short, clipped nail on the big black headlines in *The Times*.

This remark did little to calm Sable's strained nerves, so she sprang up to do her pacing.

"There's something we've got to do about this disaster, Elrod. I can't just let Freddie die there. I can't."

"Well, they're working on an evacuation plan from Dover," Elrod read. "It's all rather hush-hush, but apparently a fleet of ships is going to cross the Channel to pick up the stranded soldiers."

"A fleet?" Sable's eyes widened. "Crossing over and evacuating them? That's a brilliant idea. I'd like to go there myself."

"Are you mad, Miss Sable? The Germans drop bombs on every British vessel they can spot. The RAF—sad to admit it—is no worthy adversary for the Luftwaffe."

Elrod looked positively shocked at the idea, but a germ of a plan formed in Sable's quick mind.

"Leave the papers here, Elrod, and bring me some tea." Sable turned to get back to her father's papers.

"I will do as you please, if you promise me not to do anything foolish, Miss Sable."

She turned to smile at the loyal butler, adding mockingly, "I promise, Elrod. You know how trustworthy I am."

The old man raised his eyebrows, then just sighed, mumbling a dry "yeah, yeah" to himself as he left the room.

Sable sat down at her father's secretaire and with rapid fingers ruffled through the stack she'd just laid aside to throw away. Where was Capt. Hancock's condolence card? She couldn't find it anywhere, searched through all the drawers, even emptied the paper basket, but to no avail.

A surge of remorse swept through her at having been so indifferent about her father's condolence messages. What kind of daughter had she been? What kind of heiress to his name and title? These were his people, people who had been important to him, people he had cared for. Circles she may never have been part of, but all these letters had spoken with such deep respect and admiration for Earl Archibald Montgomery, 6th Baron of Alnor.

Sable sighed. She'd try harder from now on.

Now, losing one card almost threw her in a panic. Capt. Hancock's last farewell to his friend seemed the only lifesaver she could think of, but she had so loosely cut the ties of her father's former friends and colleagues, not caring to pay attention to any of them.

She sat and smoked, the frown between her eyes only deepening. Then she suddenly shot up and ran to her room, emptying the contents of her handbag on her bed. Old lipsticks, half-smoked Craven A packages, one golden earring, a broken tortoise-shell comb, a letter from Freddie, a note from Egbert, an empty liquor cask.

But there ... there it was. Capt. Hancock's card that he'd given her in the *Canterbury* mess when she was on her way to Le Manoir. Triumphantly she held it between thumb and forefinger. Though the business card was crumpled and stained, she could still make out the captain's Dover address.

Sable was all frenzy and fury now. She knew she had to convince the old sailor to steer the *Canterbury* across the Channel to save Freddie's life. And that of David and of others, of course. There was no doubt in her mind that Hancock—if he still was captain of the *Canterbury*—would want to cooperate.

Sprinting back to the black telephone, she dialed the operator and within seconds possessed the captain's phone number. It took her several deep breaths to pluck up the courage to dial the number.

"Malcolm speaking." Silence.

Sable had an attack of the wobblies but squeaked, "Sorry, Sir, but I'm looking for Captain Hancock. Any idea where I might find him? It's kind of urgent. A real emergency. Let me give you my number and please ask hi—"

"Is that you, Lady Montgomery?"

Now she recognized his baritone voice and added with anticipation, "Captain?"

"Yes, it's me. I'm so sorry about the loss of your father, Miss. Really struck me very hard." He paused and she could feel his emotion without seeing his face.

"I know, Sir, but that's not why I'm calling, though your card was kindly received by the family." *Terrible liar*—the thought shot through her before she added in haste, "Are you still the captain of the *Canterbury*?"

"I am, but she's no longer a ferry. She's the *SS Canterbury* now, a troop ship that will be employed in the war effort." He sounded unhappy about the fact.

"Oh good, excellent!" Sable shouted. She heard the old seaman clear his throat. He must think her dead from the neck up, but she couldn't care less.

"I'm not sure war's a good thing, and my ship is old and not really fit for battle." He sounded sad.

"Listen, Captain." Sable totally ignored his sensitivities about his ship. "Have you perhaps heard of the plan to evacuate soldiers from Dunkirk with vessels sailing from England? One of my best friends is stuck there. He phoned me, but they need help. That's when I thought of you and the *Canterbury*."

"Wait a moment, Miss. You're talking too fast for my old ears, but it's true. Vice Admiral Bertram Ramsay has already contacted me from his headquarters below Dover Castle. It's all cloak-and-dagger, but he's asked me to keep her ready to sail." He sighed; it was clearly not what Captain Hancock had in mind for his beloved ship, but Sable was unstoppable now.

"Excellent!" she cried again.

"I don't think you know what you're saying, dear girl. It's pure suicide to make that trip. Let me tell you that. Those Bochs are hitting every ship that comes close to the Belgian or French coast. Our pilots may be involved in dogfights with the Germans, but the enemy has an advantage not only on the ground, but also in the air."

"Still, will you go if you're asked, Captain Hancock?" Sable was almost begging him.

"To pick up your friend? He must be very special to you." A small chuckle.

"Oh no, it's not romantic or anything. Freddie is a friend from childhood. He's ... he's not like that," she added in her confusion.

"I can't promise anything. I'll do my duty when I'm ordered to, but I assume it's complete chaos there, and I won't be able to give lottery tickets to this poor bugger, or the other." The captain seemed to get used to the idea of his ship's mission. He sounded less defensive.

"I want to come with you. Can I come?" There. It was said.

"Are you away with the fairies? Of course not, Lady Sable. Your father would turn over in his grave if I consented to that." The resoluteness of his tone made Sable frown. It sounded so definitive. Then the words of Filippo Maltese sprang to mind. *I'm sure that one day—it may not be your happiest day—you will remember the words of that simple Italian chauffeur at your posh finishing school, and you'll be terribly proud of yourself.* This was her moment, but how could she convince the old seaman that this wasn't just a whim?

"I'm coming whether you say yes or no. I'll do everything you say, from handing out food, to helping the wounded men. Everything."

"No." It was a tinge less resolute, though.

With a sliver of hope and plenty of persuasive force, she proclaimed, "Listen a moment. My father would be proud of me, and I'll make you proud as well. I've been waiting for something to find out what I wanted to do, and now I know. After we've picked up Freddie, I'll join the WAAF and make myself useful in this bloody war."

She spoke with so much confidence that the captain remained silent for a long minute. Then he said,

"Let me think on it. Come to Dover, and I'll show you the ins and out of the ship, so you know where everything is. I'm short for staff because all the men have enlisted. But I want to talk with you first. Nothing is promised, understood?"

He sighed audibly, but she discerned an undertone of admiration for her persistency.

"Understood. I'll be at your house tomorrow morning. I'll ask Elrod to drive me down."

"Don't bring ten suitcases and fifteen hatboxes. It won't be the luxury trip you're accustomed to." Again, that dry chuckle.

"I know. I'll only bring the essentials for myself, but as many medical supplies as I can transport."

16

OPERATION DYNAMO

The English Channel, 29 May 1940

It was a brilliant end of May morning, clear blue skies, dotted with small cotton balls of clouds, the cliff flowers bursting in bloom, swallows skimming along the steep chalk cliffs hunting for insects.

Not a day for war, and yet the sky was full of it. Lysanders and Spitfires skimmed over the coastline, just like the swallows, to steer their propellor noses toward mainland Europe. Hundreds of vessels from destroyers to trawlers to private yachts lay bobbing in the Dover docks, while others already bravely took to the briny deep, hoping for victory but fearing extinction.

Sable, dressed in her customary black slacks and pullover, over which she'd slung a khaki jacket, stood on *SS Canterbury's* bridge with field glasses in her hands and a cigarette dangling between her lips. Her face was white but determined. A tin helmet sat firmly on top of her black locks.

Bringing the heavy binoculars into focus, she scanned the Channel waters. Billowing black plumes as high as the atmosphere rose in the east. A sure sign that a hellish fight was taking place only twenty-five miles from where she was standing. As yet, she couldn't get the carnage the Germans were causing into view, but the forebodings were apocalyptic.

Without her noticing his arrival, Captain Hancock stood next to her on the bridge. She was startled when he suddenly spoke.

"You've still got time to put your feet safely on English soil, Sable. I'm about to give orders to unmoor."

She ignored this remark, just scoffed. Glad that the captain finally just called her Sable and dropped all that silly decorum of "milady" or "Miss," but annoyed at his constant reminder of her "present danger."

It wasn't the first time the white-haired sailor attempted to discourage her plans, but they'd come to an understanding that she would join if she stayed out of harm's way as much as possible. The old man was just overly protective.

"Here." She handed him the binoculars. "Look. What d'you make of that? I can't make head or tail of it."

Taking the field glasses from her, he studied the overseas battlefield for a long couple of minutes, then handed them back to her.

"Well, my dear, that is the product of war. Just what I wanted to save you from."

Sable scoffed once more. "We've gone through that. Just please give me the details of what the black smoke is, Captain Hancock."

He hesitated, scratching his white beard. "What it is exactly, I can't say for sure, but it looks like ships sailing in that direction are being hit by German artillery or aircraft. It's too far from the shore to be seeing Dunkirk, so it must be on the sea. Not a pleasant prospect as we're sailing right in that direction."

For one minute Sable was the bolder one. "We knew all along we could be hit and perish, didn't we? We'll just pray we won't."

"Ai, you're right there, my dear. You heard what the Archbishop of Canterbury said before King George in Sunday's special service in Westminster. We're all praying "for our soldiers in dire peril in France." It's just the same for us now, trying to save our poor troops. If we cannot bring the poor buggers home, we won't have a choice but to surrender to the Nazis. And Winston's told us that can't happen. Under no circumstances. So, off we go!"

"You really think we're that close to capitulation, Cap, without even a fight on British soil?" The odious thought struck Sable harder than the idea of their upcoming sea voyage and those perils. She was horrified. Great Britain becoming German? She clenched her teeth. Never! Now she had even more reason to be here at this important turning point in history.

"Yes, my dear, that's what is at stake here. Now, into my cabin, and we'll lift anchor."

The journey out of Dover harbor was chaotic but Captain Hancock, with his long-time friend and helmsman Norman Potter by his side, maneuvered the large ferry boat out of the harbor and into open sea where it moved alongside an odd collection of trawlers, coasters, yachts, and minesweepers, all setting sail toward the Northern French port city of Dunkirk, though they went by different routes.

Sable could hardly breathe from excitement, a constant quivering cigarette between her lips. A skewed, longing eye went to the bottle of Madeira that stood in between the dashboard's knobs and switches. But no! She could do without, despite the terrible jitters.

When they left Dover harbor and were at open sea, she breathed a little freer, but her nerves were like jumpy cats in a bag. She felt the two men at her side equally terse and taciturn and was sure that just like she, they were thinking of the awful pictures of burnt bodies and exploding ships that the evening paper had brought them. She jumped at every distant explosion until she spoke firmly to herself to have "none of that nonsense."

The weather continued to behave as if nothing was afoot, with the North Sea calm and glistening in the morning sun. Sable thought it must be a favorable sign.

The SS Canterbury was one of the largest ships in the fleet, sailing among the smaller vessels like a mother duck with her young. But being so prominent, she was much more vulnerable to German bombardments. On the other hand, she was also sturdier and more steadfast. It would take longer to sink than that tiny sailing boat on her right. She waved at the skipper in the small boat, who nodded back at her.

Stop your worrying, Sable! You knew what you were getting into!

Next thing she knew, a gigantic blast sounded close by. The explosion shook the *Canterbury* over its entire length and rippled on. Sable stood gawking at the sight of a fountain of gray seawater sprouting meters high into the air, blocking the sunlight. A small sailing boat was washed over with a gush of water, but somehow stayed afloat.

Then came a new explosion and a new sky-high wave, which engulfed a large steamer sailing on the *Canterbury*'s starboard. Sable saw with non-believing eyes how the ship was pushed upward as if it weighed nothing. Then the stern slowly heaved backward. Explosions crackling loud as fireworks continued to deafen her ears.

Still not understanding what was happening as there were no planes or enemies in sight, she assumed the ship's bow had just hit a gigantic wave ahead. But when the stern disappeared under water, slowly and majestically as if collapsing under its own weight, she understood this was not a freak of nature but a manmade disaster.

She was aware Captain Hancock was giving Potter instructions to stay at the steering wheel and Sable to stay put, as he disappeared from the hut to take stock.

"Hold her steady, mate. Sable, stay where you are. If we tell you, dive under the switchboard." And gone was her prop and stay. No words had been shared about the cause of the accident.

Circular waves pushed out a tidal swell that came rolling toward them. As it reached the *Canterbury*, the ship started rocking like an invisibly shaken mass of jelly. Sable, who'd jumped at the blast of the explosion, now gripped firmly onto the railing around the control panel and stood nailed to the cabin's floor, ready to hold firm should they, too, go under.

With eyes wide and temporarily too stunned for words, she took in the debris that drifted in the water, the tilted mast, the bow pointing to the heavens, the big patch of black oil that was spilling around the sinking ship, while her stomach reeled at the rolling of the deck beneath her.

It seemed she and Potter were fighting the enormous waves for hours, he swearing under his breath with the steering wheel clamped between his big tanned hands, she fighting nausea and sweat trickling down her brow.

"Hold on, Potter," was all Sable could pray, "just hold on!"

"What the Devil," Hancock cursed, coming back into the cabin again and taking over the wheel from Potter. The helmsman wiped his brow and took a swig from the Madeira bottle, as his boss remarked, "It's the *Mona Queen* from the Isle of Man's Steam Packet Company? Dear God, she's hit a mine. What a darn shame. Never saw a prettier ship."

"She was, Cap," Potter agreed, staring in grim dismay at the fast-sinking ship but instantly returning his eyes back to the signal board. "I'm telling you, these mines will be the death of us more so than the nosediving Junkers. Are you keeping her stationary for a while to see if there's crew to be saved?"

"As short as possible, Norman; we've got to keep her moving. I'll signal the coastguard we'll rescue anyone in the lifeboats seeing that we're closest to the *Mona Queen*."

The elderly captain was all busyness but meanwhile monitored the capsized ship half under water, its bow sinking deeper and deeper. Small, manned rowing boats came in their direction.

Sable strained her eyes. She'd never seen such frenzied and frightful activity in her life. The lifeboats seemed to move through burning water. It was terrifying. Prayer seemed to come as if automatically.

"Just hope they've all escaped." The captain's voice sounded doubtful, which made Sable peer even harder. As if the sheer act of her eyes might keep the men alive.

"Downed too fast, I'm afraid," Potter observed. Hancock scratched his beard and nodded.

"The coastguard will have to take care of the rescue operation. We simply don't have the time."

Sable still stood frozen on the spot, her eyes fixed on the first horror of war she was witnessing. Her brain couldn't grasp it; it seemed more like something from the movies, as if the windows she was looking through gave view to a screen on which this film was projected. The captain's voice, right next to her, made her jump, her nerves strained to the utmost.

"Sable, go help the floaters to safety. Potter and I need to stay here. We're in treacherous waters. You oversee the rescue team. Cook will know what to do, and so will the medics. Come back as soon as you can to report on the number of saved and wounded men. Ask if the captain and the helmsman are amidst them. I'll meet with them later."

Sable came into action as if a figure on a spring. She now flew down the stairs as fast as her legs could carry her, holding on to both railings as the waves were still causing havoc to her stability.

Glad the captain had made such a fuss of showing her every nook and cranny of the *Canterbury*, she could find her way about the ship almost blindfolded. The old seaman had even quizzed her on the different floors, the spaces, the mess, the kitchen, the boiler room, the cabins, the first-aid room.

Knowing instinctively where she needed to go, she felt her way down the swaying ship, feeling better about being useful. Work distracted her from the thumping of her heartbeat in her throat and the queasiness in her stomach. No time to think ahead, she could only focus on the here and now. It was a novel sensation brought to her by war, but something she felt she could become addicted to. Adrenaline coupled with deadly fear.

They weren't halfway across the Channel on their outbound journey yet, and she was right in the middle of it. Racing to the middle part of the ship on the lower floor where the gangway was situated, she knew it to be the place where the rope ladders were lowered for the rescue operation. She'd practiced throwing the heavy ropes overboard with boatman Larry.

As she arrived at the assigned spot, Sable saw her presence wasn't as necessary as she'd hoped. The protocol was already rolled out as the entire crew had come into action the moment the explosion rang out.

The young boatman who'd also accompanied the captain on his tours with Sable, and who was to be her anchor point in the real evacuation later, greeted her with a lopsided smile. Larry was long, lanky, and lighthearted, coming from a long line of maritime males and determined to make a fast naval career.

"Hi, Miss, glad to see you. Be careful though. The big Missus hasn't found her equilibrium yet. What a blast. Almost knocked me off my feet. Here, help these lads to get a dry blanket and then escort them to the boiler room to get out of their wet things. Make sure they get something hot to drink. When you've done that, come back up again and we'll see what's next. Can you manage on your own? Got to stay here, to note down the lads' details."

Sable nodded. The next moment she was preceding four dripping wet sailors who looked almost as stricken as she felt to the boiler room. Not knowing how to comfort them in their sorry state, she kept her head down and just mumbled some words about soup and dry clothes as the *Mona Queen* sailors plonk-plonk-plonked after her in their sopping shoes.

When she was sure they were comfortable enough to undress, she left them to find Cook, whom everyone called Poddy, as he was of substantial form and size.

On her return, the four crew members had made themselves as comfortable as they could, huddled in their blankets, and seemed to revive when she entered with hot tea and sandwiches. She'd tried hard to keep the content inside the mugs, but it had sloshed all over the tray. The men were just pleased to see her, and grinned bare their clattering teeth.

The oldest of them, a man of about forty with a prominent chin and icy-blue eyes in a rugose face, jumped to his feet and said in a husky voice, "Listen Miss, we're very grateful for all this, but please tell your captain that we'll be doing our bit together with you at Dunkirk. We were heading there ourselves. Aren't here for a free ride.

It's bad as it is that we're taking up soldiers' places and run with one less ship."

"I'll tell him," Sable assured them, handing around the refreshments. "Got to go now. More work to do. You come up when your clothes are dry enough."

Larry provided her with a list of names of twelve crew members, including the captain and the helmsman. Sable now understood the man with the blue eyes, who'd addressed her, was the *Mona Queen's* captain. She made a mental note to ask Larry to teach her about the various naval uniforms.

With her first task completed, Sable returned to her post in the cabin and what she hoped would be a short period of reasonable normality.

And that was just what she got. For a very short time.

17

DUNKIRK

T he *Canterbury* was steaming ahead, inching closer to the black smoke on the horizon. The men in the cabin had returned to their level-headed conversation. Sable pulled herself up at their resilience while she was still coming to terms with the horrific explosion and complete disappearance of what one moment had been a gigantic ship and the next minute a shipwreck sinking to the bottom of the North Sea.

"Narrow escape for us, too. Those damned mines. Hope I navigate around the stinkers," Potter grumbled, sucking ferociously on his billiard pipe, and sending a huge plume of toffee-scented smoke into the air.

"You can if you use your wits. That's what you have them for," Hancock replied good-naturedly.

"Can't blame me for nature endowing you with more gray cells than me," his friend quipped.

"Don't worry. We've got our mascot back, our scout Sable, daughter of my dear late friend, the Earl Montgomery."

"Ai!" Potter gave Sable a wink. "There you're uttering a wise saying."

"Everything under control with the lads, Sable?" Hancock gave her an intent and friendly gaze. She knew he was testing her spunk after this first clash in the war.

"Yes, it seems the entire crew is saved. That's at least something." She hoped her voice didn't sound too shaky.

"Wish I could go down and greet the fellows, but they'll have to wait until we're back in Dover. Can't keep my eye off our target now."

"The captain of the *Mona Queen* told me they will do their bit in Dunkirk with us, Cap," Sable said, proud to deliver such an important message.

"You're doing great, boatman. You're hired!" He shot her another glance and grinned.

The amity in the confined cabin, with its large display of knobs and switches and flickering green and red lights, the timbered brown walls, and wide windows giving a view to the sea on all sides, gave Sable a sense of reassurance.

"The Missus," as she now also inwardly called the *Canterbury,* was sailing smoothly at some twenty knots. Sable's stomach settled and she accepted an offered ham and pickle sandwich and a mug of tea. The chirpy mood of the men at her side made her believe they could sail the highest waves together.

All she could think of now was the noble work that lay ahead of them. Hadn't thousands of men, whose last resorts were the Dunkirk beaches, been rescued by ships just like the Missus in the past four days? Now they were also doing their bit to prevent Hitler from forcing Britain on its knees. It was, with all its danger and setbacks, a glorious moment in time.

But Sable's mood fell as fast as it had just risen. There was no saying if Freddie and David were among the saved souls or still on that beach, or, Heaven forbid, killed by the Germans. There hadn't been another sign of life from her friend. The troops who'd so far been rescued in the evacuation effort had been taken straight out of Dover for recovery in other parts of the country. No information had reached her ears and when she phoned Freddie's parents, they had no word of their son either. There was no way of knowing if he and David were dead or alive.

"Sea legs working better, boatman?"

Hancock's voice interrupted her musings. She realized how dangerous it was to daydream in a situation like this. There was still a lot to learn about vigilance in wartime. What a lousy scout she'd make in her current state.

"I'm fine, Cap. What do you want me to do?"

"I count on your sharp eyes through those binoculars. We've been allocated Route X, apparently safer than Route Z, which is the shortest but follows the French coastline and is under heavy attack from shore batteries. I'd hoped to take the Missus across on the shortest route despite the dangers, but orders are orders."

Captain Hancock talked of this large ferry as if she was his beloved mistress. Men were funny, and some were quite endearing, like the white-haired sailor. She did not know what the different sailing routes or their associated dangers were. Seeing the *Canterbury* now cruising straight across the Channel, she asked.

"What course does Route X follow, and what are our dangers? And is there also a Route Y?"

"Our boatman's waking up," Potter joked. With more seriousness, he explained to her.

"Yes, there are Routes X, Y and Z. Z is only 39 nautical miles, but, as Malcolm said, dangerous because of sailing under the French coast. Y is the longest, some 87 miles. It increases the sailing time by four hours, so then you're much more vulnerable to come under German attack. They have so many warships and submarines, and the *Luftwaffe* is relentless. Our Route X is the safest, some 55 miles. We stay in open waters for most of the time until we reach north of Dunkirk, but we have to pay close attention to the mines that are scattered everywhere."

Sable nodded; they'd already encountered the results of hitting a mine and seeing the *Mona Queen* go under.

Hancock added in his deep voice, "We also have to steer around the many sandbanks. Another treacherous secret of the sea. You'd better pray for us hitting neither mine nor sandbank, Mascot. Don't want to get stuck on one of those on our first adventure trip together, now do we?"

All this was so fascinating to Sable. She was excited to feel a part of such a vast men's world with that expert knowledge. As if she finally belonged. Dadaigh would be proud of her if he saw her now. She bit her lip. No show of emotions now. He would have told her that too.

"What am I supposed to focus on through my binoculars, boss?"

"You report any suspicious movement you encounter, whether in the water, on land or in the air. Not that we can duck away from these bloody Junkers or U-boats. Also keep an eye out for a long, stone breakwater, where we're supposed to moor. Think it will be easy to spot as there will be more boats. We're heading for the East Mole, not the West Mole. Tide's high, so we should be able to moor at the mole and pick up these poor buggers."

The captain bared yellowing teeth as he smiled encouragingly at his pupil. Sable immediately glued her field glasses to her eyes, knowing very well it was just to keep her busy as both the captain and the helmsman regularly peered through their own binoculars.

Everything seemed to go smoothly on their end, but they came dangerously closer to the menacing-looking black smoke that spread out over the horizon like a rampant thunderstorm.

Over the drumming of the ship's engine, the vague *rat-tat-tat* of machineguns and cracking of explosions on the French coast were audibly present. Meanwhile, the men in the cabin drank their lukewarm coffee, while Sable smoked her cigarette and now and then took a sip from her tea. She cast one last glance over her shoulder, but the white cliffs of safety were out of sight. There was only blackness ahead of them.

Until they reached the mole, and the full extent of the horror became clear to the three people standing side by side in the *Canterbury's* cabin. It dawned on Sable that it was a wonder that ships were still in the water and people, thousands of them on the beach and wading through the water, like trickles of olive-green beetles. All kept moving, alive until one black spot toppled and fell. Like many did.

Wave after wave of German airplanes came, the plane at the front making a nosedive and dropping the bombs, sending ships and men down as if they were shreds of rubber. After one attack, they retreated, soon to be back for more carnage.

From the ground, German tanks positioned around the beaches fired relentlessly on the unprotected khaki figures on the long strip of sand. For every two men who fell, one walked, or crawled on.

Too many never got up again. Sable clamped her hand over her mouth, feeling the ham sandwich come back up the wrong way. The sight was just too gruesome. She lowered her binoculars, turning scared eyes to Hancock, who muttered, "There, there now, my dear. Focus on the moving ones, only on the moving ones."

And she did just that, willing with all her power that Freddie and David were among the moving beetles.

A BITING, high-pitched screech flashed through the air and over their heads. Sable's heart almost stopped beating and for a moment all she could think was a place to hide, readying herself to take a dive under the switchboard. Seconds later, the first screech was followed by a crashing blow to their left.

Forcing herself to stay upright with the men, she peered with fearful eyes around her to locate what the cause of that awful sound was. Next to them, another ship was hit. It was the cargo ship that had been sailing next to them for the last leg of the journey.

The cargo ship shuddered, shook, and shivered, then sank faster than her eyes could follow it, while flames shot into the air and a huge oil spill formed in the surrounding water.

She was tongue-tied and wide-eyed as she heard Hancock say softly, "That was fast. Nothing we can do there. Don't recognize the ship."

"It's one of the rail-owned ships, the *SS Lorina*," Potter remarked sadly.

"You're right," Hancock agreed. "But whatever happens, we must keep focused on the job at hand. Really in the middle of the spectacle now. Stay tough, boatman."

SABLE TRIED to take in everything that was happening before her eyes but the chaos, the noise, the utter confusion, and despair stretched all her senses to the maximum. The *Canterbury* slowly made her way toward the East mole, where ships were mooring, sinking, and burning while hundreds and hundreds of soldiers with tin helmets and khaki uniforms waded in long rows behind each other to reach the ships, being shot down, wounded, screaming and hollering.

It was time to leave the cabin and take up her position next to Larry, but she would much rather have crept underneath the switchboard and stay there curled up like a puppy.

"Go!" she ordered herself as her legs, rubbery and reluctant, almost refused to carry her to the gangplank.

Larry gave her a comradely punch.

"You're a tough cookie, Miss. Got to admire you for it."

"You don't know how frightened I am," she wanted to say, but taking heart from his words, she resolved to stand tall.

Standing next to the rope ladder with Larry on the other side, they pulled the shivering, wet and heavy-weighing men on board. All her muscles strained, giving it her all, Sable no longer felt pain nor fear. Despite the heavy shelling, despite the men who fell dead out of her hands, despite her own clothes getting soaking wet and bloodstained from taking hold of the drenched uniforms and the waves gushing overboard.

It was sheer perplexity and adrenaline that kept her on her post, with a crystal-clear awareness she could be dead any second now. With the awareness of death so close, Sable had never felt more alive, more dedicated to staying alive.

THIS! This was life.

· · ·

SHE SAW herself as if outside of herself, strong, determined, in charge. Lucid enough to realize her brain was shell-shocked and her body had taken over, functioning automatically as it knew what to do. Survive, never give up, keep going. She would deal with her brain later.

Clear as daylight, at a snap of her fingers, Sable Montgomery was calm, collected, complete. Dragging one man after the other on board, seeing them scurry to temporary safety, hope in their eyes. Her job, her responsibility.

When finally, Larry signaled the boat was full, she was the one to draw in the rope ladder, blind and deaf to the horrendous cries of the men in the cold water who still wanted a place to safety. A job was a job. They had to wait for the next boat.

But only then, as she turned to help the ones on board, the wounded and the sick, she realized she'd missed one face in the crowd of men who had lifted their haggard, sunken faces to her.

Freddie!

SHE FEVERISHLY SEARCHED for him amidst the hundreds of men on deck, peeked under blankets, stepped over half-dead bodies. Gazed into hollow eyes with black rings around them, men not over twenty looking over sixty. All exhausted, most already asleep where they had fallen, others crying out in pain or praying rosaries and Our Father, some grabbing her ankle to thank her.

But now her restlessness was back as she kept clawing her way through the men, hundreds and hundreds of them. Where was Freddie? All her power seeped out of her, though she knew it was madness. He could be anywhere, on the beach, on another ship, at the bottom of the sea. She'd done what she could. She hadn't failed him.

"We're unmooring." Larry stood next to her. "Could you give me a hand with the hawsers?"

"Sure."

Sable looked up into the blue sky, tainted with gray and black smoke, and saw them coming, a fleet of German airplanes flying in formation. And then the first one nosedived as usual and released a plethora of bombs.

She screamed, felt how the young boatman pulled her away from the railing. A gigantic explosion, more screams. The *Canterbury* creaked and shuddered.

"It's not us!" The young officer screamed in her ear. "It's the one next to us. I believe Hancock is right that you are our lucky charm."

But Sable had her eyes fixed on something in the water.

"Freddie!"

Her voice couldn't be heard over the explosions and screams, but she saw him trying to dash for her ship, carrying over his shoulder a tall man with a mop of dark-blonde hair and his arm in a sling, who seemed unconscious. The ship was already drifting away.

"Wait!" she screamed again and ran back to the railing and flung the rope ladder overboard.

"Wait!"

Larry seemed to understand her without asking who Freddie was. He was back by her side in no time and grabbed the man with his bulky unconscious load by the shoulders with two strong hands. Sable tried to keep them from slipping back into the water, but as they were away from the mole, she had no solid footing from where they could pull. The men hung alongside the side of the ship, slipping out of her hands inch by inch. Her arms ached as David kept sliding from Freddie's back.

"Don't give up," she screamed in a voice not her own, "Larry, please hold them!" But they kept slipping, drawn by the strong pull of the water. Tears were blinding her eyes; all the war around her was gone. She had only one thing to achieve. One thing. Fighting like a terrier, she felt how next to her Larry put in his last force as well, but the double load was unmanageable.

Just when she was sure they'd never get them on board alive, the *Canterbury* already sailing meters away from the mole, the two wet men fell together over the ridge, reaching the planked floor with a dull thud. Sable cried from exhaustion and relief. She'd achieved her most valiant deed so far in the war. Now it was her duty to keep them both alive.

While Larry plucked David off Freddie and called for a medic, Sable took Freddie in her arms, crying and cheering at the same time.

"This is my childhood friend with his pal," she explained to Larry, who stood regaining his own strength for a moment. Sable felt jubilant, a Hercules in her own right. Larry nodded and gasped. "Time to fix them up, Miss. Glad your mission was successful. Now, let's get the heck back to Dover. I'll signal Hancock and Potter, don't worry. And I'll be back in a sec."

"Thank you, Larry!"

The lanky man saluted her with a warm grin.

Sable turned her attention to Freddie. He was almost passing out as well, but she gave him small sips of water, seeing his parched lips, the bruises on his face, the black mane full of David's blood.

Just before Freddie closed his eyes and dozed off, she heard him gasp, "Sabbo, you're the best!"

And for once Sable believed he was right.

18

A FANY GIRL

London, 4 days later

"Minnie, do you remember that lemon meringue pie you made for my father when he was in hospital?"

Sable was bent over the sink, cleaning the breakfast dishes, but turned to face the housekeeper, who was standing at the large kitchen table, stuffing a chicken that was to be their lunch.

Wiping a lock of black hair from her eyes with her pink kitchen glove, Sable's face was both resolute and serious. Still with her pink gloved hand on, she picked up a smoldering cigarette from the ashtray and took a puff.

"I do, Miss, but it was not that successful as you may remembe'. 'Is Grace passed away that same night."

"Don't get all suspicious now, Minnie dear. It was the last food my father enjoyed, and that's why I thought you could make it for Freddie and David. They need perking up as well. Just make it."

"I will, Miss."

The bond between the two women, which had been rocky over the past years, was a good way on the mend. Sable's hazardous trip to Dunkirk had changed her from a languid reader into an activist. She felt Elrod and Minnie must have wondered what had brought about the change, but even if they'd asked her, she wouldn't have been able to give them the reason. Dunkirk had just opened Sable's eyes to the truth they were all living in. War.

When the *Canterbury* had—in the eleventh hour—reached its Dover port of destiny, its last working engine was faltering, and the ship was taking in large quantities of water because of several holes as large as cannon balls in its hull.

At least a dozen men had died from their wounds and exhaustion during the seven-hour journey, in which they'd been under constant attack from whatever the Germans could throw at them. David's life had been hanging on a thread as well, but with a stiff dose of morphine and sufficient hydration, he'd survived.

Sable's sea voyage into the war zone had been a sobering experience. It mellowed and toughened her in equal measure. And there had been no doubt in her mind. Freddie and David were staying at Cavendish Square until they were fully recovered. She couldn't care less that it was against the rules, as the RAF pilots had to report to their base.

"There's all the time in the world for hanging around RAF Abingdon in Oxfordshire when you're better!" she'd protested. Then added as if she was an expert on military discipline, "I don't think they'll fire pilots who're already veterans in this war. They will need your knowledge of occupied territory. It's vital to them. You're both staying here, where my trusted Doctor Howe can monitor you. He's much more qualified than those military sawbones."

And with affection, she remembered how the old family doctor had nursed her back to health after her pitfall into the abyss of alcoholism. Straightening her back, she took another puff and dipped her hands back into the dishwater.

Having finished with the dishes, she arranged the daisies Minnie had bought at the Berwick Street Market and left the kitchen. While plucking her apron, which was actually Minnie's, from her slender hips, she made her way to the living room.

At nine in the morning, the men would still be resting upstairs.

But to her surprise she saw Freddie lounging on the mauve sofa, his long legs stretched out the full length of the couch. He was holding an earmarked volume of Christopher Isherwood's *Goodbye to Berlin* between his slender fingers.

The clear blue eyes lifted from the page to meet Sable's. A broad smile broke over his somber face and, swinging his slippered feet to the floor, he exclaimed, "Sabbo, my *inamorata*! I was hoping to catch you for a moment, but I see you're busy with your housewifery hardships."

"Not at all!" Sable giggled, hanging the apron over the back of a chair and placing the flowers on the sideboard. Then she poured Freddie a coffee from the percolator that Minnie always had ready. Lighting two Craven A's, she handed him the cup and one of the burning cigarettes. After taking up a position opposite him, she pulled her legs under her in her characteristic Sable way with the ashtray positioned on the top knee. Through the smoke, she was gauging his health and mood with cat-like eyes.

He looked thin, off-color. The scar above his left eye that had ripped away half of his eyebrow was bright red, becoming infected. The swelling on the left side of his face malformed his otherwise purely symmetrical features.

At twenty-three, Freddie Frinton-Smith looked twice his age, and the utter devastation of his looks and spirit shocked Sable. Freddie represented youth to her, as much his as hers. Was she getting old as well?

The blue eyes were lusterless, expressing the unspoken horrors they'd seen in wartime Belgium, but his movements were swift and agile as ever. Propped up against the cushions, he drank his coffee with eager sips while his hand with the burning cigarette quivered, littering his Burberry cardigan, a hand-me-down from Sable's father, with ashes.

She waited for him to start the conversation as he'd intimated he wanted to talk with her. Though close as ever, Sable felt Freddie's loyalty and concern lay with the sick David lying motionless upstairs. She was playing second fiddle in this relationship now. Not that she minded. It was just plain heaven to have him under her roof.

Her roof.

Nobody kicking her out and about. A luxury neither she nor Freddie had known for many years. To Sable, her house was his house, and she thought she'd made that clear to both. So, it shocked her when she heard him say,

"Listen, Sabbo, I think David and I are on the verge of overstaying our welcome here." He raised his hand as she wanted to protest. "Let me explain. David needs a specialist's care. He needs to go to a military hospital and get proper treatment. He's not taking a turn for the better, despite our spoon-feeding him. And I'm not bowled over staying away from my regiment any longer."

"Freddie, you're not well!" Sable banged the ashtray on the table, got up and took to her pacing, an exasperated look on her unhappy face.

"But I am. Just some minor scratches! There's the war, my dear. France is about to collapse, and then it's our turn. Dunkirk was the Brits' narrow escape. This time we won't have that window of opportunity, and then there will be no more Great Britain. I can't let that happen. I am fit to fly again." He looked ashen for a moment and added in a low voice, "Well almost, I guess."

Sable shook her head. "No, Freddie. I agree with you about David. We can get him to a hospital, for sure, military or civilian. I've been worrying about him losing consciousness from time to time. That's not good. But you, you are also not well." Her voice gained more confidence as she gathered her thoughts.

Freddie was as low as she'd ever seen him when he said in a toneless voice, "I also counted on having a little more time with you, after we've gone through the mill together."

Sable sat down again, feeling defeated in her mission to take care of other people.

"I don't even know what happened to you in Belgium. Now I'm all confused. I just thought you were happy staying here with me in London, you know, recuperating, gaining strength when apparently you weren't. I thought we had so much more to discuss; so much happened to me as well ..."

Her voice trailed off, ending in a half sob. Here she would be, alone in the big house, cut off from everything and everyone. Sable, the cast-off. After she'd fought so hard to get on top again.

Freddie looked hit over the head as Sable rose once more from her chair to continue her plagued pacing. She avoided his imploring gaze. The room was thick with smoke, the atmosphere too hot and stifling for early June.

"It's not that, Sabbo, and you know it. These past days have been swell despite David and me being in such rotten shape. You're a delight to be with, my very best pal. And you look so well. You've changed. I don't know what. I'm so grateful to you. Please don't be disheartened. The way you've carried the torch for David shows how big a heart you have in that small rib case of yours."

He got up as well, feeble on his feet, stumbling toward her and taking both her hands in his. Hands so similar, their touch so familiar.

"Don't take this personal, Sabbo, because it isn't! Duty is calling, that's all."

"But you're not well, Freddo! Don't fool yourself. The wound above your eye is festering, you have a broken rib, you're full of cuts and bruises."

"I've seen men in worse conditions do much harder jobs than fly planes."

This was Freddie's death-or-glory face, presenting her with a lay-it-on-the-line, indisputable fact. Freddie would even leave his beloved David in a hospital bed to get back to his war duties.

Under his unyielding attitude, Sable felt her resistance slacken. This was a different Freddie than the languid, easy-is-as-easy-does student. The man who stood opposite her was a toughened fighter.

But was it he that changed?

She suddenly remembered that stalwart little face when he wanted to catch a fish, ride a bike, hit the wicket with his cricket ball.

Gazing up into his eyes, she saw her own reflection. She was as stalwart. They were like two peas in a pod.

"Will you tell me before you go? You know, about Belgium? How you two ended up there? I must know." Sable smiled up at him, already forgiving him his torpedoing of her own plans and the hated idea of being alone and useless in London. If war was indeed washing up their shores soon too, everybody had to be ready.

"Of course. Come and sit with me on the sofa."

Sipping coffee and smoking cigarettes, he told her how he, as David's co-pilot, had taken off from RAF Marham in Norfolk on 25 May for a routine patrol flight in their Lysander. They were supposed to collect information on the positions of the British Expeditionary Forces stationed along the KW line between Antwerp and Wavre, which was supposed to protect Brussels, and the advancing German forces coming from Holland and Germany.

With his arm around her shoulder and Sable resting comfortably in his armpit, he told the rest of his tale.

"You have to understand Lysanders aren't bombers. This was purely for reconnaissance flight. Somewhere near Antwerp, we saw this squadron of Heinkels touching in on us. The two Wellingtons that were supposed to protect us were shot down before our very eyes. David did everything right. He saved our lives. Did I tell you before what a cardinal wingman David Southgate really is? Well, he certainly showed it when it mattered most!" Freddie's gaunt face lit up with pride and love.

"While I used all my power to keep my wits about me, he just slowed the plane down and opened up the canopy. He even took the time to make sure I wasn't instinctively using my foot to jump from the side of the cockpit, which would've exposed me to the slipstream and led to colliding with the Lysander's tail. Anyway, this all sounds way too technical, but it was a vital reminder. I was a mess, you see. Not something to be proud of. I may even have been screaming."

Freddie stopped talking, pulled Sable closer, heaving a deep sigh of disappointment in himself. How Sable recognized that trait.

"Come off it! You're far from a milksop yourself, Freddo!"

"Thanks." He gave her arm a gentle squeeze and continued his tale. "Here we are rolling over the so-called wall by using our hands. Even in the deafening roar of planes around us, I hear David count to ten, waiting to clear the plane before giving the order to pull the ripcord and deploy our parachutes."

Freddie's voice was thick with emotion as he remembered that perilous moment on which his life and that of his friend depended.

Sable listened intently, her thoughts going in two directions, helping Freddie get his head sorted and soaking up all information on warfare that might one day be even helpful to her. Anything could happen in this war. Operation Dynamo had blown the lid off life as she'd known it.

Freddie's memories now came clear as they were freed from the toils of time.

"I was overjoyed as we reached Mother Earth, quite oblivious the worst was yet to come. Thought we'd bailed out, you know, survived, David had his head seriously injured upon landing in some Belgium woodlands. The trees were our protection, but they don't provide the most perfect landing spot. I helped him as best I could. My compass told me to go in a southwestern direction. I was the one carrying the load from then on, as David had a severe concussion and a twisted ankle. He was not well." Freddie's face contorted.

"One of my ribs was broken, which wasn't a lot of fun, I can tell you. Also had quite some cuts and bruises, like this pretty one." He pointed to his swollen brow.

"I took to carrying David for long stretches, and, man, that boy's a heavy load on a broken rib. God knows how many days we were wading through the carnage that Belgium had become, following the other British troops and Belgians fleeing their own homes. On boots with no soles left, no water, no food, scorching sun. But do you know what the worst was?"

Sable shook her head.

"Because we were in RAF uniform, we were cold-shouldered by the Brits and French. They took out their frustration at not being protected by the RAF on us. They'd withhold from us a resting place, a shelter, a scrap of food, cigarettes. But it wasn't our fault, and the planes didn't come to our rescue either, now did they?" Freddie sounded embittered.

"Go on."

"David desperately needed medical help, but he wasn't the only one and there wasn't a medic in sight who wasn't totally overworked. So, I took to praying, Sable, day and night I prayed, and by God you know I'm not the praying kind. But in hell, prayer happens of its own accord. It's the only thing you've got left when you're stripped of everything humane. Prayer."

Prayer, Sable thought, *when did I last pray?* White walls, the wail of a baby. Prayer. Unanswered prayer. Dadaigh. Useless prayer. She couldn't imagine ever wanting to invoke a higher power again.

"Luck was with me one day. David was about to give up the ghost. I knew I had to let the home front know what our gruesome fate was. Then I bumped into this one commander, Major Jack Palmer, jolly fellow from Ipswich, long, twisting mustache, pockmarked face. He'd fought the Bochs in the Great War. Jack had an operating field phone. He let me use it. Hope to thank that man properly one day. The rest is no secret to you."

Freddie kissed her cheek. "I'll never forget how we met again, Sab, not as long as I live."

"Neither will I."

They sat silent for a while until Freddie jumped up from the sofa.

"I'm going to see if David is awake."

"I'll phone Doctor Howe. Ask his advice." Sable made her way to the Bakelite phone.

"Yes! Let's get the ball rolling. David is written off as a pilot for the foreseeable future, but I'll report to my regiment. And what about you, my dear? What will you do?" Freddie fixed her with his blue stare, his head slightly tilted as he studied her. "You want to rally round as well, don't you?"

"Of course! Strange as it sounds, I never felt more alive than during the Dunkirk evacuation." Her cheeks reddened, ashamed to admit she'd felt so alive in the middle of terrible suffering.

"I saw that! Now, as your surrogate older brother, I have a proposition to make." He grinned his white teeth bare, not saying anything until Sable cried out.

"Stop doing that. What is it?"

"The developments are all still very hush-hush right now, but I don't want to remain an ordinary pilot during this war. Flying hither and thither, dropping bombs and dogfighting Nazis in the air. No, no! Unorthodox warfare is the future."

Sable was puzzled. What was he talking about, and what did it have to do with her?

"Winston Churchill's putting together a secret organization to train a new type of resistance fighters, a guerrilla type of style."

Sable's eyes opened wide. Freddie shook his head.

"No, no, no, sweet Sabbo! I don't mean you becoming a secret spy. How about a secretary for the organization? You stand a good chance with your knowledge of languages and your finishing school background."

Frustrated and disappointed, Sable snapped, "I can't type, and it sounds boring. Sitting in an office all day."

"You'll be close to the fire, Sab. It would also mean being trained as a FANY, you know, the First Aid Nursing Yeomanry."

That didn't make it much better for her.

"I have no nursing skills. I can ride a horse, but I suppose these nurses ride cars rather than horses into war these days?"

Freddie chuckled. "True! But let me tell you this, Sabbo. They'll come knocking on your door soon to take part in the war effort. If you're to choose between the WAAF and the FANY, choose the FANY."

Sable interrupted him. "Why the FANY? What's better about them?"

Freddie adopted that older-brotherly attitude that Sable usually found endearing but now made her impatient. He grinned.

"I've heard rumors these girls will be getting the more daring jobs should England's shores become swarmed by Nazis. I mean even better than driving lorries and flying planes. The sabotage kind of stuff. Things you'd be good at."

Now he had her attention. This sounded already a lot better.

"But why would I be selected for these tasks when they had men to do that?" She wasn't convinced.

"Because the men all have to enlist, silly. At some point, the British women will be taking over the jobs that used to be done by men." His enthusiasm was infectious, but Sable still bumped into one obstacle.

"But I'd have to start in a boring office?"

"Sure. Everybody must start at the bottom of the ladder. Now, do you want me to present your name to the leadership or not?" His eyes danced over her face while she contemplated his proposal with a frown between her brows.

"I know nothing about FANY except for what I've been taught at school. Nurses in long skirts tending to the wounded in the trenches, driving old-fashioned ambulances, all that first-aid stuff. Nothing that held my interest."

"Oh, but that's all old-fashioned bollocks," Freddie assured her. "They now have beautiful uniforms, much more practical and less womanly."

"Would I be wearing such a uniform?" Now this *was* an appealing thought.

"Every day! Even at night if you choose to." They both chuckled.

"Then yes!" she said first hesitantly and then again with more heart. "Yes, present my name to the board."

And with that, Sable pictured herself as a FANY girl.

19

EVERYTHING HAS CHANGED

The Rings, Beaulieu Estate, December 1940

"Sable, can you come here, please?"

The familiar booming voice of Commandant Jock Woolworth sounded from the next-door office. Sable had been busy scheduling the next shift of new recruits for their training and housing, but instantly left her chalkboard that was fitted to one wall of her cramped office. Smoothing her khaki dress and checking if the top-button of her blouse was done up, she swiftly walked on her high heels to her boss's office.

A robust man with a mop of rampant reddish hair in civilian clothes stood at the window overlooking the estate. As Major Woolworth often had visitors in his office, she didn't pay more attention to the man's back and he didn't turn, so she walked to her boss's desk, fully expecting to be given another urgent task.

Everything was urgent with the major and everything had to be done yesterday. How many times Sable had complained to her boss that she needed an extra secretary if he wanted to have everything done this fast, but he kept saying,

"War Office won't pay for it, sugar. SOE is not their priority." So

Sable struggled on, working as hard as she could, thanking every night she put her head to her pillow that she'd managed another day.

"What is it, Commandant? What can I do for you?"

Sable liked the Major, whom the staff affectionately called Wooly, and it was the reason she worked so hard just to make his work more bearable for him. She admired his leadership. Strict and sharp, but never without his offhand sense of humor.

Wooly was a rather short, heavyset man approaching fifty, with a balding scalp and decades of experience in the Secret Services. A Great War veteran, he'd started out as the chief instructor at the Beaulieu training center for SOE and was now its Commandant. He was likable, agreeable, clumsy, and a local Hampshire bacon-face.

"Ah, sugar, there you are!" The Major looked up from the document he was reading; his sharp light-green eyes lit up at seeing her. He was the only one Sable had no qualms letting call her "sugar." though she was very strict with the mostly male population at Beaulieu never giving her derogative names.

To everyone else she was Miss Montgomery, the Commandant's secretary, and if necessary, she even resorted to Lady Montgomery if one of them tried to be too familiar with her.

"It's about Captain Mitchell. He's got a request." The major informed her.

"What unit and nationality is Captain Mitchell from, Commandant? I haven't seen that name on the lists."

"No, sugar, it's him." The Major pointed to the man at the window. Sable swiveled around on her heels. The man turned to face her as well. Feeling her jaw drop, she was vaguely aware how fatally stupid she must look staring up at him with her mouth half open. She closed it like a fish, skillfully slipping back into the neutral and professional posture she'd adopted as Woolworth's secretary.

After six months of training by the seasoned industrial spy, role-playing came at a snap of the fingers to Sable. This time around she wasn't the half-drunk, half-crazy society peeress in a West-End club or Amsterdam dancehall.

Sable stood tall, defying the cyanic blue gaze that was taking her measure. But she couldn't help feeling a quiver in her stomach, her breath hitch. Under the carefully applied artificial blush, her cheeks developed a red of their own. A confusing sense of shame and excitement mingled underneath her stoic outward appearance.

I did nothing wrong. I have nothing to be ashamed of, she reminded herself, stretching herself even a notch taller and giving him an eye for an eye.

With triumph, she registered he was as unprepared for this meeting as she was. So, he hadn't come here to make a fool of her all over again. She let out a small breath of relief. What had happened in Amsterdam was in the past. She'd learned her lesson and turned that leaf.

Scrutinizing him before they were introduced to each other, she saw the eyelid twitch under the reddish brow, a drawing in of a deeper breath. *Good.* He'd not forgotten her. Quickly, before Wooly could spoil her moment, she stretched out her hand.

"Egbert's pilot, a pleasure." That would set the stakes.

As Bill shook her hand, it was as if her hand remembered his, its firmness, the non-tolerance of excuses. She gave it a little squeeze. *No excuses*, was her answer.

"Egbert's pilot? Please explain yourself, Sable. You're talking in riddles." Woolworth heaved his stocky body from behind his desk and, lighting a cigar, glanced from his secretary to the tall visitor. A question mark on the shrewd face that had missed nothing, not even the tension that hung between these two young cockfighters.

"I think Mr. Mitchell can explain that to you, Major. Now, what is it you need from me?"

Her boss didn't answer directly. He'd come to stand next to the Scotsman, who seemed like a towering giant next to the bald Commandant. Neither took their eyes off Sable. She finally cast hers down, slipping back into studied neutrality.

She realized why her boss was looking her up and down like this. It made her feel shy, strangely exposed. Any hint at romantic feelings between men and women at Beaulieu were a no-go.

They'd even discussed that possibility, Sable being an attractive,

young, single woman of considerable means. The wise old fox had
had a hunch about Sable's susceptibility to male attention and he'd
weaned her off it, showing how she could stand on her own two feet,
be her own woman.

He was ready to nip anything that might arise between his new
instructor and Miss Sable in the bud. His voice showed just its
normal sense of jocularity, but she didn't miss the undertone of
surprise at what he was seeing before his eyes. So much for restraint.
It was indeed a virtue worth having.

"Nothing in particular, sugar. Just arrange for accommodation for
Captain Mitchell at the Boarmans's. He's here to help train the
French section. I did not know you two knew each other. Well, let me
not keep you from your work any longer. I've got to quiz Bill on being
Egbert's pilot."

"Very well, Sir. It will be arranged straightaway. I'll ring the Boarmans' housemaster to come and collect the captain. Is there any
luggage that needs transporting?"

Bill now spoke for the first time. His voice was less intimidating
than she remembered but still had that sound-from-home ring.

"Just one suitcase, Ma'am. And thank ye."

They nodded politely at each other and Sable, straight-backed
and with as little swinging of her hips as she could muster on her
high heels, left the Major's office.

On entering her own office, she flung the door shut and sank at
her desk. *Him!* Why him? Of all the people in the world, why did
Wooly recruit him?

*Don't exaggerate, Sable. He's nothing to you. He will always be nothing
to you.*

But the memories came flooding back as she lit a cigarette and
cupped her head in her shaking hands. Unable to go back to work,
she was catapulted back into a life she'd thought she had shut the
door on for good. Just one cigarette before she straightened herself
out and could ring the Boarmans's housemaster to tell him about the
new arrival.

Bill!

If there was anyone in the world, it would be "wild" Bill Mitchell to bring the darkness back to her at this unwanted moment.

What a fool she'd made of herself, accompanying Egbert to Amsterdam with Bill in the cockpit. Her father had just died, and she was a constant mess, drunk night and day, wanting to end it all. To kill herself. With Dadaigh dead, without having had the time to reconnect properly with him, what was the use of it all? Sable had lost the last hope of having a family. The hollowness of her aloneness was simply unbearable without copious amounts of liquor in her system.

As she now recalled that dazed state on a clear, crispy December day in the pine-scented area of Beaulieu, sober and satisfied, it was as if she was a raven hovering way above herself, looking down on that "poor thing from the past."

Egbert, the kind, soft, only half-adult soul, couldn't handle her out-of-control behavior. Though, by God, Sable knew he'd tried. She was just too wild and broken, sure nobody could save her anymore. Certainly not money. His or hers. Both Egbert and she had copious amounts of cash.

It had only made it worse. There was always more money to spend on parties and pubs. Then, one night, also in December, on a slippery, snowy bridge in the middle of the Dutch capital, Bill had grabbed her wrists and told her to pull herself together. She'd flung herself in his arms, cried against that hard, broad chest, and he'd let her for a moment.

Sable shuddered at the thought of her strange behavior. She was Egbert's girl. Another pull on her cigarette as the scene played itself out before her eyes—what she remembered of it, which was only flashes.

Bill had turned to the bewildered Egbert, who stood on that nightly Amsterdam canal street looking like a dog whose bone has just been stolen by another dog.

"I'm flyin' 'er back to London tomorrow, Egbert. The girl needs help. She needs to check into a clinic of some sort."

Sable hadn't even protested, which she normally did when her alcohol consumption was mentioned. She'd... she'd felt a flicker of hope. Like when Dadaigh was still home and would reprimand her. That authority. How had Bill managed it?

Egbert had just nodded. And that's what had unfolded. She'd said goodbye to Egbert, no promises. Just goodbye. The stolen-bone expression permanently on his broad face. Then more shards of mist, of which Sable remembered little.

Not a word had been exchanged between Bill and her as he flew her back to London in the Van Eijk's Ford Tri-Motor. Despite her drunken state and her physical sickness, Sable had been grateful for someone taking control. She didn't know why he took the trouble, just sensed a depth and steadying force radiating from this tall Scotsman at her side. She could relax for the very first time in years.

Bill had dropped her off at Cavendish Square. Vaguely, she remembered him discoursing with Elrod, while Minnie took her to bed. Then there was Doctor Howe, his genteel, elderly face looking sorrowfully at her but taking over the authority from Bill. Then a long, long spell of sickness and darkness until she'd finally dried out. Accepted she was still alive. Wanted to be alive.

And here she was now. Different life, changed girl.

But somehow, she knew William "wild Bill" Mitchell's reappearance in her life was about to rehash her carefully constructed equilibrium. It made her blood flow faster but gave her head a warning.

Why in the world this stick-in-the-mud Scotsman was donned with the nickname "wild" was a mystery to Sable. He reminded her of her father, that same right-is-right-and-wrong-is-wrong attitude. Old-fashioned men with outdated habits.

She just hoped she wouldn't run into Capt'n Mitchell too often. She couldn't afford to lose what she'd built up since they last parted.

20

ANNA ADAMS

London, late April 1941

It was a great feeling to be back in London and stroll through Hyde Park in her FANY uniform.

Sable took it all in, the sweet scent of the hyacinths, the fresh green livery on the trees, the majestic swans gliding through the Serpentine as if they owned it, girls in flowery dresses and cardigans hanging on the arm of their soldier fiancés, the foreign nannies pushing prams and scolding sticky-fingered kids not their own, businessmen in bowler hats, black umbrella over the arm, crossing the park on their way to their favorite club.

Nobody knew if Hitler's bombings had stopped plaguing and destroying London for just a short while, or if he'd given up on conquering Britain altogether. For now, the sirens and the bombers were silent, and life had resumed as normal. Almost as normal.

The craters and torn-apart buildings on nearly every London corner and street were stark reminders that England had been hurt in its very heart. The photographs of a stricken King George VI in his naval uniform stepping over the rubble with his stylish Queen Elizabeth at his side, the repeated bombings of Buckingham Palace, it was all fresh on the British mind.

Sable had been out of town for months, leaving Cavendish Square in the capable hands of Elrod and Minnie, who'd withstood the first waves of German bombings as best as they could, though several houses on either side of Sable's property had taken a beating. Poor or rich quarters, Hitler's Heinkels, Dorniers and Junkers had made no distinction in the Battle of Britain.

London life certainly felt more skittish and cheerless since the last time Sable visited, though there was still a semblance of glitter and glamor in the West End jazz clubs and at the many high-class soirees held behind blackout windows.

Up till recently, she might have still felt a pull toward those leisure pursuits, but eighteen months of sobriety and a year under Wooly's strict training had produced a changed Sable. As the London gravel park crunched under her high-heeled shoes, she felt she had life under control. Well, almost. What she was about to do would not be easy. But it was necessary. She was on leave for business purposes: a visit to her solicitor, and a meeting at the SOE Headquarters in Baker Street.

Leaving Hyde Park at Bayswater Road, Sable continued her march onto Edgware Road. There, behind a gleaming maroon-colored door, was the glitzy office of Mr. Moses Brown. For two decades he had been the prime solicitor of Earl Archibald Montgomery, 6th Baron of Alnor, and now of the Earl's only child, the revered Lady Sable Montgomery, her father's *Bhobain*.

"Milady, what an honor! Do take a seat!" The spindly solicitor, well into his fifties but still with a decorative mop of dark hair on his gleaming head, and fine silver-rimmed spectacles on a thin elongated nose, snapped his fingers. A typewriter that had been rattling in the adjacent open-door office stopped, and a woman in a tailored, navy-blue dress with stylish curled blonde hair and a round childish face with a charming, snubbed nose came hastening to the solicitor's side.

"Coffee, tea, a bourbon?" The short-sighted, nickel-gray eyes looked at Sable almost impatiently, as if she had to decide that second or the moment would be lost. Mr. Brown was a hell-will-break-loose type of person, Sable knew, so to not further aggravate her host, she quickly replied to the woman with a kind nod.

"Tea will be fine. Thank you."

As soon as the refreshment department was settled, Brown opened the file on his desk and contrary to his usual haste, stared at the document, clearly contemplating something he found hard to put into words.

"Are you sure, Milady?"

"Absolutely sure, Sir."

"You know it will have major implications, not just for your mother but for the entire estate?"

"I'm aware of it."

"There are other properties the War Office could investigate in."

"Are you afraid of telling my mother to pack her bags? Because I have no scruples about doing so myself, but I'll need the legal document to wave under her nose."

It was Sable's turn to become impatient. As the elderly solicitor was beating around the bush, she wondered if her mother had contacted him or, even worse, bribed the fellow. But then he explained his point, always the proper middleman.

"Lady Montgomery, your father had a reason to lease Alnor Castle to his ex-wife, I mean your mother. You're aware of that, aren't you?" He cleared his throat, evidently very uncomfortable with the thought of bringing up anything remotely personal and emotional regarding her family.

"I'm not my father, Mr. Brown. It's my property now and the times have changed. We're at war, and as you may well realize…" She stopped here, giving the solicitor, whom she knew was Jewish, an intense stare. "We can't afford to lose this war. Should my mother wish to return to Alnor after the war, we will reconsider the lease." She took a deep breath. Bringing up the tender family ties about her parental home wasn't as easy as she'd expected.

"As far as my information goes, my mother is living alternatively in Monte Carlo and Wiesbaden as Frau Werner von Bissing, the name of her Nazi husband, Misty Fletcher's fifth husband. She's not been back at Alnor Castle since the beginning of the war, and she'd probably be ripped to pieces by the locals if she showed her face in Scotland, anyway. So whence your scruples, Sir?"

The harshness of her voice shocked Sable herself. She saw the nickel-gray eyes narrow. *Bingo.* She'd spoken directly to his Jewish heart.

"I've drawn up the document for the discontinuation of the lease to Mrs Von Bissing." Mr. Brown's voice was almost soft as he added, "You're so like His Grace, your late father in business matters, Lady Montgomery, and an asset to him, if I may say so."

"Thank you, sir." Sable smiled for the first time. If only she wasn't this tired, with the immense burden of her estate resting on her shoulders. The solicitor's compliment helped her to gather her strength.

"Would you break the news to my mother? I want to be spared the drama. And I haven't got her address abroad."

"Of course! And I'll contact Colonel Gibbins about the new lease for the War Office. When do you think they will need Alnor Castle as a training center?"

"I'm on my way to the headquarters on Baker Street to discuss the details. They should contact you. You should be able to take care of all the details. I will travel to Alnor myself to prepare for the arrival of training staff and the first batch of agents."

"Very well, Lady Sable." He hesitated a moment and then said in that same soft voice, "You're not just an asset to your late father but to the entire nation, Ma'am."

"Thank you kindly. I'm only doing my duty."

Filippo Maltese's words rang in Sable's ears and tears sprang to her eyes.

"Family is a great place to start with the patching up, Sable. And I wish you luck. I've seen you from your arrival, I've seen your struggle to adjust, and all the while I knew there was something special in you, but that you had first to find out you were your own worst enemy. I see great things for you in your future."

She was sure Dadaigh was smiling down on her from the heavens as she left Mr. Brown's office and the maroon-colored door clicked shut behind her. Another chapter closed. Her mother was now banned from using her legacy.

AN HOUR later Sable sounded the doorbell of 64 Baker Street, a regular-looking premise, no nameplate, nothing that suggested that behind these walls was housed the headquarters of the organization that Winston Churchill had given but one order: *set Europe ablaze*.

Sable waited with trepidation for the door to open. Though she'd been in the middle of Secret Service instructors and secret agents for almost a year now, most of the activities involving these undercover instructions had taken place outside her view.

The people who pulled the strings on the London hub of the organization were so far unknown to her. She was about to meet the head of SOE, Colonel Stanley Gibbins, the man responsible for making dirty warfare. Time to straighten her freshly dry-cleaned FANY uniform one last time.

A pretty woman in an identical uniform to hers opened the door, her eyes nicely made up and her soft auburn hair combed in neat curls around her oval face, pearl earrings, coral lipstick.

"Yes?" She raised penciled eyebrows, keeping the door ajar as if she was afraid Sable would storm it.

For a moment, Sable resorted to her haughty former self. "Colonel Gibbins is expecting me. Lady Sable Montgomery."

The woman adopted an expression that was just a tad too condescending. Sable wasn't just a random passerby; she was an important contributor to this organization.

"Of course, Lady Montgomery, do come in. I'm Dorothy Perkins, the secretary." A perfumed hand with a wedding band shook Sable's. "I'm sorry, but the Colonel is still in a meeting. Would you care to wait for him in the waiting room?"

"How long do you think it will take? I have to get back to Beaulieu tonight." Sable wasn't planning on being kept waiting when the Colonel himself had requested the temporary confiscation of Alnor Castle as a training ground for his international secret agents.

Dorothy raised the penciled crescents above her blue eyes anew. "I do not know, Miss. Let me check for you."

Sable took to pacing the sparsely furnished and ill-lit waiting room that Dorothy led her into. Stacks of papers on chairs, blacked-out windows and a smell of mold and stale cigarettes. The furniture was drab, the carpet soiled. Sable didn't intend to sit down on one of the tacky chairs and risk staining her skirt.

A female voice sounded behind her. "Sable Montgomery?"

Sable spun around. The frown between the dark brows deepened while her blue eyes held an expression of disbelief. "Anna? Anna Adams?"

"Yes, Sable."

Before her stood her former Le Manoir co-student in the steel-blue uniform of a flight officer in the Women's Auxiliary Air Force. Straight, closed-mouthed and closed-lipped Anna, still wearing the same glasses but with a totally different bearing. Anna clearly had come out of her hiding place and lost her former introversion. Though, after a second glance, Sable saw the dark lashes blink a few times and there was a slight hunching of the perfect blue shoulders. The slight evidence of insecurity that Sable, as a trained agent, instantly perceived.

Good. I still have some influence over her, Sable observed, as Anna informed her,

"I am the principal assistant to Colonel Gibbins. And as he's busy right now, please follow me to my office, and we can sort out this Alnor Castle business together."

The words were spoken in that clipped voice that betrayed her German-language background. Sable thought fast. This was far from her liking. Handing over the keys to her family estate would not happen with a girl who'd cold-shouldered her at the Swiss finishing school.

As Anna preceded her up the stairs, the seam in her silk stockings as straight as a yard of pump water, she seemed to sense Sable's discomfort.

"Don't worry, Sable, the colonel will see you in a minute and discuss the rudimentary ideas we've mapped out for Alnor Castle. It's not like I have the last say in it."

You have no say whatsoever in my estate, Miss Anna Adams, Sable fumed inwardly.

They entered a narrow room with a window that overlooked Baker Street and somehow reminded Sable of the bedrooms at Le Manoir, sparsely furnished, almost austere, certainly an environment in which the enigmatic Anna seemed to thrive. Sable was on the qui vive. Was Anna going to make her pay for her bossy behavior at the finishing school, or had she forgotten all about it?

"Sit down." Anna took a seat on her straight chair and pointed to the identical one for visitors on the other side of what was more a table than a desk. Her gaze adopted the quizzical look that Sable suddenly remembered, the chocolate-brown eyes not revealing any secret. They stared at each other, Sable wondering who would speak first.

For a moment it seemed Anna had to pull herself out of a memory, but her voice had the same level, clipped intonation as she spoke.

"It is very kind of you, Sable, to give SOE access to your family property. We are always short of training grounds and especially those where we can train far away from prying eyes."

"I know. That's why I suggested Alnor Castle to Major Woolworth." *If we're going to play nice and professional, I can do that too*, Sable thought, lighting a cigarette and inhaling the smoke with pleasure. Anna clearly still didn't smoke, and the freckled nose wrinkled slightly.

Then the bespectacled eyes went to a document lying on the table in front of her, which she studied intently. Sable took to studying Anna's office. The most prominent object was a huge chalkboard, much larger than the one she used for staffing in Beaulieu, with names, numbers, and codes on it, all in Anna's neat, straight-up hand-writing.

For the rest, there were three indistinguishable brown cabinets filled with hanging files, one with a dying plant on top. Anna's gabardine coat hung on a coatrack next to the door. Nothing personal, no photos, not even a handbag.

"The signing over of Alnor Castle to the War Office is just a matter of your signature, which will presently take place in Colonel Gibbins' office. In the meantime, I have another question for you, Sable."

Returning her focus to Anna again, she realized the other woman had been scrutinizing her. Looking for a place to tip the ash from her cigarette, she saw none. When she was just about ready to scatter it on the floor, Anna took the saucer from underneath her coffee cup and pushed it over the table in her direction.

"What did you want to ask?"

Sable thought they sounded like two strangers who'd never met before.

"You speak fluent French and reasonable German, don't you?"

How does she know? Sable wondered, but answered with a curt, "I do." She wished the colonel would return from his meeting, so she could sign the document and leave this stuffy office with this uptight woman.

"To what extent have you had an insight into the courses taught at Beaulieu?" The brown eyes with the dark lashes were way too prominently examining her. Sable longed to take to her pacing but forced herself to remain seated.

"None." She'd lost all interest in replying with niceties.

"I see." The dark head bowed over the file in front of her again, and Sable got the eerie feeling it held information about her. Wooly wouldn't have been shooting the breeze about her to Anna Adams? If he did, she needed to have a serious talk with her boss.

"May I ask what this is all about, Anna? I feel you're being very secretive with me." Better grab the bull by the horns.

A tiny smile quivered in the corner of Anna's pressed-together lips.

"Sorry, Sable. I wasn't trying to be uncommunicative. I suppose working for the Secret Services has endowed us all with an occupational hazard. Like second nature."

To this Sable had to agree, a smile hovering on her lips. Maybe war had done this to them. She nodded.

"I'm tasked with interviewing potential secret agents," Anna explained with the narrowest of warmth in her voice. "They say I'm good at it, but most of the interviewing is done by not speaking but observing candidates."

"Are you...?" Sable started, but Anna quickly waved her freckled hand.

"No, no, no! Don't misunderstand me. We're not recruiting women as secret agents. At least, not yet. I would be in favor of it but the Minister of Economic Warfare, Hugh Dalton, is fiercely against it and the colonel is on the fence." Anna stopped abruptly, rethinking her words in mid-air. Probably thinking this was too wide a glimpse behind the scenes for an outsider.

Sable understood Anna was cut out for her job, the seeds of which had been sown at Le Manoir. There was something to learn here, and she was ready for it.

"I see. So, what is it you propose to me, then?"

"To get involved at Alnor training school as much as you can. I honestly believe it won't be long until the men in high places will resort to the use of women like us. Two reasons for that. There simply aren't enough recruitable, fit men as they're all called under the arms, and women will be much less conspicuous moving behind enemy lines."

"Behind enemy lines?" Sable almost choked on her own saliva. "Do you mean the men trained at Beaulieu go into enemy territory?"

Anna deliberated for a moment, shoved the heavy glasses further up the bridge of her freckled nose, shot Sable another penetrating look and then added in only a whisper, "I thought you knew that part. I mean, I had supposed that Major Woolworth had told you something, or that you had asked questions. I did not know you really knew zero about... uh... our clandestine operations. A grave error on my behalf." Briefly, Anna looked lost for words, rebounding to the introverted, silent girl she'd been when Sable first met her. "I... I've made a grave error here. Forgive me."

"Not at all." Sable settled herself on the hard chair, one slender leg over the other, her khaki skirt pulled down just below the knee. If they were to work together in SOE, she'd better let Anna know exactly what she knew.

"I assumed the policy was not to ask questions, but of course, I kept my eyes open. So many nationalities, men in uniform, in civilian clothes, mostly young, grim-looking men. And then there are the instructors, who have been trickling in since January 1941. They, for sure, are an odd kettle of fish. Some veterans from the Great War. Then there are playwrights and diplomats. The housemaster of The House in The Wood told me one of them is or was a notorious burglar, who's sent straight back behind bars after he's delivered his lesson." Sable stopped, giggled, but saw Anna's expression become serious.

"You know more than you think you do."

"I suppose so. After all, I have to organize the timetables divided over our different houses and allot trainers for them. I know what type of subjects are taught and for what purpose. I only assumed it was to prepare us in case Hitler invaded Britain. Not, you know, to take these skills abroad."

"Well, now you know."

"Yes. So, please tell me what you're expecting from me next...?"

At that moment, a fair-sized man in an imposing uniform with rows of ribbons and other decorations on his lapel stood wide-legged in the doorway. With thickset, gray hair and almost black eyes under bristly eyebrows, Stanley Gibbins appeared a bit of a dark horse.

Wooly had told her Colonel Gibbins was an old spy catcher and spymaster with a long career in the Intelligence Corps and very hanky-panky with Churchill himself. He looked just like an old-boys'-network type of man, she concluded, indecisive whether she liked or disliked him. She'd give him a chance.

"Lady Sable, I'm glad you've been able to get to know my right-hand, Miss Adams. Do follow me into my office now. I'm all yours." The voice was upper-crust, a manner of speech Sable had heard all around her since birth.

Before following the colonel, she turned to Anna. "Do you expect me back here afterwards?"

Anna was already engaged in reading a thick file on her table-desk. "No, that will not be necessary. Colonel Gibbins will tell you everything you need to know. Goodbye, Sable, and good luck."

The smidgen of cordiality they seemed to have shared for a moment in that cramped office had already evaporated. The face behind the dark-rimmed glasses closed as a shrine. Sable shrugged. Who cares? She had no further dealings with Anna Adams. The indifference was mutual.

21

THE NEW TRAINING CENTER

O n the train journey back from Waterloo Station to Southampton-Central, there was so much for Sable to digest that she was thankful to have the first-class carriage to herself. It was after eight, the sun already sinking behind the forested hills of the South Downs, forecasting a crystalline but chilly spring night.

This time the trip to London had been life-changing, even more than when she'd taken this very same train down from London to Beaulieu almost a year earlier, to accept a position as Woolworth's secretary. And, as usual, every pivotal change in her life revolved around Freddie.

As promised, he'd used his Oxford connections to get her the job with SOE and then disappeared—with David—from her life for many long months. It was a pattern Sable was accustomed to by now. And then, this.

She retrieved the brief note in his elegant handwriting from her handbag, bringing it close to her nose. Dior Homme. Her favorite male perfume. Not a scent Wild Bill would choose. But no thinking of that individual right now.

· · ·

Lunna House, Shetland Isles, 2 April 1941

Dearest Sabbo,

Do you remember how—as the Freddo-Sabbo team—we'd arm-wrestle for hours and run for miles to see who was the strongest and the fastest? You often won, no matter you being a girl and three years my junior. Not being considered masculine and muscular, but frail and foppish was the stigma of my youth. And you, with your tomboy toughness, rubbed that into my vexed pride as a bonus.

David—himself strong as Zeus before his brain injury—was the first person to believe in my physical strength, and he always encourages me to challenge myself, whether it's as a pilot or now as—yes, you better believe it!—a resistance fighter trainer. I pegged away at becoming stronger, smarter, and sturdier in the past year and it's panned out well.

This lightweight slugabed is now training Norwegian commandos on the Shetland isles. These lads are twice my size, and three times my strength. They're blond Viking gods, but they listen to me. Apparently, I'm an excellent instructor. So, you can plume your old friend, Sabbo.

Enough about me. Hope you're still enjoying Beaulieu! Sure you're the best of the best as well. One thing that crossed my mind. Lunna House is getting way too crowded as these Norwegians keep coming in hordes. Just like the Vikings in the old days with their boats. It's called the Shetland Bus, by the way.

Thing is, we're running out of space and then I thought of Alnor Castle. Its location would be excellent for secret agent training. Secluded terrain with housing accommodation in a remote part of Scotland.

Last time you told me your mother wasn't using it anymore, so it's basically empty.

Just a thought! If you like the idea, you could discuss it with Stanley Gibbins in London. And it would throw you even deeper into the thick of it all.

Just give it a thought. As I'll give you a thought, or two.

· · ·

Love, as always.
   Your Freddo

P.S. David is still not well. He's in our house in Oxford, slow, slow convalescence. He'll get there! Sends his love.

Freddie's letter had arrived a week earlier, and Sable had instantly loved the idea. She'd galloped into Wooly's office, quickly spying around that Bill wasn't hiding somewhere in the woodworks.

Nodding, the old spy had commented, "Good thinking of the lad. Gibbins keeps pestering me to come up with new training places as if I have a magic wand. These foreign agents keep falling from the sky like dead leaves in the autumn. Don't know what to do with them all. It's great that there's such an eagerness to strangle Hitler's war machine, but we simply don't have enough places or trainers to equip them for their tasks."

"So Alnor would qualify, you think?" Sable's eyes had shone at the idea.

"Why not, sugar? But you'll have to make it legal with your solicitor. If War Office wants to lease it, there can't be any claims from others on the property."

Sable had been surprised. "But I thought you said that the government could claim any building when it was for the war effort?"

"Just do as you're told. With these old aristocratic families, you'd better make sure the small lettering is in place. Just in case."

The train was swaying softly on its tracks through the golden evening light as Sable rewound the conversation that had led to today's trip. How pleased as punch Wooly would be when she showed him the documents. She even dismissed the long wait before the Colonel was ready, and that not so friendly but useful meeting with Anna.

Sable sighed. Was she finally ready to return to Alnor? Her mother had no claim to the property anymore. So yes, she would go north again. Accompanied by some of the best Beaulieu training staff, Lady Sable Montgomery would set up the new training school, and follow in Freddie's footsteps on her own terrain. How smashing was that!

With Wooly, she had already discussed the specialities on which her center would focus—survival techniques, stealth killing of enemy forces, shooting practice, and detonation. Alnor was so far away from civilization that it was perfect for these terrain practices, much better than the Beaulieu forests that stood amid great, stately mansions.

But the message she'd be returning to her roots, even without her mother and the Germans there, weighed heavily on Sable's mind. Now that she finally had her head and life together, she had no clue how she would deal with the ghosts of the past. What she did know was that she had no choice. In this business, orders were orders. And after all, Alnor Castle was hers.

Which instructors would follow her had not yet been discussed. If it was up to Sable, she knew exactly who she wanted and for what. She'd have Cuthbert "Killer" Drake, the instructor who taught living off the land, field craft, and how to move through woodland and open field without being seen.

Everybody at Beaulieu liked Killer despite his ferocious appearance, a big, burly man with hands the size of fat hams, black hairs not only on his head and face but seemingly everywhere, and a complexion that Wooly jokingly called *teinte Vin Rouge*—the color of red wine.

There was a consistent whisper among the secretaries that Killer had been "inside," but Wooly had assured her he was a Chartered Accountant with an inclination for the great outdoors.

The second instructor who Sable thought would be a great asset at Alnor was a man even more nefarious than Killer. His name was Johnny "Lock" Clark, a Scot from Glasgow, originally a burglar and safebreaker. But after joining the army as a young lad, he'd become a master at explosives and detonators.

Until Bill had showed up, Sable, as the only other Scot at Beaulieu, was the only one who fully understood Lock's thick Glaswegian accent. She loved playing his interpreter. At five feet ten, heavily built and having served in several army deployments, he'd be excellent at protecting her. And she always was amused to hear him say, if interrupted during a demonstration, "'Hush yer greetin'."

With a jolt, Sable snapped out of her pipe dreams as she recognized the white-washed station building of Brockenhurst coming into view. Her port of call. Staff didn't call out the names of destinations anymore, and station platforms were rid of their names. All measures to prevent possible enemy interlopers from knowing their whereabouts, but a hindrance to the population who weren't local here.

Not losing a second, she galloped out of the train that was already starting up again, dragging her overnight bag and handbag with her. She only slowed down as she came to the front of the station, looking for a bus that would take her back to The Rings.

Private Pip Flockhart, the Commandant's chauffeur, stood short-legged and widely smiling next to the Hudson Terraplane motor car.

"Welcome back, Miss Sable. We've all missed you."

"Thank you, Pip. How kind of you to motor up all this way to collect me."

"Commandant's orders, Miss."

As Sable sat on the back seat of the luxurious car that whizzed down the country lanes to Beaulieu, smooth like a flock of birds in flight, her heart filled with melancholy. Beaulieu had given her the best year of her life, and now she had to let it go. Start anew. Up north.

22

DID YOU MEAN IT WHEN YOU KISSED ME?

May 1941

For more than a week, London dillydallied with the decision to make Alnor Castle a new training ground for SOE agents, much to Sable's discontent. Now that she'd planned to go north, she wanted to see action.

Venturing into Major Woolworth's office just to see if there was news from Baker Street, she couldn't help asking again. "What's holding them up?"

"Ah, sugar. That's the Colonel to a tee. Capital guy, but so slow. Didn't you notice?"

Sable had to agree Stanley Gibbins had come across as quiet and contemplative, but not as inactive.

"Maybe he's got too much on his plate. He seemed sort of exhausted."

"Well, don't fret, Sable. You'll get the green light soon. Mark my words. Meanwhile, I've cut Killer and Lock free from their commitments for two months, so you'll get your way. They'll be your first instructors at Alnor. But I'll need them back as soon as you can spare them."

"Oh, Wooly, thank you. You're the best!" Sable made a triumphant dance around his desk. "Now I feel London can't deny me my own school."

"Your own school, ha?" The bald major winked. "That'll be a handful for a young woman like you!"

"Don't underestimate me!" Sable cheered. "I'm stronger than I look."

"True!" Her boss gave her a lopsided grin. "Now listen, strong lady. The first female agent is expected to arrive today. Miss Adams seemed to have coaxed the old fox into letting a woman give the SOE a spin. Can you welcome her?"

"Of course. But where can she sleep? She's not supposed to be mixing with the men."

"With you for the time being. I know your room is cramped as it is, but we both believe you'll be moving out soon, right?"

Sable's face fell. Though she'd come a long way since her finishing school days, she still wasn't keen on sharing digs with another woman.

"Oh, I know that face!" Wooly shook his broad jaws. "But I tell you, I think you'll get along with Maureen Knight like a house on fire."

"Who's using my name in vain?"

Against the doorpost leaned a fiery redhead, the navy WAAF jacket slung casually over her white silk blouse, a perfect hour-glass figure, red lips, stockings and a laconic, laissez-aller expression in the mint-green eyes.

"Aha, Miss Knight, welcome. Sable and I were just..."

"... referring to the devil?" Maureen grinned bare her perfect white teeth, and Sable instantly liked her.

"I would never refer to an Irish woman as the devil." Wooly grinned back in mock protest.

"Ná amadán mé!" Maureen wagged a long index finger and took the seat opposite the major.

"I'm not fooling you!" Wooly clearly liked Maureen too.

"Aha, no secrets here. You speak Gaelic."

Wooly waved his hand. "Wouldn't go as far as that, but I understand some after years with Irishmen in the army."

Sable was standing next to her boss following the conversation and taking in the glamorous new woman who apparently had guts alongside good looks. The first female secret agent. The Germans certainly would have their hands full with Maureen Knight.

Maureen turned her light eyes to Sable.

"Oh, I adore your uniform. I'd have preferred khaki to dull navy too, but they left me no choice."

"Let me show you to your room," Sable suggested, looking forward to a tête-à-tête with the redhead.

They walked out of the Major's office as the phone rang. Wooly's friendly bark called out, "Come back, sugar, London's finally given us a jingle."

Sable apologized to Maureen.

"So sorry. It's an emergency. Let me call Boarmans's housemaster. He'll take you to the room. I'll see you later. All right?"

"Sure, no worries. I'll wait on the bench here."

Sable rushed back to Wooly, who had a broad smile on his fleshy face, the bald scalp gleaming under the electric light. He waved a paper in his hand with much enthusiasm.

"What is it?" Eagerness clashed with edginess.

"What do you think, Captain? New rank, new salary, your own car. And the best man I can send with you." The major's grin widened, and the light-green eyes sparkled. Sable stared at him in puzzlement.

"That took some massaging of the chaps at the Ministry of Economic Warfare, sugar, but you're worth it. That's what took so much time." He looked very proud at what he clearly thought he'd accomplished.

"I still don't understand it, Sir." Sable sank down on the chair where Maureen had just sat and searched her pockets for her cigarettes. Relieved, she took in the smoke and felt her body relax.

"You've been given the rank of Captain. You're Captain Montgomery now, and you'll earn twice as much. Lots of responsibility setting up the new training school in Inveraray, but I have complete confidence in you. Of course, you'll run the logistics, not the courses, but I want you to sit in with the trainees. I think you have it in you to become an instructor in organizational warfare."

Her boss was lavishing so much new information on her that Sable's brain couldn't take it all in at once. But slowly something swelled in her chest, and she felt herself growing to new proportions.

"Thank you so much, Wooly." It sounded modest, but then she added with much emotion, "I'll miss you so much!"

"You'll be back, sugar! Mark my words. This is lesson one in warfare. Never become too attached to your fellow fighters. They may be transferred or killed in the blink of an eye. That said, I'll miss you too. You're a hell of a hardworking secretary and I'll have a hard time replacing you. I could do with a redhead like Maureen, but she's here for other reasons than typing. Ah, you warrior girls will one day be the death of me." He shook his head wearily.

"So, when am I leaving, Sir, and will Killer and Lock go with me immediately?"

"Easy, easy now. I know we're in dire need of a new training school as we keep getting more and more agents and the places everywhere are restricted, but we need to do this properly. For that reason, you'll first go to Alnor Castle with Captain Mitchell. He'll oversee setting up the training school, while you are..."

He stopped in mid-sentence as Sable was shaking her head wildly. "What's wrong, sugar?"

"Can't it be Killer or Lock or any of the others?" Sable's voice raced ahead of her.

A benign smile curled the major's lips. "Aha! Well, listen to me, Captain Montgomery. Lesson two in warfare: never let your sympathy or antipathy for a fellow fighter muddle your perception. As the head of the logistics operations, you must be able to deal with everyone, whether you think they're an odd kettle of fish, or not."

The last words were spoken with more authority than Wooly usually larded his words with. Sable nodded, biting her lip. What did this bachelor in his fifties know about the tender relationships between men and women? Just as she contemplated this, she heard her boss say in a softer voice,

"I have my reasons for sending Captain Mitchell with you, Sable. Not only is he a Scot like you, who knows the terrain like no other, he's the very best trainer SOE has had so far. He's done some reconnaissance missions abroad, and he's sharp, trustworthy and a hell of a fighter. I have absolute trust he will keep you safe under all circumstances. And I mean *all* circumstances. Attacks not always only come from our military enemies; they can also come from our own past."

Sable didn't see how William "Wild Bill" Mitchell would be of any help in facing the ghosts of her past, but she knew orders were orders and that she had to accept there was no escape from having daily encounters with Egbert's pilot. She just hoped the other trainers and students would arrive soon.

"I see. Will you visit the new school, Sir?"

"Am I invited?"

This brought a smile to Sable's face. "Open invitation!"

It WAS A DISMAL, drizzly day when the Austin Tilly, with Sable at the wheel, slowly made its way north along the A34 toward Oxford. There was an uneasy silence in the car, with Bill's tall posture slammed in the passenger seat. He was reading Robert Burn's Kilmarnock Volume and seemed totally engrossed in it.

The only thing he'd asked before departing was whether she was sure she wanted to drive the first stint. After that, nothing.

The Tilly went slow as the roads were wet and it was loaded with traps, knives, ammunition, and rifles, which were in fact only the first batch. Lock and Killer would soon follow with more supplies, and there had also been an offer from London to stock up the new center. Everybody had been excited to finally have the use of a vast estate in rural Scotland.

Sable focused on driving, a burning cigarette between the index and middle fingers of her left hand. Firmly holding onto the wheel with two hands, she only took quick moments to bring the cigarette to her lips, meanwhile trying to think positive thoughts that wouldn't come. Anything not to pay attention to her taciturn passenger, who clearly wanted to have nothing to do with her.

It was the first time she had to disagree with Wooly. This man was not a protection to her, and he never would be.

She thought of Freddie and missed him dearly. They would have had so much fun driving up together, chattering all the time, stopping for drinks and sandwiches. With this deadweight next to her, fun was another world.

Maybe she should have said no to going to Alnor. Maybe she should have been firmer with Wooly and insisted on replacing Bill as the head instructor. It was clearly not going to work between them.

"Yer an excellent driver."

Completely immersed in her negative head trips, his voice made her jump, ashes spraying over her khaki jacket.

"What's that?" The car made a sudden swerve, bouncing over a pothole. Sable needed all her attention to keep the heavy vehicle steady, while big fumes from her cigarette blurred her vision. Her cheeks reddened in embarrassment.

"When ye're concentratin'," he added with a dry chuckle.

"Well, thanks. My father taught me to drive around Alnor in his Rolls when Elrod, our chauffeur, wasn't looking."

Sable muzzled herself, took another firm drag. *No personal memories, certainly not now and certainly not with him!* Routinely slipping into the new Sable, she pronounced in a more composed, professional voice, "Most of my driving experience was gained this past year. The distance between our premises on the Beaulieu estate made the use of a car indispensable."

"I'm much more interested in yer racin' around the Highlands in a Rolls." There was something in his voice, light and jocular at the surface but with a deeper, edgy tone underneath, of pain understood and complex family ties. Without a change in intonation, Bill started to read.

Ye banks and braes o' bonnie Doon,

How can ye bloom sae fresh and fair?
How can ye chant, ye little birds,
And I sae weary fu' o' care!
Thou'll break my heart, thou warbling bird,
That wantons thro' the flowering thorn:
Thou minds me o' departed joys,
Departed never to return...

Both his reading and the poem struck at the foundations of Sable's thin-veiled balance.

"Don't! Please?" It was a mere whisper.

"A'rite, I won't. Now stop the car. I'm hungry. Then I'll drive."

With a frown and a muttered protest, Sable pulled over and parked the Tilly on the banks of the river Thames south of Oxford. She'd rather have carried on as it was still a long way to their first overnight stop near Manchester. The shorter the time with him beside her in the car, the better.

Whenever the Scotsman came into her orbit, he made her feel cornered. How he did that or whether she was doing it herself, she didn't know. There was so much confusion, wanting to confide in him, wanting to trust him as Wooly had suggested, and keeping him as far away from her as possible. Sable had never before dealt with real, pure attraction to a member of the male species. But here it was, and it sent her longing to run for the hills.

And there was more. Wild Bill stirred up the old Sable, the one she thought she'd lain to rest; the out-of-control damsel that didn't care where she laid down her head the next night, forever tottering on the edge because of toxic levels of liquor, malnutrition, and death-dealing thoughts. He had been part of that past, and she wanted to forget all about it.

After the belladonna elixir treatment by Doctor Howe and Wooly's guidance and constant encouragement, Sable had been sure she'd come to grips with that damsel, had changed, buried the old ghosts. But here they were again, worming a way into her carefully constructed picture of self-defense.

All she could think right now was, *I need a drink.* Even her hands experienced the old tremor, the evidence of which she hid in the pockets of her gabardine coat.

The fine rain had stopped, but the sky above them was leaden-gray and all of nature gleamed with a sheath of moisture. Big, fat drops trickled down from leaves that were already turning yellow. Certainly not a day for an outdoor picnic.

Bill had collected one of the horse blankets from the car and spread it out over the seat of a bench overlooking the equally gray water of the river Thames—no boats, no birds, not a sign of other human life either.

They ate the bacon sandwiches that Dorothy, The Rings' maid, had prepared for them straight out of the paper bags. The surrogate coffee in her flask was lukewarm and not sweetened enough. She had no appetite and instead lit a cigarette, observing Bill didn't smoke after the meal, which was as rare for a soldier as snow at Midsummer.

They didn't speak but being outside of the car, Sable sensed the atmosphere between them was a touch less tetchy. Maybe she was getting used to him? Maybe his clear signal he wouldn't bring up the past made her less edgy?

The rain cut their picnic short. Bill's firm hands gripped the leather wheel and steered the Tilly back onto the road and northwards.

Sable, with Burns' volume of poetry in her lap, was still struggling with all her might against the longing for a swig of whiskey. Why had she given Freddie's flask with the FFS lettering in custody to Doctor Howe? What had she been thinking? How could she survive without her liquor? It had all been for naught. For naught!

"I'll make you one promise, Sable. I'll never drink in yer presence. For a Scotsman I aint a great drinker anyway, so ye don't have to feel sorry fer me."

The cyanide-blue eyes shot her a quick sideways glance. Sable pressed her hands and her lips together not to scream. The man was intolerable. Could he read her mind now on top of everything else? And as if she wasn't in enough turmoil yet, he continued in that rippling Scot voice of his, the one that went through the very marrow of her bones.

"I've seen the destruction of John Barleycorn in my own family. That's why I recognized it in yer case. Only tried to help. Yer worth it, my bonnie lass."

"Don't call me that! I'm not your bonnie lass come hell or high water," she lashed out, using his endearment label as the coat hanger to hang her anger on.

"Sorry. Is that reserved for another chap?"

"None of your business."

He chuckled, rubbing a hand over his dark-red beard.

"Correct! Stand yer ground, gal!"

Sable took to focusing her mind on their mission ahead, calming her breath as Doctor Howe had taught her. As she held Burns' leather-bound volume between her fingers as if it was a prayer book, she decided they needed to clear the air.

"Bill, can we try to lay the past to rest and concentrate on what lies ahead of us? Setting up the training school at Alnor Castle... I know it will be cumbersome as it is, and we won't help the process by flying in each other's hair all the time."

He didn't answer for a long-drawn minute, the blue eyes focused on the road. Then he said, "Ai, agreed. But I've got two questions for ye."

"What are they?" Her voice was all suspicion again.

"Tell me if ye're still angry with me fo interferin' with yer life back in Amsterdam?"

Now it was Sable's turn to deliberate a while before answering. Her heart screamed, *Yes, you stole a possible future with Egbert from me.* Her head responded, *No, you saved my life.* Which was it? She felt she'd nothing to lose, so answered the truth.

"Yes and no. The most important is that the outcome of your intervention was effective. I no longer self-destruct. What's the second question?"

"Did ye mean it when ye kissed me?"

23

GOING BACK TO ALNOR

A dark, noisy space occupied Sable's brain, dragged her down, absorbed her. She was desperately fighting to escape from ... what? She couldn't remember. She knew she was sick, constantly sick, and kept sinking back into that black hole that was everywhere. It only became bearable down here if she drank.

Something had to be done, someone had to help her, but she couldn't even scream for help. Her voice was gone. Not knowing where she was—that was the worst of all. Losing consciousness was too dangerous. But she was so tired of fighting the blackness and the deafening noise in her ear. She had to throw up, wanted to turn around, but her body refused to obey her.

I've been in this space so often, *a voice inside her said,* and there's nothing to be found here. It's neither life nor death, it's just terrible.

When she lost consciousness, it was heaven for a while. Oblivion was being spared the pain and when she woke again, some of the noise was gone. A weak ray of sunlight even glimpsed through a narrow window above her. As if it winked at her, promising better times. The space reeked of kerosene and rubber, and she was dying for a drink.

Feeling for the flask in her pocket, she gulped its contents. The whiskey burnt into her soul as a curse, made her choke until her eyes bulged in their sockets, but stopped the nauseating rumble in her stomach. Now she *wanted to sleep again, inviting the non-existence that always awaited around the corner.*

"We're back in London, Sable. Sable, can ye hear me?"

Whose voice was that? It sounded familiar. It made her drift back home to the Highlands. The green mountains, Loch Lomond, a hovering eagle watching her from above.

"Sable! Wake up, Sable!"

The male voice again. Shaking her arm. What did he want? Then something shifted, and she was lifted, carried, boink, boink, boink the footsteps went and she bobbed along, feeling light as a feather.

"Yer in a terrible state, lass."

She was put down again but felt she was now in the back seat of a car. The scent of leather. No! She sat up, dizzy and broken! Screaming.

"Not that! Not that."

Someone held her arms and then she screamed even louder. "Please, no!"

"Hold yer tongue, woman. What's wrong with ye? Stop fightin' me!"

Why was the German speaking Scottish?

She couldn't let it happen again. It was no holds barred.

"Not again!" *She begged, pleading, tears streaming down her face.*

She felt how suddenly his anger subsided, as if he'd understood something vital. He took her face in both hands, softly, tenderly, soothing her, "I won't hurt ye. Please don't be afraid. Whoever did this to ye, he'll pay, lass. He'll pay."

Had she kissed him then?

Fragments, bits and pieces glued together, always this voice, Scottish, close, talking to her, she did not know whence it came. She was less afraid now. As if he shared her burden. Then someone else took her hand. She hung onto the warmth of the grip.

Another familiar voice. "Do you remember me, Sable? I'm Doctor Howe."

Doctor Howe? Dadaigh's physician, what was he doing here with her? Was she really home? And she drifted off again.

༄

"I DIDN'T KISS YOU!"

Sable opened her eyes again. She was sitting in the Tilly on her way to Scotland with Bill at the wheel, still trying to piece together the storm that had taken over her life in those first days after he'd flown her back to London in Egbert's plane, leaving her in Doctor Howe's care. Her memory was blotchy, but Bill's recurring presence was like a leitmotiv through those days. Had he visited her after he'd dropped her off? She didn't dare to ask him, shame coloring her cheeks.

"Ye kissed me a'write, but ye sufficiently answered my question. Ye didn't mean it." She heard the slight intake in breath, a sign she'd learn to read in Bill. He did that when emotions ran higher.

"I was sick, Bill. Much of what happened those days is a total blur to me. I honestly don't recall kissing you. Did you kiss *me*?" In her embarrassment, she blurted out the last thing she wanted to ask.

"I'm not goin' to tell ye!"

"Thank you!" She was let off the hook, at least for now.

"Thank ye fer what?"

"For everything you did for me. You probably saved my life. I was in a dark spot in those days."

"I know all about dark days, Sable, so if ye ever want to talk about it, I'm yer man."

"Why would I?" It sounded ruder than she intended as she wondered what his own dark days might be. He seemed unperturbed by her answer, though.

"I'll tell ye why. As Anna told ye, the first female agents like Maureen are startin' to join SOE. And it's about time. Yer women folk can move much freer behind enemy lines."

Sable was surprised Bill brought up Anna. There was something in the way he pronounced her name.

"You mean Anna Adams?"

"Yes, Anna Adams."

"How do you know her?"

Bill smiled warmly. "Everybody knows Anna Adams, Sable. The

lass is as high up in the organization as ye get them. And a lofty lass at that!"

"Heavens, I didn't know that. So, you like her?"

The cyanide-blue gaze took a shot at Sable. "Yer changin' the subject, but yes, I like her. There's nothin' unlikeable about Anna."

A pinprick of jealousy. Sable told herself it was because of Anna's position, not because Bill liked her.

"Sorry, go ahead with your sermon." She couldn't help it; she just felt competitive around him.

"Aye. Bein' a secret agent isn't fer everyone. One of my tasks is to test how potential agents will react under pressure. Carryin' heavy things from the past with ye can be a burden. Say yer caught by the Gestapo and interrogated in one of their nasty manners. Who will break and who won't?"

"Crikey!" Sable didn't know what else to say.

"It's the only reason I told ye I'm yer man if ye ever feel ye want to unburden yerself. It ain't nosiness on my behalf, it's purely professional." Another pinprick. He wasn't interested in her.

"Wait a moment. It hasn't been decided that I'll be a secret agent at some point. Wooly told me to set up the Alnor school and run the logistics, so that doesn't make you my trainer, right?"

"There's no one else, Sable. Don't forget Major Woolworth has been coachin' ye fer a year. Ye've been promoted to the rank of Captain. They've got their eyes on ye, lass."

"Really?" She gasped in surprise, felt that swell in her heart region, then quickly added, "But why? And you yourself tell me my past is my weakness."

"Yer weakness and yer strength, Sable. Ye have both in equal doses, and we're here to make ye as strong as Flora MacDonald."

Being compared to Bonnie Prince Charles's rescuer was a big compliment for a Scotswoman.

Sable looked doubtful. It was an honor that both Wooly and the man her boss had called "the best SOE trainer we've had so far" thought she had the capacities to do fieldwork herself, but if it meant talking about her past, she'd much rather stay in Scotland and run her school. Again, she had that eerie feeling he could read her mind.

"Ye don't have to decide or say anythin', Sable. I just wanted ye to know I believe in ye, too."

She couldn't help herself. "How can you say that when you've seen me in my most rotten state? A drunkard and a shipwreck?"

"Aye, I can. Precisely because I've seen ye like that."

"Don't talk tommyrot!"

That made Bill laugh out loud, a roar that rang through the entire Tilly. He even slapped the wheel, still laughing. Sable looked at him in dismay.

"Yer a character, lass! I like ye."

"Stop showering me with compliments! And stop rattling me, you impossible man!" she shrieked over his laughter. He cooled down again, looked her full in the face. The ice-blue eyes twinkling, a mischievous grin on his bearded mouth.

"I'd give my good name and my fortune to kiss ye right here and now, Captain Montgomery."

"Well, you can't! I won't permit it." But Sable felt a rush of giddy blood swirl through her veins. The prospect of being together with Wild Bill Mitchell at Alnor was suddenly less daunting but increasingly more dangerous.

"Yer a'rite?"

The closer they came to Inveraray and especially after Glasgow, Sable felt more strung up. Bill had been driving most of the way, but now she was at the wheel with Loch Lomond glittering to her left and the Arrochar Alps looming up in front of them. Everything breathed home, but that also meant the treacherous past coming closer and a home she would never again share with her Dadaigh. Sable swallowed, aware her voice was tiny and girlish when she answered.

"Sort of."

"It's mighty beautiful up here."

"I've never even asked which part of Scotland you're from. The accent is certainly northern, east coast I guess, perhaps even Orkney?"

"Good guess, my fellow Celt. I'm from John o' Groats, Clan Sinclair." Bill's voice was coated with pride.

"Gosh, from a clan?"

Clinging to the desire to keep the lighthearted conversation going, Sable racked her brain for questions about his background, not just for the sake of their newly found balance, but certainly also to pacify her growing fear of coming home to Alnor. Her insides felt fraught. Even the scar on her belly burned like a heated opal.

It was good to hear Bill's voice, which—when it didn't infuriate her—calmed her. *No more silences, please.* But she was really surprised to hear him say,

"Yer from a clan too, Captain Montgomery. I guess yer father must have told ye?"

"I guess he did, but it's never stuck with me. Never had a head for history."

"Clan Campbell, 'tis. One of the most powerful Scottish clans. Beat mine in a second."

"All right, I like the sound of that." Sable snorted.

"I thought ye would. Ye need some pep, don't ye?"

There it was again, as if he could read her like an open book.

"It ain't easy! But you just told me I'm from a mighty clan, so I'll survive."

Bill changed the subject. "Who is goin' to be our reception team at Alnor Castle?"

"The few staff who've not left the place. The old steward, Donald Stacey, who's run the place since I can remember. And then there's Jack Durey, the gamekeeper. I think he was given special permission to stay on as he has an elderly mother to look after. Then probably two or three maids. Not sure I know them." Sable sighed, thinking of that wretched maid, Nellie Simpson, her mother's accomplice. Hopefully, that wispy creature had left in her mother's wake.

"Well, we'll see how they all fit in," Bill remarked. "Just like at

Beaulieu, staff livin' on the estate are not supposed to know what sort of irregular warfare we're preparin'.'"

"I'm sad my loyal butler, Elrod, and my housekeeper, Minnie, aren't coming up. They run the London house. We'll probably have to interview some local staff, but I know they need to be close-lipped and reliable."

"I already looked into the matter. Got my eye on some local lads who're still too young to enlist but old enough to know how to hold their blab."

Sable frowned. "Why did you do that without informing me? It's my school, too!"

"Let's say instructions from above, Captain. Nothin' to muddy the waters."

Sable was still annoyed. "But could you not have discussed it with me before?"

"That's what I'm doin' right now."

Impossible man!

"Fine, who are they? I know most locals and can tell you if they're to be trusted."

"I was told to contact the West brothers and John Hatfield. Listen, Sable, I wasn't goin' to do anythin' without ye. I just didn't think the issue of personnel would come up before we arrived. Baker Street actually told me to take a week off to study the lay of the land before setting up anythin'." "Now, did they? And why didn't they tell me?"

"Ye had yer instructions from Major Woolworth. They were identical. Take a break."

Sable had nothing to bring in against that. And on second thought, she could do with a quick break from the intense work she'd been involved in during the past year. It would only mean spending more time with Bill. She didn't know if that was a good thing or a bad thing.

He did it again. Found her emotional wavelength.

"It'll also give ye time to face yer demons, Sable. With or without me."

"And what do you know about my so-called demons? I suppose you've also investigated my past?"

Bill shifted in the passenger seat, and she heard that peculiar intake of breath.

"Aye, lass, not the details but enough to make a grown man weep."

With the steering wheel firmly in her control, and taking heart from her surroundings, Sable tried very hard to rise above that past. Though she didn't know what exactly this fox-like agent knew or didn't know, he was surely clever enough to piece some parts together. Especially if, as he had hinted at, he knew a thing or two about complicated families himself.

Sable thought fast. Bill had a point suggesting she should clear the debris that still weighed her down, but where to start? She began with the one that troubled her most before their arrival.

"I don't know in what state my mother has left Alnor Castle. According to Donald, she'd last been there in June 1940, before they chased her off the land with her Nazi husband. Since then, she's been mostly living in Monaco, but as I said, I don't know how dilapidated or disorganized the estate is."

"Don't worry about that right now. We'll fix it, no matter. Yes, I found it interestin' to read about yer mother's affiliations with high-ranking Nazis before the war."

"Interesting? Are you mad? It's disgusting! Unforgivable!" Sable spat out the words, nervous fingers getting hold of a cigarette to calm her down.

"And she married one?" His voice was level.

"Yes, after a string of affairs with several of them, she let her eyes fall on a wealthy blue-blooded general from Wiesbaden. Werner von Bissing. One of Hitler's cronies." Tears stung Sable's eyes.

"Aye, lass, yer mother sounds like a great disappoint to ye."

"Disappointment? Choose your words more strongly, Captain Bill. My mother is a... a Nazi floozie, who betrayed my father and who... who..."

"What?"

A soft lilt, like a nimble caress but she was so hurt, so wrecked inside. *Don't make it worse!*

"Who tried to sell her daughter for her dirty cause." There. It was said. Some of it, at least.

"She did what?" Bill whistled between his teeth. "I'm really sorry fer ye, Sable. Yer a strong lass, I can tell ye that. To be where yer now."

As they inched closer to Alnor Castle and Sable glimpsed the familiar lime-gray Gothic turrets rise above the tall Scotch pines, she knew Wooly had been right from the beginning.

She must have needed to traverse over five hundred miles with the fiery-eyed, silver-tongued Scotsman before she now understood that—under the circumstances—Captain William Mitchell was the best person for the job. Their relationship might have started on a rocky footing, and it was probably never going to be smooth sailing between them, but the man knew what he was doing and, more importantly, what he was saying.

"Welcome to Alnor Castle, Bill. I hope we'll make Winston proud."

"I'm sure we will, Sable. We'll show them we're a grand team together." He instantly picked up on her warmth and it made her feel good, more than good. A team! How much she'd longed to be part of a team. Different from Beaulieu. Her own team.

24

GHOSTS FROM THE PAST

Sable inhaled her homeland. Malt, pine and peat in a bottle, Dadaigh used to say. It had been raining steadily here as well, but now the sun showed its face and the water drops gave the plants and trees fairy-tale garlands of diamonds. She inhaled deeper. Home.

The house stood silent as a tomb, though Donald Stacey's Jeep stood parked in the courtyard, which pointed to his presence as he lived in a cottage further away on the estate. The steward was nowhere in sight, and neither was his wife Flora or any of the maids. An operational butler had not been in place for years.

On opening the front door to the Castle with her latchkey, she stepped into the unheated, tiled entrance hall. A quiver cold as a snake curled down her spine. She called out.

"Hello, anybody there?"

Her body slackened, but her mind was firm. *This is it. No going back now.* Next to her, tall as a Scotch Pine himself, Bill stood in civilian clothes, a navy-blue turtleneck jumper and gray flannel pants, looking around him. He didn't stray away from her and, with hands clasped on his back, took in the impressive hall decorated with oil paintings of Sable's forefathers, the Barons of Alnor.

At her second calling, an elderly lady whom Sable recognized as Stacey's wife, Flora came toward them, gray-haired and shriveled, drying her hands on her apron, a wronged look on her face that seemed to be permanent.

"Didn't expect you yet, Milady. Ye know how my Donald is. Only told me this mornin' ye were arrivin'. Come in! Ye've had a long trip. And who's the gentleman, if I may ask?"

"Hello, Flora, so good to see you. Gosh, it's been years." She shook the elderly lady's bony hand and added with a wink, in vain hope for some warmth, "I guess Donald also didn't tell you I would bring the head instructor with me. This is Captain Mitchell."

"No, he didn't, Milady. Been married to the fella for over forty years, but he never tells me anythin'." The steward's wife shook Bill's hand and ushered them into the room where the Earl used to hold his court.

Flora busied herself around them, doffing up cushions and opening shutters while continuing her aggrieved apologies. Sable saw the room was well-kept and all the dust swept. There was even a vase with wildflowers on the table. Suddenly, it came back to her how Flora had always been a grumbling wife, but a perfect housekeeper. Only during her mother's reign, the steward's wife had extended her grumbling to her housekeeper duties as well.

"Had to do most of the work myself, Milady, and you know I never had to do the handiwork myself. That wasn't my task. I suppose times have changed, but ye'll must make do with my incompetent elbow grease."

"You've never been incompetent in your life, Flora, and we're not here to be served and pampered. We're here to work. I'm used to making my own bed and filling my own tub these days. We also don't expect you to do anything you're not accustomed to."

No smile, a brief nod.

"I'll get ye some tea."

Sable lit a cigarette while she surveyed the room. This was a room with no negative connotation. It wasn't even a room she'd been in that often, but everything still seemed to be where Dadaigh had left it, including his court chair at the head with the family emblem, the boar's head with the fiery red tongue and long white tusks. The head had frightened Sable as a child, and she now smiled at that memory. No wonder she'd not listened to being a Campbell. Their emblem was just too horrifying. *Ne Obliviscaris.* Do Not Forget. How fitting a motto. Dadaigh's courtroom would serve perfectly as her office.

Memories came flooding in, pleasant ones this time. She'd sneaked into The Courtroom as a little girl, listening behind the curtains to her father talking about the poaching of partridges and the stealing of bicycles. She'd been so proud of her Dadaigh, sitting there in that impressive chair as if he was the King himself. She sighed at its emptiness, the barony in decline without an heir. Turning to the housekeeper, she cleared her throat and announced,

"I'll have this room as my office, Mrs. Stacey. It will be perfect and a worthy remembrance to my late father."

"Aye, Milady, we were all so saddened by his Grace's passin'. So saddened. That reminds me. A letter arrived from yer mother last week. It had been traveling for quite some time. Do ye want me to fetch it fer ye?"

"Not at this moment, thank you. After tea, Captain Mitchell and I will take stock of the premises, make a preliminary plan. It would be great if your husband could accompany us."

"Sure, sure! Donald was gone to give a-talkin' to that lazy, good-fer-nothin' Jack Durey. It's perhaps a good thin' yer here, milady, as we don't know whether the fella's a gamekeeper or a poacher anymore. Yer father would turn around in his grave if he knew of the man's wheelings and dealings."

Sable sensed Bill was paying close attention to the conversation between the two women, but as she got set to leave the room to fetch their tea, he asked in a reverent tone,

"Do ye want me to unload the car first, Capt'n Montgomery?"

Sable perceived a stir in Flora when Bill addressed her by her formal rank, but she had no time to explain all that to the elderly lady, who wouldn't understand it, anyway.

"Thank you, Captain Mitchell. That would be great."

The stakes were planted.

"I hope you've planned for dinner and prepared our bedrooms, Mrs Stacey?" Her voice had more authority now.

"Ai, naturally. The maids, Janet and Helen, are busy with that as we speak. It's all rather haphazard, as we weren't told by the lord and master himself. Talkin' of the devil..."

In the door opening stood Donald Stacey, red-faced and weather-beaten, with a tweed cap on his head and dressed in a tweed suit that had seen better times. He had dark, brooding eyes and full lips, a nose that wasn't just red from the cold.

Sable could see his watery blue eyes going from his wife to her, the daughter of his former employer, no longer a wild teen, and someone for whom he had nothing but disdain. Hence the tardy reaction to their arrival. Well, he'd have to make up for it.

"Donald, what a pleasure. Time to revive some good times at Alnor Castle." She took the lead, shook his hand, matched his stare. He toned down his attitude rapidly. With a warm smile, Sable added, "And thank you again for making the hazardous trip to my father's funeral. I think I haven't thanked either of you for attending. It's meant a lot to me and, of course, to Elrod." Her voice was a tad too chirpy, the role as head of her father's estate still a very new one.

"Aye, Milady, 'twas a great loss. Still is. Welcome back."

She saw how moved he became, talking about her father. The expression on the steward's face spoke volumes. How saddened and neglected, maybe even overseen, he must have felt after her father had left the castle in her mother's unfit hands. Well, the full-blooded daughter of Earl Montgomery was back, and they'd rectify all that from now on.

"I'm afraid there's lots of arrears in repairs." He looked at her rather sheepishly.

"Like what?" Sable stood in her father's office, straight as a ruler.

"Uh... some ceilings are leakin', there are rotten windowsills, holes in the fences, and... uh... the roof of one stable has collapsed, but as there were no more hors..."

"Wait a moment, Donald. I've given my solicitor, Mr. Brown,

explicit instructions to send two thousand pounds for repairs to you every month. What did you do with that money?"

"I'm out of here," the steward's wife mumbled as her husband turned his tweed cap in his rough working hands.

"I did what I could, milady, honest to heart, but with all the men gone off to war, I couldn't handle it all on my own. It's in the account. Don't ye worry about the money."

Sable's cheeks flushed. How could she have forgotten? In an apologetic voice, she replied, "Well, we'll see to the repairs later, Donald. It's also my fault. I've been neglecting Alnor Castle over Cavendish Square. But I'm here to make amends. Let's start the tour."

LATER THAT EVENING, as Sable lay in her bed in the bedroom she'd used as her own ever since she could remember, she felt torn by deep and dangerous emotions. Drifting above everything, she tried to steer her course, think of all the plans she and Bill had already discussed for the training center, but the truth was, that facade was left at the designing table and here she was. Alone and small in a room that had too many ghosts.

Two hands on her belly, flat on her back, she tried all the tips and tricks Doctor Howe had taught her, but to no avail. With sleep elusive and her body restless, she slipped out of bed and into her woolen dressing gown, deciding to make herself some hot milk in the kitchen and have a last cigarette. And no, she wouldn't pass by her father's liquor cabinet, though the temptation was palpable.

Sitting on the kitchen top, just as she had done as a girl, watching Mrs. Gibson hit the batter or fry onions, Sable sat swinging her legs, smoking, and sipping the hot milk. Suddenly she sat upright, tight as a rod. There was a sound, footsteps. She looked around her and sped over to the corner to pick up the waiting broom. Ready to hit, she stood behind the door.

In stepped... Bill. His mass of auburn hair tousled, an open bathrobe over blue cotton pyjamas. He was as startled as she was, seeing her standing ready to hit him over the head. They stared at each other for a moment, then cracked up like two schemers.

"Ye couldn't sleep? I heard a sound and then saw a light down here. That's why I checked."

"You weren't in bed, yet?" Sable was confused. It was after midnight.

"Nay, I never sleep much. I was workin' in the small office ye allotted to me."

"Ah, you're jealous that I took the big room. Let me make you some hot cocoa for your bruised ego."

"That would be great. I'm thirsty as a dry road."

As they sat opposite each other at the kitchen table, Sable with her cigarette and Bill sipping his cocoa, the blue eyes flickered, harnessing their knock-down-drag-out expression.

"Spit it out, Sable! Have it over and done with. It'll lift yer heart as the sun risin' over Ben Nevis."

She fiddled with her sash, pondered, then replied at warp speed. "On one condition."

"Bein'?" He lifted a reddish brow.

"That you tell me your story as well?"

"Promised, though I'm sure my history ain't half as gut-churnin' as yours."

SABLE TOOK A DEEP BREATH.

"It all started seriously in 1937. My mother's never hid her predilection for Nazism, but after she'd been to Hitler's tea party in Berchtesgaden on the invitation of ... uh... Joachim von Henkell, she was completely in rhapsodies."

"Wait, you mean Von Henkell, that fellow that was the German ambassador to Great Britain until Churchill kicked him out?" Bill interrupted. Sable shivered all over, her eyes wide. All she could bring out in a sob was, "I can't, I can't."

Bill was at her side in two steps, lifted her from her chair and took her in his arms.

"Yer not telling me it was him?"

Sable could feel Bill's anger for her plight through his bathrobe but also his warm body underneath and the promise of protection. She leaned into its welcoming embrace, easier in her mind with the two powerful arms around her, arms that wouldn't hurt her, wouldn't take anything away from her she wasn't ready to give.

A GOLDEN SPRING sun pushed to penetrate the edges around the thick velvet curtains still closed in front of the three bay windows of Sable's highland bedroom. A room in the west wing with morning sun, as she liked it. The sun cast playful strobes of light among the shadows of the spacious room, kindling it with its warm aura. The new morning promised a fine day for outdoor activities, inspecting the various buildings on the estate, repairing fences, preparing the fields for shooting lessons. Health and fresh air.

Sable lay breathing easily, feeling rested for the very first time in ages, warm and secluded in ... *yes* ... Bill's bear hug. From his warm chest to the length of his muscled legs, he was nuzzled against her backside. Not daring to move but longing to look at him, she just imagined him, still asleep, breathing with contentment, journeying toward her soul from the Bay of Sannick to the shores of Loch Lomond. She knew him, and he knew her.

They hadn't talked in the night as he'd followed her to her bedroom with her complete consent. They hadn't made love, had just lain there as they were doing now, easy, easy, so much to explore, but only after the ghosts of the past had been laid to rest.

THE ONLY THING they'd agreed on before falling asleep was that they would tell the staff they'd been lovers for a year. There was no need to overthrow any apple carts and give the household the idea a new version of Misty Fletcher had descended upon them.

But the whole reason for this new intimacy had been for Sable to clear the cobwebs, as she would do this morning. She was ready for it. Not everything. Not yet. Not at this stage. Not that which gnawed at the core of her soul every waking moment. But that which would give Bill the contours of her dismay and the reason for her hatred of the Nazis.

Bill stirred, mumbling *"m'aingeal,"* which made Sable nudge his ribs with her elbow.

"Are you addressing me?"

"Huh? What? No, of course not! I was talkin' about my Mam." He tightened his clasp around her and tickled her sides.

Sable squealed with laughter. "Stop it, I believe you!"

"You'd better, lass." He turned her around to face him, a more serious expression on the wild, beautiful face. "But are ye sure ye'd not rather be Egbert's girl?"

"I never *was* Egbert's girl. I just liked him. He's a good friend." Their gaze met, testing each other's resolve.

"I'm glad to hear the coast is clear, as Egbert will probably show up here one of these days. He's joined the Dutch Resistance."

Sable's eyes lit up. "That's wonderful news! What will he do?"

"Set up his own cell in Amsterdam. At least that's the last news I heard."

It was Sable's turn to probe in his past. "And what about you? Is there a special girl in *your* life?" She wasn't prepared for the wounded look on his face.

"There was. There isn't now. I'll tell ye all about it in due time."

HIS VOICE WAS CLIPPED and closed her out. It set her on high alert, but then he added in a softer voice, pulling her closer, "There's no one else, Sable. There never was anyone else since I clapped eyes on ye in Shim Sham Club on Warbour Street, but I'd never dared to dream of... this."

He kissed her, warm and deep, but still restraining his passion and hers while Sable melted further into his arms. She pulled back so she could talk with him before they would have to get up and face the staff.

"Bill, listen."

"Hmmm... one more." He opened one eye halfway, grinning like a Cheshire cat.

"No, not now, later."

"A'rite, Captain, you're the boss."

Sable sat up, lighting a Craven A. Looking at him through the smoke, she said imploringly, "You know why you're here? I mean, here in my bed? I wouldn't have let you unless I was sure I could trust you."

Now Bill opened both eyes and the dozing glance vanished like the shadow of a cloud.

"Ye can trust me as ye trust yerself, Sable. There's nothin' I'd ever do to harm ye."

"Good!" She took a drag. "Then listen carefully, William Mitchell, as I'm only going to talk about it once. To you and to nobody else. My secret must remain safe with you. Do you promise?"

"On one condition."

As she pushed more cushions behind her back and pulled in her legs, her lower arms clasped around her knees, she chuckled. "Oh us, with our conditions! What's it this time?"

Bill turned on his side, lifting his gaze to hers. "Tell me, why *me*?"

She stared down at him, clearly hesitating what to answer, then bowed her head to his and kissed him on the lips.

"This is why."

"Condition accepted."

A silence followed in which Sable smoked and searched for words.

"Ambassador Von Henkell was a constant visitor here at Alnor. He was absolutely in my mother's inner circle. They may or may not have been lovers, that I don't know, but at some point, my mother's attention shifted toward me and him, always making sure I sat at the dinner table next to him. Of course, I tried to escape as often as I could. Claim a headache or just outright refuse to come down to dinner."

Suddenly she stopped, extinguished her cigarette, and leaped out of bed. With swift movements, she opened the heavy curtains, saturating the walls, the furniture, the carpets, and the four-poster bed with an abundance of bright sunlight.

"I need to see when I talk. This half-dusk makes my story seem even more ghoulish and detestable."

After she'd taken her former position on the bed, Bill pulled himself up and sat next to her, lighting the first cigarette she'd ever seen him smoke, the hand with the burning cigarette resting on her leg. A comforting contact she needed.

"At the time, I had no idea what was behind my mother's plan. She was trying to keep me in her Nazi circle, you know, and I thought she was just henpecking me. I hated it, I hated the entire ambiance, but my father was gone, and I had nowhere else to go. I think most of the staff played along with my mother's crazy ideas. I don't mean the Staceys, but the indoor staff, maids, and male staff she'd employed after my parents separated." She took a deep breath.

"Go on, lass. Ye can do this."

"All right, I won't digress any further. My mother started to suggest to me this absolutely bonkers idea that I should marry that awful Von Henkell. I mean, the man was at least twice my age and— though in his own way perhaps quite good-looking—not at all my type, not to mention the fact that he was a staunch Nazi. For all I knew the man was married already, but who cares?" Sable bit on the inside of her lip. The words came with more difficulty.

"I honestly think my mother had some political plan. It had nothing to do with a good match, or something like that. And she's never cared about my well-being or happiness, but this was something she was pursuing with great tenacity. I really got scared, because Von Henkell started paying more and more attention to me. I desperately tried to get in touch with my father, but he was abroad at the time and so was the best friend of my youth, Freddie Frinton-Smith. I felt so alone. I've never been a very girlfriendly, social type of girl, making only superficial contacts at the boarding schools, so there were no locals or girlfriends who could help me. I was trapped at Alnor. Here."

Sable's voice became very soft, and tears ran down her cheeks. Bill gave her knee a squeeze but didn't interrupt the flow of her words.

"I'm a fighter. It was absolutely clear in my head that I would *not* marry Von Henkell or become his mistress. So, I devised a plan to escape from Alnor. I would take one of my father's smaller cars that were still there in the garage and just flee to London, whether or not he was home. So, I had it all arranged, packed my bag. I would slip out in the night when everyone was asleep, which, mind you, could be three or four in the morning as my mother's parties went on into the wee hours. I would be ready. I could do this. There was petrol in the car. I had taken the keys from my father's desk.

"To conceal my plans, I played along that evening, so I went to dinner and went through the charade of sitting next to Von Henkell and listening to their foul Nazi propaganda. When he offered me a drive in his Mercedes, I thought, *why not?* There's nothing he can do to me now. How wrong I was." A sob, another comforting squeeze.

"One maid, her name was Nellie, had blabbed to my mother. She'd seen my packed bag. At least I think it was she who betrayed me. Even before we came to his car with the Swastikas upfront, I began to feel dizzy, but I thought it was because I was so excited about my plan." Sable swallowed hard.

"After that, I only know flashes. The smell of leather on the back seat of that Mercedes, his breath in my face, a struggle. They must have put something in my wine."

"No!" An agonized groan escaped from Bill's throat. Sable sat straighter.

"The abuse wasn't the only thing, though it was the worst, the little I remember of it. Still gives me nightmares. Afterwards, my mother effectively locked me up at Alnor. Here in this room. I've spent almost a year between these walls."

She made a wide wave with her arm, encompassing it all.

"Only that horrible maid, Nellie, had access to me. I wasn't allowed down at dinner. I lived in my room. But now and then the gamekeeper, Jack Durey... He really isn't as bad as Flora describes him. He must have gotten wind of my imprisonment. He used to pull up newspapers and chocolate via a rope we'd attached to the latch on my window. So, I read the papers. I knew that the situation with Hitler and the Nazis was becoming worse and that much of that scheming was taking place here at Alnor. It made me so ashamed of my father's lineage. So ashamed. But there was nothing I could do but hate mother and the Nazis with every fiber of my being. And I swore the next time I'd lay eyes on Von Henkell, I would kill him with my own hands."

Sable stopped, hesitated, wanted to go on, but something in her felt blocked. She couldn't share her entire story, not even with Bill. Not even with the man who'd promised to protect her.

How trustworthy were men, ultimately?

25

SABLE'S MEN

Alnor Castle, July 1941

For weeks, Sable and Bill applied themselves to repairing and preparing Alnor Castle so the first batch of July secret agent students could be welcomed. They mended roofs and fences, tackled unmowed grass, milked livestock, and trimmed shrubbery. With the help of Stacey and Jack, who seemed to revive under the duo's leadership, Alnor slowly returned to its former gothic glory.

Sable, in overalls and with a handkerchief around her long hair, tried as best as she could to keep up with the men. Though in much better shape than during her partying days, it was a challenge she good-humoredly accepted.

When they didn't squabble over futilities, she and Bill worked well together and gave each other enough space to do things their own way. Sable was a pull-it-all-off-in-one-go type of worker, who kept going until she collapsed as her body simply gave up despite her mental tenacity, whereas Bill proved to be a steady, meticulous worker, untirable and unstoppable because of his robust Highland blood and years of training in the army.

Sable worked alongside Bill and the local staff, cutting down dead trees and wiring fences, shooting her Colt Commando .38 revolver until she hit the target, but her slight build and untrained condition blackballed her, to her immense frustration.

And that's when they squabbled. Bill never told her to pull in her horns. He let her go to her own limits. Only Sable refused to accept her limits.

THEY WERE SITTING on a log overlooking Loch Lomond, drinking coffee, and having thick slices of cold pie the maids had prepared for their lunch. It was a sunny day after a long spell of rain, warm, with the blackbirds singing in the trees overhead and the distant flapping of a heron's wings over the water.

"So, Lock and Killer will be here tonight? And they'll bring the first students?" Sable remarked, brushing the crumbs from her overalls. She was sweating under her headband and her hands were full of blisters and scratches.

"Correct! There's only one problem." Bill stared into the distance, looking unhappy.

"What's that?"

"Yer friend, Freddie Frinton-Smith, who's been trainin' the Norwegian Commandos in the Shetlands, has a mission in France next week."

"Freddie?" Sable gazed at Bill in astonishment, a frown between her brows. "Why do you know that, and I don't? He's *my* friend!"

"For God's sake, Sable, who got the message or not is not worth botherin' about. The bedevilin' thing is that I have orders to replace Captain Frinton-Smith in the Shetlands. I don't know fer how long. The Norwegians are preparin' an important raid on their coastline."

The message sank in. Bill would leave. She would be alone at Alnor. Well, not really alone, but without his support, his friendship, his strength.

"Oh."

It sounded spiritless. Bill was poking angrily with a stick in the mud at his feet. Sable took to her Craven A.

"I know, I'm devastated. Sometimes I hate Baker Street overrulin' everythin'. I mean, what do they think? That I can just leave ye here on yer own to make a success of Alnor from scratch? I don't mean that ye can't, Sable, but it's not fair on ye either."

"Can't they find someone else to train Norwegians? How hard can that be?" Sable was equally angry.

"Ye know, in this business orders are orders."

"Then I'll come with you?" Her face lit up. She saw a way out of the peril.

"I wish ye could, lass. I hate bein' away from ye even fer a couple of hours."

"That bad, huh?" Sable gave him a friendly nudge, but he pulled her in his arms and kissed her, unlocking a feverish passion in both of them. Then suddenly he let her go, took her face between his hands.

"Yer my blue-eyed girl, Sable, never forget that."

"When are you leaving?" It had to be asked.

"Day after tomorrow. Flyin' there myself."

"For how long?"

"No idea. Couple of weeks, I suppose."

Sable nodded, chewed on the inside of her cheek. "So, we've got two days left. Better make the most of it!"

She jumped up from the log and pulled him to his feet.

"Yer right, sulkin' won't get me anywhere. Damn jealous, though, that Egbert is comin' tonight."

"Ah! That's why you've been moodily brooding." Sable grinned "To tell you the truth, I'm very much looking forward to seeing Egbert again, but I never had and never will have any romantic feelings for him."

"Yer a stinkin' liar, even to yerself, Lady Montgomery."

"Oh, I'm in danger now, am I? When you start calling me by my titled name? You never do that."

"I'm sort of honest," Bill agreed, picking up the axe to chop up the trunk of the mountain birch they'd just taken down.

"It was a different time, Bill. I was a different girl, and remember, I was always drunk."

SABLE WAS OVERJOYED to receive three of her former friends at Alnor Castle, where she'd worked so hard in the past weeks together with Bill to turn it into a training school SOE Headquarters could be proud of.

Johnny "Lock" Clark, Cuthbert "Killer" Drake and Egbert Van Eijck were men Sable admired and to each of them, in their own way, she'd been close.

Though endowed with a pockmarked exterior, a cunning look in his ocean-gray eyes, and an impressive criminal record, Lock was the archetypal gentle giant, who'd not only shared many a dirty joke in Gaelic with Sable to snub the rest of the mostly Eton-educated trainers, but had also sought her out to teach her what he knew about explosives and detonators.

"Always handy to have one of them lovelies in yer handbag, Miss," he'd joke, showing her the inside of a plastic explosive he called a CLAM MKIII.

Like Sable, Lock had been at Beaulieu almost from the beginning in the summer of 1940, when relationships between administrative staff and trainers had not yet been pegged. As they smoked and joked together, Lock became Sable's first unofficial instructor in guerrilla warfare. The rest of the Beaulieu clique referred to them as Lock and Miss. Though on the opposite spectrum of maleness, Lock gave Sable some of the lighthearted comradery she'd so loved with Freddie.

Killer was a totally different man, taciturn, red-faced and with hands that could snap anyone's neck with only two fingers. His black-haired, rough, burly exterior actually hid a learned man who read Tolstoy and Kierkegaard in his free time. Killer was passionate about living off the land, a romantic à la Thomas Hardy.

Sable would sit next to him as his fat, yet deft fingers created a trap to catch a hare, or watched as he sketched ways to move from a secluded place over an open field. Killer never taught Sable what he knew, but she became calm and centered when near him, and he accepted her presence unconditionally.

And then, of course foremost, her old friend from her wild London days, rich kid Egbert Van Eijk. He'd changed so much over the course of two years, it looked as if he'd had a makeover. Having lost his former chubbiness, here was a proud, well-trained man, whose blue eyes were no longer engaged in reading the labels of champagne bottles and wooing equally rich heiresses but rather took the measure of Gestapo agents and looked after the oppressed Dutch people.

Though still white-skinned and with that thick, straight hair the color of Sahara sand, Egbert had, just like Sable, checked out from their pre-war bohemian lifestyle. Extending both his hands, adorned with a diamond-studded signet ring on his right little finger, Egbert marched toward her while Sable felt Bill's cyanic-blue eyes pricking in her back.

"Sable, my love, I was so excited to hear we'd be reunited. Look at you, damsel of the North. You look more spectacular in overalls than in a Schiaparelli dress!"

Fat kisses landed on either of her cheeks, and with his arm possessively around her shoulders, Egbert turned to Bill, shaking his hand heartily and slapping him on the back. He still didn't let go of Sable, who, with her cheeks red, tried to dive from under his embrace.

It was all there again, right before her, Egbert's bred-in-the-bone apprehension about rivals. But he was mistaken. She was no longer an accident waiting to happen, in need of a man to fend off other men on her behalf.

Abruptly, she ripped herself loose from the Dutchman's embrace and, turning to shake hands with Lock, told him in thick Glaswegian accent that he'd trained her well on how to escape in the case of being caught. She double-checked that Bill also got the message, as she said, *"Bha sin na teicheadh cumhang. Theagaisg thu mi gu math dhomh."*

With a smirk on his pocky face, Lock replied he was glad to have helped her in delicate matters. *"Tha mi toilichte a chluinntinn gu bheil mi air a bhith na neach-cuideachaidh ann an cùisean finealta."*

Relieved, Sable saw Bill's slight intake of breath. Good. He got her point. Whatever there had been between her and Egbert was in the past. Only Egbert still needed to get that message.

To Cuthbert Drake, Sable turned with her usual reverence, as she considered the fieldwork's instructor a scholar of stature. "Welcome to Alnor Castle. Have you ever been to my remote part of the world, Cuthbert?"

"I have not, Sable. I've seen the steppes of Mongolia and the great rivers of South America and yet I've never been to Inveraray. It's a great pleasure!"

In their wake, Lock and Killer had brought the first six Alnor trainees. Three Dutchmen, of which Egbert was one, and three Frenchmen.

Though surrounded by a motley group of members of the male species, Sable felt totally at ease. How far she'd come from loathing and fearing the Nazi bunch at her mother's dinner table. Perhaps men were better company than women. Except women like Maureen and... perhaps... Esther.

LATER THAT EVENING, they were all sitting around the elongated, rectangular dinner table in Alnor's main dining room, Sable snuggled in between Bill and Lock, with Egbert and Killer across from them. The other students sat further down the table, talking among themselves in their own tongues. Mostly Sable was silent, listening to the lively chatter of the men, who all at some point had crossed each other's paths.

When only she and Bill had been at Alnor together, they'd eaten with the staff in the kitchen, making the least fuss for them as possible, though the real reason had been that Sable avoided this room like the plague.

Now she was back in the center of the castle with this rowdy, robust brotherhood of resistance fighters, each of whom she instinctively knew would protect her with their own body. But Sable couldn't help remembering the times when the terse, guttural twang of German voices, the fake, over-the-top Valhalla evenings her mother presided over, were the rule at Alnor Castle.

There couldn't be a sharper contrast. It made her feel good, and yet she missed her father with a pang. Would the 6th Baron of Alnor have approved of what his Bhobain was doing with his heritage?

"Dadaigh," she whispered to herself, "please, give Alnor training school your blessing. May my work erase the stain of Nazism mother tried to stamp on it."

Sable sipped her water and smoked her Craven A. The men were drinking red wine and whiskey, getting louder and funnier. Bill kept his promise and stuck to water, giving her hand a squeeze under the table.

She smiled up at him, love in her eyes. He caught her eye and smiled back. At that moment, Sable realized she felt happy, really, really happy, and it struck her like a thunderbolt. That this was possible. And here at Alnor. Had the ghosts been finally laid to rest?

26

ESTHER

August 1941

"Miss Sable, phone call from Lunna House, Shetland Isles!"

Sable looked up from the fur coat of a dead rabbit she was holding in her hands, her first catch with a trap she'd made herself. Killer, beside her, was grinning from ear to ear.

Helen, the newly appointed Alnor maid, stood squarely on the lawn, scanning the surroundings with a hand above her eyes against the bright sunlight.

"Miss Sable, telephone!" she called again.

Sable dropped the rabbit in Killer's lap and, brushing the thin gray-brown hairs from her hands, jogged back to the house.

It must be Bill! she thought, rather panicked. *Bill's phoning me. Is that good or bad?*

He'd been gone for three weeks now and though she managed with the instructors and an increasing number of students, not a moment to herself from dawn to dusk, she missed him like the sky misses the stars.

"Coming! Is it Captain Bill, Helen?"

"Aye, tis! Quickly, Miss, the Captain says these calls are expensive."

Sable took up the receiver, her heart in her throat. "Yes? Are you there, Bill?"

"Hello, Sable dear. Yes. Just a quick call. I miss ye so much."

"I miss you too, Bill. Everything all right? You gave me a fright, thought something had happened."

"Yes, everythin's a'rite. Just thought that we're doin' a type of commando trainin' here that I'd like to show ye. Maybe we could introduce it at Alnor. Are you interested? There's a Norwegian girl comin' here today, so ye wouldn't be the only female. I know it's a lousy excuse to see ye."

"I'd love to, Bill, but I can't simply walk away from here. There're more agents arriving every day. We now have Poles and Czechs as well, and you know how small the staff is. We're expecting a new shooting instructor by the end of the week." Sable was terribly tempted to just shout 'yes!' but then Egbert called her from the schoolroom.

"Sable, got any more chalk for the chalkboard?"

"Just a sec, Bill!" And with her hand over the receiver, she called back, "In the sideboard drawer!" The lack of training staff meant Egbert was teaching temporarily as well.

Then Helen pulled on her sleeve. "I need two men to help dig up more potatoes for lunch."

Sable's head buzzed, as it continuously did these days. How on earth could she leave now?

"I can't, Bill. I want to, but you hear how it is here. Crazy busy."

"It would only be for one week, Sable. Ye could hand over the management to Lock and Killer."

She was so tempted. Longed for his embrace so much. Only a quick break with the one man who filled her dreams at night? Rubbing her tired forehead, she protested less strongly.

"How would I get to the Shetlands?"

"By plane, of course. I can collect ye from RAF Inveraray tomorrow mornin'."

∽

It was Sable's first time aboard a plane, and she was in raptures, not just because of the view and the thrill of flying over Scotland and then over the Atlantic Ocean to the west and the North Sea to the east. It was being with Bill, who was such an experienced flyer that he completely put her at ease.

Gazing down from the cockpit window, she couldn't repress her oohs and ahs as Bill seemed to bask in her delight. The world below was like a puzzle of colorful elements—greens, yellows, blues, and blacks. Yet so fresh and alive! Green hills, then rocky formations and then the gleaming blue sea, tiny cows and trees, and even tinier humans who trudged the earth like mini versions of themselves.

The occasional cloud they flew through was a new delight, not as fluffy and cottonwool as she'd expected but sturdy, giving the Lysander some friction as she glided through.

The world was a spell of light and dark, of changing landscapes, while safe and high up, she saw how beautiful her homeland was from the sky.

"Look, John o' Groats! On a clearer day, ye can almost see my house." There was something in his tone, a ring of sadness and anger that didn't make Sable ask any further, but she studied the isthmus with great interest. One day, she'd ask which dark secret he had buried there, but not now.

As the Lysander descended slowly and steadily to the narrow airstrip on Lunna, Sable felt Bill's mood improve. The smile returned on his bearded face; his shoulders relaxed. As he helped her jump onto the tarmac from the cockpit, he held her in his arms, kissing her passionately.

"Welcome to Lunna, *mo ghràidh*."

My love! He'd never called her *my love* before. Sable felt light and giddy, as if she'd suddenly been invited on her honeymoon. Hand in hand, they walked to the hangar, where Bill gave instructions to the mechanics to check the plane and fill her up.

"Come now," he said, grinning that endearing lopsided smile, "it's all rather basic here, but Lunna House's a sight for sore eyes."

"Prettier than Alnor?" Sable teased.

"Nah, that never, but that has mostly to do with the owner. A capital lass!" He kissed her again and Sable kissed him back, not caring that some of the Norwegians who were doing a ground training exercise whistled at them.

"Did you see Freddie before he left?" Sable was dying to get news about her old friend.

"Aye, Major Frinton-Smith took a day to hand over the lead to me. Nice fella. Would never have expected such a fine-built, delicate man to be such a cutthroat in the fields. Really surprised the tarradiddle out of me. I can be such a boor in judging other men."

"Ah, he's a major now, is he? Never told me." She looked wistful for a second. "How was he doing?"

"He was fine, my dear. He left a note for ye."

"Oh great! Can't wait to read it. I so hope I'll see Freddie soon. I miss him. Hope David is also well."

"There was no David," Bill observed. "But I'm afraid Frinton-Smith will have to survive the Jerries in France before comin' to visit ye." Bill stopped, looked at her, saw her concern, as she asked,

"He will survive, won't he?"

"Sure. Both yer friends will be fine. Don't fret, my girl. Frinton-Smith kinda reminded me of ye. Same built, same glance, same tenacity."

They had meanwhile arrived at Lunna house, which Sable thought was like a relic from the past, the type of Gothic mansion from the nineteenth century.

Taking in its weather-beaten front, paint peeling off and side-boards sagging, Sable wasn't sure she shared Bill's view on architectural prettiness. It looked desolate on a desolate island that was pummeled by wind and water, year-round, not the lush and majestic landscape she loved in Scotland.

It was nothing like her grand, sturdy neo-Gothic castle in green-gray stone, the many windows adorned with red-and-white shutters and the elegant turrets covered with gray slate roofing.

Bill led her through the dilapidated front door through a long, narrow hall that led to a large office space, where, despite it being August, a fire was lit in the dusty fireplace.

"By the way, the Norwegian gal arrived yesterday. Caught my eye immediately. Strong, tall, blonde as you get them. First-rate shot, too. Ye'll like her." Bill went over to the percolator and poured two cups of coffees.

"Do I have reasons to be jealous?" Sable lit a cigarette as she took the coffee from him.

"Nah, I love them tawny and black as a raven."

"Good! So, what do I do now?"

"I'll show ye our room and then ye can freshen up and have a look around. I'll meet you fer lunch, a'rite? And then this afternoon ye can look at the trainin'. Tonight, I'll introduce ye to everyone."

"Are you the only instructor here?"

"Aye, but these Norwegians need little instruction. They're true Vikings. Used to survive under extreme weather. A tough lot. It's just a matter of softenin' the edges with them."

"Okay, sounds like a plan."

He kissed her warmly again and let go of her with difficulty. Savoring the lingering of his lips on hers, Sable sat down and sipped her coffee, content to be free of duty for a little while.

DRESSED IN HER KHAKI OVERALLS, she stood at the window, studying her boyfriend. Bill was instructing the commandos to sneak through tall grass on their bellies and then quickly get up and shoot at a target. It was fascinating to watch and though she had by now quite a lot of physical training under her belt, this seemed really hard.

Behind her, she heard the plonk-plonk-plonk of army boots and, thinking it was the orderly with the soup she'd requested for lunch, she turned around. She blinked, thought the daylight had caught in her eye. A fully armed, tall woman in camouflage clothes hesitated to enter, then paused in her tracks.

"Esther? Esther Weiss?"

"Sable?"

They stood gaping at each other, not understanding how this was possible.

"What are *you* doing here?" It came as if out of one mouth.

Sable hesitated whether to greet her or run away and hide. Esther had changed. The sea-green eyes had a hard ring to them. She looked even taller, menacing, tormented. Was she that angry with her?

"Did... did you get my apology letter?" Sable hated herself for sounding so weak, but then saw a glimpse of the lovely, social Esther as she replied.

"I did! But there was no need for it. Le Manoir was another epoch, wasn't it?"

Sable nodded, glad, as they closed the distance between them and hugged each other tightly. Gosh, this woman was strong. Someone to look up to.

"I'm still sorry for my behavior," she murmured, as they let each other go. "I was a horrible person and yet you saved my life. You need to tell me what happened in that ravine, because it's all a blur to me." *As are so many other patches of my life*, Sable thought sadly.

"I guess you had your reasons." Esther shrugged. "But listen, what are you doing here? I guess you know my mission." She pointed to her commando outfit.

"I'm Captain Mitchell's girlfriend." Sable explained, and quickly added, "but I'm training as well, probably to go into France as I'm fluent in French. Stupid international boarding school doll, you know."

At that moment, the orderly came in with Sable's lunch.

"Would you like something as well, or do you have to go somewhere?"

"Yes, I have training."

Sable saw Esther look longingly at the soup.

"Wait a sec. I'm going to tell Bill we're taking the day off. Time to catch up!"

"Would you?" For one moment Esther was again the hesitant, shy girl from Vienna and Sable ruling the roost.

"Of course! France and Norway will just have to wait a little longer before we create havoc there," Sable announced with a wink as she slipped out the door.

SITTING opposite each other with the steaming leek soup and thick slices of buttered brown bread, Sable wondered if she should ask what happened to Esther after the war started. She bit the bullet.

"So, you went to Norway instead of back home to Vienna?"

"Yes, my family had moved there during the time I was in Switzerland. But they weren't safe there either. I'm the only one left." Esther paused, the jewel-like eyes filling up with tears, which made Sable grab her hand over the table.

"Oh no!"

"Yes. That's when I joined the Norwegian resistance." Esther stared out of the window, then wiped her eyes with the sleeve of her jacket.

"Heavens!" Sable didn't know what to say to console her. She rumbled around in her pockets in search of her cigarettes. Made some awkward movements. The next moment, she was holding Esther's Enfield gun in the air with a triumphant smile. This trick was the only thing she could think of to cheer the sad girl up.

"Gracious sakes," Sable exclaimed, nodding her head in pseudo-disapproval, "what would the Sphinx have said if she'd found you armed to the teeth like this?"

Sable saw it worked. Esther looked puzzled, forgot her pain, her hand going to her empty holster. Then the beautiful eyes fixed on Sable inspecting her weapon.

"How did you do that?"

"Remember, I'm Bill's girlfriend," Sable joked. "No, I'm pretty good myself. Trained by Cuthbert 'Killer' Drake. Taught me tricks like this."

She handed the gun back across the table. As Esther shoved it in its place, she grinned. "You'll have to teach me your tricks."

"I will. Feeling better now?"

Esther looked at her with the warmth she'd radiated at Le Manoir and that, even then, had tempted Sable to become friends with her.

"We're getting a second chance," she threw out. "Who'd have thought?"

"War's a beast and a blessing," Esther agreed.

"I've been praying for an opportunity to do something back for you after you saved my life. Bill can train you to become the best agent in the Norwegian resistance. And I can become your friend. And I'll teach you the dirty tricks. How to kill Nazis without a sound, detonation devices, that sort of thing."

A shadow slid over Esther's face and Sable stopped talking, saw the raw pain reappear on her friend's face. She was mentioning killing people in cold blood. What had happened to them? They were young women in their twenties in the middle of the twentieth century, talking about murdering grown men.

"I know it's not a joke," Sable added more soberly. "It's dire need."

Esther nodded. "I know. They deported my whole family. I have no other choice."

"What about your fiancé?"

Esther shook her head, new tears welling up. Sable slipped from her chair and crossed the table to sink at her feet, taking the firm hands in hers.

"Oh no, oh no, oh no!" she kept repeating, now sobbing herself. "The bastards, the rotten bastards! We'll get them, Es. Each one of them."

"I've killed one already." It was only a whisper.

Sable gazed up into Esther's tear-smeared face.

"Golly, you did? What happened? Wait, do you want to go for a stroll along the beach? I feel like we need some fresh air. It's suffocating in here. Then talk some more?"

"Good idea. Plenty to catch up on."

They both got to their feet and walked the short distance west-ward to a large inlet called Lunna Sound. The tall house, high on the rugged grassland above, stood watching over them. After years of pent-up silence and regret, there was so much to recount, like old school friends having missed out on important developments in each other's lives.

Hands in their pockets, they walked and talked for hours, trying to find a new balance in which Sable hoped they would become life-long friends.

There had never been another woman in her life that she admired like Esther. There had never been a woman in Sable's life that she admired, full stop. A poor example of a mother in Misty Fletcher had made her suspicious of her own sex. By adopting a bossy and inapproachable demeanor, Sable had for two decades steered clear from real women friends.

Female friendship? Prematurely ended with Maureen, but perhaps here it was. The longing for this feeling had been in her since Esther sat majestically alone on that stone at Lake Geneva's shore. It was a different love, but as deep and as tender as what she felt for Bill, for Freddie. Another human speaking directly to Sable's tormented heart. Here it was.

Now don't squander it.

Sable cracked as many jokes as she knew, Killer's entire arsenal, to lift Esther's spirits. Then she held extensive lectures on irregular warfare, to share everything she learned. Sometimes cussing, some-times using posh words, she still did most of the talking.

At some point, Esther interrupted Sable's long-winding digres-sion on lock-picking and lock replacements. Standing stable-legged in the sand, she took Sable's measure, laughed out loud and proclaimed in that sweet voice of hers,

"You may wear the baggiest clothes in the world and have a cigarette hanging sailor-like from the corner of your cupid-bowed painted lips. But you will always and everywhere be Lady Sable Montgomery. Every inch of you! You're delightful. But also, a bit of an enigma to me. I still picture you more at the Moulin Rouge in Paris or the Monte Carlo casinos than trudging around the Shetland Isles in search of sabotage."

"Please don't say that!"

Sable felt as if Esther had hit her in the face with a wet newspaper. She wanted to stamp her foot, scream into the wind she was no longer that girl, the lost one. The one who had lost everything but had returned, carved out a life for herself, a mission, a man. Was she still a fraud, no better than her mother?

She felt all the life seep out of her, while in the distance Esther's voice sounded apologetic.

"What's wrong? I didn't mean to hurt you. What did I say that was wrong?"

Sable stood stock-still in the sand, pasty-faced and played-out. She couldn't answer. There it was. Women, real women like Esther, saw through facades much better than men ever could.

Lifting the wondrous light-blue eyes in search of Esther's green gaze, Sable chewed on the inside of her cheek, doubted, weighed. Should she tell her? Tell someone everything, share the burden, the pain, the loss?

Confession?

But instead, she said in a bitter but anger-free tone, "I'm not my mother!"

Esther protested, "I don't know your mother, only what you wrote about her in your letter, which wasn't very favorable. But how could I compare the two of you? It's just like I said. You are an enigma to me, always were. I'd just like to get to know the real Sable."

Esther looked lost as well, as if she'd burnt the thin bridge of trust between them.

"So, you still don't like me?" Sable kicked the tip of her boot into the wet sand. "Well, I guess I'm not very likable. And I certainly didn't behave like a nice person in the past."

"But I do like you, Sable! And I admire you. You've got spunk. I totally see why Captain Bill is smitten with you, like every man and woman you come in touch with. You're special, Sable. That's not it. It's just … that you seem to hide something, but maybe I'm reading way too much into it."

Sable drew in a long breath between half-closed lips, then fished a packet of Craven As from her pocket and took a fresh cigarette. Looking askew at Esther as she lit it, she felt her heart swell.

Maybe Esther was right. Maybe she was both a lady and a vagabond. But she was still struggling with her longing to tell Esther the truth. After all, this girl knew what loss was, what it was to lose loved ones who were like a part of your own soul.

"You're way too sharp, Jeger, and I think you know it."

"I didn't know you knew my code name?"

"Sure. It suits you, the huntress!"

"All right." Esther let down her guard again. "I'm not trying to be sharp, or anything, Sable. And you don't have to tell me if you don't want to."

Drawing a long and deep haul on her cigarette, Sable made an impatient movement with her hand. "Well, as we are in the middle of nowhere and there are no unwelcome ears, I might as well tell you my story. I've got a child. A girl. Already had her before I came to Switzerland."

Almost choking on her cigarette, Sable was convinced she would die of shame or the wrath of the gods on the spot. Feeble and broken, she knew only Esther's verdict could keep her together now.

"Heavens, I didn't know you were married."

The remark was so ludicrous that Sable, despite herself, uttered a wry laugh. "I wasn't and I ain't."

Now it would come. The Verdict. But Esther only asked in that sweet, melodious voice, "Then where is she? I mean, your daughter? Is she with the father?"

Sable stared out over the gray sea that rolled its powerful waves over the strip of sand. The tide was rising.

"I don't know. No, not with the father. They took her away from me at birth. I named her Isabella, but she probably now is Gertie or Marie or something else drab. She was given away in adoption and I was packed off to Switzerland."

"But how?" Esther's mind clearly couldn't fit the pieces of the puzzle. "Who did that to you, and why? What *about* the father?"

"Who did it? My mother and her then-boyfriend, some Nazi officer she was involved with, that's who. Why? I have no clue. Probably just to spite me. The father never knew I was pregnant."

"But why, Sable? And why didn't you tell him? He would've married you."

"Oh Esther, you're such a goose. He might have, but I didn't want him. It was... it was... very complicated. Oh, I don't know why I told you all this. I never told it to anyone." Sable's eyes filled with tears. Her hands were fists in her pockets, as she marched the strip of sand, over and over.

"It was complicated. It was complicated! I hated him!"

"All right, Sable, please calm down. I'm sorry I'm asking the wrong questions. I thought... I thought a baby meant happiness. You're right. I *am* a goose. I wish I had Carl's baby in me now. I don't care about marriage either. We're beyond these things in war. I'm sorry for what they did to you. Whatever it was. But you're a mother. That's like a dream to me. Sorry, I'm rambling."

"It's okay, Esther." Sable fought her tears, helpless in her inability to explain the context of her pregnancy to Esther. *That* she certainly wouldn't understand. It was her own fault, going for a drive with the German. She might not have known she was drugged, but she shouldn't have gone.

"I shouldn't have! I shouldn't have." Furious as a wounded bull in an arena, she kept stamping through the sand.

"Please, Sable, it's all right you told me, really it is. I won't tell anyone else. I think it's a good thing you *did* tell me." Esther misunderstood her fury, and suddenly Sable's wild pacing slowed.

"I didn't mean that, Esther. I know. I've been walking around with this kick in the teeth for three years now. It will give me an ulcer someday soon."

"Have you not told Bill?"

The blue eyes flashed. "No, Bill knows nothing about my child, and don't you dare tell him! It will all be over between him and me if he finds out."

Esther backed away from the fury in Sable's gaze. "I never would tell him. But maybe you could trust him. After all, he's your boyfriend, maybe more in the future. Why *me*?"

"Because you asked, or at least you hinted at a secret. I thought you'd care." It sounded defiant and dejected.

"I do care, Sable, of course, I do. I'm so sorry."

"Isabella will be four this Christmas. I have no clue where she is. If she's even been told she's not living with her birth parents. Probably not, and probably for the best. But it might explain to you why I went wild at times at Le Manoir. I shouldn't have taken it out on you, I know. Like I shouldn't have told you my burden now, but there's something so darn disarming about you."

"Come here." Esther took the cigarette from her fingers and stamped it out with her shoe. "Come here! Words don't help in a situation like this."

Sable felt how she was pulled into a warm female embrace. Esther was holding her tight, muscular arms, enveloping her slender frame. There was no holding back now. First, her body started shaking in ripples, but the convulsions took over more and more until she cried against Esther's chest with every fiber of her being.

For the abuse, for the imprisonment, for the lonely pregnancy, for the horrible delivery, for the last glimpse of her dark-haired, cooing baby being ripped from her arms. A white frilly blanket. All she had left of her.

Nothing else. Nothing at all. Not a name, not an address, only the knowledge of a father who should not have been the father of her child. It was such a mess, such an incredible mess. Nobody could ever make head or tail of it.

Sable didn't know how long she had been crying against Esther's chest, but when she was finally wasted, she heard Esther say in her gentle tone,

"Cry as much as you want, Sable. It's all right. We both hurt so much. But we'll get through it. I will get my family back, and you your little girl. Maybe not during the war, but one day this hell will be over, and we will be reunited with our loved ones."

"But how?" Sable sniffed. "How can I find out where my little girl is?"

"Well, you've come to the right profession, dear. You must tell Bill if you're serious with him. Then trust the intelligence services. They are so smart. People everywhere can be tracked. Just start at the hospital where she was born. Trust the process. She's legally your child and now you've reached adult age, you can claim her back."

The crying had stopped. Soon, Sable restored some of her former equilibrium, though she felt her face was puffy and warm.

"I will try to tell Bill, not now, but one day. Perhaps when the war is over. It's no use now." Peeking at her watch, she exclaimed, "Heavens, this late. We must get back to base. They'll think we've drowned or gotten lost. It's almost dinnertime." She kissed Esther on the cheek.

"Thank you, Esther Weiss. I knew you were gold from the very first moment I laid eyes on you. Will you be my friend?"

"I loved you from the first time I saw you, Lady Sable. No matter how horrible you tried to be, you were always so endearing, and I think I gravitated to your vulnerability under that hard veneer. Yes, we're friends. We'll always be friends."

The sun slowly sank lower over the barren Shetland landscape, still radiating warmth on their backs.

A friend, Sable pondered. *I have a friend who knows my secret. At least part of it. The only good part. Isabella.*

A female harrier hawk flew up from the field, screaming *kee-kee-kee-kee,* her message ending in a sharp whistle. The mother bird was protecting its nest.

27

THE BREAK-UP

That evening at the Lunna House dinner table, Sable felt enveloped in a balmy gush of warmth, doubly so when she glanced across the table and caught Esther's eye. It signaled a forever friendship. She hadn't experienced this kind of heartwarming affection before—maybe only now and then with Dadaigh in her youth, and glimpses of it with Freddie—but certainly not since her downfall.

It was as if the wall had been broken down inside of her that had stood between her and the world, the one that had prevented her from really associating with other people, from letting anyone in.

It gave Sable a new sense of liberation, as if she'd already won the war, if only her own personal war. Yet despite the wonderful, fresh feeling of connection, her busy mind wondered how this new self would pair with Bill. What should she disclose to her boyfriend without giving him the full truth?

For telling Bill she had a three-year-old daughter with a high-ranking German Nazi was off the cards. Still. Probably forever. That was *her* albatross. Sable didn't know why, but her intuition told their relationship wouldn't survive that blow. So, what then? Would only

Esther ever know? Even Freddie, who, she knew, was guessing more than she'd told him, kept quiet, didn't ask.

Sable was still entangled in her deliberations when she and Bill were climbing up to their very Spartan but clean bedroom on the top floor of the big drafty house. Bill seemed in a totally different mood, still as affectionate as he'd been that morning when he picked her up. He clearly was determined to continue his wooing of her. He kept circling around her, touching her hair, wanting a kiss.

"I've missed ye so much."

Sable answered his embrace on automatic pilot, which, instead of pushing him away, made him only more fervent in his advances.

"Kiss yer man back. We're finally together. Let ye hair down, *Mo Chridhe*."

The word *chridhe* made her giggle despite her preoccupations.

"Why are you calling me 'your heart'?" But she knew what he meant by it. It made her cheeks flush and her heart race.

Looking around the strangely impersonal room where only two small electric lights were lit, she wondered. Would this be it? The sealing of their love? It had just two single beds with white bedspreads, a washstand, and an old-fashioned armoire.

In the open windows a gentle North Sea breeze billowed the thin curtains, while the distant crashing of the waves on the shore had a rhythmic, soothing lull. Little spoke of the brutal, bloody battle being fought on the shores across the waves.

The night was full of summer, flirtatious grasshoppers bringing an evening serenade, a gentle buzz as if emanating from the very ground, interspersed by the screeching chirp of beetles and the occasional hoot of a night owl. No human sounds. On Shetland by night, only nature had free play.

The smell of fresh hay mingled with Bill's scent of musk, silt air and the sulfurous, metallic smell of ammunition. Sable drank it all in, especially his masculine smell—a far cry from Dior Homme and sophistication—drawing strength from his love for her as he kept rounding on her, touching her, kissing her face and neck.

"Maybe it was a good thin' we were deprived of each other's

company. Absence makes the heart grow fonder, that sort of thin'."
He kissed her again, tenderly, then venturing further.

Sable half wriggled herself out of his embrace. It was hard. She
loved what he was doing to her, how his caresses and mouth made
her body tingle and glow, but she was also scared. And the beach talk
with Esther was still very much occupying her mind.

"Bill," she tried, "can we sit down and talk for a moment? I need...
I need..."

"Can't it wait? I just need to kiss this spot and this one." His
mouth traversed down her neckline, reaching the first heaving of her
breast.

"Bill," she began again, but then faltered. How on earth was she
going to let him know now? It would spoil everything. Everything!

"Yes?" he asked, momentarily letting her go to take off his
uniform, but keeping her constantly in his view, the intense blue eyes
filled with dreamy amorousness. He was totally in his game of
winning her over.

She, too, kept taking in the beauty of this powerful man, a body
like a Nordic god that made her go weak in the knees. She loved him
so much, yearned for him, with body and soul. But so far, they'd just
been dating, gone no further than kissing and sleeping together in
the same bed. Her female intuition told her Bill wanted more tonight,
and it made her body freeze.

She wavered between impatient fervor and infused fear, while her
secret hung over them like a snowy cloud over the Arrochar Alps. Bill
knew of Von Henkell's bodily claim on her. He'd accepted that.
Maybe he assumed she'd had other lovers. Surely, he too had lain
with other women.

That discussion hadn't come up between them. It hadn't—yet—
been part of their relationship. To Sable, every step with Bill had
needed to be valuable and real.

He kept eyeing her with those penetrative eyes, searching for her
yes, but at the same time respecting her space. "What's it ye wanted to
tell me?"

What is it exactly you want to tell him, Sable? Stop stringing him along. She became angry with herself for her dillydallying. It wasn't fair to him, but something in her balked. An impenetrable bulwark of pain and mistrust. She heard herself say, as if from another planet,

"Nothing. Only that I missed you too, William Mitchell."

The moment had passed. She had let it slip. It was just too darn difficult. The scrutinizing gaze was still on her as she took off her overalls and slipped into her nightgown over her underwear, then quickly dove under the bedclothes of one bed.

Bill lifted the other bed as if it weighed nothing and pushed it against hers. Then sat down on her side and took her hand, kissing every finger one by one.

"I don't know what it is with us, but when I'm not around ye, it feels like some part of me is missin'."

"Your best part?" she managed to joke.

"Aye, my best part."

He took her in his arms, lying beside her, stroking her face with fingers rough from terrain work.

"Sorry for that."

"Never mind, I love sandpaper fingers. Especially yours."

She didn't know where this lighthearted Sable came from, while her real heart grieved. His mouth sought hers, testing her resolve. She tried to feel it, do the normal thing, but the frigid fear took over again. Without alcohol, all this seemed to have become impossible for her.

"Dearest." He stopped kissing her, lay his bearded cheek against her smooth one. "Dear Sable, my girl, I would love for us to be even closer than we are now, but I feel I need to tell ye my story first. I promised ye. It is time."

Sable felt a deep, rosy love engulf her, swell through her like a warm tidal flow of water, washing her ashore, near him, with him. He would go first. Then she could too.

"Please," she whispered.

"On one condition."

They locked eyes again. This time, it wasn't a joke. It was dead serious. Sable was shocked. The look on Bill's face was one of total haggardness, a broken man, aged, devoid of all his former strength and luster. Yet his pain was their bond, her opening to do the same. She held her breath.

"What's the condition?"

"That ye'll be my woman after I tell ye." The words were simple, unadorned, raw, and real. She just nodded.

Still lying next to her, their bodies entwined, Bill took a deep breath.

"I married Suzanna when I was twenty and she was nineteen. Suzanna had been my sweetheart since forever. She wasn't from John o' Groats, but a Morgan from Clan Mackay, born in Durness. Both her parents died in the influenza epidemic of 1918, and that's when she came to live with her aunt Maud, who'd married into the Sinclair clan. Maud and Alex Brown were our neighbors, so Suzanna lived next door to us."

Bill stopped talking, tightened his embrace around Sable, clearly overtaken by memories of this period.

"If it's too hard for ye to hear I loved another woman, ye must tell me."

"Go on," Sable urged, though it made her swallow hard, learning Bill had been married to the love of his life.

"So, where's Suzanna now?" Her voice was small but determined.

"I'll come to that in a bit. I need a cigarette. Have ye got one for me?" Bill sat up, combed two hands through his long auburn hair.

"Sure." She grabbed for her package of cigarettes, lit two, and gave him one. He lay back down on his back, staring at the ceiling, smoking in silence. Sable felt his tenseness, so like hers. Fighting the battles that had scarred you to the core was so much harder than fighting any physical enemy.

"If you're not ready to tell me, Bill, it's all right. I understand." She gave him the leeway she needed herself.

"Nah. Ye need to know." It was terse, almost angry.

"Suzanna and I married on 23 March 1933, the day that blasted Hitler took control of Germany. But that was far from our minds. We were happy. At least I thought so. We lived in a small cottage on my father's estate. I was trainin' to become a pilot with the RAF, so I was away from home a lot, stationed at RAF Dyce in Aberdeenshire. Maisie, our daughter, was born in the summer of 1934."

Bill's voice was monotonous and dispassionate, as if he was reading a prewritten script. In the temporary pause, he took another drag on the cigarette. Sable felt a shock, as if touching an electric wire. *A daughter called Maisie.* She bit her lip.

As he did so often when they lay together, he put a hand on her leg, ritualizing their connection. It was little comfort this time.

"There had always been the mention of a Richard Mackenzie, Suzanna's second cousin back in Durness, who'd pestered Aunt Maud and Uncle Alex for years, telling them to send Suzanna back to her own clan after she'd come of age. I'd taken none of it seriously and we were legally married," Bill scoffed. "These clan claims seemed outright ridiculous in the twentieth century. And Suzanna hardly remembered livin' anywhere else but in John o' Groats." Sable listened to Bill's intake of breath.

"It did happen, though. While I was away on trainin' in England, I got a distraught phone call from my mother that strange men had lifted Suzanna and Maisie from their beds and taken them away in some old van. My Ma said she could still hear the screams in her ears."

"How awful!" Sable grabbed Bill's hand for support. "What happened to them?"

He sighed sorrowfully. "I wasn't to find out until weeks later. The RAF is strict about taking leave. I wasn't allowed any, no matter that I couldn't concentrate, and was a mental and physical wreck. When I finally returned home, I went straight to Durness. The reception wasn't very friendly as ye can imagine, but I demanded to see my wife and child." Another deep sigh.

"What?" A heavy weight settled in the pit of Sable's stomach.

"I don't know what'd happened, but when they finally granted me some time with Suzanna somewhere in a dingy cottage on the coast, she'd changed. Her relatives must have put pressure on her, or even worse. I don't know. She wouldn't look at me, told me she wanted to stay where she was. That she was happy, and so was Maisie. Maisie was only ten months at the time and, with me regularly away, didn't recognize me. I felt like the Devil took possession of me. I was so angry, so disappointed. I threatened Suzanna, tried to coerce her, tried to kiss her. Everything. But it was like she was cast in stone. I didn't know this woman whom I had loved and who had loved me. I went mad."

Sable thought Bill was going to cry, something she couldn't imagine he'd ever do. There was a sob, then he continued.

"I screamed at her I would be back. That I'd collect her and Maisie and bring her home. I just saw no way of doin' that at that moment, so returned to John o' Groats to figure out a plan of how to release Suzanna from her captors. Because that was what I believed was the case."

"Was it?" Sable asked in a low voice.

"I'll never know." Bill sounded defeated.

"How so?"

"When I returned to Durness, they were no longer there." The curtain rustled in a sudden breeze; the electric lamp on the bedside table flickered. Sable's insides froze.

"Where were they?"

"Drowned."

"Oh, no!"

"I was too late. Suzanna had pushed a dilapidated rowin' boat into the sea. Maisie was lyin' in her little yellow coat on the bottom. It was a dark, stormy day in November. The sea was wild. I ran over the sand and jumped into the waves in my uniform, not feelin' the cold or my heavy boots. They were out at the open sea already. I swam and swam until I got hold of the boat and then... and then... it toppled over, and they disappeared underwater. I dove after them until I had no more breath. Maisie's yellow coat and Suzanna's black velvet coat were the last I saw, goin' down and down and down. I'll never forgive myself for goin' back to the surface and survivin'. I should have drowned with them. That's why I can never join the RAF again."

Sable was stupefied, still, shocked to her core. It seemed irrelevant, but she asked, "What's it got to do with the RAF?"

"I tried to commit suicide by bringin' down my plane. But I survived. Then I tried to kill myself with liquor. That didn't work either. Egbert van Eijck sort of pulled me up on my shoelaces durin' my gallivantin' in the London whorehouses, found out I could fly a plane. Offered me the job. Now ye know why they call me 'Wild Bill' and I assume ye'll stop wantin' to associate with me."

A long silence followed. Sable felt as if her own gruesome history paled compared to Bill's loss. None had died in her case.

"Why... why do you think Suzanna went into that boat and took your daughter with her?"

Bill rubbed his forehead.

"I'll never know. When I returned to the Mackenzie property, all wet and shaken to the bone, they shot me off their premises with a huntin' gun. Maybe it was Suzanna herself; maybe her relatives had done somethin' to her. I'll never know, and I've given up tryin' to break my head over it. It's no use. She's gone and so is my daughter. Well, that's my sad story, Sable. It took me years to want any other woman, but ye caught my eye immediately in that London bar. I think I recognized the brittle beauty of yer soul underneath the darkness."

"I don't know what to say, Bill. Your story is so harrowing, and I am cold from it. I'm sorry, but I know my sorry is as empty as the arms of the wind."

He took his former position alongside her body, his face buried against hers.

"My condition."

They kissed, and he slowly undressed her, looked at her naked body in the light of the single lamp. Traced his finger over her curves until he came to the scar that ran almost from one hipbone to the other.

"What is this?"

Sable withdrew from his touch, tried to hide her nakedness from his staring at her disfigurement. "Nothing!" She drew the bedclothes around her, backing away from him like a frightened deer.

"Sable!" His voice was harsh, his gaze telling her he failed to understand her sudden reaction.

"I was... I had an operation. My intestines." She yammered, "It's nothing, nothing like you went through."

"Come back here, Sable, let me have a look." His voice was commanding, which only made her more afraid.

"No, no, no. Please let me be. This was a mistake. Can we just go to sleep and forget about it?"

"Forget about what, Sable? About us? After what I told ye?" Bill now seemed furious. She saw the power of his body, the wild look of hurt in his eyes that hadn't been there before. He'd warned her. He was Wild Bill.

Though she knew he'd never force himself on her, she'd broken their condition. Their conditions weren't just for fun. They made up their intimate rules of the game. And she had broken their rule without an explanation. He would not forgive her. Sable began to cry.

"Please, Bill, I'm just tired and rattled after your story. Can you just hold me, just hold me, please?"

"Why can ye not be honest with me, Sable? If ye had an operation, tell me about it. It seems serious. Let me in."

"No, no, no!" she cried, hiding her face in the cushion. "Please just hold me."

"I can't, Sable. Ye must talk to me. Ye're breechin' our trust."

He had already gotten up and pushed the bed away from hers, slumped his body on it and turned his back to her. Sable cried softly for a very long time. She saw dawn break over Lunna Ness when she dried her eyes.

Still and white-faced, she rose from her lonely bed. Bill was still lying with his face away from her. She didn't know if he was awake or asleep. It didn't matter. Not anymore. It was over between her and William Wild Bill Mitchell.

AT LEAST, that was what Sable read in his turned-away backside.

28

EVEN IF IT'S THE LAST THING I DO
BEFORE I DIE

London, March 1943

I t still was never a pleasure for Sable to come into the orbit of the unfathomable Anna Adams, but every female SOE agent knew there was no way around the Head of Operations at Baker Street. Sable studied her former finishing school fellow-student as she was sitting across from her at Manetta's, a restaurant in Clarges Street, Mayfair, where Anna had ordered her to meet for lunch.

She was convinced Anna was studying her in every respect, though the brown eyes behind the thick glasses appeared to be taking in the establishment around Sable. Then Anna brushed an invisible hair from her blue uniform before taking a file from her handbag.

"You've finished all the courses at Beaulieu." She kept reading, pushing the heavy glasses up her nose. To Sable, it wasn't clear if she was making a statement or asking a question.

Read for yourself, was all she could think, but didn't say aloud. Nobody challenged Miss Adams, certainly not before you had at least one successful mission in France under your belt. And that was the precise reason Sable was here in London. To get Anna's formal consent. Sable was ready. Wooly had told her so, and that was tenfold more important to her than haughty Miss Anna's signature.

She was dying to get away from this place, from London, from Britain, and to show she was worthy of being sent behind enemy lines as one of Churchill's secret agents. Then there was also, always, that raw feeling in her heart that told her to head for the Continent and make the distance between her and Bill as large as possible.

Her contribution to the actual war had taken long enough. And there was a chance she'd become part of Freddie's LANTERN circuit in Clermont-Ferrand as a courier.

"Your report says you've done excellent work at organizing, disguise, lock-picking, survival, adjusting to new identities, interrogations, but your hand at coding and morse is below average. You will not be used as a W/T, wireless operator."

Anna seemed annoyed at this, and Sable knew why. These agents were needed the most, and they lasted the shortest.

"I've tried hard, Anna. Honestly, I have, but have you ever tried your hand at it yourself? It's sheer undoable, especially reaching the speed of sixty signs per minute."

"The largest part of my job is staying in touch with my agents in France via wireless, so yes, I'm accomplished at it, Sable."

"All right, you were perhaps always cleverer than I was." Sable was totally done with the cold, formal high-ranking agent.

With a stab of pain in her heart, she thought of Esther and how different the meeting with that former Le Manoir student had been. But Lunna House was shrouded in pain now as well, and Sable didn't want her thoughts to return there. Done was done.

Sweet, dapper Esther. She hadn't heard of her again and did not know if she was alive or dead. The valiant Jeger. Sable hoped she was giving the Nazis hell in Norway and that they would meet up after the war and rekindle that budding friendship. But first, she—the Raven —was ready to give the Nazis hell in France, too.

Sable smoked, drank her black coffee, looked taut but strong, the lines in her pretty face even adding to her unique beauty. She was a hard woman now, or rather less and less woman and more captain and soldier. A leader if need be.

Anna seemed to have discerned some of Sable's inner thoughts as she shifted on the red-leather seat that was pushed up against the wall.

"There's been brought up something of a concern regarding your departure, Sable." The tone was different, softer, less commandeering. Sable looked up from the figures she'd been drawing on the tablecloth with her red nail. The blue gaze held Anna's dark one steadily.

"Being?"

"We usually give agents a couple of days to spend with their family before they leave. Of course, not to tell them the actual story of what they are about to do, but to say goodbye and to put them at ease. Where would you want to go? I understand you have a mother who's abroad and with whom you're not close?"

Sable was prepared for this one. All the agents knew. Her tongue burned to say William Mitchell, but she didn't even know where he was right now. And it was over. Over.

Anna was as good at her job as Sable was at hers. They both were trained to read others, read fear and trustworthiness. The very thing she'd broken with Bill.

"There's no one. I'll spend a day or two at my house in Cavendish Square. Instruct the staff. My other property, Alnor Castle, is looked after as a training school. As you know yourself. It's all right, Anna. I've been on my own as long as I can remember."

Her table companion nodded, made a note. Seemed to sympathize. And Sable wondered if behind that cold facade was a lonely woman as well, without family and with few friends. It would explain the attitude.

"Next question." Anna looked up from her scribbling. "It is my job to regularly keep family updated. You know—the vague letters about their son or daughter, husband, wife doing well. But I also need to inform the family in case... you don't come back, or it's unsure whether you're captured."

Sable cleared her throat. "The paperwork is all in order. Contact my solicitor Mr. Moses Brown on Edgware Road. He'll know what to do. It's all been discussed with him. Inform my staff at the London House. You've got both addresses in my file."

This was the tough question she'd dreaded, but she'd got through it without showing what she really felt on the inside. She swallowed, lit another cigarette. Would Bill and Freddie accept her offers? If not, Brown knew what to do. Anna nodded and wrote on her notepad again.

"Last question about your family. Do you want me to inform your mother should you not come back?"

"No!"

The dark eyes held Sable's for a longer time. They were unreadable. Then Anna continued. "My next and last concern is also connected to your personal situation."

Sable made an impatient movement with her hand as if saying, *What else have you got up your sleeve, woman? Spit it out.*

Anna thought for a moment, then dropped her notepad on the table and planted both elbows on top of it, her hands together as if in prayer.

"Unstable family backgrounds and traumas can trigger agents at unexpected moments. When things go right during the mission, we're not that concerned, but in case agents are captured and put under pressure, they may snap. I've discussed this at length with Major Woolworth, and he thinks you'll do fine just because of that. Because you're incredibly resilient and independent." Anna stopped, hesitated.

"But *you* have your doubts?" Sable filled in the blanks for the Head of Operations.

"I don't know," Anna answered honestly. "We know each other from other circumstances before the war. You were too hard and uncompromising then. I've seen no weakness in you, Sable, and strange as that may sound, that is what I'm worried about. There's a rumor circling around at Baker Street about an incomprehensible breakup between Captain Mitchell and you during your stay in the Shetlands..."

The dark eyes flickered, discerned something Sable was sure Anna wanted to see. She fought with all her might to keep her gaze unwavering but failed. Anna had cornered her, after all. Had Bill talked to Anna about them? He'd told her he knew Anna well. *Ignore it. Bluff your way through this*, her inner voice whispered.

"There's nothing to it." Her voice was flat. "We were just dating for a while. Nothing serious. Rumors are just that, rumors."

"All right. That's it then. Now your mission." Anna looked at her notepad again.

"Yes?" Sable was eager to get away from sensitivities.

"You've practiced your cover name and status over and over?"

Sable scrambled through it for the hundredth time. "I'm Madame Jacqueline Brisse, a widow and a private English tutor living in Suresnes, Paris. Code name Raven."

Anna smiled. "I didn't mean for you to dish that up. I know all that. Heard you did excellent in the Gestapo interrogation training."

"Oh, sorry." Sable smiled back. "Yes, it was quite scary, especially because it was the middle of the night, and they kept my head under water until I really thought I'd choke."

Anna nodded, the freckled face wrinkling in sympathy. "I agree. It's one of the worst parts of our training. But necessary. I hope you'll not come anywhere near such a treatment in reality."

"I'm prepared for it." Sable sounded defiant.

"You'll join the CHASSIS network in Bordeaux as a courier. Your organiser is Henri de Bonheur, code name Joseph. You'll be flown to Gibraltar in a Whitley Bomber on March 20 at three p.m. together with two male agents. From Gibraltar, you'll be taken by a felucca called the Seadog, which will land secretly in the moonlight on the Riviera coast between Bijou-sur-er and Pointe-Fourcade. You go to the hotel in Nice. I'll give you the address, in code, at departure. You stay there until you are contacted by one of De Bonheur's couriers. The code sentence will also be given to you on departure. I will personally accompany you to the airfield at Tangmere. The taxi will arrive at your house in Cavendish Square at ten in the morning. It will pick me up at Baker Street after that. Is all this clear?"

"Yes."

"Good." Anna closed her notepad. Cold and professional. "Do you have any more questions for *me*?"

"Yes."

Sable didn't continue, thus forcing Anna to look up from storing her notepad in her handbag.

"So, what did you want to ask, Sable?"

"It's about two male agents. One with section N and one with section F."

Anna looked slightly worried. "I'm not allowed to talk about other agents, and I only know about our own section F."

Sable shrugged this off. This was her chance. Anna was high in the SOE hierarchy.

"My friend Egbert Van Eijck trained with us at Alnor and was sent to Holland as an organizer last fall, but I was told the Germans have rolled up the entire Section N. Is that true?" Sable's eyes pleaded. She saw Anna think hard.

"It doesn't look good in Holland," she answered softly. "Nazi infiltrators created havoc among the agent networks, but I really know little about it. The country sections operate separately. I'll ask for you and let you know the day after tomorrow."

Egbert, Sable thought. Brave, wonderful Egbert would've been such a pal to her when she returned home to Alnor with a broken heart. But he'd left for Holland in a hurry, and now she'd probably never see him again. What had Wooly said? *Don't become too attached to other fighters. They may be dead the next day. Oh, Bill!*

"I hope your friend is still alive. I really do," Anna offered. "What was your other question, Sable?"

The Head of Operations clearly thought they'd spent enough time together and wanted to go.

"It's Freddie Frinton-Smith, codename Whiskey, I think he's with the LANTERN circuit in Clermont-Ferrand. He left in January. He's one of my best friends. Is there a chance I can meet up with him?"

"Freddie?" Anna's eyes lit up and a small smile curled her usually closed lips. "He's supposed to fly back to England in a week, so I'm afraid you'll miss him. You can leave a letter for him, and I'll make sure he gets it."

"That would be grand. Thank you. I'm done now."

Now it was Anna's time to linger, shifting her position but not leaving the red leather chair. Sable was already buttoning up her trench coat and adjusting the beret on her raven hair.

"Anything else?"

Anna slowly rose as well.

"I don't know if I should tell you this. It's probably not of any interest to you as you... uh... weren't very involved in what went on at Le Manoir except being in Madame Paul's good books and... uh... harassing the less popular girls."

"That's not true, Anna. Well... I may have been at the beginning, you know, when you and I fell out, but I definitely gave the Sphinx a piece of my mind before I left. Has she died, or something?"

"No. It's the chauffeur, whom you probably don't remember. Filippo Maltese. He was murdered."

Sable felt all the blood drain from her face and had to clasp two hands around the back of her seat. The red of her nails matched the red leather.

"Filippo," she stammered, "I really, really liked him. Oh my God, how do you know? What happened?"

"We read the French communist bulletins at Baker Street because —as you've been taught—many of the local resistance fighters are with Franc-Tireur, the communists. Filippo Maltese was a high-ranking Italian communist who'd fled Mussolini's Italy and worked with the resistance in the southeastern, Italian-occupied part of France, Monaco, and such. His work as the Le Manoir chauffeur was just a cover."

Sable's eyes widened. "Did the Sphinx know? She was a Nazi as far as I could read her."

Anna shared a small grin. "No, I don't assume she did. Filippo slipped away from his position after the school was closed on the outbreak of war at the beginning of September 1939."

"So, what happened? Do you know?"

Sable's mind was flooded with memories of two special car rides in the black Renault in the middle of winter and snow, with Filippo at the wheel. How cold and ill she'd been, and how the stocky Italian had turned out to be a mentor and a friend. Filippo had been as instrumental in the course her life had taken after he dropped her off at Lausanne Station as Operation Dynamo had been. She felt bad for never trying to get in touch with him. And now it was too late.

Anna continued. "The story in the bulletin was short and gave very few details. It really was more of an obituary. He was killed at the beginning of the war in Dunkirk. Even before the Brits were evacuated. The two things were unrelated, as far as I can tell. Filippo was shot by what was believed to be Italian black shirts. They'd been on his heels and had driven him first to Paris, where he had to disguise himself as a chauffeur once again."

"Dunkirk?" Sable interrupted. "How odd. Do you know the exact date of his assassination?"

Anna shook her head. "No. I just read the article with more than usual interest, not only because we'd known Mr. Maltese in a quite different role, but also because he apparently was dropping off an English girl who came to Le Manoir really late, in the summer of 1939. Lili Hamilton. She had communist sympathies herself and for a time was Leo Oppenheim's girlfriend, you know, the leader of the British Communist Party. Lili isn't part of SOE. I don't know what she was doing in Northern France, but circles around her Conservative MP father whisper she was smuggling Jewish diamonds from Antwerp to London. Well, I don't know why I'm telling you all this," Anna wrapped up, pushing her glasses up her nose and extending her hand to say goodbye.

"Oh, but it's vital you tell me all this, Anna. I had some great conversations with Mr. Maltese, not about communism but about fighting for your country. Do you know where I could find that English girl? I mean, not now, but perhaps when I come back from

France? She should tell me more about our friend. I really became very fond of our chauffeur-in-disguise in the end."

"I'll find Miss Hamilton's address for you, Sable. Her family is from Kent."

"I'd appreciate that."

THE CURTAINS in the sitting room were drawn. A cozy fire crackled in the background. Sable was seated on the mauve settee, smoking, thinking. She looked up when there was a knock on the door.

"Would you like your tea now, Miss Sable?" It was Elrod, now in his sixties, white-haired and more bent, but as subservient and precise as he'd been in all the decades of service in the Montgomery family. First father, now daughter. She sent him a warm smile. He and Minnie were so good to her and to the house.

Though she was always on the move, from Alnor to Beaulieu and now soon into France, they never asked questions, just held the fort.

"I'd love to, Elrod. Thank you. Just bring it in here. No use to heat the dining room. And please take the rest of the day off. I won't be needing anything else."

"Thank you, Miss. I will. And I'll ask Minnie to switch on the electric heater in your bedroom in an hour."

Sable nodded. Her mind was elsewhere. There were so many matters to consider before she put her life on the line in France. All the technicalities had been taken care of, but the emotional decisions still weighed heavily on her.

First there was Bill. The scar just wouldn't heal. She kept revisiting their last conversation, her refusal to trust in him. Why had she backed out? He'd been so open with her. Maybe sharing the loss of a child would have strengthened their bond instead of broken it?

Her hands itched to reach for the phone, hear that voice, be comforted before she was about to do the most dangerous thing she'd probably do in her entire life. If she died, she'd die with this stab in her heart. Was her pride worth it?

But then she'd see his naked back turned from her. He didn't want her anymore. But then why had he called twice, and she'd refused to talk to him?

"No!" she said firmly. "You've gone over this matter often enough. I can't take in another wound. I have to go as I am now and forget Bill. It's too late. He's at Lunna House; I'll soon be in Bordeaux."

And how hard she'd worked to be sent aboard. Stacking as many training courses as possible in as short a time as possible. Despite her haste, it had taken her almost a year, and all those months she'd managed not to run into him. She crammed her fingernails into her palms. No phone call! End of story.

As with a mantra, the words soothed her, covered the raw wound of her lost love with a soft protective layer. From there she could act. From there she could be strong again.

But there was one piece of the puzzle that kept nagging at her. She'd arranged with Solicitor Brown that Bill would be offered the rights to govern Alnor Castle if she died in the war. Maybe he didn't want it? Maybe he wouldn't understand despite the long explanatory letter that came with the offer?

In that letter, which had taken Sable months to craft, she revealed the truth of their breakup, the entire sordid truth, not leaving out the traumatic Caesarean delivery nor the shocking forced adoption of her daughter. And yes, she revealed that Joachim von Henkell was the unwanted father after he'd drugged and abused her.

She'd made Moses Brown swear on her father's King James Bible that he would only release that letter to the addressee if Sable's death was certain and verified by the War Office.

And yet, she still considered revising her will once again on the last day before her departure. Maybe she wanted to let bygones be bygones and offer Freddie custody over Alnor Castle?

But Sable had decided to leave Cavendish Square to the friend of her youth. The London house seemed more befitting his taste. He and David loved the city, whereas Bill loved the highlands.

And then there was Isabella. Sable's greatest agony. Isabella could never be found, no matter what Esther had told her about intelligence services. And certainly not after she, as her mother, was gone. There was no possibility of leaving her property to the blood of her blood. The Montgomery line would die with her.

"Let it rest, for God's sake! What does it all matter when you're dead and buried?" Sable lit another cigarette, hating her dillydallying and the loneliness that came with having no relatives with whom to discuss these important hurdles.

There was one more emotional piece of barbed wire that Sable had to hurt herself on. It couldn't be put off in the face of her own diminished life expectancy. Wooly's advice still ringed in her ears.

"Make a clean sweep before you go, sugar, and carry as little emotional burden as you can. It will enlarge your chances of survival, traveling light, so to speak. Take the days before you leave to make sure you have no unfinished business in your life. I don't want to scare you, but you have a fifty percent chance of coming back in one piece. I want to be the one to pin that MBE award on your lapel. Do you understand?"

She'd nodded, had done her best to clear all the cobwebs. There was just one left.

"Time to face it, Captain Sable Montgomery!"

Two years earlier, Flora Stacey had given her the letter from her mother addressed to her and sent to Alnor. Sable had never opened it. Now she would land not over fifty miles from Monaco and have a few days in Nice. Not that she felt a need to see her mother, but she had some questions for her. This was perhaps her last chance to find out what had happened to Isabella.

After Elrod had brought her tea, two slices of bread with cheddar cheese and a jam tart, Sable gazed at the envelope with her name written in her mother's flimsy handwriting. The ink had faded; the S in Sable was almost gone, which made it read 'able Montgomery'.

Turning the envelope in her hands, she studied the red seal with which it was closed. Frau Werner von Bissing. Somehow, that seemed so wrong. Who was this person? A total stranger to her. With swift fingers, she broke the seal and read the two-year-old letter.

·   ·   ·

Hôtel Hermitage Monte-Carlo, 25 March 1941

Sable,

I know you're not waiting for a letter from me. You've made clear you didn't want to stay in touch when you left home in January 1938, which—by the way—was without my permission. Since then, I haven't heard from you. Over three years!

I know it was you who changed your father's will and ended my lifelong lease on Alnor Castle. You were always more vengeful than Archibald. This sudden change forced me to marry Werner von Bissing because I had nowhere else to stay. As you may have understood from the staff, I moved to Monaco and the summers we spend in Wiesbaden.

The reason I'm writing to you is to let you know that I'm ill. I have thyroid cancer, but I'm treated by the best doctors, and I may still have years to live.

I don't expect you to come and visit me, but I'll give you my address, anyway.

Your Mother

P.S. Hôtel Hermitage Monte-Carlo
  Sq. Beaumarchais
  98000 Monaco
Sable folded the letter in four and stuck it back in the envelope,

then tucked it into her handbag. She sat still, very still for a long time, trained as she was to reflect on how she'd react to an attack from outside. There was no need to read the letter twice. The tone was obvious. Her mother felt victimized. She'd probably felt that way all her life. No emotion, no mention of love or a bond. Just accusations. The illness didn't bother Sable. Despite her unhealthy diet of cigarettes and champagne, so she'd keep her slim, flapper girl figure, Misty Fletcher was as strong as an ox.

But how to approach her? And how to get out of this cold, calculating woman the information she, Sable, wanted?

I'll cross that bridge when I get to it.

This was the only sensible path ahead. It would be a struggle, probably almost a physical one, but Sable was sure she'd get the name of the adoption center where her baby daughter had been taken.

EVEN IF IT'S *the last thing I do before I die!*

29

FRANCE

28 March 1943

I t was a chilly but clear morning in late March when the taxi pulled up in front of the dark-red door on Cavendish Square and Sable, white-faced and with lips thin as a line, descended the stone steps, wearing a neutral dark-brown women's suit of French making, and carrying a large valise with all her belongings.

Elrod, bent and looking crestfallen, stood in the doorway, waving goodbye with a white handkerchief. In a state of nerves, Minnie peered over his shoulder and shouted after her. "Enjoy your stay in Cornwall! 'ope the writin' of the book goes well."

"Do send us a postcard," Elrod chimed in.

"I will!"

One last wave through the back window of the black Austin, and she was off. Sable swallowed, feeling a traitor. At this stage of her trip, there was no need to tell the staff the truth, not here and not at Alnor. Anna would take the necessary steps should she get stranded in France. But Sable suspected her loyal staff had pieced two and two together and just played along for her sake. She'd been traipsing around the country in her FANY uniform for almost three years now;

Elrod and Minnie must have known their employer was involved in the Secret Service.

But no uniform now. Now she was Madame Jacqueline Brisse, a twenty-five-year-old war widow, who lived in an apartment in Suresnes, Paris, and had been an English tutor before the war. The documents to prove her new identity rested securely in her handbag, her real passport in a hidden compartment, to be stored in a French anonymous postal box.

Sable was as calm and prepared as she looked. This was the day she'd been waiting for since her return from Dunkirk, but certainly after the breakup with Bill. It had almost taken too long.

Now she couldn't wait to be in France, to experience what it was like to move around in an occupied country, where the presence of the enemy was real and not a phantom like here on the British Isles. How were the French holding out and how could she, with her long training in secret warfare, be useful to them and to her CHASSIS network?

Personally, Sable had felt no need to be waved off by Anna Adams, not particularly the last face she fancied to see on British soil, but from other F Section female agents who'd been dropped into France before, she'd drawn the conclusion this was the customary thing, and she couldn't wriggle out of it. Apparently, this was Anna's way of showing her closeness to the female agents she was responsible for.

They arrived at RAF Tangmere at the beginning of the afternoon. Little had been said in the car, which to Sable was as well. Relieved, she got out, stretched her legs and back and took in the smell of sea air and kerosene. It gave her a first taste of impending action. Small clouds were forming over the English Channel, looking as innocent as merino lambs.

Anna ushered Sable toward the hangar and into the shade, while the taxi driver dropped her luggage at her feet and took off in a cloud of dry dust.

"Let me introduce you to Flight Lt. John Murphy," Anna said in her clipped voice as a tall, middle-aged man in RAF overalls with ash-blonde whiskers and brows under his leather helmet strode their way. The camouflage paint on the Whitley Bomber, its three twin engines already droning, shone dimly in the full sun.

"The weather holding out, Lieutenant?" Anna asked, with Sable at her side. The tall pilot grinned, showing two rows of white teeth and lots of tiny wrinkles in a tanned face.

"Couldn't be better, Miss Adams. So, this is the new Joe?" With that, he shook Sable's hand, in a firm grip, and gave her a wink.

Lieutenant Murphy was clearly in an excellent mood, still grinning widely as he gave Sable a once-over. Then he refocused his attention on Anna.

"Flying over the English Channel will be a piece of cake. Forecast for the Gulf of Biscay is a bit rough, not just weather-wise. The Germans have intensified their targeting of British aircraft down to the coast from Bordeaux. I'll try to stay as far from the coast as possible and go down to Portugal before we cross the land. Don't worry, I'll keep the new miss safe, so at least you can't blame me for not putting her feet on solid soil."

Anna gave him a coy smile, almost flirtatious, which Sable had never seen before. There appeared to be a woman in Anna Adams, after all.

"I entrust my agent into your capable hands, Lieutenant."

At that moment a new taxi arrived, delivering the two male agents who were to accompany Sable on the March drop.

Anna also introduced Sable and Lieutenant Murphy to them, checking her clipboard. The first man was René Savy, a dark-haired, fine-boned Manchester lawyer, born in France, who was to join the SYLVESTER network in Vichy as a W/T, a wireless operator. Next to his rucksack, Rene was lugging around the heavy suitcase with his wireless set.

The second man, Sable recognized as the large-set Frenchman from Brest, Marcel Norman, who'd been with her at Beaulieu. He was to join the CHEVAL circuit in Rennes to train local resistance fighters.

"All three agents are to be dropped off at Gibraltar, and from there you'll take the same felucca to the south of France. Is that clear, everyone?" Anna said after a double check on her schedule. The three agents nodded.

"All righty. All aboard then." The pilot clapped his tanned hands.

"Anything else you need, Sable?" Anna turned to Sable, seemingly more forthcoming today with even an aura of restlessness in her manner. The dark eyes went all over the place and though she was not responsible for the male agents, she seemed to fuss over them as well.

"I'm fine. Just want to go now," Sable responded.

And then she understood. Anna hated being superfluous. She also had difficulty being the boss when people put their lives on the line, and *she* stayed behind, safely and cozily, in her apartment in London while her agents did the dirty work.

This was Anna's Achilles' heel but also a kind of self-torture. There was no reason for her to be here, to feel diminished, no longer necessary. Only employed to send out the fake postcards that the agents had written from places they weren't visiting before leaving and that Anna would regularly post to the ones who stayed behind.

No action for her, just dull office work.

The former finishing school students shook hands. There was a tremor in Anna's face. She cared. She did care.

"I'll be all right, Anna. I'll stay in touch."

These were Sable's last words on the relative safety of the British territory.

SAFELY BUT AFTER a long detour toward the Atlantic Ocean and therefore short of fuel, Flight Lt. John Murphy put his aircraft on the ground at the RAF North Front, a landing strip created in the Bay of Gibraltar. Sable's watch told her it was past ten in the night.

The pilot cheered, "She's been a good girl, right? Drank all of her lemonade."

Men and their transportation means! Sable thought not without

irony, recalling how the white-haired Captain Hancock also talked of
the MS Canterbury as if the ship was his mistress.

A LITTLE RED-NOSED and feeling cold, she peered down through the
small plane window, but apart from some landing lights, it was pitch-
black outside. She was tired, shaken, but knew this had probably
been the easiest part of the trip. The ten-day sea voyage with the
Seadog was a known nightmare among agents who'd been subjected
to it before and reappeared in England to tell the tale.

"Well, folks, that's all I could do for you!" The jolly lieutenant
saluted them. "I hope you all return to the motherland safely and
bring victory in your wake."

"*Vive La France*," the two French agents replied, with Sable
following suit.

"Long live the King!" the pilot replied, which she also repeated.

The three agents made their way to the harbor on foot. Marcel
was lagging, muttering French swear words under his breath at the
heavy load he was carrying. In the safety of the dark, Sable was grinning at his expanding vulgar arsenal, repeating them softly to herself.
Merde, Nom de Dieu, bordel, saloperie, These words could come in
useful, like many other French oddities she'd have to pick up to pass
off as *une vraie Française.*

"Come on, *mon vieux*, keep up the pace." René urged Marcel on.
"The Seadog is sailing in an hour. We're told to make headway during
the night when the Jerries are all tucked up in their beddies."

"Give me a hand then," Marcel panted. "This load weighs a man
down like a hod of mortar."

They arrived at the still and unlit ship softly swaying on its ropes
in the ink-black water. The Seadog was a majestic wooden sailing
ship, only used in the Mediterranean, and Sable was glad to notice it
looked adequately seaworthy.

It would be her first boat trip since the blood-and-thunder
journey aboard the MS Canterbury. The stillness of this ship in the
night compared to the chaos of screaming men, whizzing bullets,

booming cannons, and roaring planes in the blaring sunlight couldn't be bigger.

Yet Sable felt a strong repulsion to the waves that would keep her captive for the next ten days.

"It's this or nothing," she told herself, and with that, went up the gangplank after the men.

HÔTEL NICE EXCELSIOR, 10 April 1943

An exhausted and worn-to-a-frazzle Sable checked into the Excelsior Hotel on the Avenue Durante on a late Saturday afternoon and collapsed on her hotel bed to sleep for the next fourteen hours. She woke to a knock on the door and an anxious French female voice asking if she was awake.

"*Vous êtes-vous réveillée, madame?*"

Still half in her dream, Sable answered in English, "Yes, I'm coming!" Immediately scolding herself for her *bêtise,* hastily adding that she had overslept but was coming.

"*Merci beaucoup, je viens de suite.*"

This clumsiness was her first reminder to be constantly on the alert. While she dressed, she invented a story that she had been preparing an English lesson for one of her pupils and had accidentally answered the maid in English. Just in case questions were raised about her foreign behavior.

Sable rushed around the room, checking all her disguises were securely locked in her valise before she left. Standing in front of the gilded mirror in a flared, floral Schiaparelli dress she'd found hanging in tissue paper in her London closet, Sable gazed at herself for a long time. Underneath her white lace gloves, there were two identical wedding bands, hers and that of her deceased husband. On top of her raven-black hair, she'd planted a broad-rimmed burgundy velvet hat that matched the flowers in the fabric of her dress.

After years in either the FANY uniform or combat overalls, she hardly recognized herself. The woman who used to dress like this had been a debacle and a drunkard. How far had she'd come since these days? Now she was Captain Montgomery and this dress meant business, not seduction.

Never since had she dressed up, felt womanly... been beautiful. For, despite her tiredness and a terseness in her face, eyes on the qui vive, Sable had to admit she looked grand. Dressing up would help her on this difficult mission. She vowed that whenever circumstances permitted it, she would use her French couture dresses.

"Thank you, *Dadaigh*, for always giving me the opportunity to wear beautiful clothes." It felt only normal to think of her father at that moment.

Descending the carpeted staircase of the Excelsior Hotel on her way to the dining room, Sable saw guests turn their heads to gaze at her and she wondered if she'd made a second mistake. During all the trainings, the message had been, blend in, act like the locals, don't draw any attention to your person.

But this was Nice, and Nice was synonymous with elegance and luxury. At least it had been before the war, before the Italians had taken over command of the French Riviera. A place to show yourself and watch others show themselves. Was all the pre-war allure gone?

On entering the belle époque dining room, Sable heaved a breath of relief. She would have stood out in her simple brown traveling suit. Now she was just one of the elegant women trying to forget that only a hundred miles north, the Germans ruled the roost. In the Italian part of France there was a more relaxed atmosphere, and no matter that Mussolini wasn't exactly a nice guy, Il Duce had so far refused the German command to round up Jews, many of whom had found a haven on the Cote d'Azure. As long as it would last.

After a copious meal of veal steaks, green beans, and potatoes, followed by a dessert of crepe suzette, Sable ambled toward the post office to see if there was a message from her CHASSIS network.

The evening was cool but pleasant, and people were walking along the promenade in a leisurely manner. The climate, the language, the elegance, somehow revived her, and for the first time in many months she felt the scar on her heart might heal here.

As there was no message back, she decided to ring the hotel in Monaco and make the dreaded appointment with her mother.

Better have it over and done with, she thought, turning the curling wire of the telephone cord between her fingers as she waited for the phone to be picked up.

"*Reception de l'Hôtel Hermitage Monte-Carlo.*"

She explained to the receptionist that she was looking for Madame Werner von Bissing, a long-staying guest at the hotel.

"*Madame von Bissing? Un moment, s'il vous plaît.*"

Sable waited, taking one deep breath after the other, and when there was still no answer, she lit a cigarette. The receptionist at the Excelsior Hotel was eyeing her with suspicion. International phone calls were expensive these days.

"*Merci pour votre patience, Madame. Je suis vraiment desolée mais Madame Misty Fletcher est décédée.*"

Passed away? Using her own maiden name. How could that have happened? It felt as if the earth would swallow her. Out the window went her last opportunity to find Isabella's whereabouts. Vaguely, she was aware she'd also lost her last parent, but that seemed unimportant to her right now. Her child, her alive child, mattered, not her dead mother.

With the self-control of a trained agent, and because she was keenly aware of the Excelsior having eyes and ears, Sable replied in a level voice. "Merci beaucoup." She was just about to put the receiver down when the voice on the other end said.,

"I see a note attached to Madame Fletcher's file. It says that there was no return address to send her last belongings to. Are you a relative, by any chance?"

A tiny sparkle of hope sprang up in Sable's chest.

"Yes, I'm her daughter." This was tricky information to be giving in front of the listening Excelsior receptionist, but Sable felt she had no choice. "Could I come and pick it up? I'm currently in Nice?"

"À toute heure, Madame. The parcel will be waiting for you."

30

THE END OF MISTY FLETCHER

S able was in an incredible hurry with her head in a spin. Although it was only a thirty-mile drive to Monte Carlo, and she wouldn't have to venture outside Italian-occupied territory, she had to travel with her legitimate passport so she could prove her identity at the Hermitage Hotel as her mother's daughter.

Les Corniches, as the coastal road was called, was a tricky and dangerous route even outside wartime. Now, the Cliff Roads were heavily guarded with road blocks every two kilometers and menacing gray warships bobbing in the Mediterranean Sea at close distance, their cannons directed landward.

But Sable's greatest worry was that she was on duty for the SOE and therefore could be called up at any moment to board a train to Bordeaux. What if she messed up on her first mission? It would be the end of her career with the Secret Service.

The ambivalence of cutting out a couple of hours of her time for personal affairs niggled at her. Yet Sable felt she had to take this one chance, not to collect her mother's belongings, about which she couldn't care less, but to dash for that one last hope to find out more about Isabella.

"I'll be a better agent as a result," she promised herself, remembering how Wooly ... and even Bill ... had urged her to purge her demons.

She swallowed the exorbitant sum of one hundred francs, which the French taxi driver demanded upfront to take her to Monaco and back. Another brief prayer went up. She couldn't spend SOE pocket money on private affairs.

"Thank you, Dadaigh, for leaving me well off."

Thinking of her father in the back of the French taxi meandering along the breathtaking cliff road, with its steep ravines and narrow passes, Sable pondered if her father would've been the only one to approve of her personal mission. If only he'd known what had really happened to her. That he was a grandfather. That his blood lived on through his Bhobain.

As the taxi pulled up at the Square Beaumarchais, Sable eyed the exorbitant l'Hotel Hermitage Monte-Carlo with mounting disbelief. Her own Hotel Excelsior in Nice wasn't a poor example of belle époque architecture itself, but paled into insignificance compared to this white-stuccoed giant from the hand of architect Nicolas Marquet and Gustave Eiffel. Overlooking Monaco harbor and the shimmering Mediterranean, yes, she could perfectly understand how her peacocky mother would fall for such grandeur. And die in it as a fit place for a flapper girl.

Sable instructed the grumpy taxi driver to wait for her.

"I'll be back as fast as I can."

"Remember curfew starts at eight."

"I will."

She rushed into the lobby that looked more like a palace than a hotel and sped to the marble reception desk. Luck was on her side. When she introduced herself, the receptionist smiled at her.

"Oh, I had you on the phone an hour ago. Let me get your mother's... pardon... your late mother's belongings."

The dark curly haired receptionist rang a bell and summoned the doorman to collect Madame Fletcher's suitcase from the storage.

It arrived, and Sable immediately recognized it. An old-fashioned yellow leather suitcase with brown leather straps, embossed with gold-metal triangles at every corner and decorated with her mother's name when still married to the Baron of Alnor, Countess Misty Montgomery, Baroness of Alnor. Certainly, her mother's most prestigious marriage in her multi-married life.

On examining the suitcase she'd unconsciously seen so often as a child, Sable's legs felt wobbly, but she kept her back straight and her eyes dry. *Just handle this, Captain Montgomery!*

To her surprise, the bulky suitcase wasn't heavy, but its size would pose a difficulty lugging it around on her secret missions. That was a problem she'd figure out after her return to Nice. Thanking the friendly receptionist, she had one more question for her.

"Do you have any idea where my mother was interred?"

"As a matter of fact, I do. It was quite a problem at the time, as Madame had died in her room, but we couldn't get hold of any direct family at first. You know, with the war going on. So, the hotel's manager Monsieur La Planche decided she'd be buried at La Colle. Later, we managed to get in touch with your mother's ex-husband, Herr von Bissing, when he paid us another visit. He kindly settled her outstanding bill for the hotel and for the funeral. Would you like Herr von Bissing's address for further information?"

The receptionist looked a little lost, clearly understanding from the name on the suitcase and Sable's passport that Von Bissing was not her father.

"No, thank you. No need. But I do what to thank you for all you've done for my mother and ..." Sable quickly scribbled her signature on another check. "Just treat the staff to something nice from me and please thank Monsieur La Planche. You've been nothing but kind to me, Mademoiselle Bernard."

A bewildered Sable descended the marble steps of the grand hotel, hauling the monstrous valise with her. There was so much to digest, first and foremost that her mother had even managed to divorce husband number six. And she'd probably died as penniless as she was born. *Pauvre Maman,* she thought in her new language. It somehow sounded less painful than "poor Mommie."

The taxi driver got even grumpier when he had to fit the large suitcase into the trunk of his gleaming automobile without scratching the lacquer. And then she ordered him to stop at a flower shop to give his demanding customer the time to select a bouquet and then drive up to the Monaco graveyard.

He growled, "That will be fifty francs extra!"

"Fine!" Sable snapped, as she darted out of the car to find her mother's simple grave without a headstone. Just a small plate.

Misty Fletcher

Born London 2 April, 1900

Died Monte Carlo 2 April, 1942

Died on her 42nd birthday. Alone, friendless, and cheerless. Sable felt no tears, no anger, nothing.

She arranged the flowers over the gravel near her mother's name plate. Took a step back and said a last goodbye to a person who'd always been a stranger to her. No fond memories. A mother who'd taken away from her own daughter the possibility of being a mother.

"Bye, mother. May God protect you!"

It was ten in the evening when Sable returned to the Excelsior Hotel —after curfew, but no one seemed to care much about this in Nice. The post office was closed and there was no note for her. She hauled the bulky suitcase up in the elevator herself and dragged it to her room.

"No thoughts and no dilly dallying," she told herself, as she unbuckled the leather straps and clicked open the valise.

Most of its content were her mother's clothes, underwear, and shoes, all rather worn out and stained. Nothing that Sable wanted to keep. No jewelry, not even a wedding ring, which pointed to her mother having pawned everything of value. Probably to pay for her medical bills.

Sable almost gave up. There was nothing of worth here and nothing personal until, at the very bottom of the valise, she found a black case that was locked. No key.

"This is where my training comes in handy!" she said aloud as she took a hairpin from her hair and, with a little wriggling, the lock sprang open.

Her mother's English passport, a couple of letters and postcards from people she didn't know, and then, Sable gasped, a file with a photo of a baby pinned to it. The baby's face was hardly visible under the frilly bonnet, but Sable would have recognized her from a million babies. Her heart cried out, her child, her bonnie lass. Forcing herself to stop staring at the days' old child, she glanced at the file.

Unnamed girl, born 25 December 1937, 11.55 am, weight 6 pounds, length 20 in, healthy.

Out of wedlock

Mother: Sable Montgomery, underage

Father: Unknown

Place of birth: The Elsie Inglis Memorial Maternity Hospital, Edinburgh

Giving up for adoption on 28 December 1937
    Adoptive parents: Mr and Mrs Daniel Carter, 15 Queen Victoria Street WW2, London.

SABLE STARED at the document and then from the document to the photo. Kissed it cautiously, stared at her daughter again. Unable to let go of the file, of the photo.

It finally, finally sunk in that she, Sable, hadn't made this baby up. The birth had really happened. She hadn't dreamed it. Somehow, she'd become more and more afraid that it had all been a hallucination, that she had given up Bill for a baby she'd imagined. There was no other proof then...

Of course, there was the caesarean, but everything had been so muddled in her brain from the moment she was drugged and abused to that dark, gloomy time in her father's library at Alnor when Freddie had come to save her.

Here she had her definitive answer. Now it was time to store reality away for the duration of the war.

The photo of her daughter went in her wallet, but the documents she hid in the secret stitched-in double layer of her rucksack.

SABLE WAS NOW ready as a primed cannon to be transformed in Madame Jacqueline Brisse, Code Name Raven.

LADY SABLE MONTGOMERY was no more.

31

CODE NAME RAVEN

"**P**hone call for Madame Brisse, phone call for Madame Brisse!" The junior receptionist entered the breakfast room in a trot, shouting her name as he went along the tables. Sable got up, her serviette slipping to the floor, as she jogged after the young man to the lobby. This was it. This was what she'd been waiting for. Her call to action.

"Madame Brisse ici. Here!" It was almost breathless; she was so excited.

"*Venez certainement visiter*," a male voice said rapidly. Then *click,* and the connection was broken.

Do come by all means. The message wasn't good. This was the agreed code meaning the opposite. Danger. Betrayal or arrests. Her network might have been destroyed. What now?

As Sable slowly made her way back to the breakfast room and finished her lukewarm coffee, she debated with herself. Going to Bordeaux might be suicide, but she needed to get information on her CHASSIS network to find out if repairs could still be made. And if not, London needed to know.

"Lyon!" she decided. "I'll travel to Lyon first. Our agents are always passing through there. I'll certainly be able to connect with one of them and see if anyone knows what happened."

LYON WAS MUCH BIGGER and more chaotic than Sable had expected, a labyrinth-like network of interconnecting passages through and between buildings, which the French called *traboules*. Her eye, trained for Secret Service, immediately understood how invaluable such a city plan was to a resistance movement. A confusing layout was also a perfect hiding place. Sable liked this city, or rather Madame Brisse did. She felt unnoticed, independent, strong.

Walking from the local train station, she studied every important building and street name, ingraining the map in her mind. She recognized the Hôtel Terminus, where, since the German occupation of the French Free Zone in November 1942, the Gestapo Headquarters was housed. Headed by Klaus Barbie. Not a man to come face-to-face with.

There was one trail Sable wanted to follow. She'd heard of a small café on the Quai Perrache where she might get the sign out that she was an agent in need of a safe house or a hotel. Walking up and down Quai Perrache, where men and women sat at outdoor cafes, drinking Pastis or a café crème as if there was no war, Sable scanned all the faces. And there was her luck.

She recognized the brave and fierce redhead, Maureen Knight, code name Adèle, posing as an Irish journalist married to a French newspaper owner. They'd only briefly crossed paths when Maureen had arrived at Beaulieu to be trained as the first female SOE agent. As far as Sable had heard, she'd done exceedingly well and had been in France for over a year now.

Maureen was talking with a dark-haired man in a khaki turtleneck and brown corduroy pants who could well be an agent too in a bar called Perrache Charlemagne, which supposedly was the meeting place Sable had heard talked about.

Maureen was laughing, the mint-green eyes squinting, at something the man was telling her and though she looked relaxed, Sable uncovered the woman's meticulous scanning of the surroundings around her and the bags under her too bright eyes that signaled she was taking the Benzedrine pills to keep awake and alert. Too thin and wearing a thick cardigan despite the mild weather, sure signals life had been tough on the Irish agent.

Sable sat down some tables away from them, facing Maureen. Her plan worked. Maureen kept engaging in the talk with the dark-haired Frenchman but made a V-sign to show recognition. As she rounded off her conversation and got up, Sable quickly paid for her coffee and, walking behind Maureen, followed her at a distance through a criss-cross of streets until they came to the Grand Nouvel Hotel in the center of Lyon.

As they arrived at the entrance, Maureen amicably put her arm through Sable's and, shouting a merry *"Bonjour Philippe, j'ai une copine avec moi,"* ushered her new friend to the elevator, to the third floor, quickly opened one of the identical doors with her latchkey and closed it firmly behind them. Maureen did not let a moment pass.

"What's your cover name?"

"Madame Jacqueline Brisse."

"Good. Mine is Madame Marcelle Gautier. We only use Jacqueline and Marcelle. Understood? All the other names that circulate are our cover names or code names."

Sable nodded, though she felt the tone of the more experienced agent a little overbearing.

"Do you know anything about the CHASSIS circuit? I got a disturbing phone call this morning when I was still in Nice. That's why I decided to come here."

"Yes, wise thing to come here to Lyon. We're the hub for the south and middle part of the country, as Paris is for the north half. Things aren't looking well in Bordeaux, but we don't know exactly what happened. There are rumors that Henri de Bonheur's W/T operator Philippe Arnault was arrested last week and that Henri himself went into hiding. The man I was talking to in our meeting place, Claude Bardet, who's part of the CEREBRAL circuit near Clermont-Ferrand, told me about it. I guess you were to be a courier to Henri?"

"Yes, that was the plan."

"So, this is what I suggest," Maureen continued in her rapid Irish lilt. "You travel to Bordeaux to take stock. As you've just arrived in France and haven't been in touch with any of the networks yet, the Germans won't be on your trail. You can still maneuver a little freer than most of us. What do you think?"

"My idea too," Sable agreed, "I just wanted to be sure I was doing the right thing."

"Clear thinking. I am, or actually I was, part of the PROFESSION network here in Lyon, but I'm moving south to Perpignan tomorrow. Barbie's breath is a little too hot on my neck to stay here any longer." Maureen offered her a cigarette and took one herself. The women smoked in silence for a while.

"My notoriety with the Gestapo means it's the last time we can meet, Jacqueline. You don't want me to put them on your trail. I'll try to stick it out south for a while, but if they're still sure they want to catch 'the Red Fury' as they've labeled me, I'll cross into Spain and get back to England. As soon as I hook up with a W/T, I'll notify London that you're here and doing field research. You should do the same, but be careful which operator you use. Send a message to London as soon as you find out what happened to CHASSIS."

"I will. And thanks again for showing me how to use my own brain to get around here." Sable felt she had already learned more in the half hour she'd spent in Maureen's presence than during all the Beaulieu theory lessons about secret movements in enemy territory.

Then she added, "Do you know a place where I can stay tonight? I left my luggage in a locker at the station, as I didn't want to draw any attention to myself."

"I'll arrange a room for you here at the Grand Nouvel Hotel. The owners support the cause. They'll drive you to the station to collect your luggage. Then we'll get you the necessary permits, passes and ration cards. After that I'm gone, and remember, you never met Madame Marchelle Gautier, code name Adèle, nor heard of me. Understood?"

"Understood" seemed Maureen's top favorite word, and the hurry and commanding tone in which she spread around her instructions chafed Sable's own rulership personality. Maybe it was a good thing that the old captain was abandoning the ship.

"Promised. And thanks for everything, Marcelle. I'm glad I ran into you." Sable's voice was sincere, despite the friction she felt. On the scale of dislike of women, Anna still scored lower than Maureen. It all depended on guts.

"Always a pleasure to help a novice," Maureen remarked. Then she took a long moment to scrutinize Sable, as if she was reading her between the lines. "One more thing, if you find the CHASSIS network is beyond repair, return to Lyon. You can fill in for me."

"Sure, but who would I contact?" Sable liked the idea, more than going to Bordeaux. Lyon seemed her place. Maureen fixed her with her Celtic green eyes.

"No one in particular. I'll leave a message here at the hotel, or at Perrache Charlemagne. And always stay clear of a man by the name of Jacques Déricourt. He's a double agent operating here in Lyon. Suave and social, but a rat."

As there was no direct train from Lyon to Bordeaux, Sable had to travel the circumspect way of going some 500 miles via the northern part of the Massif Central. A hazardous journey that, with the many stops on the way, was going to take her two days aboard the rambling, drafty SNCF trains, the French railroad company.

There were uncountable screeching stops and stuttering starts, loud German voices and stamping boots through the gangway, not only at stations but sometimes in the middle of a cornfield, and unreliable timetables that made her miss connections.

Inconspicuous and unpretentious, this time in her brown traveling suit, hatless and without makeup, Sable mingled amidst the local French, who were traveling in silent communion with heads bowed down to their knees. The noise only rose from the random cackling cock in a farmer's wife's cage and the rowdy German officers who ruled the roost.

Their favorite sport seemed to be harassing young girls traveling alone or in pairs until their cheeks turned red and they didn't know where to look for safety, their lips pressed, their eyes huge with fear. It angered Sable to the bone.

She was prepared for this unwanted treatment and determined to escape the Germans' attention at all costs. Hiding behind thick, fake spectacles that would've befitted Anna, her long dark hair in a modest bun and her nose in Proust's *À la Recherche du Temps Perdu*, Sable pretended to read but all her senses were on high alert. The Frenchmen's famous 1913 novel, *In Search of Lost Times*, was a secret sign among agents to connect.

Her secret code worked. As the train left Clermont-Ferrand for Limoges, a young, spindly man with thin black hair combed backwards and a yellowish complexion, sporting an ill-fitting, pre-war costume, seated himself across the corridor from her and disappeared behind one of the few authorized French newspapers in Vichy France, Le Figaro.

Sable deliberated with herself, but decided she'd take the risk. Any information about networks in this part of France might help her get a clearer view. She'd take the next train to Périgieux as soon as possible.

Descending the Limoges train station with a smaller suitcase and slipping through the German checkpoint without further trouble, she walked straight to the front of the station, sat down on her valise, and took out a Gitane. After five years of daily Craven As, she found the French cigarettes *déguelasse*, disgusting, but it was the price Jacqueline Brisse had to pay. Before she could light it, she heard,

"*Pardon, vous avez du feu?*"

Another code sentence at which she followed the gangly man away from the station, still without speaking a word, and into a narrow street where he rapped three times with his knuckles on an old wooden door.

A female voice from inside requested their code names.

"Antoine."

"Raven."

The door was held ajar, and they slipped through to enter a low-ceilinged office room with several typewriters, a simple printing press, and a stack of folders on a table. A man came out of the shadows at the back and quickly threw the papers into a burlap sack.

"Follow me, Raven." The man code-named Antoine preceded her to a small office space next to the press office. Just a table, four dissimilar chairs, an overflowing, smoldering ashtray, and the smell of ink, Gauloises and lack of air.

"Sit here, please." He dropped more folders from a chair and took another chair at the other side of the table. "I'd hoped to run into you."

"What's your cover name?" Sable couldn't place the Frenchman.

"I am Henri de Bonheur."

Sable thought her eyes would pop out of their sockets. "But I was told your code name was Joseph?"

"Big deal!" Henri sounded irritated. "Sometimes you have to change your identity before London knows. It's confusing, but for your own safety."

Sable still wasn't convinced the man was speaking the truth.

"So, who am I, according to you?"

"Don't play these games with me, Miss Brisse. You were supposed to join my CHASSIS network, as you damn well know, but my best operator, Arnault, got caught and is God-knows-where. And now I've got those German idiots on my heels as well. Can't stay here long. There's nothing for you in Bordeaux. The network is burnt, twenty arrests in one week. I have to flee the Pyrenees myself if I am to make it out in one piece."

Sable thought of Maureen's offer to go back to Lyon, and she was tempted, but something flickered in her, a tiny voice that told her to go to Bordeaux first. She doubted if she'd share her thoughts with De Bonheur.

"What about the armament drops that are scheduled for mid-May in the Bordeaux area? Someone must be there, or has London canceled?"

Bonheur was starting to lose his patience with her. "Without a W/T, I couldn't bloody well let them know, could I?"

Sable lit another cigarette, though the air was so dense she started coughing.

"Did the Germans confiscate Arnault's wireless?"

"Woman, you're working on my nerves. I told you what I know and that you shouldn't go near the area. Just trying to help."

The more De Bonheur became aggrieved, the calmer Sable became and the surer she had to see what could be solved. On a silk lining inside her coat, she had the coordinates of the place where the armament would be dropped. If only she could get hold of a wireless herself or an operator to inform Baker Street.

Resolute, she got up from her chair, inwardly thankful she didn't have to work with this disagreeable fellow.

"Thanks for the information and the advice. I wish you luck."

"Where are you going?" De Bonheur also raised from his chair, looking at her suspiciously.

"As you told me, back to Lyon."

"All right. Take care."

They didn't even shake hands.

WHEN SHE WAS BACK on the train, which was first chugging toward Périgieux and then onwards to Libourne with the final destination Bordeaux, Sable tormented herself over her rash decision to operate completely on her own. No network, no wireless, no organizer, just her maps, her common sense, and her steely reserve not to leave the British pilots and the French reception team on their own, or they'd most certainly fall into the hands of the Germans.

Whether or not De Bonheur was a traitor was not important right now.

32

THE PAPILLON NETWORK

Two weeks later

Sable was cycling from the Lefort farm along the vineyards of the Haute Médoc toward Lesparre-Médoc, where she had stored her wireless set in a cabin in the fields behind Château Escot.

The breezy wind played with her long hair, waving it hither and thither as at one time the wind was blowing from the Atlantic and the next moment from the majestic Gironne river on her left. The bicycle was an old, rackety thing without gears, which made it heavy to peddle forward, and Sable wasn't an experienced cyclist. Determined to show her grit, she'd mastered the rusty two-wheeler that had proved to be a slow but reliable means of transport.

Her hosts were the farmer Jean Lefort and his wife Christine, who ran both a sizable vineyard and a considerable resistance network. They'd met on the Saturday market in Lesparre-Medoc and the signals had worked also here. The couple had hidden Philippe Arnault's wireless when he was captured during one of his rare visits to Bordeaux.

Sable had found the CHASSIS network broken but not destroyed and she'd worked hard and diligently to repair whatever she could. There were no other British trained agents but plenty of French resistance fighters, mostly from the Maquis. The weakest link was the transmissions to London, as Sable had never been adept at coding and wasn't trained as a W/T.

Desperate times call for desperate means and she'd managed to let Baker Street know what had happened to Henri and Philippe and that she was in great need of a new pianist, as the W/T operators were called, and new crystals for the set. And at least one courier who could travel the country for her.

That she was going to lead the network, now renamed PAPILLON, for as long as it was safe enough to stay in one place, was clear to her. Her plan was to set up the new network and then return to Lyon.

Yet Sable knew all the signs pointed to her running out of time. The hefty thirty-pound Type 3 Mark II set had to be transported to a new place every day, and she knew the German Radio Intelligence was on her heels. Every time she attached the seventy-foot flexible aerial to a rooftop or in a field, she shuddered at the idea this would be the last time. Her clumsiness at tapping the keys also made the transmission last way too long, which exacerbated the danger.

But today might be a good day. She was to hear if the drop was going to take place tonight. Hopefully, all her wishes would be granted and PAPILLON would carry the day.

Sable was impatiently waiting for her message—*The life that I have is all that I have*—to transmit, to see if the plan tonight would go through as planned. She sat still as if spellbound, every nerve in her body ready to jump while her blue gaze scanned the only road that led to the ruin, her ears pricked up for sounds and her nostrils for a change in smell.

It was a still morning. A church bell rang nine in the distance; a humming bee buzzed by; to her right, the vague crashing of the waves. No sound of war or Germans, though they were everywhere, also around her.

The all-clear message came back: *And the life that I have is yours.*

As fast as she could, Sable closed off with her own code and the safety code before quickly dismantling the set. Just as she was about to haul it onto the back of her bike, covered as a potato sack, she saw a dust cloud come up the trail.

A German patrol. She'd been on the air too long, or the Funkabwehr had been too close. Either way, there was no saving her precious potatoes. Leaving the case where it lay in the grass, grabbing only her code book, Sable jumped on her bike and cycled as fast as she could in between the rows of vines that were sprouting tiny green leaves and gave little cover.

She'd studied the terrain intensively and had spotted the slow-moving Armorara in time, a gray-green solid van with an antenna looking like a many-sided kite on its roof.

When she was certain she'd shaken off her followers, having found cover in a dry ditch, she contemplated her next step. It didn't worry or frighten Sable that the Germans were on her trail; it only made her more vigilant and careful. She had her Welrod 7.65mm silent sleeve gun and her L pill, filled with arsenicum, neither of which she hoped she'd have to use soon.

There was no going back to the Lefort farm. Peering over the edge, she waited until the German Radio Defense Corps was well out of sight before yanking the heavy bike back on the trail again. Tempted to return to the ruin to see if her wireless set was still there, Sable argued against it. What if the Germans expected that and returned? Better cycle the other way and ask one of the French fighters to collect it under cover of night.

Ten minutes later, Sable was on her bike again, peddling toward a safe house owned by an elderly doctor's widow in the small village of Renard, knocking on Mme Marie Dandicolle's backdoor.

"Come in, come in." The tiny woman dressed in reverend black, her hair pinned up under a white bonnet, ushered Sable into her spacious living room. It had closed, top-to-floor gauze curtains in front of the three bay windows, but still gave an excellent view to both sides of the main street. Marie Dandicolle moved around restlessly, casting quick glances Sable's way, partly maternal, partly anxious.

"I've been expecting you, Jacqueline. I need to warn you. The Milice were asking after you in Madame Pousse's bar the other day. They kept asking everyone to keep out an eye on 'Le Corbeau Noir.' Apparently, they've dubbed you The Black Raven. You must be careful, ma chérie!"

"I know," Sable acknowledged, as she watched Madame Dandicolle's busy hands pour her a cup of coffee. She was dying for a cigarette, but the doctor's wife was strictly anti-smoking.

Flopping down in one of the sumptuous fauteuils, she was overcome with a deep longing to close her eyes and take a nap. Somehow being in the presence of Marie Dandicolle made her want to let down her guard, if even for a brief time, but she forced herself to stay awake. She'd take a Benzedrine pill later, as the night ahead would be long.

With a deep sigh, enjoying the black drink, she said to the straight-up widow now sitting vigilantly at her window, "My network is just growing, Marie. I can't let my group down now. It would collapse again like the CHASSIS network did."

"Pah!" The tiny woman waved an angry hand. "I never trusted that Henri de Bonheur. I think he works for the Germans."

Marie diverted her outside gaze to look straight at Sable, the beady black eyes hard, vexed. At first, Sable was taken aback at the open accusation *la petite Française* launched at one of the SOE trained agents. London had trusted Henri de Bonheur as an organizer, leading an important network for the whole Bordeaux region. Yet she recalled her own misgivings about the spindly, ill-dressed man.

"You think so?"

"I'm sure. He just let that wonderful Philippe Arnault, a boy from this region, the son of the Gaillan pharmacist, walk into a Gestapo trap. I tell you, De Bonheur is an eel. Steer clear of him."

Sable looked doubtful. If what Marie said was true, she needed to warn Baker Street as quickly as possible. But how? She couldn't go near her wireless set right now. She'd have to wait for her new operator, who hopefully was part of the mission that would arrive that very night.

IT WAS A MOONLESS NIGHT. Cold and dewy despite it being mid-May, no wind. A perfect night for a drop. Sable was hiding in the shrubbery around the makeshift airfield where two airplanes were expected, one with supplies and one with agents. Fifteen of her men and women were at equal distance from her, dispersed around the field. Two of them, local French girls, with code names Marianne and Delphine, were at her side, ready to flip on their battery-operating flashlights the moment the roaring of the planes came close enough.

Though this wasn't Sable's first drop and the responsibility that came with such a night-time event was never a picnic, she was shaking in her combat boots as she squatted next to the girls. Her ears were alert as the birds in springtime, ready to whistle the "withdraw" tune at any sign of German approach.

Marie Dandicolle's words were still fresh on her mind and all day, wherever she went, she bumped into German officers that appeared like machinations on her path. Had they followed her here? She'd even considered diverting to another reception field, but it was impossible to notify London at such a late moment.

"You hear anything?" she whispered to Marianne for the second time.

"Not yet." The same answer. The night was still but for the rustle of the leaves in the treetops and the sound of the ocean in the distance. The scuffling of a wood mouse scurrying past sent Sable's heart to her throat, and she almost jumped up in fright as the tiny animal disappeared again in the undergrowth. *Stop being so tense, or you'll make mistakes*, she scolded herself, concentrating again on the sound of plane engines.

She panted with relief when a dark silhouetted plane came into sight and the girls flashed on their lights.

Thud, thud, thud.

Three loads of small parachutes landed on the soft grass and shadows appeared from the bushes to unhook the parachutes, store them away and carry the heavy crates back to the bushes from where they would be gathered and taken to Lefort's farm. That part organized, Sable strained her ears for the sound of the next plane, inwardly crying, *Come on, hurry!*

Any minute longer was a danger, and she prayed the Maquis fighters could bring their loot to safety. That part was beyond her control.

She needed the new agents more than anything. Working with the local French, arming them, and helping them organize themselves for the liberation of their country was all great and honorable, but the exclusive burden on her shoulders was too heavy. Especially as the Germans might be closing in on her and she might bring the entire new network down.

"I hear something, Jacqueline," whispered Marianne, who had excellent hearing. Sable listened again. Yes, there it was, unmistakably the soft roar of a Lysander. Her heart jumped up in relief. *Now let it all go according to plan. Please, God!* She prayed, not knowing where the sudden religious stint came from, but attributing it to her extreme strain.

Another dark silhouette of a plane dove and took off again, disappearing before the three parachutes had even touched the ground. *Hurray!*

The remaining reception party crawled closer, helped to press together the parachutes, and accompanied the three dark-clad agents to the relative safety of the woods. Sable was at their side in a jiffy. She couldn't see the agents, so used their pre-agreed code sentence.

"*Mary had a little lamb.*"

The first agent answered, "*Itz fleece waz white az snow.* George Dumont, code name Hector." Correct English, French accent. Good.

The second agent answered with a high French voice, "*And ev'rywher zat Marie went.* Bernadette Mulsant, code name Lucienne." Sable rejoiced at having a female agent, someone to talk with about other stuff than just ammunition and cleaning revolvers.

The third agent answered, "*The lamb was sure to go.* Maurice Suttill, code name Whis..."

Sable would have recognized the voice out of thousands even in the dark.

"Freddie!"

"Sabbo!"

They hugged, forgot for a moment their cover, who they were and where they were. Tears streamed down Sable's face as she clung to her friend. He smelled like Freddie, Dior Homme, and English leather.

"Now, I'll be all right," she kept repeating as the French fighters urged them to go back into their roles and start moving.

"I volunteered for this mission," Freddie told her in a low voice as they made their way on the footpath through the woods, preceded by the French who knew the way as no other. "When Anna told me what you were trying to accomplish here in Bordeaux, I couldn't let you do it on your own."

Sable whispered back, "But I was told you'd just finished a mission in Clermont-Ferrand and were on leave for a while."

"I was, and I really wanted to stay with David, who's still struggling with his health but what choice did I have, huh? My Raven, here in danger on her own, or David safely propped up in a revalidation pension in Oxford?"

She squeezed his hand. "I couldn't be happier. What a lonely job this is!"

"Not anymore, Madame Brisse," Freddie chuckled, "and George is the best W/T in the business. He loves playing his piano like nothing else."

George grumbled an affirmation in the dark.

"Chut..." The Frenchman upfront hushed them, and Sable had to agree with him. They were being reckless even at whisper level. Every sound, a voice, the snap of a twig, could give them away.

With difficulty, they held their tongue until they came to an abandoned barn where Sable had arranged for them to spend the night. She couldn't wait to hear all Freddie's stories, and she also had so much to share with him. It had been over two years since they parted. It seemed like a lifetime.

Unable to light a fire for illumination and warmth, they sat in a circle, close so they could continue their conversation in a whisper. Marianne and Delphine kept watch at the door.

Sable huddled near to Freddie, glad as spring's earliest rose that he'd taken the pains to come and support her. Gladness and gratitude. She felt a strength return to her she hadn't found since... since she was with Bill.

The female agent had not spoken yet, apart from giving her name and the code sentence, so despite her longing for a talk with Freddie, as the organizer Sable addressed the slight silhouette sitting across from her in the dusk.

"Are you all right, Bernadette?"

"I will be, zank you. I am Phillipe Arnault's sister. I am also 'ere to find out what 'appened to 'im."

"Oh my," Sable whispered back. "So, you're from the region? That will be mighty helpful. Of course, we'll help you any way we can. I've tried my best, and there is a possibility he managed to escape and took the route over the Pyrenees into Spain. My contacts have been asking at all the prisons, but only had a lot of no answers."

"London iz trying to find out if 'Enri Bon'eur iz a traitor," she said in her lilting French voice.

That was good to hear. Doubt about the man's reliability had trickled over to London. Then she could let it rest now.

"That's why I set up the new PAPILLON network," Sable explained. "CHASSIS is no more. Whether De Bonheur is a traitor, time will tell, but he has no access to my team anymore."

"Three cheers for Madame Jacqueline Brisse!" Freddie hoorayed. "I'm so incredibly proud of you!"

He kissed her on the cheek.

33

BOUND BY BLOOD

"We have to take one day off! Just to talk and laugh and eat!" Sable was lying on her stomach on a bed in Hotel La Poste in Saint-Trélody, smoking a deliciously fragrant Craven A that Freddie had smuggled for her from England. She felt safe, at least for now, knowing the owners of La Poste would give them a signal to flee through the ground-floor window, if necessary.

"I agree." Freddie was sitting in the open windowsill, one leg drawn in, the other dangling outside, a glass of Pastiche in one hand, a cigarette in the other. A long lock of silky black hair fell over one bright-blue eye. He was clad in an expensive French summer costume, but his feet were bare.

How she loved his fine elegance, that well-bred, stuck-up type of Britishness. She'd not realized how much she missed home, thinking she was adapting well amid the loud-spoken, wildly gesticulating Frenchmen. *I'm a featherhead for the Fatherland*, she thought, already falling back in their alliteration game. She didn't say it aloud, though. Too many emotions would leave her weak.

"Tell me, how's David? I'm so glad you guys are still together."

"Oh, I'll tell you all about us in a couple of shakes, old girl. Not much blew in for us, except for David's creepingly slow convalescence, which he finds hard to square up to, especially with me flying hither and thither and being a hero avant la lettre. David wants a piece of the pudding as well." Freddie turned his gaze from studying the massive trunks of pine trees outside the window to Sable on the bed.

"But tell me about you. I barreled into William Mitchell when I was relocating some Norwegian commandos from the Shetlands to Beaulieu. Only then found out that you guys had severed ties. Slap in the face, that was. You never told me. Bill was also not very communicative about it. What happened?"

The mentioning of Bill's name sent such a shot of pain through Sable's body that she curled up in a ball as if hit in the stomach. Freddie was by her side in two steps, putting his arm around the rolled-up figure on the bed.

"Oh my, that bad, huh? Tell me, old girl. You know you can trust your Freddo."

To her surprise Sable started crying, first softly and then louder, her body shaking all over. Freddie patted her back, mumbling repetitively, "There, there now. I didn't know your love for that Scotsman ran that deep."

He retrieved a white handkerchief from his pocket and gave it to her. Sable blew her nose in Dior Homme, then sat up.

"Sorry," she sniffled. "I'm overreacting. Must be because I'm tired and strained. I thought I was over him."

"Aha," Freddie mused. "You can't even jaw his name. Speaks volumes in Freddo's love dictionary. Let me tell you, you can't bend love like you can iron. When it's solid, it's solid."

Despite herself, this made Sable laugh. "You have such odd comparisons. They leak like a sieve."

"Whatever lets the sunshine in, I'm all for it. Now spill the beans, honey! What really happened? Or do you need a pep Pastiche first?"

"I don't do alcohol anymore."

Freddie took her by the chin and gazed into her eyes. His were incredulous.

"What? Are you a bluestocking now? Glad we didn't get yoked. You can't marry the son of a whiskey distiller as a teetotaller!"

Freddie's attempt at cheering her up worked well.

"We would never get married. With or without intoxicants."

"Stop going off topic, old girl."

She slapped him fraternally. "You accuse me? You're the one who goes off topic because you're tipsy!" Sable giggled.

"Legally responsible." Freddie grinned as he hopped over to the table to pour himself another drink. When he turned around, he studied her for a while with that well-known frown between his dark brows.

"Love of my early life, you've changed so much. I mean, not on the outside. You still eternally look like Sabbo the Superb, but for the rest..." He shook his head, then added in a soft, emotional voice, "Was it Bill Mitchell? Please, tell me. I promise I'll stay silent and let you speak."

Sable gazed up at him, saw his love for her, and her heart melted. Freddie was the closest person in the world to her and she loved him fiercely, not as a lover but as a kind of brother.

"I don't know where to start. It's been such a turmoil."

"I know. Like old days?"

She smiled. "All right."

They sat on the bed with their backs against each other, keeping physical contact in the perfect way to speak freely without seeing each other.

"When was the first time we sat and talked like this?" Sable asked.

"The day your dad left Alnor. What age were you? I think I was about thirteen."

"I was eleven."

"Let's see if we still can do this, Sabbo."

Sable felt Freddie's warm back, the reassurance of his nearness. Soon, the words came of their own accord.

"It was love at first sight with Bill. Yes, it was, though we fought a lot at the beginning. We're both rather stubborn and scarred by life. I really fell for him, the first man in my life who wouldn't leave my feelings alone. Bill also had a stabilizing effect on me, and he pointed out not so much in words but in what he showed to me that I was an alcoholic. That I wouldn't make much of my life if I continued to drink and party. I couldn't see it myself, but I needed substantial quantities of alcohol to numb my pain after... you know... that thing with Von Henkell."

She lit another of her precious Craven As. Blew out the smoke. "I thought that our love for each other, which was growing every day, would be enough to face the past. Bill was the first man, besides you, with whom I wasn't, you know ... loose. We took it slowly, getting to know each other first. Then he told me in the Shetlands how he'd lost his wife and daughter before the war. They drowned under tragic circumstances."

"Oh, no!" Freddie groaned. "I expected a splash of something bad had happened to the fellow, but not anything that brutish. There's a dark depth there. You two are well-suited."

"Yes, I thought so too. After his openness, the dynamics between us changed. And I was so in love that... you know... I wanted us to be intimate, but then... but then..."

"What, Sabbo?" Freddie grabbed her hand and held it. "Spit it out, my dapper demoiselle."

But Sable couldn't go on. Freddie didn't know of her caesarean, of her daughter, of the adoption. When she remained silent, he tried again. "Listen carefully, Sable Montgomery, for once I'm dead serious and in no way joking. You know as well as I that you can die tomorrow. Do you want to take your secret to your grave? Is that it?"

His question jolted like a solitary penny in an iron bank. Then the penny dropped. Did she want to end up like her mother? Misty Fletcher, the flapper girl, who took her secrets to her lonely grave?

"No!" It sounded resolute and forceful. "I'll tell you. Just be patient and gentle with me, will you?"

"Have I ever been anything else?" He gave her hand a little squeeze. "I may be far away and unavailable, but I'll always be gentle with you. You're my best friend."

"And you are mine." Sable took heart from Freddie's kindness.

And then, so she had no time to think again, she scrambled through words, fast as the streaming rain. "Somehow, Von Henkell got me pregnant. My mother wanted me to marry him, but I refused. Then she said I would have to give up the child after it was born. I didn't care. I didn't want a baby and certainly not with a Nazi."

Freddie pushed his back harder against hers and squeezed her hand tighter until it was almost hurtful, but Sable clung to his support.

"My mother shut me up at Alnor when I grew bigger with child, and I wasn't allowed out of my room anymore. When the baby was due, I was taken to a clinic in an ambulance. It was freezing cold, around Christmas. I didn't know where they were taking me. Nobody told me anything. My mother wasn't there. I had no clue what was going to happen to me or to the baby. And then the pain started, first doable, but after a while it came in waves, bigger and harder. It was terrible."

Almost screaming again like she had done then, Sable clenched her fist in Freddie's hand.

"It went on and on and on. I was sure I was going to die and, frankly, I didn't care. I was out of my mind with pain and exhaustion. Then everything went white. I don't know for how long." She stopped, swallowed hard.

"Go on, Sab. You can do this!"

"When I came around, the first thing I heard were these tiny gurgling sounds. I thought I was in heaven. Everything was white and peaceful except for these sweet little sounds. I just lay there on my back listening, but then suddenly I had a stabbing pain in my abdomen, as if it was being torn apart. I put my hand under the blanket and felt my entire tummy was bandaged. Then the pain only increased. I did not know what it was. I cried and cried for help. Then that other little voice started crying, and I understood it was my child."

How Sable now longed for a sip of Freddie's Pastiche, but she thought of Doctor's Howe's breathing techniques and calmed herself enough to go on.

"I turned my head and there she was. I was sure it was a she. She was looking at me with these round dark eyes, dark lashes with tears like dewdrops on them. Oh Freddie, you cannot imagine how divine she looked. I was instantly in love.

"'Isabella,' I whispered, 'I'll call you Isabella.'

"She winked at me. I swear it! I felt so much love that despite the pain and weakness, I slid out of bed and took her out of the little crib and with me into bed. She instantly sought my breast and started drinking. Then she fell asleep. I think I slept as well, despite the pain."

"Oh Sabbo, oh my dear, dear Sabbo!"

She could hear Freddie was close to tears.

"When I woke, there was a nurse at my bed taking my temperature. She was nice. She smiled at us and took a chair to sit down for a while. She asked my name and how I felt. Then she told me I had had a caesarean. They feared the baby would not get enough oxygen because the delivery was taking too long. That I would have a scar on my tummy for all my life. That it would hurt very much for a couple of days, but that I could still have more children later in life if I wanted.

"The nurse never told me anything about the baby being taken away from me soon. Just told me that she was healthy and could stay in my room with me." Sable took a deep breath. The hardest part was yet to come.

"The next two days were the most sacred days of my life. Despite the pain, despite Isabella starting to wail every time I wanted to take a nap, despite the horrible hospital food that tasted of sawdust. I was happy, Freddie, really happy, and for brief moments I didn't even care that the child was unwanted and fathered by a Nazi. I made plans to escape with her to the Continent and forget all about the horrors of that past year. Of course, I fully intended to include you as the only person in on it!" She pressed his hand again. Then her voice fell.

"It was not to be, of course. On the third day, a stern-looking man came in and he told me to sign a document to hand over my child for adoption. I started to scream at him, threw a plate of porridge at his head. Isabella was wailing like mad. I took her in my arms and tried to flee, but he grabbed me by my dressing gown and hauled me back. I was beside myself, scratched his face, tried to escape again. Then... then..." Her voice trailed off.

"Go on, Sab, go on."

"Then two doctors came, their white coats flying wide, and they seized me forcefully. Jammed a needle in my arm and I collapsed with Isabella in my arms. The last thing I saw was her frilly bonnet and that sweet, sweet face. Then it was dark. It was dark for a very, very long time."

"But you never signed the document?" Freddie asked.

"What does it matter, Freddo? I was underage. And I did not know where they had taken her." Sable sniffed loudly.

"Then what happened?"

"You know most of the rest. When my wound was healed, I was sent back to mother at Alnor. I refused to see her and refused to sleep in my bedroom, where she'd locked me up. You found me in the library, remember? That's when I started drinking."

It was silent for a while. Children's voices wafted through the open window. *Un, deux, trois... je viens.* They were playing tag.

"I still don't understand how it made you and Bill say adieu to each other."

"Simple," Sable observed. "When I undressed, I froze and when he asked after my scar, I couldn't tell him. I'm sure he'd not want anything to do with me when he found out I had a child with the enemy, even if I couldn't be held accountable."

"I think you're underestimating Wild Bill."

"Even if he'd accept my fate, I felt I couldn't make love to a man anymore. So, it wasn't fair to stay with him. He deserves a woman who can be totally his."

"He would have waited in the wings for you, Sabbo, and you know it. You got cold feet, but that's not a reason to take a hike and leave. Not when love plays a role."

"Whatever. There's no turning back. Bill and I are no more. But there might be a way I can find Isabella."

"How?"

Sable whizzed off the bed and spun to her suitcase. Triumphantly, she held the file in the air.

"Something's dipping to the floor, Sabbo."

"Not important! This is."

She showed him the details of Isabella's birth and her adoptive parents. Then the photo she carried in her purse.

"Where did you confiscate this, Miss Secret Agent?" Freddie looked slightly spooked at the document.

"My dead mother!"

"Pardon, your what?"

"Oh Freddie, that's a whole other story, but the long and the short of it is that my mother died in a hotel in Monte Carlo and when I landed in Nice a month ago, I went to collect her belongings and that's when I found this file. The only thing of consequence she'd kept. Isn't it fantastic? When I'm back in London, I'm going to find my daughter. That's why I must stay alive. I want to see Isabella again, even if she's called Marie or Betsy, even if she doesn't recognize me and calls someone else Mummy. She'll be five this Christmas, Freddie. Can you imagine? She can walk and talk and maybe even read and write a little. She'll be a prime little madam."

Freddie stared at the photo in disbelief. Sable saw he tried to be enthusiastic for her sake but also envisioned all the obstacles between her and a reunion with her little girl. And he had nothing in common with children.

"I truly hope it will happen, Sabbo. And I will help you in whatever way I can. Maybe David can do some groundwork for you?"

"No, no, no! I don't want anyone else but you to know for now, and I will find her myself. God willing!"

Sable took the file from Freddie again, gave her little daughter another loving look and put the file back in her suitcase. Then picked up the envelope that had fallen out. She turned it around and went white as chalk.

"It's... it's addressed to your father, Freddie." She was gobsmacked.

"How can I not have seen this before in my mother's things? I thought the rest was just postcards and whatnot."

On eggshells, she went to the bed where Freddie had swung his long legs to the ground. She handed him the letter. It had an unstamped Monaco stamp, which meant her mother had never sent it.

"To my father?" he uttered, equally perplexed.

"Open it!" Sable ordered.

She saw him break the Frau Werner von Bissing seal and take out a short lavender colored note that was folded in half. He read aloud.

Hôtel Hermitage Monte-Carlo, 25 September 1942

Dear Francis,

*I don't have long to live. The cancer is eating me, but I want to let you know that if you go ahead and tell Frederick that he is **our** son, you have my blessing. One day, he may want to understand the barren Gertrude is not his biological mother.*

I think we've kept our secret pretty well hidden from everyone. Archibald never wondered, and he's dead too.

I cared little for Sable or Frederick, as you well know, and I know the boy's been quite a handful to both of you.

Adieu,
   Your Misty.

· · ·

"You're my brother?"
 "You're my sister?"

Identical blue eyes locked on each other, too stupefied for words.

They hugged, they kissed—they'd always known.

There was a knock on the door.

34

THE REAL FIGHT BEGINS

"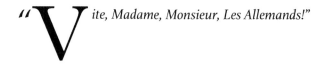Vite, Madame, Monsieur, Les Allemands!"

THE GERMANS?

WITHOUT THINKING TWICE—SABLE grabbing the photo of her baby and Freddie still clutching the letter—they slid in their shoes before leaping out of the window. Then took the prearranged escape route through the Rue Victor Hugo toward the village church.

Sable made three quick raps on the side door that led into a Virgin Maria alcove. She found the heavy oak door open, and they slipped into the sanctuary of the cool church. Pasteur Antoine Dedieu was in Sable's network of French resisters and had already helped many agents in trouble escape from the area via his church.

Wringing his big, white hands, his heavy golden cross dangling against his black chasuble, the priest with his ring of black hair on a bald cranium and large, soulful light-gray eyes approached the panting pair noiselessly.

"I was expecting you, Madame." His French was warm and round. "Ever since the drop last night, the Germans have been questioning villagers on the whereabouts of *Le Corbeau Noir*. But who is the gentleman?" The friendly priest took in Freddie with his intelligent light gaze.

"Oh, Pasteur Dedieu," Sable exclaimed, quite shaken. "This is Maurice Suttill. We just found out he's my half-brother. Can you bless us?"

"Biensûr, I would be delighted, but after that, you must run. It's no longer safe for you to stay here. I have a car waiting to take you to Lesparre-Medoc. We'll see how this pans out today, but if the Gestapo rounds up too many locals for interrogation, you must drop your network here, Madame Brisse."

"I understand, Father. But what about our luggage?"

"That is already in the car's boot. Don't worry. Now, both bend on these prie-dieu so I can bless you with the power and love of the holy Virgin Mary."

Though neither of them Catholic, it felt like an honor to hear the priest mumble his prayers over them while he put a warm, fleshy hand on the crowns of their heads. Sable felt the energy pulse through the priest's hands, and she'd never in her life felt so bonded together with another person.

I have a brother.

I have a daughter.

I am no longer alone.

I have a reason to live.

I am blessed.

"May God bless you both and protect you." The priest's touch disappeared, and both siblings remained in their kneeled position for some long moments, savoring the blood tie that bound them for good and vowing they would stand for peace and liberty.

~

THE GRAY CITROËN TUB with farmer Lefort's farm hand at the wheel raced the winding roads from Saint-Trélody to Lesparre-Medoc. Jolting in the back sat Sable and Freddie, hand in hand, with their suitcases between their legs.

"Are you afraid?" Sable shouted over the roar of the van's engine.

"Not really." Freddie shook his dark head. "I'm just racking my brain what is the best way forward for us. I know you put a lot of elbow grease in rekindling the CHASSIS network by developing it into PAPILLON. I guess you're disinclined to abolish your hard work just yet?"

"I am," Sable confirmed, "but I'm also wary of putting my people in danger."

"I still have my contacts with the LANTERN circuit in Clermont-Ferrand. We could hitch up with the folks there. Just to get out of the hair of the SS in this region?" Freddie suggested.

Sable shook her head.

"I hope they'll send my W/T George Dumond and the new courier Bernadette Mulsant our way. Let's consult with them first. We could also relocate to south of Bordeaux, if necessary. As long as we're together, Fre-, Maurice."

"Yes, Madame Brisse!" It was hard to remember to call her brother by his agent's name, but it was crucial to stick to this protocol out of doors.

"Madame," the farm hand bellowed over the noise in his cabin, "I think we're being followed. Hold tight, I'm taking a detour. It might be a bit bumpy."

It was as well that he'd warned them because, though Sable held tight to the bench on which she was sitting, she thought her stomach would come out of her mouth any second. One moment the van spun in the air, then hit the ground hard, went through craters and over rocky plots while branches hit the roof and the sides. First it zigzagged, and then it felt like it was going in circles, on and on.

As there were no windows in the back, they couldn't see where they were going and had to trust the local man at the wheel to take them to safety. At some point, Freddie groaned.

"If the Germans will not polish me off, this field trip will. Heavens, man, can't you slow down for a second?"

Sable was much too knocked around to utter a single word. The ride through hell seemed to have no end, but then suddenly the car stopped. Its engine died, heaved, and sighed for a moment and then *tic tic tic*. Silence. No more foraying into the territory, as if they were in a tank instead of a Citroën van.

The farm boy's round face appeared in front of the tiny window between the cabin and the back. Rather laconically, he remarked, "At your destination, Madame, Monsieur. It was my pleasure."

A little later, he opened the backdoor of the van for them. Sable stared at a long-stretched field with grass and a large and lonely chestnut tree in early foliage. No houses, no nothing. Just morning sun and chirping birds.

"What is this?" she asked, suspicion in her voice.

"I can't take you to Lesparre-Medoc, Madame. The Germans know my van. I'm going to drive back straight into their nets and let them search my van to their hearts' content. Your next escort will arrive here any minute. Just sit under the tree. I assure you the Germans don't know about this place. You're safe here. Guaranteed."

"Thank you." Sable smiled at the young man, who had beads of sweat on his dark forehead but wore a triumphant expression. "Good work, Nathan, very good work. Now be careful on the way back."

"I will, Madame. Au revoir, Madame, Monsieur."

"Holy Mother of God," Freddie observed as they sat on their valises under the lonesome tree in the middle of nowhere, "these French are first-class race monsters. I thought I could handle my Morris 8, but the way he took this parcourse was in a class of its own."

Sable was still recovering from the trip when she heard another car come closer in the distance.

"We will have to disguise ourselves before we leave. I can wear one of my expensive French dresses and you should wear another suit. I've got a stylish blond wig in my suitcase. For now, I'll just put a hat on top of my head and a pair of sunglasses."

"I have a fake moustache." Freddie was already rummaging in his suitcase. They stripped to their underwear and even giggled as Sable toppled in the grass, trying to get quickly out of her trousers and got caught in one leg.

"Do you remember the Christmas fancy dress..." They said it at the same time.

"You had roses from your aunt's hat pinned over your cherry-coloured velvet jacket." Sable giggled.

"You were a garden boy with white kid leggings cut above your knees," Freddie added.

"Maybe our mother cared enough about us to let us spend so much time together," Sable observed as she planted a red velvet hat on top of her head and scanned the dark-green Renault that drove over the grass toward them.

"Maybe," Freddie replied, rather in a low mood. "Yet I cannot recall exchanging over two or three words with your mother in my whole life."

"She was your mother, too."

"No, maybe biologically, but I had a great momma in what I thought was my mother."

Only then it dawned on Sable that the revelation that Misty Fletcher was also his parent was much more of a shock to Freddy than to her. She'd lived with the notion that the flapper girl was her unreliable mother all her life. Freddie had had a loving and doting Momma, who was still alive and whom he'd have to face one day.

But there was no more time to go back to the past. They had to tackle the future with full force.

SABLE WAS RELIEVED to find George and Bernadette waiting for them at a safehouse in a quiet residential area in Lesparre-Medoc. They found themselves in a kind of scullery that smelled of garlic and onions, a rather tight square room with a black-white tiled floor and brown storage cupboards along the three walls that had no windows. The scullery led to a garden, through which they'd come in, preceded by the thin man dressed in black who had picked Sable and Freddie up but who hadn't introduced himself.

Sable did not know if he was the owner of the house, or whether he'd just dropped them off. Neither did she know if they could stay there for the night, which would be rather cramped, and the floor looked uncomfortable.

For now, it was important that George got a message out to London. He was already busy attaching the long transmission wire to one pole of the washing line.

George was a slight, already graying man, though still in his early forties, wiry and taciturn. He worked with swift, capable hands, an excellent wireless operator who would blend in in every community without attracting attention to him. Yet, it wasn't his personality that could bring them into danger. It was his transmission from the middle of a larger town. Sable was on her qui vive but knew they had no choice. London had to know PAPILLON was in danger. Yet before George sent his message, she wanted to discuss with her core team what the best way forward was. Maybe she herself should disappear for a while.

Bernadette was a lovely, voluptuous girl with lots of tiny strawberry-blond corkscrew ringlets and a fresh, ruddy face with doll-like, china-blue eyes. She danced more than walked, but Sable soon found out that behind this attractive exterior was a shy yet shrewd girl, very attached to her missing brother and set on making the best of her job as a courier. Bernadette would be of good use now.

"The Germans have my code name and they're actively searching for me," Sable began. "The last thing I want to do is put you in danger. But I suggest I try one more time with a total disguise. I really don't want to abandon my circuit, now it's finally growing. We have at least two hundred fighters and we've planned a big sabotage at Gare Coutras next week."

"You can do it, Jacqueline," Freddie encouraged her.

"Okay, Maurice, thank you. George, I see no need to alarm London just yet. Let them know we've got the supply we needed.

Bernadette, please go to the post office and see what's in the mailbox. Then see if someone can loan you a bicycle and find us a safehouse."

FOR A FEW DAYS, things seemed to calm down, as if the Germans were no longer on her trail. Sable was busy organizing the next big sabotage PAPILLON would claim, blowing up the rail relay between Bordeaux and Paris. It would be a sensitive blast to the German supply route.

Traveling to Coutras by train, Sable felt more relaxed, reading her Stendhal novel, and airily looking forward to the nightly activity. With her hair in a peroxide blond wig and sufficient makeup to look like a modern French woman, the disguise helped her to feel different, act differently, even speak differently.

There was the prospect of some nice fireworks to tickle the Germans and demolish one of their vital railroad arteries. Freddie would follow on the next train. The demolition expert team would take yet another train.

Two SS officers took a seat on the other side of the aisle and started talking about the weekend in Paris they were looking forward to. Now and then they glanced in her direction, but Sable stayed firmly behind her book. They seemed normal, no buffoons, just young men a long way from home, looking for some fun. It would just not be with her.

Then the two men made her the topic of their conversation. Whether she was really reading, whether she was going to Paris as well, if she had a boyfriend. Sable understood enough German after her mother's dinner parties. She willed the next station to come into sight, but the train was slow. It seemed wisest to move to another carriage, away from these increasingly pushy officers.

The next station could only be another couple of minutes away. Putting the book in her handbag, Sable got up, slipped on her coat, and made for the door as if she planned to descend at the next station.

"Hallo, Miss, your papers." One of them called her back. She thought about dashing for the door, but the train was not yet at the next stop. She turned around and handed him her Reisedocument. The officer who had ordered her to show it glanced at her travel document without interest.

"Passport!" he yapped, feeling emboldened by his colleague to keep her there. He was a chubby man with very thin white hair. His skin and eyes were very pale as well, almost albino. Very uneasy with the situation, she scolded herself for staying too long in their orbit. Things so easily got out of hand.

She tried to get rid of them. "*Das ist meine Station!*"

"*Wir sind noch nicht da!*" The reddish eyes fixed on her. She handed him her passport.

"Widow?" He showed the passport to his pal, who sniggered along with the white guy.

"You look too young and dolled up for a widow." The pale eyes scanned her. Maybe the new disguise hadn't been thought out enough for a widow who taught rich kids English. She tried to snatch her passport back.

"I need to go now."

The train was indeed rolling into a deserted little station.

"Wait a moment, Madame. It's not up to you to call the shots. It's up to us."

Sable assessed her chances when the train came to a full stop. There were no other passengers in the carriage. Would they shoot her if she took to her heels?

There was no time to think. Before she knew what she was doing, with one eye on the exit and her ears pinned on the screeching brakes of the train, Sable retrieved her bottle of powdered glass from her pocket, and with two quick, precise movements, aimed the contents at their hands and holster bags. She dove to pick up the documents the white man instantly dropped.

The last thing she saw and heard as she leapt backwards out of the carriage were their bleeding fingers and cries of pain. Then there was a single shot, but it hit the train door.

She was out of the train, whizzing down the empty platform like a roebuck down the plains, stunned at her own response but clear-minded and determined to stay out of their control.

Sable didn't stop running until she was way beyond the sleepy village, but made sure she kept the train and the station in sight. Her luck was that the station sat at an elevated place, as she lay hiding in a small plot of shrubbery, her sleeve gun already in her hand.

The train stayed at the station for a long time, but no search command for her seemed to have gone out. The damage to the SS officers' hands was clearly minor and after what seemed an endless time, the train rolled out of the station to its destination: Paris.

Only then Sable let out a long, deep breath and lit a cigarette.

I've blown my cover, she thought sadly. *I need another cover name and passport. That is my priority now.*

She had forty minutes until the next train would arrive with Freddie on it. Time for a meager but hopefully successful temporary coverup. Changing into the dark clothes she'd brought for the upcoming raid, she hid the fake blonde hair under a polka-dot Chanel scarf and her nicely done up eyes behind dark sunglasses. The sleeve gun went back into place. She realized she was probably attracting quite some attention in this rural area, half combat outfit, half ladylike and, despite herself, it made her chuckle.

Exactly what you are, Sable Montgomery. Lady turned tomboy. It's usually the other way around, but you've always had a knack for eccentricity.

None of the villagers seemed to pay any special attention to her as she marched through their dusty main street on the way to the station. She knew she'd have to bluff her way through this. If anyone asked her for her passport this time around, she'd be captured and thrown in jail. That couldn't happen. Her freedom was crucial to her now. With Freddie, and with the attack they'd planned.

FOUR HOURS later and in a roundabout way, Sable arrived at Coutras on her own. Confident she'd meet up with her team later, she set out to meet a contact in the town who could provide her with a new passport. Emile was supposed to be good at it and luckily, he was home.

"Of course," he beamed, "I'd be delighted. What shall we make it?"

"Mademoiselle Violette Bernard, a traveling saleswoman for Triumph typewriters in France. I know a thing or two about typewriters because we studied them during my SOE training. I can invent any story I want around Triumphs."

Emile listened intently, his one good ear toward her. A grenade exploding next to him in the trench wars of 1918 had left him deaf and blind on one side of his face. But he was as alert as a fox at mealtime and certainly as cunning.

"Got it. Please take a seat, Mademoiselle Bernard, and I'll get going right away. Would you like to leave your former cover passport here? Just in case?"

"Sure. If I can't use it again, you may forge it slightly for someone else."

"My thinking exactly!"

Still nodding, he went to his presses and stamps in the back room.

"Could you also get me a stamped Laissez-Passer permanent document, Emile? And new food coupons?"

"Sure, sure. You ask, we deliver."

"I've got the money to compensate you for your trouble. And don't say no. They're not my own francs. It's what the British government gave me to pay local helpers."

"In that case, your francs are welcome, mademoiselle, but it's no trouble at all to me. Makes an invalid like myself still feel useful."

"Without people like you, we would be nowhere," Sable assured him.

IT WAS A MUCH BETTER feeling to have a new identity to prove who she was, at least to the occupiers. Her hair could be washed in a different color. Then all her recent troubles would be gone. With a fresh spring in her step, Sable made her way back to the station. Evening was falling, and it promised to be a dry night, clouded enough for the moon to be invisible.

Nothing could go wrong now.

35

EVERYTHING GOES WRONG

I t was a perfect night for an act of sabotage to be executed slick as a whistle. The night was dry and humid, windless, with no rain, no stars, and sufficient fog to see for those who wanted to see but not to be seen. The station was half a mile away from the village town center on an elevated embankment, at a suitable distance from prying eyes.

Total silence reigned because of the curfew. Only one car rambled by on the ring road on its way to Libourne. In this remote part of France, German officers preferred to wine and dine in the nearby town of Libourne or even travel down to Bordeaux.

There was no need for night vigilance here. No one suspected anything to happen in Coutras, which made it a perfect place to destruct the Germans' vital rail artery to the south-west coast.

Sable and Freddie lay side-by-side on their stomachs on a knoll of grass surveying the *Kriegslokomotive* of the DRB Class 52. They were waiting for two Frenchmen of the Résistance-Fer, the so-called *cheminots*, who would instruct Sable in placing the explosives.

She felt it was her duty to take the responsibility for the sabotage so that the local men who worked on the French rail system would technically be in the clear. All her Beaulieu training would prove if it was ultimately useful for actual operations.

Freddie had insisted on being there with her.

"Wouldn't want to miss my blue-blooded sister dynamite a Nazi iron horse."

Sable had protested. "Why endanger both of us? There's no need, Maurice. It's a hit-and-run act and these men know what they are doing. One's on watch; the other checks my work. The fewer people involved, the better."

But there had been no changing Freddie's mind, so Sable had conceded and now was actually glad to have her brother nearby during her first big mission on her own.

The raspy croak of a night heron sounded once. Her sign. Two dark shadows crept along the railroad track, only visible to those who knew what to look for. Her *cheminots*, men from the village Sable had never met but trusted as underground resistance fighters. Simple workers, men, and women, who obstructed the occupiers wherever they could, as thousands of French citizens did day by day all over France. The very foundation on which the SOE could function.

"Good luck," Freddie whispered. "I'll keep my eyes peeled."

"Night owl hoot twice in case of danger," Sable whispered, as she was already crawling forward toward the stolid locomotive, silhouetted as a massive black apparatus against the charcoal, starless sky.

No words were exchanged. The silence of the night reigned as Sable took the plastic explosives from her backpack. A tall shadow beckoned her to come closer while the other shadow went to the locomotive's front and stationed himself in the middle of the tracks, from where he could stake out the entire region.

Both at Beaulieu and again that morning, Sable had studied the various components of the steam engine so closely that she'd be able to find the red cylinder blocks low near the wheels even with a blindfold. The explosives would crack the cast iron blocks. It was vital to break this part of the engine, as the Germans didn't keep spare cylinder blocks since they hardly ever wore out on their own. The blast would not only wreck the locomotive but have enough power to deform the railroad itself.

With swift hands, she attached the innocent-looking plastic bars to the cylinders with sturdy tie wraps. The *cheminot* was close at hand and checked her every action. His whispered *"parfait"* gave her the confidence she needed; she was now an adroit explosives expert. One last check and she was at the ready. The shadow insisted on giving her the all-clear she didn't need.

"Ignite the wick and run as fast as your legs can carry you. You've got eighty seconds before the flame reaches the blasting cap."

"I know. You do the same. *A bientôt.*" Sable couldn't help sounding indignant. Who was in charge of this operation?

IT WAS THE FASTEST EIGHTY-SECONDS' run of her life. Not even bothering to check if her accomplices had also left the scene of the crime, Sable ran with all she had inside of her, away from the village and away from the expected explosion. The team would meet at a pre-agreed place at dawn. Until then, it was everyone for themselves.

The shock waves of sound and the flames shooting high into the sky temporarily deafened and blinded Sable, but she kept running, low to the ground, leaping like a mountain cat. The explosions were still ringing out with debris landing everywhere, but she managed to increase the distance between her and the station, away from the built areas. The blackout made lights inside houses unseen, but she heard French voices, villagers daring to withstand the curfew to see what had caused the blow-up. Dogs barked and rattled on chains. Then the siren of a fire engine sounded, coming nearer.

Her lungs burnt; her legs were as lead while her rucksack felt as if filled with fifty-stone bricks. Still, she urged herself on, not daring to stop until she was well out of earshot and protected by the thick forest around her. Only then did she allow herself to slow down.

A blast so forceful must mean the dynamite had done its righteous, ruining job. The mission's success made Sable feel victorious, full of vim and vigor, though at the same time she was aware how odd it was to feel so pumped up after an act of destruction.

"It's what I came here for!" she reminded herself, still panting from the run, her heart thumping, and her throat dry. What a crazy day it had been!

IN THE FOREST a couple of miles west of Coutras, Sable made herself a bed of leaves near the shore of the Dronne River. During her SOE training, she'd taken part in a variety of survival trips, some of them for several days, with only a compass and the bare minimum to find her way back to camp.

So, sleeping in the open air and creating a warm and safe hiding place was not the issue. The only difference was that it had been in the safe homeland and not in a strange country under enemy occupation.

Knowing she would have to sleep with only half her brain, so she'd wake to the slightest sound, Sable lay down on her back, her hands folded on her stomach under the leaves, her Colt Commando .38 revolver at close reach. She relaxed her body while her head was awake. It worked the first hours, waking and listening, listening and waking, but in the end, she was so exhausted that she missed a vigil... and slept a little longer.

SHE WOKE to something wet in her face, a sniffing dog, then heard voices. *Blast!* On opening her eyes, her hand going to her gun, she looked straight up into the snout of a black-eyed German Shepherd. Stealthily, she shoved the gun back in her pocket. It was no use shooting now. A rough German voice called out.

"*Gefunden!*"

Before she knew what was happening, two Germans in Wehrmacht uniforms dragged her to her feet. Thank God she'd slept with her rucksack as a cushion. It eased down her back and sank into place. The layer of leaves she'd used to cover herself fell around her feet as if she'd let drop a colorful skirt. Fully awake now, she registered two Germans, a dog, and a Kubelwagen in between the trees. Not good news by any measure.

She quickly scanned the officers, who were wearing the gray-green uniforms of the Wehrmacht Heer. Both with two-stripes on their uniform, thus not very high in the hierarchy, lads too young and too green for the job. The dog might be more of a danger. For now, it was held on a short leash by the taller of the two, a stocky figure with an unhappy, pimple-skinned face. The shepherd kept barking as if it had found a rabbit.

On a *"halts maul"* from its surly owner, the animal sat on its behind and calmed down.

"Qu'est-ce qu'il se passe?" Sable pulled herself free with not too much effort. She decided that asking them in angry French what the heck they were doing would be the best tactic. Stay on the offense. The men could hold nothing against her.

"Kommen Sie mit," ordered the other officer. He had a peculiarly small head which made his huge cap sink almost down to his eyes, so that he kept pushing it back or wriggled his eyebrows in an attempt to keep his vision.

"Why?" Sable was still standing her ground. "If you want to know why I was sleeping outside, the answer is that my boss pays me so little that I have no money for a hotel. *Pauvre moi!*"

"Shut up!" The man with the dog eyed her suspiciously and felt a need to exercise his authority.

"Please be more polite, Sir. *Ich bin kein Hund!*" she protested, changing to German.

"She's clearly a handful." The small-headed man shook his head. Sable made use of their confusion and lack of experience. She had one eye on the road where their Jeep was parked, the other on the river. If she had to make a dash, it would be back into the woods. The dog, however, was the real hindrance. Without doubt, they would let it loose on her. It seemed wiser to cooperate for now.

"In the car!" number one ordered.

"Why?" She struggled as they grabbed her again. "Just tell me why you're taking me. What have I done? I'm just a poor woman on my way to earn some money in Bordeaux."

Still focused on escape, she agreed to let them escort her halfway toward the Kubelwagen. The dog snarled and the hairs on its back stood upright, which was not a good sign.

"The dog picked up your trail, Miss. There's been an explosion at the station last night."

"That dog of yours is rabid," Sable snarled. "I know nothing of explosions at stations. Now let me go. I'm an honest woman."

"The Lieutenant will decide on that, Miss. Hector has never led us to the wrong suspect before. His nose is perfect."

Sable understood that at this point further protest would only be counterproductive. She'd come up with a plan when she was confronted with their boss. It was a good thing she had a new cover. There would at least be no connection to Jacqueline Brisse, aka the Raven. Somehow, she'd wriggle herself out of this, one way or the other. Of that, she was sure. This wasn't Paris or Lyon or Bordeaux. Only second-class German officers would be stationed in Coutras. They might even be susceptible to bribes.

The hood of the camel-colored Kübelwagen was closed. Sable was handcuffed, much to her dislike, and ordered to sit in the back with the small-headed man, who chained himself to her. The dog went in the upfront passenger seat and the poor-complexioned officer heaved himself behind the wheel.

After a short, bumpy track through the woods, they came back on the single-track road to Coutras. Sable stared demurely out of the window, but her brain was working at top speed. By all appearances, and as her instinct had told her, the lowly officers were taking her back to Coutras.

They clearly had no orders to transport her elsewhere. It was only the dog that had connected her to the act of sabotage, but in concrete terms, they had nothing on her. She'd be free as a bird in the next hour, on her way to her meeting point with Freddie and the cheminots.

"Can I have a cigarette?" She sent her chainer a coy smile. Dipping the green packet from his breast-pocket, he offered her an Eckstein cigarette.

"Please take these silly handcuffs off. I won't take a runner. I promise."

Without questioning his actions, the young officer clicked the lock open, took a cigarette himself and proffered her a light. Then lit his own. Sable inhaled deeply, bestowing the German with a warmer smile, but not in any way flirtatious.

"Thank you! Though I prefer my French Gauloises, these aren't too bad, either."

It was a blatant lie but for a good cause as Sable detested the French cigarettes. What a treat to enjoy a normal tasting smoke. She meanwhile studied the soldier with his small moustache and small eyes through the smoke as the Jeep hobbled over the cobbled streets of Coutras.

"Where're you from, soldier?" Sable talked in such a low voice that the man upfront couldn't overhear her and perhaps see through her tactics.

"Wiesbaden."

"You're joking."

"Why would I?" He looked at her as if she'd lost her marbles.

"Nothing!" She'd almost given herself away, bit her tongue.

"What's your name?"

"SS-Untersturmführer Henrik Braun." Sable filed this name away for potential future use.

"And your buddy? Is he also from Wiesbaden?" She pointed her chin toward the thickset neck of the man upfront.

"No, Karl's from Köln. He's SS-Untersturmführer Schmidt."

"Good, good." Sable nodded as she thought Henrik so far rather stupid, but in no way violent. He raised no questions about her identity, didn't seem interested in her as a potential saboteur, but certainly sat up straighter, showing he was flattered by her female quizzing of his person. It was plain as pie that the Untersturmführer left interrogations to his superiors.

"You've got a girl in Wiesbaden, Henrik?"

No protest at her addressing him by his first name.

"Yes. My fiancée, Ann-Marie Doust." He glanced at her with his small-set eyes, as if trying to figure out what she was all about but failed to grasp her strange femininity. Sable grinned inwardly at her game and the success it had.

"Good for you!" she answered with a longing sigh. "I have a beau in Bordeaux. His name is Georges. He will wonder what keeps me so long. Now, can you let me go? I really need to be getting on my way."

Talking about a distant lover with languish would hopefully mellow the dimwit enough to decide she was as innocent as a wayside fly.

"Sorry, Fraulein, but we're here."

Sable looked out of the window. The Kübelwagen stopped in front of a perfectly symmetrical Mairie, built in that warm, elusive, cream-gray limestone of most French town halls, with a small balcony and built-in clock on the first floor. Two Swastika flags on either side of the balcony hung limply on their poles.

"This is it?" she asked, play-acting disbelief. "Awfully nice place. Do you live here?"

"Out!" the small-headed man ordered, clearly exasperated by this fickle-tongued prisoner. The other German got out of the front seat, looking puzzled as the dog sniffed Sable's pants.

"Why is she not handcuffed?"

The small-headed one eyed his colleague rather sheepishly. "This one's not dangerous, Karl. She promised not to escape. She's... a little crazy, but otherwise rather nice."

Sable peered around her, left and right down the high street for a way to escape, but saw none in the middle of town with the dog at her heels. There was no other choice than to follow the lowly officers through the front door and into the town hall. At least they didn't handcuff her again, so she hoped for the shortest of visits and a quick exit.

Sable's mood fell when she was escorted into the visitors' room at the front, where not only a Lieutenant sat writing in a logbook behind a large mahogany desk, but also Freddie sat, with his head down, the black mane over his eye, on a bench placed against one wall.

He looked up as she walked in flanked by her captors and the light, but also the worry shone in his blue eyes. Sable registered there was no sight of the *cheminots*. She had a speck of hope they'd escaped. Sable and Freddie shared a covert V-sign but didn't show they knew each other.

Two steps further into the room, Sable stopped in her tracks. Her anger flared up despite her well-chosen cover of a rather dewy-eyed mademoiselle who understood little of the German occupation and even less of danger and destruction. Coming in through a side door and walking up to the SS-officer sitting at the desk was no other than... Henri de Bonheur.

The expletive that came from her mouth and the staring down she gave the treacherous double agent was enough to make all in the room look at her in surprise. She saw him narrow his eyes, hug his ill-fitting jacket around his thin frame. There was triumph there, but also something Sable couldn't read. Almost as if he was jealous of her.

Fast and fluid as mercury, she spun around to her adopted sweet self while inwardly swearing, "I'll get you." With a smile coated in that childlike simplicity, she apologized.

"Sorry for my *merde*. I just realized I've forgotten my mother's birthday. It's today. I must get her a present now. Please, let me go."

It was a lousy excuse, but it even distracted De Bonheur from the fact she'd almost blown her cover by showing recognition of him. While she was forced to march to the desk and stand close to the hideous man who now was her worst enemy, Sable swore to herself and to God above, this would not be her imprisonment. It would, however, be Henri de Bonheur's end.

THE INTERROGATION WAS short and simple. To Sable's content, the superior to her two captors wasn't a bright button either, not even making the effort of searching her or her rucksack, just shooting some vague questions about explosives and sabotage at her that were easy to ward off. De Bonheur kept silent during the questioning but remained the chink in her armor. He complicated matters of escape, as he knew she and Freddie were British agents.

Yet why he stayed silent and didn't feed the SS-officer more in-depth questions was beyond her. Freddie clearly had undergone the same shallow treatment as he signaled to her in an underhand matter.

"That will be all for now," The SS-Oberleutnant declared, scribbling some more on his pad, and dismissing them with an away-away wave of his hand.

Sable was trying to read Freddie's expression as they were brought to the back of the building by her two captors and placed together in a cell that, before the war, most likely had been the nightly cool-off lockup for drunkards and petty thieves.

Being together with Freddie in the cell was De Bonheur's doing. They both understood that without exchanging one word. The recording device was not well hidden. It would have to be code language and gestures between them. The question was if De Bonheur knew they were acquainted. Better keep that vague as well.

Freddie looked shaken but not broken. Dark rings under his eyes showed he'd had an early and rough awakening as well.

"*Comment allez*-vous?" A neutral start, asking how he felt as she sat down next to him and pressed his hand, signaling, *I'll find us a way.*

Freddie shrugged. "I've had better days. I'd rather have a *petit-dejeuner* with lots of *café noir*, instead of being in a prison cell."

"Alas," Sable agreed, "same here! Are you traveling through?"

"Yes, I was on my way to Paris. Wanted to take the early train, but apparently there was a sabotage last night so there is no train today."

"That's what my German captors told me, too. I was on my way to Bordeaux for work, but also to celebrate my mother's birthday."

With another squeeze, she was communicating they were doing fine. Sable let her eyes roam around the cramped cell that smelled of stale cigarette smoke and rancid sausages. There was one small window high up on the wall with iron bars in front. Not an inviting place to escape from, but somehow, she knew she'd find them a way out. If she let traitors like De Bonheur win, all the hard and dangerous work of the Section F SOE agents would have been for naught.

In the meantime, it was important to keep up the small talk, as she was sure they were listening to their conversation in the main hall and silence would be detrimental to their case. Yet it was a fine line. Surely De Bonheur knew too much and possibly had informed the Germans. If so, they were playing a game with them, trying to extract information without having to do anything themselves.

"Are you from Paris?" As she talked her nonsense talk, she got up and stood on the bunkbed under the high-up window, signaling to Freddie to fold his hands and let her stand in it. This way, she could peer outside. Ground floor, back of the building, plenty of shrubbery outside, a sloping lawn that ran down to the riverbed amidst tall trees in full foliage, no buildings. Perfect.

"My mother is, but my father is English," Freddie meanwhile lied, concocting a story about his family so wild and exotic, Sable had difficulty not bursting into laughter. They were both endowed with a vivid imagination, which was only a good thing considering their situation.

While listening to Freddie inventing his backstory about a famous Parisian Cubist painter mother and an English Lord father, who'd almost drowned in the Seine and was laid up to dry in Madame de Pompadour's gallery, Sable seized the rusty bars to test them. Not overly solid. The stones around the metal rods were crumbling.

The maintenance of the Mairie's back side was clearly of less importance than its facade and was simply left to rot. Whether she could remove the bars or bend them with her hands, she was still unsure.

She wanted Freddie to check their escape route as well, but he was now so engrossed in his own story that she had to jump off his folded hands to get to the floor, meanwhile *uh-ing* and *aha-ing* at his ever-wilder roots.

She pointed to the window and stood ready for Freddie to test the bars. He grinned down on her, nodded, and came down, all the while inventing ten brothers and sisters and more boat trips on the Seine.

One ear listening for approaching footsteps, Sable got hold of her rucksack. The lazy officers hadn't even cared to inspect the contents. Unbelievable, but true.

Her possessions might have looked innocent enough to untrained eyes. They certainly weren't. A pen that could shoot one bullet, tear gas in a capsule, her Colt, a portion of ground glass, her compass, maps printed on silk, and everything needed to survive in outdoor conditions. She also still had her sleeve gun and a file in her boot. Showing it wordlessly to her brother, she nodded he had his gear still as well.

"What about your family?" Freddie asked.

"Oh, I want to get married to my Georges this summer. He's so handsome and such a fine man. But right now, I'm more concerned about my mother giving me a piece of my mind about forgetting her birthday." While she chattered, Sable became more anxious that their senseless talk was going to irritate their audience and that they would come to their cell any minute now.

To dampen the screeching of her file, she put a handkerchief around the blade while talking loudly about the splendor of Bordeaux and her wine merchant fiancé. After one rod was out, she could bend and break the others with her hands.

Thank god, we're both slight, she thought as she first threw her rucksack out of the window and then pushed herself out. Freddie had to clamber up the wall himself, but soon he fell next to her in the tall grass.

Still dazed at their sudden escape, they hid in the bushes underneath the cell for a moment. Then staying low, they pressed themselves against the wall as they came to the rhododendrons that led down to the river below.

There was only one bullet left in her sleeve gun, but she'd use it if a guard would come in sight. But that wasn't their primary concern. It would be just about impossible to lose Hector, the trained tracking dog, if what his proud owner, Karl, had claimed was true. Move downwind, cross the river, make sharp edges and above all, be fast and far away. Karl didn't seem like a long-distance runner, so even if Hector could catch up with them, the pockmarked second lieutenant would slow down his hunting dog.

"We will have to run for many miles," Sable observed, spurting ahead.

"As fast and as far away from the Coutras Mairie as we can," Freddie agreed. It was a good thing they'd followed the same training and only needed half a word to do what was required.

"An amazing escape, by all means," she panted.

"Save your energy, Sab!"

But she couldn't stop herself from crying out, "If I do only one more thing in my life, it's killing Henri de Bonheur with my own hands."

"Let's focus on staying alive yourself," Freddie remarked rather drily.

They'd meanwhile arrived at the riverbank. The Dronne was wild and ice-cold, but they plunged in, glad to reach the steep mountain ridge on the other side that would be hard for Hector to climb. Sable retrieved her compass from her rucksack to orient where best to go. Freddie was already climbing. So far, no dog barking or angry German voices. Would they really be able to escape so easily?

By mid-morning, the sun was hot and plentiful. They'd cleared a good ten miles away from the town. High on the mountain peak of Cimes de Graves, Sable stared down at the shimmering rooftops of Coutras down in the valley.

"Time for a quick break. I see some red berries there." She went over to pick a handful.

"Yes, let's rest our weary limbs for a spell." Freddie dropped in the grass, lying on his back with his arms and legs stretched out like a scarecrow.

Sable didn't feel exhaustion. Her system was filled to the brim with adrenaline. But the thirst was acute. The grouse whortleberries were unripe and tasted sour, but she sucked them up, anyway. She kept picking more, some for Freddie and for the trip ahead.

"Did you also have Killer Drake for survival classes at Beaulieu? He made me taste these berries for the first time. As a kid, I always thought they looked poisonous."

"I never went to Beaulieu, remember?" Freddie was stuffing some whortleberries in his mouth and spit them out after two chews. "Argh, they're caustic."

Sable pricked up her ears.

"I hear water." Following the sound, she moved further over the plateau and came to a tiny stream trickling down from the next mountain top. "Over here, Freddo!"

They threw themselves on their stomachs and dipped handfuls of the cold water into their mouths, on their faces, in their hair.

In a roundabout way Sable felt happy in that instant, lying side-by-side with her brother as if they were home again at Inveraray. Without a care in the world. No war. No Germans. No betrayal. But soon the reality of their precarious situation in a faraway hostile country, on the run, dawned on her again. She spoke the inevitable words.

"We have to split up."

"I know." Freddie sounded equally unhappy.

"Do you have a plan?"

"I do. This time I'll go to Paris. Clermont-Ferrand would be my first choice, but I think it's wiser to mingle in and hide in a big city for now. I've got contacts there. What about you?"

"I'll go to Lyon. I liked it when I first came here, and I have a meeting point, a cafe where I know I can get in touch with other resisters," Sable lied. She had another mission first. "Just give us one more minute together. I love you, Freddo."

"I worship you, my darling little sister."

THEY HUGGED, they kissed, they tried not to cry.

"Be in touch when you can," Sable shouted after him, as his back disappeared. But she knew she'd either meet in London after the war, or... in death.

36

THE RAVEN'S REVENGE

Dry-eyed and tired to the bone, too highly wired not to be affected by her anger at the traitor, Sable sat in the shadow of a large oak until the late afternoon sun sunk over the mountain ridge. Though the weather was still fine, Sable was shivering, her body weary, but her mind forged in steel resolve.

Then slowly, but certainly, she made her way back the way she and Freddie had come. It would be death or glory; she would accept either. What she couldn't accept was that Henri de Bonheur made one more SOE victim. If London didn't know or wouldn't listen, she would take matters into her own hand.

As she arrived in the shrubbery, underneath the Coutras Mairie, Sable called herself crazy in every term she knew. De Bonheur was probably long gone to another place to betray other agents, and she'd be detained all over again—and no escape would be possible this time.

"So, what's the plan, sugar?" Sable asked in Wooly's thick voice. Thinking of the Beaulieu commandant at this moment dynamized her.

"Follow your instinct," answered the Raven.

She'd checked that the Kübelwagen was gone from the square upfront, probably searching for the escapees.

"He's still here, licking his wounds while they search for me. He wants his treat. Well, so do I," the Raven spoke.

It was still a long wait until night fell and the town became quiet under curfew. Sable was hungry and thirsty but pushed all discomfort aside. The worst recurring pang was her yearning for a cigarette. For years she hadn't gone this long without a smoke, but she told herself over and over that everything... everything was worth this wait.

Having no clue what was going on at the front of the building, who was in and who was out, Sable lay in her secluded spot in the shrubbery. As no one came for her, she surmised the second lieutenants with the dog had probably not returned. Without a doubt, Hector would have led them straight to her. And she would have shot them on the spot—Karl, Henrik, and Hector. The Colt was without fail in her right hand, directed at the now shadowy corner of the town hall's wall.

To pass the time, Sable created a detailed map in her mind of the rooms and corridors in the Mairie that she'd seen and of the surrounding grounds. Approach, enter, attack, escape. Over and over, she painted the picture in her head until she could almost see it play out.

As the town hall clock sounded eleven times, she got up and moved. A shadow among shadows, edging around the corner to the front of the building.

The streetlamps were out, and the square was only lit by one electric light above the double front doors that illuminated the stone steps to the entrance. Not a soul in sight. The building was quiet, but Sable knew there were Germans keeping watch.

The Kübelwagen and one French private Renault were parked side-by-side. As they seemed to expect no threat from the outside, they'd withdrawn inside. No extra activity in the square or elsewhere probably meant they'd given up on recapturing *Le Corbeau Noir* and her partner in crime, Jacques.

Sable's major worry was whether Henri de Bonheur was still inside. Was that Renault his car? Was that her luck? If they'd given up on putting Freddie and herself in shackles again, the rat had probably moved on to betray others in other regions.

Biting her lip, Sable hesitated about retracing her steps and taking to the road again. She reckoned the Germans would try to chase them for at least twenty-four hours, and that De Bonheur would want to be present for their recapture.

That was the whole reason for her swift return to Coutras. The disgrace of the agents' escape wouldn't sit well with De Bonheur's German masters. He'd press for finding them, yet stay put in the Mairie himself. But did he remain there? Or couldn't they all care less? Or was he not a traitor, after all? Everything was confused in Sable's overstretched mind, but her intuition was crystal clear. He'd thrown sawdust in everyone's eyes, including London, but Marie Dandicolle had known as well.

Well, there was only one way to find out what the truth was.

Sable had the luck she'd been praying for. Soon after she'd taken up her position flat against the wall and next to the front doors, she heard footsteps inside and the door creak open. She turned her head in the sound's direction, so the whites of her eyes wouldn't show.

It was small-headed Henrik, whose Ann-Marie was waiting for him back in Wiesbaden. Sable followed him, still as a ghostly lake as he headed toward the Jeep. When he was about to open the car door, she stood right behind him with her knife. Seconds later, Second Lieutenant Henrik Braun slid out of her arms and to the ground as noiselessly and unobtrusively as a sack of potatoes.

Sable felt sorry for the forever-waiting fiancé, but there was no time to mourn either her loss or that of Henrik Braun. In war, sometimes the innocent must die. It was them or her.

Her first throat-slicing kill had been near perfect. No blood on her, not even on her hands. Killer would be proud of her, but Sable didn't feel proud. She felt disgusted.

Grabbing Henrik's Walther P-38 pistol and, stuffing it between her belt, she plucked the car keys from his already stiff fingers and returned to her shadows next to the front doors. Now it was a matter of moving fast.

CRAWLING along with her back against the wall, she cracked opened the front door and slipped inside. The Walther P-38 was now securely in both her hands. Checking the hall, she saw it was empty, but subdued voices sounded from the room where she'd been interrogated that morning. She inched to where the voices were coming from and stepped inside, feet firmly on the ground, the black balaclava hiding her face except for her eyes and mouth. Only two men, as she'd hoped. Karl and De Bonheur.

"*Mains en l'air!*" She almost choked as she spit out the words, but they had the desired effect.

Both men gazed at her as if she was a being from another planet but raised their hands up in the air. However, she saw Karl change his mind. His hand went down, down to his gun. She fired once, planting the German bullet from his colleague's gun straight into his heart. Karl's body sank sideways, staring at her French resister disguise with a non-plussed look on his scarred face.

He was dead within the next ten seconds. De Bonheur was about to jump to his feet, but she fired again, the bullet whizzing past him and hitting the wall, where it collided and dropped to the stone floor, spinning for a while, then fell still.

"Don't you dare!" Sable snarled in English, "you despicable traitor, get up and move!" The spindly man, still wearing the ill-fitting pre-war costume he'd worn when they first met on the train to Bordeaux, got up from his chair, ashen and wobbly, clearly less of a hero now his protectors were dead.

"Leave your gun on the table, and move over to the wall," Sable continued. "No games, or you're a dead man too."

"*Mademoiselle, je vous en prie,*" De Bonheur started, falling back in his native tongue, his voice hoarse and shaken.

"No! There's no mercy for what you've done to Phillipe Arnault and possibly many more!" Sable was adamant. He placed his Welrod suppressed pistol on the table. This act, the pistol itself moved Sable more than all the other dramatic things that had flashed by in the past five minutes. The fact this traitor still used the weapon the Brits had supplied him with. It was the proof of ultimate betrayal.

"Outside with you."

"I've done nothing. You'll find nothing." He walked in a peculiar sideways gait but held his arms away from his body, his tone more defiant.

All Sable's senses were on high alert. Henri de Bonheur was an agent who was certainly as well trained as she was, so he could pull any trick on her any time. Yet he moved rather meekly to the door and out of the building.

"Is the Renault Juvaquatre yours?"

"Yes."

"Have you got your car key with you?"

"Yes."

This spiritless man was a totally different character from the impatient and unfriendly agent she'd encountered on the train. She put even more vigilance into monitoring his every move. He was a chameleon, totally untrustworthy.

"Sit at the steering wheel. I'll tell you where to drive to—and no foolishness."

So far, De Bonheur did as he was told. With Sable holding the pistol at close range of his temple, he slowly navigated the lime-green car down Coutras' cobbled high street.

They were both silent apart from Sable's instructions to turn left or right. After a short drive, she ordered him to park near the Dronne river at a secluded parking place.

"Keep your hands on the wheel while you and I have that much-needed talk. You know I'll shoot you without qualms if you make one wrong move."

With the gun in one hand, Sable swiftly took the ignition key and pocketed it. De Bonheur took to staring out of the front window in the dark. He didn't reply. The streaming water could be heard outside.

"What made you change sides?" It was the plain question to which Sable desperately wanted the answer.

"I didn't." It was said in a low voice. "It may seem that way to you, but you're wrong."

"Then where's your W/T Philippe Arnault? And why were you hanging around these German officers when Maurice and I were brought in for questioning?" Her tone was caustic. Sable didn't suffer liars gladly.

"These are two separate questions, mademoiselle. Which one do you want answered?"

Some of the man's former nettlesome personality showed through. A good sign.

"Well, answer them both, Henri de Bonheur. I haven't got all night and there's a bullet in here with your name on it." Sable could do irritation as well.

"I don't know where Philippe is. I haven't spoken to him for weeks."

"But Phillipe is—or rather was—part of your CHASSIS network, remember? The one I was also supposed to join. But when I arrived in the Bordeaux area, the circuit had fallen apart. Everyone said there was a mole in the system. They were so much on tenterhooks they didn't trust me at first because I kept asking for agents from the CHASSIS network."

Sable took a breath, dying for a cigarette but unable to divert one inch of her attention away from the supposed informer in the driver's seat.

"CHASSIS was already rotten when I arrived. I had nothing to do with it." The quake in his voice told otherwise.

"Tommyrot! Then why wouldn't you have let Philippe warn London? You were the organizer, right? You let people, your own countrymen and women and Brits, be arrested by the SS. You did nothing to stop it, so it must have come from you. Your name, Monsieur de Bonheur, was front and center every time when suspicions were raised."

Angry and provoked, Sable stared at the man's profile in the slight

light of the new moon. *Keep your calm, interrogator,* she told herself but found this the most difficult part of all. This Frenchman was so clearly guilty, yet she needed hard proof. Did she turn out to be worthless at cross-questioning?

De Bonheur didn't move, showed no sign of admission or regret. The man was an eel. The exact word Marie Dandicolle had used for him. Sable's gut instincts, too, told her the man was as rotten as the gills of an old mushroom. But she wanted to hear the proof coming from his own mouth. It could become a long night.

"Whichever you believe." The tone was death-like. It raised the hairs on Sable's arms.

"Leave CHASSIS for now. Answer me: what were you doing in Coutras today?"

"Nothing in particular. I happened to be at the town hall for business."

"Rubbish!" Sable was done with his sidestepping and cocked her Colt.

This seemed to wake De Bonheur from his stupor. "You wouldn't!"

She registered the fear in his voice with a flicker of hope he'd come clean. "Now, wouldn't I? You've just seen me kill two Germans who were probably less guilty than you are."

"All right." He raised his hands from the steering wheel in a gesture of surrender.

"Hands on the wheel!' Sable snarled, making a threatening gesture with the cocked gun.

"I was captured myself last November," he semi-confessed. "I was tortured in Bordeaux and sort of snapped. Then I promised to work along with the SS in exchange for my life. I had no choice."

There was something in these smooth words that had too many holes. Sable didn't buy it but went along for the sake of the information that might follow.

"Wasn't that the easy way out?"

"Maybe. Wait till you're in that situation yourself. Then come back to me to complain."

"It doesn't look like the SS is holding you on a string any longer, so why not get back to the right side, or at least inform London?"

De Bonheur sighed, "I tried to warn them, but they won't listen. Nobody listens to me and they're all after my skin. The Bochs and the Brits. I've had enough of this whole bloody war." He was playing the victim card, but Sable wanted concrete details.

"What did you tell the Germans about CHASSIS and the SOE organization? Names, places? Be more concrete."

"I don't remember exactly. After their torture, I was a mess. I may have given some names. Not yours, because you weren't with me yet."

Sable weighed his words. They still didn't add up. Nobody had ever talked about Henri de Bonheur being arrested by the SS. It still looked like he'd walked over to the other side of his own free will.

"Did they pay you well?"

"Who?" He was taken off guard by her question.

"The Germans, of course."

"Not as well as I'd hoped, but enough to stay alive."

"So that was your reason? Money? Not ideology, but hard cash?"

"Who cares, woman! What is it you want from me?" He was clearly going up the wall, but Sable felt she was almost where she wanted to be.

"I told you what I want. Names and landing places you gave the SS."

For the first time, he locked eyes with her in the car's darkness, the whites of his eyes darting from one side to the other. The eternal water stream gurgled outside.

"What's your plan, Raven?"

"That depends on you, Joseph!"

They measured each other's strength. Sable feared for the other weapons he might suddenly whip out in the dark.

"Will you let me go if I confess?" He was trying to bribe her, but she decided to keep him in doubt. In fact, her mind was already made up.

"That depends on the truth."

"All right, I gave Phillipe's name, but I've heard he was able to escape. Then there were the couriers, Brigitte Simonet and Angèle Borrel."

"Who else?"

"I don't know. A few, I guess."

"You worked for the Germans since November? Over eight months?" Sable kept prodding him.

"I guess. So, what is it you really want, Raven? We're not having a little chit-chat for nothing. There was no reason for you to come back to Coutras unless you wanted to close a deal yourself. It's good money. I can tell you that much."

"You're even a bigger rat than I already thought." Her tone was low and steady, but it was dripping with disgust.

"Whatever you wish, fool!"

What happened next seemed to last minutes but was less than a few seconds. De Bonheur turned to face her, meanwhile slipping a gun from his right sleeve while his left hand opened the car door. The black metal glinted in the moonlight. Quick as the flash of a quail's wing, Sable hit the gun out of his hand with her own Colt. A shot rang out. The bullet punctured the front window, which cracked as a spider's web.

The next moment he was out of the car, jumping over the railing that led down to the river. Sable leapt out on the other side, went up to the railing and fired at the moving shadow disappearing in the dark. He kept moving. A second shot. His silhouette became vaguer. She aimed again, stilling the trembling of her hands. *This time*, she told herself. The bullet whizzed.

A loud wail. Then the shape stumbled and fell. Silence but for the torrent of water rushing ahead. Sable waited. Counted to ten. No movement, but he could still be tricking her.

Inching over the railing, her gun directed at the slumped body, she slowly descended to where he lay. He didn't move. She kicked him with her boot. Still no movement. It was a raw deal, but she fired once more. The bullet went straight into his head. He quivered, groaned once. Was gone.

Four shots had rung in the night. Even at a distance from the town, it meant danger. Sable knew as no other she'd have to work quicker than lightning and get away from Coutras. Emptying De Bonheur's pockets without looking at the contents, she stuffed everything in her rucksack. Then she dragged the body down ten feet and eased the dead man into the river. The corpse was swallowed instantly by the furious water. The last thing she saw of him was a flap of his old-fashioned linen jacket.

"*Plus de Bonheur*! No more luck." She couldn't help using the pun, but without wasting another second, crawled up the embankment and into the driver's seat of the Renault Juvaquatre. Sable had never driven a French car and certainly not one where the vision of the broken windshield was this poor, but she managed. Her teeth clattering and her stomach churning, she turned the car onto the main road toward Tulle.

"I'm going to Lyon," she kept repeating to herself. "I have to notify London." But her mind kept screaming at her. *You've killed three men, Sable. This is real, this is very real.*

In the glove department, she found a packet of Ecksteins. The Judas had even taken to smoking his new bosses' cigarettes. But Sable thought it a lesser crime if she took one.

Never had a cigarette tasted this good and calmed her more.

37

THE LULL BEFORE THE STORM

S able arrived in Lyon at the end of the afternoon after a sweeping four-hundred-mile drive. The spine-tingling events of the night before had followed her the entire stretch of the journey, eating into her system like a many-armed spook.

"It can't be changed anymore. I've done what I had to do." She kept assuring herself, but her conscience had more trouble processing the cold-blooded murder of three men with her own slender hands. Repeatedly she tried to bring Major Woolworth's face before her, his wise words.

"There's no clean war, sugar. Chances are that even secret agents have to kill, not once, but a slew of times. You'd better stomach that right now."

But she hadn't. It had been a theoretical yes to the veteran of the Great War, and now she had to face the consequences of not really understanding that war could scar you also as an aggressor.

Sable realized she was facing a hard time ahead, maybe even harder than her imprisonment at Alnor Castle and the forced parting with her daughter. She was no victim of the circumstances here. She herself had become a calculated and cutthroat killer. The struggle would be both inside and outside. And vigilance was paramount, as *Le Corbeau Noir* was now certainly high on the Nazis' wanted list.

Arriving at the Grand Nouvel Hotel, longing with every bone in her body for a bed and a meal, too frazzled and exhausted to make any further plans, Sable parked the lime-green Renault in the driveway and let out a deep sigh.

"I'll find a wireless operator as soon as I'm rested, but board and bed now," she promised herself as she dragged her weary feet up the stairs. Looking down, she saw smears of blood on her hands and jacket from when she'd dragged De Bonheur's body down to the river. It looked rather ghastly, but there was nothing she could do about it right now except hope no one would notice.

BLINKING INTO BRIGHT SUNLIGHT, with someone pulling her arm, Sable's awakening was rather rough and abrupt. Double quick, she grabbed her gun and sat upright. Her eyes were wild, her long black mane glued to her forehead and cheeks. Still squinting in the light, she zeroed in on her attacker.

"Who's there?"

Her arm with the gun was pushed down by a firm hand.

"Easy, easy, girl. It's only good old me." An Irish lilt. Maureen Knight, aka Madame Marcelle Gautier, code name Adèle. The details popped back from the periphery into Sable's out-of-focus mind.

Not knowing what washed over her—relief, pain, desolation, gratitude, or a mix of it all—Sable threw herself into Maureen's arms, hugging and clasping her, half sobbing, half laughing. All earlier doubts whether she liked the Irish agent were forgotten.

"I thought... I thought... you'd left Lyon for Perpignan?"

"I did, my friend, but I came back last week. Didn't like the molly-coddle I'd become. There's so much to be afraid of in wartime, so why not face it head on? It will never be a walk through a field of daisies. When presented with the option of getting a safe passage through Spain and hopping on a plane back to Britain, I did the opposite.

Much to the dislike of my hosts, I told them I'd be heading back to Lyon to take over the broken BROUILLARD network."

"I couldn't be happier to see you, Marcelle. And to be back in Lyon."

"Be careful what you wish for, Jacqueline!"

"Oh, I'm no longer Jacqueline. That cover was blown. The complete story I'll tell you later. I'm Mademoiselle Violette Bernard, a traveling saleswoman for Triumph typewriters in France."

Maureen whistled. "Ooh-la-la. You must tell me all over coffee and petit pain. I heard you're still *Le Corbeau Noir*, though. Your reputation has preceded you."

The Irish agent released Sable from her embrace, the Celtic green eyes taking her in with interest. A fresh gulf of relief and friendship filled Sable's heart. Tears came of their own accord.

"I'm so happy to see you, Marcelle. I think I've never been happier to see anyone."

"Though I know that is a pertinent lie born out of despair, I'll tuck it away as a compliment." Maureen smiled. "Now come, let's think of our physical well-being first. I've got brand-new fake food ration stamps that will buy us a decent petit déjeuner."

They were seated on either side of a minuscule wooden table on the hotel's back-side veranda. Two in-love pigeons were making a racket on the roof opposite with a lot of wing beating and cooing.

"Welcome to spring in Lyon," Maureen giggled. "You think we'll have as much luck getting wooed here as these pigeons?"

Sable lit one of her Eckstein's cigarettes, which made Maureen raise one red brow, but she didn't comment on it.

"Lesson one in elementary precautions," Sable mimicked Wooly's deep baritone, "don't share accommodation with another agent."

"We've gone wrong on that one already," Maureen smirked, but Sable stoically went on with the list.

"Commit nothing to writing, or talk about operations."

"There we go. We're useless." Maureen banged her coffee cup on its saucer and turned her eyes upwards in mock despair.

"Pay attention, sugar." Sable enjoyed playing the part of Major

Woolworth. "The most objectionable faux pas are still to come. Don't go directly to meetings or sit in a public vehicle. Don't stand near an exit."

"I don't get the last two." Maureen drew up her brows again.

"Neither do I. I just recite the list," Sable replied in her own voice and then went deeper again. "Don't disclose the name on your identity card or carry more than one identity card."

"Leads to multiple personality disorder." Maureen, who had a streak of the comedian anyway, made such a funny face that Sable snorted her coffee over the table.

"Don't interrupt my lecturing again," she squawked. "You wanted to hear if we could take a lover, didn't you?"

"All right, all right, I'll keep my Irish trap shut."

Sable continued. "Don't get drunk in public or chase the girls or sleep with another agent." She gave Maureen a stern stare before quickly scrambling to the end. "And don't use a two-way dead letter box, or somebody may use it to trap you."

Maureen looked pensive, tilting her head sideways before letting her perfect teeth sink into a jam-filled French pastry.

"Hmmm, so it's perfectly all right to sleep with someone as long as he's not an agent? That throws up some interesting possibilities."

Sable thoroughly enjoyed their lighthearted banter. It was exactly what she needed after her night from hell.

"You're impossible." She grinned. "I'm sure your head is screwed on your neck in such a way that you won't pay heed to any of Wooly's precautions if you feel like it."

"True," Maureen agreed, but then suddenly she grew more serious. "Which doesn't mean I'm reckless. Life here is just so totally different from what we were taught at agent school. So, is there a special non-agent in your life, Mademoiselle Violette?" The mist-green eyes focused on Sable with a warm smile.

Sable startled, not expecting the question. From some ill-timed, hidden source Bill's handsome face flashed in front of her, which made her shake her head, a little too vigorous for her alert friend.

"So, there was? I see pain, so I'll not ask any further. Same here. Broken heart." Maureen made a sideways cross over her modest bosom.

"Yes, once upon a time." And with a wan smile, Sable added. "He was —is—an agent, but not here in France." And to change the subject, she added, "But I have excellent news. I found out I have a half-brother and he is in France, currently on his way to Paris. He used to be with the LANTERN circuit in Clermont-Ferrand."

"How exciting!" Maureen exclaimed. "But what do you mean by, *I found out I have a half-brother?*"

Sable told her friend how her mother had revealed also being Freddie's biological mother just before her death.

"Now I need another café crème," Maureen announced, "and before we get to work, I want to hear the story about the blood on your clothes. After that, I'll disclose some pleasant surprises that have happened within the BROUILLARD network this week."

The mint-colored gaze focusing on her, Sable experienced anew how good an agent Maureen was. Nothing escaped her, and she deftly used the psychological method of small-talk and reconnection, before coming to the point. They'd be a formidable team.

"So where have you been, my dear? You look a tad better this morning, but when I found you asleep on the bed, I was shocked how straggly and hounded you looked. And blood-smeared too. You haven't been in some sort of fight, have you?"

"It's Henri de Bonheur," Sable blurted out. "He was working for the Germans. He has snitched on the entire CHASSIS circuit. And he had Maurice—you know, my half-brother—and me arrested in Coutras."

"And you...?" Maureen made a cut-throat movement. Sable nodded.

"Holy Mother of God. I knew it, I knew it!" The green eyes flashed with fury, but she immediately grabbed Sable's hand firmly across the table. "You have guts in that waifish body of you, my dear. I doff my cap to you! Does London know?"

Sable took strength from Maureen's grip as her hands were shaking. "No, that's why I came here, hoping to find a W/T. I couldn't go back to Bordeaux, but we also must get rid of the Renault. It was De Bonheur's car. Not that I think anyone knows here that I took his car, after... you know."

She was now scrambling through her words, relieved to unburden her weight but still not at ease with what she'd done.

"One thing at a time, my dear." Maureen squeezed her hands. "Let me tell you the good news that fits in perfectly with our plan. I'm working with two fantastic agents, and one, Cecil Granville, is the best W/T operator I've had so far. There's also a female agent you may remember from Beaulieu, Diana Rolfe?" Sable shook her head. Neither name rang a bell.

Maureen continued, "Before coming to Lyon, Cecil was also in the Bordeaux region and heard all the rumors about De Bonheur. He tried to warn London several times, but they wouldn't listen to him. Still had new agents dropped in the Bordeaux region. I fear for all their lives."

"So, Marcelle, do you think I did the right thing by killing him? I also killed my two German captors, young guys, not really baddies." Sable hung on to Maureen's hands for dear life. Maureen pondered her urgent plea.

"I think so. I mean, I might not have had the guts, but the rumors about De Bonheur were persistent and it's true that London didn't pick up the signals." She hesitated and then said with more conviction, "Yes, *Le Corbeau Noir*, it deserves a medal, I'm sure. Now let's get to work."

The busy city, the many undercover agents both international and French, Maureen's constant nearness and high spirits... All these markers helped Sable through the struggle of her first days in Lyon. Her assassinations were still raw as a stab wound on her conscience.

Spurred on by Maureen, who called her "string bean Sheila," she did her best to eat; but appetite was lost in another world. Even more than before, Sable singularly depended on her cigarettes. Booze was still out of the question, but she came close, especially because all the other agents consumed copious amounts of Pernod and Vin Rouge and got drunk, very offhandedly forgetting the precautions instilled in them.

Sable missed Freddie, who hopefully would now have safely landed in Paris but knew nothing of her return to Coutras. She hankered for her brother to be with her in Lyon. His presence at this difficult stage in her life would have made it all so much more bearable. *I should never have let us part*, she thought many a time, but then reminded herself she'd decided all along to keep him out of her reckoning with Henri de Bonheur.

The fewer people knew she was involved in De Bonheur's death, the better. Even London hadn't been told the whole truth. Just that he'd been exposed as a stool pigeon and killed by the French Maquis resisters.

Without being conscious of it, Sable was homesick, without family, a rudderless orphan. Telling Maureen about Bill and their painful breakup hadn't made things easier. Now she ached for his embrace even more than ever. The proud Scotsman with eyes clear as a blue-eyed eagle, his warm embrace, his unwavering strength. Oh, she could do with all that now that she felt so vulnerable.

Bill frequently materialized in her dreams and every time he appeared, she woke with her heart pounding and her hopes raised high. She would even reach for him in her sleep, spreading her arms wide, but would curl up in a ball, miserable and stranded, when the dream had once again proven to be a figment of her imagination.

Alas. No word from William "Wild Bill" Mitchell. It was as if she'd once lived in a wonderful romantic fiction, but it had completely fizzled out, no happy ending, just an unhappy emptiness. Most likely, he'd found another girl. He'd certainly forgotten all about her.

Meeting Cecil and Diana was as nice as Maureen had predicted. They were good company. Though the four of them had to make sure to only meet in twos or as a group in one of Lyon's many safe houses, they became friends and functioned as a perfect unit.

BROULLIARD's current task mainly comprised of helping downed Allied airmen, who all seemed to pass through Lyon to get to the Pyrenees and then via Spain back to England. Maureen and Sable were also busy restoring the circuit that had suffered greatly from the zealous actions of Gestapo Chief Barbie's men.

ON A SUNNY AFTERNOON at the end of May, the four of them were in a lofty apartment near le Pont Lafayette overlooking the river Rhône. It had belonged to a Jewish industrialist who'd fled with his family to London after the German occupation of Vichy in November 1942.

Before his departure, Monsieur Dreyfus had given the keys to their apartment to Giles, the owner of the Perrache Charlemagne Bar, to be used as he saw fit.

Sable loved the place. It gave her a sense of security, however false that was. The sprawling apartment, consisting of twelve rooms and two bathrooms, lay on the second floor and was lavishly furnished. It had large bay windows that opened to the buzz and the liveliness below on the Quai de Retz.

The sweet, aromatic scent of the lilac bushes on the quay wafted up into the air, mingling with gasoline, baked bread, and tangy river water. The essence of a French city in spring.

Sometimes, especially when her heart ached like this, she loved to be surrounded by a city. The Dreyfus home generated an acute anguish for life in London. For her home on the lush, leafy Cavendish Square. For the placidness and peace and simple pace that life with Elrod and Minnie had provided.

She pictured herself wearing a silver-lamé evening dress and diamond tiara, long white gloves to her elbows and her hair done up with glittering gemstones as well. Darting to the Empire Cinema on Mile End Road in her silver-heeled shoes to see the newest movie, *Between Two Women*. Of course, she was on Bill's arm, who was proudly wearing his kilt battle dress from the Clan Sinclair.

In reality, she was sitting in the open window on the lookout for potential SS officers lurking around the building. In the middle of war-torn France, where she could be arrested and killed any moment. Her knees drawn up, her eyes squinting against the sun reflecting in the river water, the eternal cigarette with a long ash stump held between her yellowed index and middle finger, wearing an old cotton dress and espadrilles. Her hair was only done up with a bandana in the same pattern as her dress.

No makeup, no jewels, no Bill. And certainly, no peace or calm routine.

Behind Monsieur Dreyfus's imposing mahogany desk with its carved lion feet at the end of every leg and an inlay of billiard green cloth, Cecil sat in a calf-leather desk chair, busily tapping his daily coded message to Baker Street. He hunched over the wireless set as if protecting it with his very body.

In his mid-twenties, Cecil Granville looked French with his dark wavy hair and brilliant desert-sand brown eyes, a full moustache on a strong, regular face, but he was, in fact, a Quebecer preacher's son. With his broody seriousness, he tried hard to pass as a true-blooded Frenchman, but his Canadian French tongue was quickly detected.

Cecil was a remarkable and likable personality with the body and posture of an athlete. At the *Université de Montréal*, where he had studied law, he'd been an ardent athlete excelling in rowing and tennis.

Whenever he walked into a room, his charisma lit up the scene and the people around him. Though modest in his manners and with the discretion and guardedness of a high-level secret agent, Cecil Granville couldn't be overlooked. Maybe not the most helpful asset for an agent, but he seemed unaware of it. Sable felt Maureen's snarky wit soften every time Cecil was on the spot.

Unlike Maureen, who she'd known before coming to France, Sable had not met Cecil and Diana during her training, so for security reasons Sable only knew and addressed them by their cover names, Cecil and Diana.

Diana was a very different personality from the dashing wireless operator and the funny Maureen, introverted and sweet with an almost unbridled closeness to both Maureen and Cecil, watching their every move and helping them wherever she could. Diana was out grocery shopping, which meant, in effect, she was dropping off messages at other safe houses.

With one ear Sable was listening to Maureen in the back room giving instructions and handing out civilian clothes to two disoriented RAF pilots. That evening they would be escorted by Diana to Ciboure in German-occupied Basque Pyrenees, where a guide would meet them and take them over the mountains.

How all the downed airmen got word of the Comet Line, as the escape route and the organization thereof in Lyon, was a mystery, but the message had clearly spread as wildfire all over France. *Go to Lyon, to the Perrache Charlemagne Bar. You'll get help there.*

They came, dozens of them, Poles, Frenchmen, Dutchmen, Brits, Canadians, Czechs, Americans, disheveled, sometimes wounded, exhausted, having walked or traveled with farmers' carts for hundreds of miles, from one safe house to the next.

Until they dropped on their doorstep, more dead than alive, in need of food, shelter and Maureen's pep talk before being ready for the treacherous trek over the Pyrenees.

Many of the pilots, some still arriving in their torn uniforms, formed a danger to themselves and to the network, but BROUILLARD turned none of them down. Not even though the foursome were running out of time, out of resources, out of ration cards, false passports and travels permits.

MAUREEN CAME INTO THE ROOM, her pale skin blotchy from fatigue and burden, though she doffed up her ginger locks when Cecil looked up from his code book and caught her eye. She marched over to the window where Sable was sitting, the slender hands visible fists in her thin cotton overalls.

"It can't go on like this anymore," she bemoaned. "I see no other choice but to instruct Giles at Perrache to send the airmen on to Valence or Toulouse. The Comet line from Lyon will collapse any time now."

"But do we have contacts in these cities?" Sable gave Maureen a quick glance before resuming her lookout post. "I could go there to connect with the circuits. Or perhaps Diana can make a stopover after she's escorted Anton and Michael to Ciboure?"

"No, Diana has to come straight back. Giles told me three Polish aviators are arriving this week that must be helped out of the country *de suite*. Plus, she must drop off the explosives for the sabotage at the Michelin factory in Le Puy. And then there's the drop of more ammunition and hopefully agents in the Givors region tomorrow night."

Sable agreed they were terribly understaffed. Working in an urban area was so different from working in the countryside. Here it was much harder to find trustworthy Frenchmen who wanted to join the fight, coupled with the Gestapo constantly trying to get on their wick.

"Cecil, can you ask London which agents we have in Valence and Toulouse?" Sable asked.

"At your service. Will do it tonight." He winked at the girls, reassuring them with his handsome smile.

"I'll do the Givors drop tomorrow night, Marcelle. You really don't need to exert yourself further," Sable declared. "I know it's on your schedule, but according to me, you need a stiff drink and an early night."

"Would you?" The green eyes lit up. "But you're overworked yourself."

"I don't depend on booze like you lot. As long as I have my ciggies and my dreams of a future soft bed, a satin nightdress and maybe a good book, I will survive."

"Is there only a book and no handsome man in your future soft bed?" Maureen quipped.

"For sure there is. Jacqueline just won't tell us about her mystery man!" Cecil chimed in, but the desert-brown eyes were all over Maureen.

Sable laughed with them, jumping off the windowsill and making a pirouette on the parquet floor, her cotton dress swirling around her slender legs.

"Who knows? Not me!"

IT WAS the lull before the storm.

38

THE NEMESIS

The next night, at the moonless and humid midnight hour, Sable left the LeBlancs' farmhouse outside Givors to go by foot through dense undergrowth to an open place close to the Rhone River, where Cecil had arranged the drops of supplies and agents. The shimmering blackness of the water was the only diffuse source of light and would guide the pilot to the assigned spot.

How many more of these armament drops? Sable wondered as she followed the shadowed back of the LeBlanc's son in front of her. The Allied forces had provided the French resistance with so many arms and ammunition already. Plane loads and plane loads. And she'd been present at scads of them.

For sure, the longed-for invasion would be at hand. She prayed for it every day. Four grueling years of war, too many resisters and agents arrested, then disappeared, and the brutality of the Nazis increasing by the day. There was even talk of immense death camps the Germans had set up in their own country and in Poland. No one knew for sure whether it was true, but the bodings were bone-chilling. It had to be over soon. Sooner than soon.

In between the nineteen-year-old, taciturn youngster and behind her, his father Gerard LeBlanc, equally closemouthed, Sable stealthed through the wet bushes, drenched by now, and cold to the bone. She endured the hardships, as always, grateful for the company of locals, who knew every bend in the path, every danger, every pitfall. At least they'd reach their destination, no matter the conditions.

It was hard to stay positive when tired, wet, cold, fighting a constant battle against an overpowering enemy. It was so much a David against Goliath tug-of-war, but they had to win. So, she focused on the outcome, more supplies and more helping hands.

Yet in the pit of her stomach there was a nagging premonition that this time made her extra edgy and out of sorts. There was no direct reason for her presentiment. She and the team had taken all the necessary safety measures, all the time, never letting their guard down. Since arriving in Lyon a couple of weeks prior, Sable had for the first time felt she could rely on her team blindly, as sure as the coat on her back that their inner and outer circle was rid of moles.

Then what?

She had the constant feeling of being shadowed, an invisible Peeping Tom who was impossible to shake off. Whether it had to do with a reckoning for Coutras, or that the actual target was Maureen, and they were trying to get to The Red Fury via her was the question. But either way, their motivation was of no importance. Staying ahead of the hunters was what matters. Her sixth sense mattered.

Why the Gestapo didn't simply strike was puzzling, but Sable knew from her intense training that tracking an agent for a longer period delivered vital information to the enemy. The threat shaped her every step, every turning of a street corner, every brief nap at night with her Colt as her companion, slowly but certainly stretching her so thin it created a sense of mounting helplessness.

An ardent believer in her own gut feelings, Sable knew she should bring up her suspicions with Maureen and the rest, but she didn't want to strain the others more than they already were. She'd have the talk tomorrow, after this drop. Maybe break up as a four-some or move together to another town.

Here in the neighborhood of Givors, away from Lyon, the edginess was slightly less predominant. Sable now put all her hope on the arrival of newly trained agents, who were still unknown to the Lyon Gestapo and who maybe, at least temporarily, could take over the BROUILLARD network.

And if Maureen doesn't want to hear about it, I will have to move on myself. Maybe go to Paris where I can be anonymous for a while. Although there, I could not stop myself from looking up Freddie, she promised herself, as the small reception team took up their positions on the edge of the woods, in sight of the calm, nightly Rhone River.

For Sable these armament and agent drops were a routine operation, but she realized every time how exciting and frightening the journey must be to each fresh batch of agents, most of whom had never set foot in occupied France before.

The drop went according to plan. Two women, one man, ready to strengthen their team, clambered out of their parachutes and on shaky legs, set their first steps on French soil, close to the clutches of the real and dangerous enemy. The Lysander took off to England again. No Germans in sight.

Sable went through all the steps with Bella, Marguerite, and Alphonse. Checked and double-checked they knew their cover stories and understood what was expected of them before putting them up for the night in a nearby safe house.

The next morning, they each made their separate way back by train to Lyon. Sable felt slightly more optimistic about sharing the workload with what seemed a capable operator and couriers. She couldn't wait for the beaming of Maureen's peaky white face when she saw their reinforcements.

But...

When Sable opened the door to her safe house in District XII, she instantly knew something was wrong. Standing stock-still on the doorstep, nostrils flaring, a vague soap scent not her own, a frequency subtle but different than before.

Without having to see the evidence, she knew someone had been there with ill intentions. Her room had been searched thoroughly, though every object was still as she'd left it. With her Colt cocked, she went from the room to the adjacent bathroom, kicking it further open with her boot. No one was in there.

Time to undertake a proper search. Apart from the soap smell, it was her book, Madame Bovary, lying in a slightly different position on her nightstand, the curtain further drawn than she'd left it. This person had wanted to leave no trace but had failed.

Having no choice, Sable quickly packed the necessary a few more items in her rucksack and grabbed her always-ready suitcase. Dragging her suitcase down the stairs, she left the apartment only five minutes after she'd entered it, locking it carefully.

There was no one lurking around, but she sensed them, and it turned her blood cold as a winter's sky. Considering it too dangerous to go to Perrache Champagne Bar in the middle of the day, she would drop off her suitcase at the Grand Nouvel Hotel and go in search of Maureen, Cecil, and Diana. Her next job would be warning the newcomers.

At the entrance of the hotel she bumped into Yvette, the chambermaid who doubled as a French resister. She immediately pushed Sable into a corner of the lobby behind some man-sized palms.

"Have you heard?" she whispered, her eyes round with fear.

"Heard what?" A new level of agitation gripped Sable by the throat.

"They've all three been arrested. Marcelle, Cecil, and Diana. We hoped you would come here. You must flee as fast as you can, Violette." The maid was pulling on her arm, as if she wanted to ship her out at that very moment. The entire conversation took place in whispers.

"They've been taken where?"

Yvette shook her head. "We don't know. Probably to Hôtel Terminus, the Gestapo Headquarters. It doesn't look good. Horrendous things go on inside there."

"Then we have to liberate them," Sable concluded.

"Silly, you can't. Barbie has turned the hotel into a fortress."

Sable's mercurial mind was already a few steps ahead.

"Take care of my suitcase for me until I return. Here are the safe-houses where the new agents are lodged. Make sure they're warned. Try to get hold of Giles at Perrache and tell them the Comet Line won't function from Lyon for a while. I'll be back as soon as I can, but I have to go into hiding for a while."

Yvette looked at her with her head slightly tilted. There were rumors about Le Corbeau Noir, and Sable could see them play through the maid's head.

"I won't do anything stupid," she lied, "don't worry. Just cover me. I'll take the back entrance and disappear from Lyon, but rest assured, I'll be back."

Liberating people from Hôtel Terminus was little short of a kiss of death, Sable conceded as she lay in an underground cellar in the 7ème arrondissement on a dingy mattress smoking a cigarette. She'd arrived at the place through the mazes of streets mapped in her head on her arrival in Lyon the first time. She was quite sure she'd shaken off her followers. Well, almost sure.

For now, there was nothing to do but kill time. It was still light outside, and she would only move after curfew. Without a detailed plan so far. Cursing herself for not studying the Hôtel Terminus plan and surroundings before, she came up with one escape plan, tossed it out, and thought of a new one. Liberating three people was sheer impossible. And were they still here or already transported to Fresnes prison or even Paris?

It was an audacious ploy, risky as hell, but she'd give it a shot. She would wait for a shift in guards, follow him, a swift kill, and then change into his uniform.

As soon as dusk had fallen, she dressed in her all-black outfit and with only her knife in her boot and her gun in her pocket, she slipped outside in the dark, walking in that circumspect, shrewd manner that Cuthbert had taught her, an urban guerrilla fighter, invisible to all but God.

It was a pleasantly warm evening, but the city was deserted save for a Jeep of jeering SS officers on their way to a bar or brothel, and a lonesome German motorcyclist riding at high speed in the middle of the *Cours de Verdun*.

When Sable finally arrived at the corner of the Gestapo head-quarters, she studied the lay of the land. Two soldiers on the doorstep, guarding the building. That was one too many. She would have to wait, despite the risk of being discovered, loitering in the dark.

Her foot crunched on a small stone. *Blast!* One guard looked in her direction. She ducked back, stumbled. Off base, she was grabbed by two brawny arms grabbed from behind. Sable yelped despite herself at the sudden attack in her back.

"*Was machts du hier?*"

She wanted to say, "Nichts" but was already dragged into the light. Eyes cold as a fish stared triumphantly into hers.

"We've got her, *Kamerad*! Great job. The General will be so happy we caught another of these agents. Maybe it's even *Le Corbeau Noir*. Anyway, no more flying free for you, little birdie!"

Sable tried to struggle free, fought with every muscle of her body, but the two men held her, pulling her along, up the steps of the former hotel, dragging her inside as she kicked and screamed.

Something teetered in her. Furious with herself for being caught, furious her instinct had not protected her this time, furious at her captors. So, they had followed her all along. They had been smarter. It was the end of the game, but she would fight till the end.

She'd always hated Germans, but this was like nothing she'd felt before. It was as if she was being injected with a fluid that poisoned her blood, her heart, the very fiber of her being.

You will pay for this!

Later she wasn't sure if she'd screamed it at the top of her lungs or had thought about it. But she had felt it, nothing else, nothing more.

Between her two captors, she was led before a simple desk behind which sat a four-star general. He looked up as they came in.

They locked eyes.

He slowly rose from behind his desk, tall, elegant, the uniform tight with a belt around his slender waist. The wide khaki trousers disappearing in shiny black boots. Powerful, robust, what people called an aesthetically appealing man, the blond-blue eyed German aristocrat.

"You?" His face twitched. "You... are *Le Corbeau Noir?*"

Sable met his eye, saw through the appeal, felt the ice in her veins.

"Yes, I am the Highland Raven. And you, Monsieur, are Hauptsturmführer Joachim von Henkell. My nemesis."

39

THE CONFRONTATION

T he slight squinting of his eyes, his lips pressed together after uttering *Le Corbeau Noir*, a hesitance in his raised posture... Sable could read Von Henkell inside and out. He was more knocked sideways at seeing her in front of him than she was. Frankly, all her training had prepared her for this moment.

As they stared each other down, she studied his every feature with meticulous care and was greatly relieved to feel no angst, no anger, no need for atonement. Whatever he could do to her now, she was above it, free from it, a soaring raven. *Hurt me if you can.*

As if her ears popped open, she became aware of the room, the rather old-fashioned, red-carpeted hotel lobby, rather haphazardly turned into a Gestapo headquarters with grey metal filing cabinets around Von Henkell's desk, two lanky SS officers looking rather aghast at their off-kilter boss and the black-clad, slight woman who seemed to challenge his very authority.

A fan hanging from the stucco ceiling whirred in slow-motion above their heads. *Tick, tick, tick.* The sound of German voices in the anteroom, one laughing out loud and then the eerie sense that there were French and international prisoners obscured from view all over the building. Hurt, bleeding, dying. That sense, that awareness, kept Sable on her toes.

She waited. Stood her ground. The ball was in Von Henkell's court.

"Sit down, pleaze, Madame," he addressed her in his clipped English. Then he made a gesture for her captors to leave the room. "*Schliesst die Tür!*"

The two officers slinked out of the room, looking dissatisfied at not being heartily congratulated for bringing in the agent on whose head was a 100,000 francs reward.

Sable sat down on the edge of the chintz-covered hotel stool. Von Henkell hesitated again before sitting down, struggling to maintain his dominance by looming above her.

A package of Chesterfield cigarettes lay nonchalantly on the table's smooth surface. Stolen from an American prisoner, no doubt.

She pointed to the package. "Can I have one?"

"Sure!"

Her hands were steady as she held the cigarette and inhaled the smoke, but her heart raced. His silence was working on her nerves, so she took the lead again, though aware his taciturnity might be a tactic to get her talking of her own accord. She'd have to be vigilant to the maximum, knowing that her cover was blown.

"Did you hear that my mother passed away?"

The bruise-blue eyes weighed her up, the tiny muscles around them twitching. He lit a cigarette from the same package.

"I did. My friend Werner von Bissing informed me. My condolences, Madame."

Sable scoffed. "Unlike you, I wasn't close to my mother. It didn't feel like an enormous loss."

While she dragged furiously on the filter of her cigarette, Von Henkell seemed to ponder her answer. Then answered in his heavily accented English.

"Ah, but you are wrong zere, Madame. Losing one'z mother iz ze greatest loss of all."

Sable wondered if the man had lost his marbles. Were they seriously discussing mothers in the wee hours of the morning, just after she'd been captured by his men? She shrugged, but he didn't let go of what apparently was an important topic to him.

"I lost my dear Mutti when I was only four years old. I only vaguely remember her, but I remember her smell like yesterday, lilies-of-the-valley."

Why on earth are you telling me all this? Sable wondered, as she had to admit the man with his handsome features and soft manners confused her. She'd expected Klaus Barbie, the Butcher of Lyon, not this rather dreamy diplomat who seemed totally unfit for interrogating and torturing foreign agents. Blabbing about his lost mother.

Von Henkell had always irritated her, even at her mother's dinner table. She'd considered him a softie then, which didn't jibe with the cruel way he'd forced himself upon her later. And the picture she'd painted of him to justify herself. *If only I hadn't been drunk and drugged, I might remember more*, she told herself.

It was tempting to ask him what had happened. He who was the only other person in the world cognizant of what had had passed between them on that fateful night on the backseat of the black Mercedes with the waves of Loch Fyne lapping the shore. But Sable knew she'd never degrade herself to ask this man even one question.

"Would you perhaps want something to drink, Madame? A glass of water or a black coffee?" The hesitant voice drew her from her befuddled thoughts.

"What do you want from me?" Sable abruptly struggled to her feet, looking at the door as if she'd take a leap and fling herself at it.

"Madame, may I remind you that you are in custody? Please sit down again." There still was no real authority in his command, so Sable remained standing on her feet.

"Only if you tell me why I'm being held. I've got more to do zan hang around Hôtel Terminus wiz you." She deliberately mocked his clipped English.

"I think you know, Madame. You're not a fool."

"Then can you not do something for me, considering we share a past?" It was an audacious proposal as she looked straight at him. She was taken aback by the distress in the milky-blue eyes. Unprepared for Nazi agony, she sank back on the hotel stool.

"I don't think so, Madame, although if it had been up to me, I might consider it."

Holy moly, Sable thought, *for some odd reason I've got this Nazi in my pocket. I need to exploit this with all I have.*

"Please stop calling me Madame. You know very well my name is Sable. And yes, I could do with a strong coffee."

Her memory catapulted her back to 1935, standing with her father across the street from the London Palladium in the afternoon sunshine. At that very spot, she'd decided to become an actress. Now the time had come to shine in her absolute star role.

Unlike in Hitchcock's *39 Steps,* she, Starlet Sable, would not die with a knife in her back, but the man across the table from her certainly would.

She had to swallow hard. What she was about to try disgusted her to her toenails. But it was worth it. Maureen and Cecil and Diana, and all the other captured and tortured agents and resistance fighters were worth it. Her sacrifice was so small in comparison, almost nil.

From very far away she heard that almost lisping voice. "Yes, I know your name is Sable. How could I ever forget?"

"I guess not."

Sable gave him her most endearing smile, counting on it that men were used to the whimsical mood changes in women. If she'd first come across as a hard-shelled resistance fighter, now she fluidly slipped into the role of seductress.

"So, what do you want me to tell you, Herr von Henkell?"

"If I may call you Sable, I guess you can call me Joachim, like in the good old days?"

"Sure, Joachim, my pleasure. Why do you call it the good old days? Heavens, I thought you Germans doted on this war?"

"Not I, Sable. Remember, I was the ambassador to the UK before the war. I love Great Britain and I love diplomacy. I feel much more at ease in a suit than in this attire." He made a cheerless gesture to his fancy uniform.

"Well, we can agree on one thing then," Sable observed drily, stirring two precious lumps of real sugar in her real coffee that had been served to her immediately. The scent made her mouth water. She continued. "To tell you the truth, Joachim, I had expected your boss, Klaus Barbie, to be here."

"He is out of town."

"All right, shall we get down to business? It's getting late and I'm tired."

It seemed so peculiar that she, as the arrestee, was calling the shots and the Nazi on the other side of the table a hesitant, huggermugger mess.

"I agree. It is late. We can do the interrogation tomorrow morning over breakfast. I will ask one of my men to accompany you to your cell."

"Am I being detained? For doing what? Breaking curfew?" Sable pouted as angelically as she could muster. The artificial smile hurt her jaw, but it was worth it.

"Alas, Sable, I cannot let you go. You know better than I your reason for being in France. But don't worry. I have had the best room in the hotel prepared for you. I will see you tomorrow at breakfast."

Sable didn't know if she was displeased or pleased with this arrangement. It meant probably options for escape, but she would never find out more about her team's presence at the Hôtel Terminus if she fled that night. There would be no turning back. But if she stayed, Barbie might return any minute, and this cat-and-mouse game between her and Von Henkell would be over.

"Thank you, Joachim, you're most attentive." Another fake smile was all she could whip up.

She was taken to the top floor of the hotel and ushered into what indeed was a lavish hotel room with sweeping gold-colored curtains and thick Persian carpets. An ornately decorated mahogany four-poster bed dominated the room.

As soon as she was left alone and the lock in the door had turned, Sable leapt to the window and tore open the heavy velvet curtains.

The windows could open but immediately banged against iron railings that served as an inaccessible mini balcony.

"Blast!" Sable muttered.

What now? She hadn't the foggiest idea if she was the only BROUILLARD agent detained at the Terminus or whether her team were still here. Or others. On the way up, she'd strained her ears on every landing to catch a sound of her friends, but the hotel had been dead quiet. Too quiet.

She was well and truly trapped now, her only viable exit Von Henkell's weird and wishy-washy approach to her. He seemed such a different man from the proud, silver-tongued diplomat who'd been at the core of Misty Fletcher's Scottish dinner parties.

The idea he'd come into her room and force himself upon her again only crossed her mind fleetingly. She'd kill him with her own hands and somehow, she felt he knew not to try his luck. But if Barbie was back in Lyon in the morning, she was doomed. That was clear as day.

She slept, one ear awake, her Colt within reach, another incomprehensible action by the Haubtsturmführer. Not having been searched, she was still in possession of her rucksack filled with incriminating articles.

40

THE SHADOW OF MISTY FLETCHER

A staccato knock on the door woke Sable from a slumber she'd fallen into long after five in the morning.

"Madame!"

Bleary-eyed, still in her crumbled black disguise, she shot out of bed.

"I'm coming."

"I'm here to escort you down," a German voice announced.

Sable raced out of the door. "Ready!"

The fake smile was already plastered on her tired, thin face.

"Hauptsturmführer Von Henkell is waiting for you in the lobby, Madame." The young SS-officer looked rather sheepishly at her and Sable thought, *what now?* The hotel still seemed deserted at this early morning hour. No sign of other occupants but the Germans.

On coming down the last flight of stairs with the officer at her heels, Sable froze in her steps. It was as if time was turned five years back. Von Henkell stood dressed in civilian clothes, just as she'd known him before the war. Instead of the high-necked SS field jacket with the hated SS and Iron Cross insignia, the puffed-up pants, and high black boots, he was wearing a light linen, Viennese-style suit with a good amount of waist suppression, wide shoulders, and full-cut pants. He'd even donned his wavy blond hair with a straw hat.

Sable raised her eyebrows but asked nothing. What did she know about the way the Nazis dressed? Neither did she care, quickly rebounding from her initial shock at the memories of his prewar presence in her life.

He greeted her with a slight bow, glancing uncomfortably at her combat outfit in plain daylight. It made Sable smile inwardly. Had he expected her to come down in one of her Chanel evening dresses?

"I hope you had some sleep?" He looked uncertain, as if he was asking her validation for something.

"I prefer my own bed, but it's been quite a while since I've seen it." Sable automatically slipped back into her rather sarcastic self, forgetting she was supposed to be endearing.

Perhaps it was his clothing compared to hers, or the almost slavish look on his clean-shaven, middle-aged face. The old repulsion she'd always felt for him reared its head, making it impossible to act as a pliant and well-bred British girl. She wasn't, never had been, and the hardships of life as an undercover agent had washed out every last trace of loveliness.

"I invite you to have breakfast wiz me at *Brasserie Georges*. I think we can talk there more freely than here at Le Terminus."

"Fine."

He held the door open for her, and Sable saw the black Mercedes with the swastika flags stand at the bottom of the stone steps, a uniformed chauffeur waiting next to it.

"No!" she balked. "I'm not going in that car!"

He misunderstood. "Oh, sorry, the swastikas. Herman, take them down!"

"No, it's the car. I'm not going in a Mercedes with you again."

Seeing her chance to get out of his clutches, Sable ran down the *Cours de Verdun,* but she had miscalculated the guards outside the hotel. A shot was fired, whizzing past her at close range. Sable stood rooted to the spot. Her first instinct was to turn around and fire herself. But she didn't. It would be suicide in this situation. Slowly turning on her heels, ready to play along for as long as it was needed, she was already grabbed forcefully by her arms.

"All right!" she spluttered. "I'll comply for now, but I don't like it one bit."

She let herself be escorted back to the hated Mercedes.

"Nothing will happen to you, Madame. I promise." Von Henkell held the backdoor open for her to slip inside.

"Your promises are nothing but smoke and mirrors," Sable grumbled, sitting down on the beige leather seat that already made her nauseous. She sat perfectly still, as far away from the German as possible. When he took his position next to her, he gave her a meek look, but said nothing more. The guard sat up front with the chauffeur. The car cruised away from the hotel like a black ship on land.

It was only a quick ride to the Brasserie Georges. Von Henkell dispatched the car and chauffeur, but the guard stayed with them. Sable wondered why he, being the Haubtsturmführer and thus the boss, wasn't policing her himself.

They sat down at a table in the winter garden room, the only two people present. The sliding doors closed behind them, but Sable was sure the guard stood outside, and she had no chance of escape for now. Still, this whole arrangement with breakfast in a posh place and Von Henkell in his civilian clothes was positively puzzling and suggestive of evil.

I'll try to find out about my friends, then excuse myself that I have to go to the bathroom and try to attract the attention of the Brasserie staff. By grace from above, they will be on my side, Sable told herself as Von Henkell studied the breakfast menu.

"What shall you have?" he asked her, switching to English. The blue eyes looked at her over the brown menu board. Again, she saw the hesitance, as if he was more afraid of her than she of him.

"Black coffee and a cigarette."

"Any particular brand?" He didn't persuade her to have any food.

"Craven A."

"Of course!" The smile he gave her showed a pained tenderness. *Heavens, the fellow's in love with me!*

The realization was so acute that it hit her as a thunderclap. It slammed her back five years in time when he'd constantly sought her company, followed by her mother's endless litanies. *"Marry Joachim, Sable! You, of all people, could do much worse!"*

At the time, she'd just assumed the two oldies conspired together to make her life miserable. As they had well managed to do. Now she understood there had been more to it. At least, from his side.

She'd been so young, so innocent, so ready to flee from Alnor and her mother's cronies. Nothing else had mattered. And it had all turned out so topsy-turvy.

Real life was weirder than fiction. Who on earth could ever have fathomed she'd be sitting with this guy in occupied France, each other's enemies in more than one way? And he fancied her!

God, it was unbearable!

She was glad the cigarettes and her coffee came quickly. Von Henkell ordered bacon and eggs on toast. The discovery of his feelings for her was such a shock that she was temporarily too baffled to talk.

He seemed to sense the change in her and concentrated on cutting his food in minuscule portions and popping them into his mouth, dabbing his lips after every mouthful with the damask napkin.

Another habit she suddenly remembered and how it had annoyed her. Was that his way of thinking he could pass for an upper-class Brit? It was pitiful.

After he'd finished his meal and she was on her third cigarette, he started the conversation she'd dreaded.

"I see that you understand why I brought you here?" It was more a question than a statement.

"No, I don't.' She blew the smoke in his direction. "Please enlighten me."

Suddenly he laughed, a rather hiccupy sound that revealed little joy.

"If you knew how much you bear resemblance to your mother now, that same sassy wittiness."

Her cheeks flushed from indignation. "I'm nothing like my mother! Nothing!"

His words were too much. It hadn't happened in a long time, but she took to the floor, fists in her pockets, marching across the room from one side to the other. "Why do you say that? You must know how much I hated my mother!"

"Sorry, Sable, I didn't mean to upset you. Please sit down. I have another apology to make."

She eyed him as if he was vermin but took her seat again, pouring herself another coffee from the glass percolator.

"Go ahead, spit it out. And let me know what this whole charade is about. I don't know about you, but I've got a country to defend. No time for tittle-tattle."

"All right. Fair enough." He lit a Craven A himself. "Did you or didn't you have my child, Sable?"

She was sure she would die on the spot. All the blood drained from her face, and she looked at him aghast, her mouth hanging open. "Did I... did I have what?"

He seemed the calmer one now. "It's the main thing I have been trying to find out these past five years, ... you know, after our ... uh... close encounter." He hesitated. "That's what this is all about, Sable, I need to know." His voice trailed off.

Too stupefied for words, she nodded, a slight bob of her head. Then, against all her powerful will, tears welled in her eyes. She felt drained, defeated, dead. Through a mist, she heard Von Henkell say,

"Believe me, I pleaded with your mother to tell me how you were, again and again, but she kept telling you wanted to have nothing to do with me anymore. So it was just rumors for me that you were pregnant."

"But you did get why I wanted to have nothing to do with you? After... after you abused me like that?" The fire was back in her bones like a finger-snap. *How dare he utter such bêtises?*

"I did what? But you... but you said you wanted it yourself?"

She saw his white cheeks redden, the bruise-blue eyes widen.

Staring back at him with hard eyes, she suddenly gasped, bewildered, thrown back upon herself.

Her voice was low, toneless. "I did not do such a thing. You took advantage of me while I was drugged."

"Drugged?" He spoke the word as if God had lashed all his anger on the mortals below.

"Yes, drugged. You drugged me, together with my mother. You two had arranged this criminal encounter all along. My mother had even had my temperature taken that afternoon to see if I was ovulating."

"She did what?" Von Henkell took his head between his hands, the diamond in his golden signet ring flashing. "I had no idea, Sable, really I hadn't. I knew you were slightly drunk, but I asked you twice if you were sure you wanted to... you know... be intimate with me and ... and you didn't fight me off like you usually do. I'm so deeply sorry."

Sable was temporarily too confused to understand what he was actually saying. That she was complicit in the sex act. Despite her distress and despite the different direction this awful episode in her life now seemed to take, the central thought fighting in her was that she had to know, had to face it.

Whatever it was.

He'd been the only other person present. He alone could clarify what had taken place on the backseat of that German Mercedes.

She took a gulp of air, fighting her vulnerability, hanging on to her cigarette.

"So what did actually pass between us?"

His voice was as toneless as hers. "I was so happy you agreed to go for a drive with me after dinner. The first time I saw you at Alnor Castle, I fell in love with you. I thought I stood no chance with you. I was forty, and you were seventeen, but I was sure I'd never seen a more beautiful and independent girl than you. Contrary to other evenings when you just mocked me or told me to go to hell, you were quiet during the drive. I asked if you were comfortable. Do you remember?"

"No!"

"I parked the Benz at the shore of Loch Fyne. It was a beautiful

April night, clear sky, millions of stars and the light of the full moon reflecting on the inky water. Not cold at all. You cradled yourself in my arm and asked for a kiss. At that moment, I thought I was the happiest man on the planet. From one thing came the next. I know I should have stopped, but I asked you if you'd consider becoming my wife and you said with your usual sarcastic wit, "*Hell ya, why not marry a Nazi?*" I remember protesting that I never was a Nazi. Still no..."

"I said what?" Sable planted both elbows on the table. "Whatever you and my mother put in my wine, I must have been hallucinating because I don't remember any of this."

"I didn't put anything in your wine."

She gauged him, full on, saw he spoke the truth, the wretched truth.

"Then my mother did."

"I honestly don't know, Sable, but I never did anything to harm you."

"You think making love to a drugged and drunk minor isn't harmful?"

He bowed his head. "Now I know it was and believe me, I am disgusted with myself. But at that moment, you seemed happy enough. I'm a poor reader of character. I should have known. But after that night, whatever I tried and in whatever way, I wasn't able to see you again. Your mother kept saying you would be down for dinner that night, but you never came. I had the documents to apply for our legal marriage with me every night. And then you disappeared out of sight completely, and your mother became cold and unwelcoming to me."

Though the words sliced through her as a butcher's knife, she knew he was giving the cruel but true story.

"What game did my mother play then? First offering me to you on a platter and then standing between us. If she was so desperate to see me married to you and she knew I was pregnant—which obviously she'd planned all along—I don't get it."

It was silent for a while. Von Henkell cleared his throat.

"I may have the answer, but it's a rotten one."

"Pray tell. It can't get worse than this."

She lit another cigarette and flung his engraved silver lighter on the table. A waiter stuck his head around the door to see if they wanted to order more.

"Nein danke!" Von Henkell snapped. The waiter's head disappeared quick as the bat of an eyelid. Von Henkell shot her a brief glance. "I told you before, I'm a poor reader of character. Probably the reason I never found a wife. But a man can learn. This must be terribly hard for you. Are you managing? Is there anything I can do for you?"

"Tell me what you know."

"Right!" He poured himself the last of the cold coffee but didn't seem to care. Drank it with small sips. "Before I met you, I had a relationship with your mother. Nothing serious. Like... uh... you must know your mother had been with many men, especially German aristocrats."

Sable shuddered. He was telling her she'd shared her body with the same man that had had his hands on her mother. The truth was truly gruesome, but she bit her lip and stayed quiet.

"The divorce from your father wasn't finalized, but your mother wanted to remarry. I didn't want to marry her, especially not after I had seen you. I think... I think... bad as it sounds, that your mother took revenge on both of us."

Sable looked up from toying with the ash on the table. Their gazes met. Two wounded people. Misty Fletcher's playthings.

"We had a daughter." There was still no timbre in Sable's voice. "But I wasn't allowed to keep her. After three days, my mother gave her up for adoption."

Von Henkell groaned, the sound of an injured animal. "What did you name her?"

"Isabella."

"My mother's middle name."

41

A BIZARRE TURN OF EVENTS

Something was amiss. They were sitting way too long in *Brasserie Georges*'s wintergarden. Sable had no clue how long they'd been there, as she didn't dare take a glimpse at her watch for risk of showing her sleeve gun. But then she shrugged and pushed the thought away.

Hauptsturmführer Joachim von Henkell could most likely do as he chose. Even if that meant sitting all morning in civilian clothes in a posh Lyon restaurant in the presence of one female member of the enemy.

The seconds crept by. The sun grew hotter on the glass roof, the space heavy with smoke. Bathing in the sunlight, the blue-breasted parakeet in a gilded cage in the corner began to let himself be heard with loud shrieks and high long-drawn yells.

At moments Sable could rise above the scene and see its absurdity, a die-hard British agent and a high-ranking Nazi SS-officer locking horns, unlocking the past. They were the parents of a little girl now living with unknown adoptive parents in London. How could this all have happened?

What was clear was that they weren't cut out to help each other in their pain. Every word spoken was hurting more as they scratched the surface off Misty Fletcher's long, poisonous tentacles into their respective lives.

She scolded herself for even forgetting her secret agent status now and then. The mission for which she'd come to Hôtel Terminus —to liberate or, at least, find out the whereabouts of her friends. Not to become entangled with this individual all over again.

But not all was lost on her. Wooly's security measures were still quietly present in the way she sized the room, the door, who came in, and what Von Henkell's movements were, while the rest of her attention was swallowed up by the revisiting of that awful past. And how her life had been thwarted by this man who now laid similar cards on *her* table.

"Do you know anything at all about our daughter?" His words were like a serrated knife cutting in her heart. *Our daughter?* Her daughter had a father who wanted to be her father.

Unexpectedly, Esther's words spoken on Lunna Beach resurfaced. *"Why Sable? Why didn't you tell him? He would've married you."*

And what had she replied? *"Oh Esther, you're such a goose. He might have but I didn't want him. It was… it was… very complicated."*

This was awkward, but the truth. She recalled having acknowledged Von Henkell's soft side to Esther. In her own mind she'd needed to vilify him, but Esther, as always, had extracted the truth from her. Sable gave Von Henkell another once-over. The depth of his pain was plain and clear.

"I found her adoptive parents in my mother's papers. They live in London."

"Oh, Sable! That's fantastic. It means we can get her back!"

"We? What do you mean by *we?*" She instantly regretted having given him her most precious information. When the war was over, she would go looking for her daughter, but not with Von Henkell in tow. But there was no stopping him now.

"After all, we are her biological parents. We can prove that."

"I don't think so," Sable retorted. "The papers state me as her mother, but say 'father unknown'."

"Oh." Another twinge distorted his face, but then he recovered with a pallid smile. "However, if we were married, that would give you a more solid footing to claim her back."

Sable didn't know whether to laugh out loud or kill him off with her sleeve gun.

"Marry you? I'll see you in hell first!"

She didn't care much for the pain she inflicted on him now. What he was suggesting was just too ludicrous. And she didn't need him. She could do this herself.

For a long time, it remained silent from the other side of the table. The parakeet was the only living being in the room to make a racket. Finally, Von Henkell clarified in that soft-spoken voice of his.

"You misunderstand me, Sable. And that's all too logical after my earlier confessions how I feel about you. But this is different. I know you don't love me, and I don't mean to force you into a traditional marriage. You wouldn't have to live with me; we could even divorce after you have your daughter back. A marriage would only serve to prove we're Isabella's legal parents. After your aim is accomplished, you'll have all the freedom in the world to go where you please and with whom. I think it's the least I can do for you."

"Well, I'll be blowed!"

Sable was aghast, not so much by his reasoning but by the repetition of moves.

"There must be something wrong with me! You're the second non-marriageable chap suggesting a marriage-of-convenience to me. The first was from my half-brother who likes men and the second from a German Nazi more than twice my age. Maybe my mother's curse on me works after all, and I'll be doomed never to marry for love."

Beyond being hurt or offended, she now considered the whole situation so bizarre that she was in a state of just-knock-me-down-and-drag-me-out shock.

Von Henkell seemed to be the one keeping the steadier course of the two as he continued, "You know what, don't decide anything for now. I have another favor to ask you, which is more urgent in fact."

"Being?" She lifted one eyebrow, ready for anything but not for this.

Von Henkell's voice went down to a whisper, which Sable found eerie.

"Could you help me flee to England via one of your escape routes? I was already planning on leaving the German army, but now I'm even more sure it's the right thing to do. I'm prepared to turn myself in and go to a British prison. I'll share all the information I have."

Her expression must have been as if she was kicked in the teeth because he added on the nail, still in that soft, lisping voice.

"Meeting you, Sable, has been the last push I needed. I've wanted to get out of this absurd, unjust war for a long time. Even before it started. I wanted to stay in England. That's where I feel I belong. And from England, I'll have a better chance at organizing a coup against Hitler."

It took all her training to pull herself together as she shook her head in disbelief, very aware of the walls having ears and this all being a possible trap. Her fine-tuned intuition, though, told her the man opposite her was sincere. So, she muttered. "I don't know what to say. I mean, we're supposed to work independently when networks break down, but in this case I'll have to consult with London. I'll risk my own integrity if I ... if I helped a Nazi escape."

"Pleas stop calling me a Nazi. I'm not!"

To Sable, that seemed a matter of less importance. She was calculating if she could pull it off. Hauptsturmführer Joachim von Henkell was not unknown in the British old boys' network. Having him on their side might even enhance her position. But could she trust him? She shot him another glance, and despite everything that had happened between them and the devastating consequences of that relationship, her gut instinct told her again he could be trusted.

Even as far back as at her mother's dinner table, she'd never heard him boasting about Germany as a superpower or Hitler as a great leader. And he'd arrived in his civilian clothes this morning. He must be serious about his desertion, and she would have to keep it under wraps until she was certain he was, in shackles, on a plane to England.

"You're a very good secret agent, Sable." There was genuine admiration in his voice. "I can almost see you check all the boxes before you make your decision. Whatever happens between us, and whether or not we see each other again, I want to tell you I'm happy you found your strength and are fighting for a rightful cause. Winston Churchill must be so proud of you."

His words made her smile, and a tiny giggle escaped her. "I doubt whether Churchill is even aware of my existence, but you're right. I was born to do this, to be a fighter. And I'll continue to be the Highland Raven until this terrible war is over and the people of Western Europe are once again liberated."

"So, you'll help me?" His eyes held love as well as admiration.

"I will, Joachim, but you'll have to do everything I tell you to."

"Don't worry. This is your expertise, not mine."

"First, I need to know how you're going to pull off getting away from Hôtel Terminus." The parakeet repeated, "'ôtel Terminus."

Von Henkell nodded. "I've thought about that. We'll have the chauffeur and the guard drive us back there. Then I tell them you have agreed to cooperate, and you'll bring me to Perrache Champagne Bar to listen in to conversations. And that is the reason I'm wearing civilian clothes and need to drive my car myself."

"You know about Perrache?" Sable shuddered. She needed to go there as quickly as possible to warn Giles and the rest. She was already on her feet.

"Alas." Von Henkell looked stricken. "But I promise we'll pass by there to warn them on our way out of Lyon. The Mercedes will be our cover car."

Sable swallowed hard. How much did the Nazis know? Maybe this was her only escape as well.

"What about the rest of my team, those who were arrested yesterday?" No names.

A shadow flittered over the German's handsome features. "That is the reason Barbie is out of town. He wanted to be present himself when they were brought to the Paris Headquarters. He called it, 'the best catch this year,' followed by saying, 'now we only need to get hold of Le Corbeau Noir and the BROUILLARD Network is extinct.' I'm sorry, Sable. I fear the worst for them. You were too late anyway."

"I could've gone to Paris if you hadn't detained me here." Her tone was acrid.

"You never give up, do you?" Again, that reverential tone.

"Not if I can help it." Her voice was small, tears pricking behind her eyes for losing her cherished friends, no matter how short their time together had been.

"Do you want to think about my request for help first, Sable? It may jeopardize your good name."

"No."

"Are you sure?" The bruise-blue eyes lit up in hope, relief emanating from every pore of his being. She was making the right choice. No matter how controversial.

"I'm sure, Joachim. Let's go."

42

THE FLIGHT

W hile Von Henkell discussed the new arrangements outside the door with his chauffeur and the guard, Sable nervously paced the wintergarden room. The guard that had been at the door all the time, what had he heard? Maybe they had spoken much too freely and for far too long.

But there was more. Getting a high-ranking German out of the country was lunacy and way beyond her responsibility. Why had she said yes? She should back out of helping a high-ranking Nazi now it was still possible, but would they lock her up then? So many questions, no answers.

Von Henkell came back into the room, looking relaxed. "All settled." He even gave her a quick wink.

With lead in her shoes, she followed the three men back to the Mercedes. Her stomach churned.

When they were seated in the same order as on the outward journey, Von Henkell said, loud enough to be heard by the men in the front, "We are not done with you yet, Madame. You will escort me to Perrache Champagne Bar. If you show willingness to cooperate, we will see about an arrangement that you work for us and have your freedom."

"All right." Sable could hardly bring herself to speak at all, let alone on the same insistent level. She felt she would choke any minute on fear and hopelessness. *I'll tell him we're not doing this as soon as we're on our way to Giles*, she promised herself and tried to take heart from it.

Arriving back at the stone-faced Hôtel Terminus, the chauffeur and the guard exited the car and went up the steps to the entrance, as had been discussed. With a gruff jerk, Von Henkell grabbed Sable by the arm and pushed her in the front seat, locking the passenger's door. In haste, he made his way around the hood to the driver's seat.

A shot rang out. And another. Von Henkell's blood spattered all over the hood and the windshield. For a split-second Sable froze in her seat, then reacted swift as a dolphin glides. She jumped over the passenger's seat, grabbed the steering wheel, pushed the car into gear, and jammed her foot on the accelerator. The heavy car lurched forward. With a quick maneuver, she only just evaded running over Von Henkell's lifeless body lying in the middle of the road, his beige Viennese suit drenched in his own blood.

More shots rang out, ricocheting on the Benz's armored chassis. Bullets aimed at the tires, failed to puncture them, and then Sable was around the corner of *cours de Verdun*. Out of sight, but not beyond pursuit.

The analytical part of her mind took over. No time for emotions. Only survival. Diagnose the situation and find a way out. The guard surely had betrayed Von Henkell. He'd been too careless and frank in their long talk. It had cost him his life. There was nothing she could do about it. She would certainly follow suit if they caught her. She should get rid of this ridiculous car with the swastikas upfront.

And yet.

Sable had been taught by her Beaulieu instructors that sometimes it was best to hide right in sight of the enemy. It was paramount she left Lyon in double-quick time, but not without a proper disguise and her valuable suitcase.

Zigzagging through the city's maze, grateful she knew it as the back of her hand, she steered the German car at the highest possible speed toward the Grand Nouvel Hotel. *Thank you, Dadaigh, for teaching me to tame the highland hairpin bends.* She sent a brief prayer upwards.

One eye glued to the rear mirror, checking and double-checking for possible pursuers, but also on the alert for everything coming from directions in front of her, Sable completed her tour de force. Safe for now. Braking abruptly, she parked the Mercedes in the hotel's courtyard and raced inside via the back entrance.

To her relief, Yvette was behind the desk, staring wide-eyed at her. "*Pour l'amour du ciel*! What has gotten into you?"

"I need to flee Lyon. Now!" Sable explained in rapid French. "Make sure you warn Giles at Perrache, Yvette. The Nazis know. I'm sorry about the German Mercedes in the drive. No time to explain. Just park it somewhere on a busy road when it's dark and leave the keys in it." She threw the car key on Yvette's desk. The French girl looked even more perplexed.

"I have no time to explain. Just that I'm in mortal danger. We all may be. I'm getting my suitcase and will leave for Paris."

Yvette nodded, asked no questions. She heaved her round body from the chair she'd been sitting on and came around the counter.

"Be safe, Mademoiselle Violette. You're the best!" Yvette hugged her with her fleshy arms and bid her goodbye.

"Thanks, Yvette, I'll never forget Grand Nouvel Hotel. I hope to be back after the war."

FIVE MINUTES LATER SABLE, wearing a red dress, her black hair covered by a blonde wig and wearing stylish sunglasses, her head high and carrying her suitcase as if on a business trip, made her way to *Gare de Lyon-Perrache* on the *cours de Verdun*. When she passed the Hôtel Terminus, she didn't falter, though the bloodstain in the middle of the road and the entrance swarming with black-clad SS Officers made her stomach go queasy and the blood in her ears ring.

If she was stopped and questioned now, all would be lost. So she wouldn't stop. Then she wouldn't be questioned. After all, she was

Mademoiselle Violette Bernard, a traveling saleswoman for Triumph typewriters in France on her way to a client in Paris.

But in her heart of hearts Sable was more than ever the Highland Raven, broken yet strong as ever, hardened by backlashes and brutal murders. But most of all her heart bled for her fellow agents, at that moment no doubt being tortured by Barbie and his gang.

SICK AS A DOG AND HEAVYHEARTED, Sable arrived at Gare de Lyon just before curfew. It had been at least nine years since she visited Paris. For one lovely year in the middle of her parents' long-drawn-out divorce battle, she'd lived as an international *étudiante* at le Lycée Molière in the 16th arrondissement. Next to freedom from strife, it had awakened in Sable a lifelong love for the French language and its capital.

But little of that bliss was now present in her. Von Henkell's gruesome, sudden murder had left her feel like a beaten dog too afraid to whine. There had been the slight possibility of him acting as the father of her child. There had at least been some mutual understanding they'd both been wrong about each other. But it was all pulp and past now. Her network blown, the price on her head probably doubled, and London wondering what had happened to the BROULLIARD now that Cecil's wireless had fallen silent. At least in Paris Sable hoped to find out more about the Lyon arrests.

But first and foremost, she wanted, needed, hankered for her brother.

She had one address in the Gare de Lyon region, on the Boulevard Diderot, and was glad to find Jean-Pierre at home. On giving him the agreed-upon code, *"Jean has a long moustache,"* he opened the door. She couldn't see him properly. She lost her focus; the world spun and spun and spun. The last she heard was Jean-Pierre calling out, *"Emilia viens ici."*

Sable collapsed on the threshold, welcoming oblivion.

.....

When she came round, there was a lightness in her head, a warm fuzzy feeling that everything would be all right.

Someone was singing and playing a guitar.

THERE WAS *a man lived in the moon, lived in the moon, lived in the moon,*
    There was a man lived in the moon,
    And his name was Aiken Drum.

AND HE PLAYED UPON A LADLE, *a ladle, a ladle,*
    And he played upon a ladle,
    and his name was Aiken Drum.

AIKEN DRUM, the most beloved nursery rhyme from her youth. The words had always made her squeal with laughter. A coat made of roast beef and a hat of cream cheese.

WAS SHE HOME? Why was she so happy? And then she knew. The voice, the singing, the guitar.

FREDDIE!

OPENING HER EYES AT ONCE, she looked straight into his gaze. Her own eyes reflected in the blue light of his, clear as a mountain stream. Tears spilled over her eyelashes, streaming down her cheeks, unstoppable and unchained. She was at once full of love and full of pain. He finished the last stanza for her with a smile on his lips.

AND HIS BREECHES *made of haggis bags, of haggis bags, of haggis bags,*

And his breeches made of haggis bags,
And his name was Aiken Drum.

FREDDIE PUT THE GUITAR DOWN. Sat on the bed next to her and stroked the raven black hair out of her damp face.

"My darling sis." He kissed her wet cheek, dried her tears. Sable buried her head in his jacket, crying louder.

The story came in fits and starts. It took a long time before Sable calmed down, but she was glad to be able to tell Freddie everything. He knew and he understood. They were two sides of the same coin.

"You have to turn your tail to London, Sabbo." He lit a cigarette for them both and handed her one. "It's become way too dangerous for you in France."

But Sable shook her head.

"I will not beat the retreat. Not now. The Allied forces have recaptured Italy. The war will be over soon. I'm needed here. More than ever."

"But you can come back. Just go home to recuperate. It would do you good. You've never been broad on the beam, but you're less than a matchstick now, Sabbo. You won't last long this way."

"I promise I'll eat." Sable meant it. She knew living on cigarettes and coffee wouldn't sustain her health much longer. And she wanted to stay and fight in Paris, not let Freddie go another time. Not after everyone else she'd lost.

"Now tell me, how's Paris treating you, brother mine?"

Freddie smiled at her again. "Busy, busy, busy. We've had some arrests, but overall, if you keep your eyes skinned and your blab shut, I feel you have a better chance of survival here than in the countryside. Jean-Pierre and his wife Emilia are class A. They simply know everyone. So glad they searched your pockets and found your Violette Bernard papers. They immediately asked around in the largest network here, the ALPHABET circuit, and that's how I was notified."

Sable listened carefully, then asked her most burning question.

"Do you know if important agents arrested elsewhere in France are always taken to Paris?"

Freddie scanned her face, looked pensive. "Your Lyon friends? They could be held at 84 Avenue Foch or Fresnes prison, but there's only a ghost of a chance you'll be able to find out, Sab. Let it ride for now. Of course, keep your eyes and ears open, but it's best to get cracking on your own activities and not mourn captured friends for too long. I know it sounds cold-hearted but believe me, now's the time to think of your own future. Make the best of a poor job."

She considered his words, thought of her impossible plan to break into Hôtel Terminus. Still, if she hadn't done that, she wouldn't have known what she now knew about Joachim von Henkell. That ghost was lying to rest for good.

Let it go, Freddie said. He was right.

"You hang loose here with Jean-Pierre and Emilia for a couple of days, Sab, and then I'll come and steal you back."

Freddie gave her a last kiss, tucked in the blanket around her, and with his elegant gait made for the door.

"Work's calling!"

"Bye, Freddo! Be careful."

"You too."

Sable slept, ate, and mourned for three days.

Then she was on her feet again.

43

PREPARATION FOR D-DAY

Paris, May 1944

In the spring of 1944, the French population was caught in the middle of what they called *le mentalité terrible*. In large parts of France, especially along the west and center, the fight between *la Milice* and *le Maquis* was relentless. The two French groups were locking horns—with the Nazi-supported, paramilitary *Milice* often even more demonic than the Germans themselves, and the *Maquis* increasingly reinforced by SOE and De Gaulle's Free French.

Both groups had thousands of members but were not well-armed. The miliciens, sporting blue uniforms with the Greek letter gamma as their symbol, brown shirts underneath, and white berets, had to make do with British weaponry confiscated after the evacuation of Dunkirk. For a long time, the German occupiers were hesitant to arm even their own conspirators.

It was only toward the end of 1943 and the first half of 1944 that the Allied forces began their frequent armament drops—Operation Carpetbagger—to bolster the French resistance.

Sable could name all the weaponry and knew in which hands the weaponry would be most beneficial. She organized and attended hundreds of armament drops of crates falling into fields all over France from the "carpetbaggers." Jokingly, she was known among the *maquisards* as Mademoiselle Sten-Gun.

But to Sable, it was all dead-serious and being a thrifty Scotswoman, she didn't want to squander any of the British and American ammunition. Each morning after a drop, she would be in the hangar where the crates were stored, always dressed in the same faded blue overalls, a sturdy belt with her own Colt secured around her small waist and a black beret atop her raven hair.

With her clipboard and pen ready, she would mark them off, 50 Sten machine guns, 25 Webley revolvers, 20 Bren machine guns, 50 Lee-Enfield rifles, 10 PIAT anti-tank grenade launchers, 5 M3 Grease-guns, 20 Browning handguns, 15 M1 rifles and 35 Bazooka anti-tank rocket launchers.

ON A LATE MONDAY morning after another night without sleep, she was busy with her distribution schedule in a hangar in Lozère, south of Paris, when Freddie stormed in.

For security reasons, they hardly saw each other in person and, as a rule, communicated via couriers. But they worked closely together, Freddie heading the ALPHABET circuit after the arrests of Jean-Pierre and Emilia, while Sable headed the newly split-off BROAD-CAST circuit. Together they commanded almost 40,000 fighters, with Freddie concentrating on the north and Sable on the south. Her territory stretched from Ile-de-France, Centre Val-de-Loire to Pays de la Loire, Bretagne and Normandie.

"What is it?" It sounded preoccupied, but the smile she gave her brother was affectionate.

"Great news, sis." Freddie came to stand really close so that walls with possible hostile ears didn't overhear him. In a low voice, he added, "Rumor has it the Allies will storm the French coast soon."

Sable drew up one eyebrow while she kept jotting down numbers. "Tell me something I don't yet know, brother, like where and when."

"Ah!" He wagged a slender, musician-like finger with its female-like long nail. "Don't act the blasé one, my dear! I'm here to tell you we must pretend it's going to happen near Calais when it's actually planned further south. Now go and blow up some more vital arteries, Madame Raven. We know you excel at those."

Despite her tiredness and the nagging workload, Sable burst out in laughter. "I'm getting more nicknames by the day. Sabotage Sally was what I heard yesterday."

Freddie, who had been laughing with her, suddenly turned more serious. "You're such a cool-headed agent, Violette, you don't even pick up the reverence the male fighters have for you. I tell you each one of them would sell their kingdom for a kiss from you. And possibly a lot more."

Sable's laughter rang through the high-ceilinged hangar. "You're such a fantasist, brother. Nobody has time for a girl in guerrilla overalls who hasn't washed her hair in two weeks."

"Those are the ones with the most sex-appeal," Freddie argued, posing as a connoisseur.

"Who cares." Sable had finished her filing and sat down on one crate with a cigarette. "Though you haven't come here to size up my marriageable status or talk romance, let me ask you how David is."

"David is fine. He's working at Beaulieu as a propaganda instructor. At this stage in the war, it's vital to throw as much dust and confusion as we can into the German machine. He sends his love." Freddie beamed at mentioning his lover.

"I'm so glad he'd finally healed from that nasty brain injury. Now tell me the real news. I still have to cycle to Orléans today."

But Freddie ignored her remark.

"What about you, sis? Any word from the Scotsman?"

It felt as if she was stabbed in the chest, although his name wasn't even mentioned. *Bill.* She had heard nothing from him in over three years and yet... and yet... she yearned for his presence, his "one condition," his encouragement and... his love.

She shook her head, unable to hide all of her sadness. Freddie gazed at her for a moment, seemed to hesitate, and spoke.

"He's at Beaulieu too, sis. They're training a whole slew of agents right now, as they'll be packed off to France before long. So, Wooly summoned him back from up north. David says he's well, but extremely solitary. He doesn't socialize with the others. You know, hang out at The Royal Oak for a pint. He's working on a volume of poetry. At least that's what he told David."

Sable drank in every word Freddie told her about her former heartthrob, picturing him at Beaulieu, the towering man with his wild red mane and fierce blue eyes. A lion among men, a wounded lion.

Well, she was a lioness too, and one with a mission.

"Got to go, bro, unless you have anything else for me?"

"I do." Freddie sat down next to her, close enough to whisper, "5 June. Normandy. But you know nothing."

He put an index finger to his lips to indicate a secret. Sable gave him a quick kiss, didn't question her brother's sources, knowing he was part of the old boys' network.

"Yet more work to be done!" she exclaimed, her face jubilant and combative. *Everything to snap out of this heartache*, she told herself. And it always worked. Wiry and muscled, Sable at twenty-three was no man's girl, a free and independent woman who headed her BROADCAST team with pride and precision.

"You know what to do?" Freddie asked, just to be sure.

"I do. As long as I have my operator Georges Cleck and my courier Ginette Butt, I can lead my men and women into battle. Heaven forbid there's a mole in the system now."

"The Germans are certainly plugging away at keeping what they've got left of occupied France. One wonders in some parts who's in charge the Bochs or SOE and the *maquisards*. Keep your eyes peeled for the *Milice* these days."

"There are still some rotten Gestapo men around as well," Sable observed. "I heard a saying that alpha male apes are most lethal when they're wounded. They're a bloodthirsty bunch, killing and torturing citizens with no evidence of them being resisters."

"Tread lightly, my dear!" Freddie hugged her tightly.

"See you in London," Sable sniffled, trying hard not to become emotional.

"Deal. Lunch on me at Kettner's Townhouse. I want to sit in Oscar Wilde's chair!" Freddie danced away from her, but she saw his shoulders were hunched. They knew the hardest battle lay ahead of them still.

"I love you! Stay safe!" she called after him.

He raised a long, slender arm, whirling his hand at the wrist but didn't look back. Sable watched him until he'd started the old Renault, and only a cloud of dust showed the path he'd gone. Out of sight.

She took a moment to recuperate. All love, all tenderness, made her weak, and she hated it. Being hard, almost insensitive, was much easier these days. And much more useful.

CYCLING WAS the way Sable got around in the present climate. Ever since Von Henkells' murder in Lyon and her narrow escape, she was aware of the price on her head and avoided public transport as much as she could.

A tendon in her right calf was inflamed from the many hundreds of miles she traversed on the old bike, and it became increasingly painful and harder to push the pedals around.

Willpower her only companion. "Give up" was no longer a phrase in Sable's vocabulary. She only accepted a motorized lift, or a free cart ride if it came from a resister she knew.

So far, her motto, if anyone in her vast network suggested lying dormant for a bit, had been, *I can't let my circuit down. Not now. I'll rest when we've pushed the Germans out.* She knew the moment was coming nearer that she'd have to give up her traipsing through the countryside and give her leg a rest. But not now. Only twenty of the eighty-two miles left. *Come on, leg!*

Arriving on the outskirts of Orléans late in the evening, Sable crept through curfew as a thief, invisible as the stars at midday. Too tired to eat, she just gulped down her flask of lukewarm tea and slept a couple of hours in the haystack of a friendly farmer. Her right leg sent agonizing shots through her entire right side, throbbed and burned, and her stomach rumbled, but Sable blacked out into the sleep of the worse for wear.

She woke with the sun in her face and her courier Ginette holding a steaming cup of coffee under her nose. Sitting up and rubbing the sleep from her eyes, she was glad to see the girl who'd become her best friend in the past year.

Ginette wasn't Maureen—who'd vanished from the earth—but Ginette, broad-hipped and glowing with goodwill and gusto, was devoted to Sable. The Normandy sailor's daughter's attitude reminded Sable of the position she'd often possessed at her boarding schools and definitely at Le Manoir, where she'd pulled the strings. As a rule.

But Sable had changed. The need to push around another female or use her for her own gain was no longer something she enjoyed. Sweet, strong Esther Weiss had taught Sable the preciousness of female bonds—something Misty Fletcher had never prepped her daughter for.

"Let me have a look at your leg." Ginette, who was also one of the team's medics, was already unlacing Sable's heavy combat boot. The latter yelped in pain. Ginette gave her a knowing look.

"What did I tell you last week, Violette? Give your leg a rest." The clear graphite-gray eyes searched Sable's, who clenched her teeth in pain. Ginette inspected her swollen leg, softly pressing it here and there, which made expletives in a mixture of French and English leave Sable's lips.

"Merde! Hell and darnation! What do I do now, Gin?"

"What do you think, Vio? I told you a few weeks ago." Ginette's face looked grave.

"All right!" Sable sat upright, pulled the leg of her overall over the swollen calf. "I promise I will not cycle for a while. Give me some more of your morphine and I'll try not to walk too much either. Will that satisfy you, doc?"

Now Ginette did smile. "It's not about satisfying me. It's about taking care of yourself, Vio."

"Ahh, you know my weaknesses better than I do myself," Sable confessed. "I'm hopeless at looking after my physical well-being. Always was."

"You mean your strict regime of coffee and cigarettes?" Ginette chortled.

"I do not know what you're hinting at," Sable retorted in mock surprise.

"I hesitate to give you more morphine when that's not the cure. Didn't you once tell me you struggled with alcohol some years back? That that's why you don't drink? I don't want you to win the war as a morphine addict. That would be losing it all over again."

"I may have an addictive tendency, but I also have a strong will to overcome it. Now give me the jab and I'll promise, no more cycling until the tendon has healed."

Ginette sighed, shook her head, but did just that. The injection was bliss, the pain receding to a nagging presence.

"I'm ready for another cup of coffee, a fresh cigarette and the morning meeting." Sable hobbled out of the barn on her way to meet her fighters.

At least two hundred eager faces looked up at her as she, limping and swearing at her injury, took to the stage in the heavily armed village hall of Fleury. With her operator Georges Cleck on her right and Ginette on her left, Sable felt bolstered enough to deliver her big speech.

The gathering was, as she hoped, a calculated risk. There was a safe passage out of the building through an underground tunnel, and she could absolutely trust the *maquisards* who stood on guard at all the doors and along the access roads to the village hall, equipped with walkie-talkies.

Delivering her message in this way was the swiftest way to instruct all the district leaders of what was expected of them. She simply didn't have a moment to lose. The invasion was due in three weeks. Wooly would've been absolutely aghast at her disregard of the protocol about large gatherings of resisters, but Sable now had to do it her own way.

Scanning the crowds, she began to speak.

"Dear BROADCAST comrades, the hour of our ultimate fight is here. The Allied forces will be landing on the French coast in the next month, though it remains a secret where and when exactly. Even to us. As BROADCAST handles the area south of Paris toward the Atlantic, including Normandy and Brittany, it means that our network must step up its activities in the entire area."

You could hear a pin drop in the barn filled with heavy-combat bodies. Dust molecules swerved around them like heaven-sent angels.

"We'll divide our upcoming resistance activities into three categories. One, we derail and destruct; two, we trick and confuse; and three, we gather intelligence. I'll explain all three to you. Also, the where and how. Mind you, these activities come on top of what was already planned, and the armament drops that are scheduled per region. We'll have to work our butts off."

Fists went into the air in silence, showing the crowd was ready for more action. Sable drew in her breath. It was a magnificent sight.

"Each operational unit is responsible for their own three-forked resistance.

"Let's start with derailment and destruction. All the main railroads, bridges, and road arteries that the Germans may use to get to Brittany and Normandy are fair game. However, always consider that when our forces land, they will need to make use of the road infrastructure as well."

Heads nodded; bearded and fair faces grinned. They were such a tough lot. Sable's heart swelled with pride. With a group of fighters like this, she could achieve anything. There was a tremor in her voice when she continued.

"Targets to hit are Le Mans, Tours, Rennes, Chartres, Dreux and Mayenne. Also manufacturing plants for car components, tires, armaments, and anything that's on your map and looks vital to the Germans, are fair game to be demolished, as well as German vehicles, tanks, and locomotives. And of course, communication lines. Be very aware that there are as few reprisals on the local population as possible, though it cannot be always avoided."

This sent a sigh of grief through the audience. So many of them had lost loved ones in the brutal reprisal actions of the Gestapo. Thousands of innocent French killed. Innocent blood, a permanent stain on history. To get them back on track, Sable brought up her second focal point.

"The trick-and-confuse game is probably the only fun part of our work. Do it to your heart's content and use your imagination. Change names of streets, even of villages, but be aware that when the Allies land, they'll have maps of routes as well. And they shouldn't be confused. Be ready to change back, if necessary.

"Put your underground presses on full steam and send out messages that seem to come from the Germans, for example, telling the Milice to lay down their arms. Spread lies and confusion, but be extra vigilant when distributing from door to door."

Sable could almost hear their minds working out strategies, and she rejoiced in it. She might be their leader, yet these men and women were also excellent at leading their own smaller units. She came to her last point.

"Finally, about infiltrating among German officers and collecting data. All information you gather, whether it's about German positions, conversations overheard, demolished sites, movement of troops, must be given to your wireless operator to send in coded messages to London, either to SOE or to the Free France headquarters. If you think the information is of vital importance, please first share it with me and Georges, my W/T here.

"That will be all. The next meeting is in two weeks in Rennes, unless otherwise communicated down the chain."

No applause, but lots of satisfied faces and more grins. Sable wiped the sweat from her forehead with the sleeve of her overalls. She gripped the chair in front of her for support. The morphine was killing the pain in her leg, but lack of a proper meal and too little sleep were taking their toll. She felt Ginette's eyes on her and sat down on the chair.

Several fighters, men and women, came up to her for clarifications or further instructions. Georges whispered in her ear, "Taking my set to send now." She nodded. From somewhere, someone handed her a plate with ham sandwiches and a mug of coffee. While eating, she oversaw the large map that was spread out on the table with a myriad of colored pins pricked all over.

"I feel like a general in the army," she laughed, swallowing a mouthful of bread, "but I'm only the BROADCAST organiser. A pinprick in the French resistance."

44

A SLOW VICTORY

Caen, 6 June 1944

In the first minutes of the new day, US pathfinders set foot on the Cotentin Peninsula to mark parachute zones for the arriving Douglas C-47 pilots. Minutes later, Lancaster bombers of the Royal Air Force attacked the German Merville Gun Battery.

The paratroopers and the British airplanes were the harbingers of a new phase in the war. The beginning of the Allied invasion. The beginning of the end of the Third Reich's hold on Western-Europe.

On a gray day with low-hanging clouds and brief spells of rain, not too much wind, the first Allied battalions reached Normandy at 6:30 in the morning. Battalion after battalion came ashore on beaches that, from that day onward, would be known by their military names, Utah Beach, Omaha Beach, Sword Beach, Juno Beach, and Gold Beach. Parallel to the attack from the sea, planeloads of paratroopers were parachuted in, scattering over the peninsula, while bombers relentlessly attacked German strongholds.

When at 6:40 a.m. General Eisenhower woke up after a quick nap, Admiral Ramsay could assure him Operation Overlord was going to plan. Hitler, in his Berlin mansion, after having listened late to his favorite composer, Wagner, was still fast asleep.

Sable was in Caen, together with Georges and Ginette. Though unaware of the scale and the exactitude of the invasion, she wanted to be as close as possible to her approaching fellow countrymen and their band of brothers—for moral support and for feeling the earth move under her with the trampling of feet of their own men.

Two long years she'd fought with every bone in her body for this day, rebuffing London's recurring offer to return to the safety of Britain for a much-needed break. Most agents accepted the offer, but not Sable. She'd never left her post, had known betrayal, arrest, hardship, and loss. But every setback became worthwhile now.

It was a relief to trust the enemy's final blow to trained military men. Let them push the Germans out of France. Sable and her band of resisters had fought their way from inland France to the coast. Now the Allies would sweep the Germans out in the opposite direction and force them back within their own borders.

She and Ginette were having morning coffee in a safe house on the south flank of Caen, while Georges was busy trying to contact London for the latest reports. They'd soon have to leave as the Allies were certain to bomb the Germans out of Caen. The double doors of the cupboard where the radio was hidden stood open. Ginette was turning the knobs, trying to get onto the BBC wavelength.

With her coffee cup in one hand and a cigarette in the other, Sable paced the room, too jittery to sit down. All the while, her mouth muttered prayers for the thousands of young men clambering up the Normandy beaches, many of whom were sure to be hacked down by German machine guns, leaving their lives for a greater cause.

She also prayed for Freddie in Paris, for Esther in Norway, for Maureen, Cecil, Diana who'd disappeared in the Nazi *Nacht und Nebel*, for Giles, Yvette and all her fighters. She prayed for her daughter in London, for David, for Elrod and Minnie in Cavendish Square, for Wooly, Killer, and Lock in Beaulieu. She prayed for her estate in Alnor. She even prayed for Anna. And finally, hesitantly, she prayed for... Bill.

It felt as if the Normandy soil was shaking under a seismic earthquake and that all the good people of France were bricking themselves over the outcome of this clash of giants. Which side would be victorious? Would they be free after four long years of war, or chained to the Nazi beast for good?

"I still can't believe we'll be in England tomorrow," Sable announced, still pacing with the cold remains of her coffee and a long-ashed cigarette.

"Hopefully, it will be hit-and-run for me. I can't wait to go back to a liberated Honfleur. See all my loved ones."

Sable stopped her pacing as if it only now dawned on her that Ginette was from the region.

"Of course, how could I forget you have no English blood like most other SOE agents? But you must stay at least a couple of nights with me in London. Promise?"

The dark-haired française looked doubtful. "I haven't been home in ages for fear of leading the wrong people to my family. One or two nights, all right?"

Sable grinned. "As long or as short as you decide, Ginette. We won't lose touch, anyway. I want to meet your family, too."

"Yes!" Ginette's sweet gray eyes lit up. "*Maman et Papa* so much want to meet Le Corbeau Noir. And I want to go sailing on the Atlantic with you in my boat *Courageux*. You do like sailing, I hope?"

"I've never given ocean sailing a try. Only motored on the lochs in Scotland, and of course, crossed the Channel many times, but with you I'll sail to America!"

At that moment Georges joined them from the backroom, a wide grin on his tired, three-day-beard face, on bare feet and with the breeches of his corduroy pants undone.

"Three hurrahs for the BROADCAST circuit! The Allied forces have apparently just captured the first bridge at Bénouville. We've been instrumental, not just in sabotage, but also in guarding the right places."

"That's wonderful news." Sable clapped her hands, spraying ash everywhere while remembering the recent nights they'd lain in wait to make sure the bridges over the river Orne and over the canal at Caen and Ranville weren't blown up, not by the Germans, not by the milice and certainly not by the maquisards.

On good authority Georges had deduced that these bridges were the first the Allies wanted to capture by surprise. Therefore, Sable had ordered and carried out the surveillance of roads and bridges on the peninsula, ducking down every time a German jeep or tank rattled past.

Ginette hushed them, putting a finger to her lips. Churchill's booming voice resonated from the cupboard. He was addressing the House of Commons, hailing the liberation of Rome. Then Winnie, the Bulldog, roared on.

"I have also to announce to the House that during the night and the early hours of this morning the first of the series of landings in force upon the European Continent has taken place.

"In this case the liberating assault fell upon the coast of France. An immense armada of upwards of four thousand ships, together with several thousand smaller craft, crossed the Channel. Massed airborne landings have been successfully effected behind the enemy lines, and landings on the beaches are proceeding at various points at the present time.

"The fire of the shore batteries has been largely quelled. The obstacles that were constructed in the sea have not proved so difficult as was apprehended. The Anglo-American Allies are sustained by about 11,000 first-line aircraft, which can be drawn upon as may be needed for the purposes of the battle.

"I cannot, of course, commit myself to any particular details. Reports are coming in in rapid succession. So far the Commanders who are engaged report that everything is proceeding according to plan.

"And what a plan!

"This vast operation is undoubtedly the most complicated and difficult that has ever taken place. It involves tides, wind, waves, visibility, both from the air and the sea standpoint, and the combined employment of land,

air and sea forces in the highest degree of intimacy and in contact with conditions which could not and cannot be fully foreseen."

Sable's breath was taken away as she listened. Somehow the affirmation of her Commander-in-Chief made all doubt evaporate that the invasion—the endlessly anticipated invasion—was a mere fairytale. She grasped both Ginette's and Georges' hands, feeling hers were clammy and trembling. They held onto each other, tears spilling, mute and humbled.

Winston told them the landings were going according to plan. That's all she wanted to hear. After all, her BROADCAST circuit had done what it could, working tirelessly to prevent the German trek up north. There had been successes and drawbacks. It was never enough.

In the past days, with all the confusion spreading about where on the coast the invasion would start, Caen had been one city festered with Wehrmacht soldiers in their tanks and jeeps, but there was fear instead of pride in their eyes now.

Despite herself, Sable had sometimes felt for them. Had Von Henkell himself not been a victim of Nazidom? The coin was now definitely rolling the Allied way. It would be the Bochs' turn to be massacred and trodden down.

"War is a beast," she voiced as they released hands.

"It always gets worse before it gets better," Georges observed in his dry, matter-of-fact voice.

"Probably, but I pray for it to go right. I've never felt this tense in my life."

"I know. Same here, also because it's my homeland," Ginette chimed in.

At that moment, their host, the local pharmacist, came in, rubbing his chinstrap beard. "It's happening, folks." His jovial red face gleamed, but the dark eyes looked worried.

"Time to instruct the citizens of Caen to stay indoors and preferably in their cellars," Sable announced. "Has the door-to-door pamphlet been printed, Monsieur Chirac?"

"It has, Madame, and the boys are ready to distribute them. Time for you to leave."

Sable sighed. She wasn't ready, but knew they'd have to retreat soon. The aerial attacks on Caen could start any minute. She had to travel the 120 miles to her destination near Rennes, where she would be picked up by a Lysander at midnight. She'd said goodbye to most of her fighters in the past days, hoping to be reunited with some of them after the war.

They'd fought together relentlessly to hamper and divert the German army. Many of the German battalion had either arrived in Normandy too late or found themselves north, near Calais.

They'd broken down as much as they could inland but also weakened the Atlantic Wall, a fortification that the Germans had built from the North of Norway to the very south of the French coast near Biarritz. Bunkers, anti-aircraft batteries, mined beaches, barbed wire, and guard posts. They'd attacked them all.

Le Corbeau Noir's job was done.

~

IN THE DEAD OF NIGHT, the Lysander with three war-weary agents of the BROADCAST circuit landed without a hitch or a bump on the airfield at Tangmere, the very place where Anna Adams had seen Sable off two years earlier. It seemed a lifetime since she'd stood there as an inexperienced, rather recalcitrant novice. There was no Anna Adams now. She was probably needed at her switchboard in Baker Street.

As the door to the plane's cargo opened, the foggy, peaty smell of rural Britain caressed Sable's nostrils. Home. No country smelled like this, of wet grass and chimney exhaust. No country.

Not sure if her legs would hold her if she jumped onto the tarmac, she wavered for a moment before tentatively setting foot on British soil. It was as if even the runway carried her in a hard embrace and her head kept repeating—*home, safe, home, safe*—over and over until her body finally believed it, too.

Her first steps on the homeland held everything. Jubilation, exhaustion, pride, and a deep and abiding love for her country. But also, for France, and all countries in the free world that had opposed the Third Reich. How much pain and suffering it had brought to the peoples.

She'd never felt herself as part of a bigger plan. She'd just done what she'd done. Her fight had been a basic instinct for survival, coming from deep within her. Now she understood the scope and magnitude of her sacrifice. It humbled her.

I'm home. I'm safe. This country loves me, and I love it so. I have defended its freedom and its right to exist as a sovereign country. Now I'm free to live my own life again.

THE JUBILATION only lasted for a brief spell, just as the wind tosses a leaf in the air before it whirls back down to earth. As the three agents made their way to the hangar, loaded with suitcases and backpacks, a new cloud of doubt spilled over Sable, thick as the night fog around her.

She wasn't free. A prickling sensation ran up her spine. Her most intense private battle was still in front of her. All on her own, she would have to go in search of her daughter.

Ginette put her free arm through hers, sure to sense her trepidation. "Where to now, Violette? You lead the way."

Sable was grateful for her friend's nearness and sixth sense. She took a deep breath.

"The name's Sable, Sable Montgomery. Violette Bernard has been left in Rennes a couple of hours ago. Oh, it's so good to be Sable again!"

"You'll never guess my name," Ginette laughed.

"I was just going to ask you. Do tell. And I want to know the real Georges as well."

"You'll never guess," Ginette repeated, still laughing.

Sable shook her head. "Please enlighten me."

"It's Violette! My real name is Violette Devereux."

"You're kidding me?" Sable was hugging her friend now.

"You're seriously telling me that my cover name was your real name? It must have been so odd to call me that all the time."

"It was actually fun, especially as I was the only one who knew."

The girls turned to Georges. "Now yours, please. Shed the Georges."

Sable added with a grin, "Georges was so wrong for you. It's a beastly name. All fluff and no substance."

Georges cracked up. "I was all right with Georges; what's wrong with him? There's George Washington and George Eliot and George Gershwin."

"George Eliot was a woman, wisecrack!" Sable jeered, "and they're all without the 's' at the end. I think that was the trouble. As if there were two of you!"

"All right," the real Violette interjected, "let go of poor Georges and show us the real man."

"You don't want to know."

"I do!" The girls cried out together.

"All right, you asked for it. My name is Francis Starr and I'm a born and bred Liverpudlian."

Sable stared at him in disbelief. "But your French is accent-free?"

"Got a French mother. Can't wait to hug her in Liverpool."

45

6 CAVENDISH SQUARE

Late August 1944

R ain was pelting the bay windows of 6 Cavendish Square. Big, fast drops chastised the stone pavement like a drummer in mid-battle. All view was barred in the barrage of the water curtain. The year 1944 had an ordinary wet English summer.

A sizable fire to repel the damp crackled in the fireplace. Sable, warm and cozy under a double eiderdown, lay propped up on cushions in the bed Elrod and Minnie had placed for her in the front parlor. Agatha Christie's *Murder on The Orient Express*—spine up—lay spread out on her stomach.

The sound of the rain and the roar of the fire had made her doze off again, but she woke as the door creaked. Lazily opening one eye, she saw Minnie, now almost thirty but still with that Cockney-style, I-know-where-my-bread-is-buttered aura, tiptoe toward her.

"'Ow are you feelin', Miss Sable?" The intent smile of her housekeeper brought waterworks to the corners of Sable's eyes.

"Sorry," she muttered, "I'm such a milksop these days." And then she laughed out loud, a high, tinkling laughter. This was Sable these days in her convalescence, cold and warm, striving hard to find a balance and continuously failing at it.

"I was just thinking of the days I'd rather kill you so I could go out to the West End, and look at me now. Just seeing you makes me overcome with emotion."

Minnie was rearranging the eiderdown around Sable's feet. The warm hazel eyes looked up, and Sable saw glistening drops in her eyes as well.

"I know, Miss. Elrod and I keep sayin' it to each other. That the Lady is back. We've been so afraid for you, so afraid. Miss Anna Adams was good at keepin' us informed about your whereabouts if she knew, but we were sure we weren't 'earing 'alf of the truth. And then when you collapsed..."

"I remember so little of it. Now that I'm home again, you must tell me, Minnie."

"I will, Miss, but let me get you some lunch fi'st. Doctor 'owe says 'ealthy meals and plenty of rest will do the trick. Though it's 'ard to come by good food with all the rationin'. Almost a day job, I can tell you."

"You never were much of an advocate for the French food that fed me for two years, were you, Minnie?" The housekeeper pulled a disgusted face. "No one should be forced on a regimen of bread long and 'ard as an arm and snakes pulled up from the grass." She shuddered. "Well, enough talk. I'll get you a propuh portion of shepherd's pie and a fresh pot of Earl Grey tea. That'll pass the doctor's judgment."

"It's so good to be back in your care, Minnie dear." Sable closed her eyes for a moment. "But we can really get rid of this bed. I don't need the extra fuss. My legs can carry me up the stairs now."

"We're not 'aving it yet. You're still too weak, Miss Sable!"

"All right, you're the boss." Sable gave up her protest, and not just for her own sake. She knew how important it was for Elrod and Minnie to watch over her now. It had been such a long and unforeseen convalescence at the Rehabilitation Center in Worcestershire.

Her London staff felt they'd somehow let her down, being unable to nurse the physically and mentally whacked-out Sable back to health.

Elrod brought her lunch, his old, wrinkled face sporting a gleeful grin. Sable was sure they'd been quarreling in the kitchen over who was about to serve her this meal.

"Oh Elrod, you shouldn't be carrying that heavy tray. Minnie could've done that." There was even a vase with daisies on it and a heavy teapot. Bent and white as washed snow, Elrod balanced on his feet to get the tray down on the coffee table.

"Nonsense, Miss! Minnie's ignoring her chores already, fussing over you every minute she can."

"You know what?" Sable sat upright, beaming suddenly. "Why don't we all have lunch together here around my bed? We're in need of a proper chat, anyway! There's so much I haven't told you, and I want to hear all that went on in London in the past years as well."

Elrod looked doubtful, the corners of his anaemic lips pulled down.

"But Miss..."

"No more Miss, either. If I learned anything in France, it is that we're a team. And in a team, there may be an organizer, but she isn't the boss. If you call me Miss, I'll start calling you Monsieur Elrod and Mademoiselle Minnie. Now, that will send the two of you up the curtains in despair."

It was the best-tasting meal Sable had enjoyed in as long as she could remember. Whether it was what Minnie had cooked up from rationed lamb and power-dry potatoes, or whether it was her mood, it didn't matter. She was on the mend. She was home and with the people she loved, who'd loved and served her father and known her from when she was still a girl and not a die-hard espionage agent who'd almost done herself in by weathering a storm that was above her might.

"I don't want to dwell too much on the past," Sable said, wiping the last crumbs from her chin. "I just take heart from the fact I wasn't the only SOE agent needing to be hospitalized on my return. And I mean, not just the women; there were plenty of male agents too. One day it will be possible to explain all we went through, and I'm sure tons of books will be written about our escapades, but for now, I want to focus on the future." Her eyes went from the elderly Elrod in her father's armchair to Minnie, sitting stolidly on the straight dinner chair next to her bed. Sable continued.

"I'll be eternally grateful for you keeping the fort here in London and for Donald and Flora Stacey looking after Alnor Castle. Without you, I wouldn't have been able to serve my country. So now it's time to give you the option to leave and do something else."

In her heart of hearts, she hoped fervently that they would rebuke her offer of dismissal. It came swifter than a shadow flees.

"I'm going nowhere unless you want me to," the old butler grumbled.

"And I can't do without my daily game of Scrabble with Elrod," Minnie protested.

Sable clapped her hands, tears spilling again. "Thank you, thank you, thank you!"

"All right, Miss, no need to featherbed us any further." The old butler rose to his feet, the joints of his knees cracking.

"Please sit down for a minute, Elrod. I've got some other announcements to make." He sank with delight back into her father's comfy chair.

"War has told us we're all equal, which means I'll do my bit in the household as well. And I'm raising your salaries and putting money away for your pensions."

"But, Miss..."

"Hush, hear me out!" Sable wagged her finger as the strict organizer she'd become. "My dear late father left me enough money to not worry one day of my life about where my next meal will come from. It's the least I can do for you both. But there's more. I already told Elrod that I'll have none of this nonsense of Ma'am-ing or Miss this or that. I'm Sable, plain Sable, and it's high time you call me that."

She paused for a minute, pure raw authority.

"I've given my own future a good thought as I lay half-paralyzed in that hospital bed. I want to follow in my father's footsteps. Not in the House of Lords, of course, but I want to make myself eligible for the Constituency of London and Westminster. And yes, Elrod, for your Labour party, not for my father's Conservative Party."

"Ohhh, Mis... Sable, you'd be an amazing MP!" Elrod's watery blue eyes lit up with pride and affection.

"We'll see about that." Sable sobered him up. "But I've realized in France I'm good at bringing people together around a common cause. And there will be so much to be done for this country when Germany's finally defeated."

"We need a toast! I'll bring out the sherry!" Minnie cheered, but then her face fell. "Oh no, Mi... Sable, I fo'got you don't drink!"

"Serve us your sweet sherry, dear Minnie! I feel on top of the world. Alcohol is no longer my enemy."

They clinked glasses. The first taste of the amber liquid was strange. It burned in her throat and wouldn't go down. When Elrod and Minnie didn't pay attention, she left the rest of the glass untouched on the table.

"I should go back to work." This time, it was Minnie to get up and smooth the creases of her cotton home dress.

"There's one more thing," Sable announced, then fell silent. Too pairs of eyes, one hazel and the other old and blue, were fixed on her face. She wrung her hands.

"Is it the little one, Sable?" It was Elrod, only a whisper, but her ears picked it up.

She was stunned. Didn't understand. "How do you know, Elrod?" He shrugged his shoulders. "We were so worried about you, Sable, not just this time but also... you know... when you returned from Amsterdam and Doctor Howe took you under his wing."

She still didn't understand. Looked at Minnie, who avoided her gaze, staring out of the window where the rain had died.

"You tell her, Minnie. I can't, you know, as a man." Elrod's face was red as a peony in full bloom.

"What is it?" Sable's voice was alarmed.

Minnie cleared her throat, her full cheeks pink and flustered. "Doctor 'owe told us you 'ad 'ad a special opuhration. That... uh... they only purform when... uh... babies can't be born the natural way..." Her voice trailed off, and she stood up abruptly to clear the lunch plates. Her hands needed something to do.

It was silent for a while. Sable lit a cigarette. Then exhaled.

"Well, I wanted to tell you just that, so it's a coincidence you bring it up. It's a long and complicated story. I owe you a full explanation, but not now. I'm too tired, as it's a lengthy story. And I'm... uh... sort of ashamed of it." She took a long haul on her Craven A, took her time to let the smoke escape from her nostrils.

"The long and the short of it is that I have a daughter. She will be seven this year on Christmas. She was adopted by people in London when she was only three days old."

Sable hung on to her cigarette for dear life. It was so darn hard and painful to disclose her secret to the people whose opinion mattered so much to her.

"Oh, Sable, a daughter! Blessed be God! You must try to find her." Elrod's eyes sparkled as she'd never seen before.

And Minnie chimed in, "Oh, and 'ere was I thinkin' you were just a pain in the butt before the war. If only I 'ad known, I'd have treated you like a lamb."

"So, you're not angry with me?" Sable dared looking at them again.

"Of course not! We'll help you find her, won't we, Minnie!" Elrod was almost dancing on his old feet.

"As sure as there's a moon in 'eaven," Minnie agreed. "We want to 'ear it all, but now you must rest, Sable. You've got red patches on your cheeks. I 'ope you're not running a fever again."

"No, it's all good." With a sense of deep gratefulness, she closed her eyes. She could only too well imagine the excited chatter that would go on in the kitchen.

. . .

"*ISABELLA!*"

THE NAME WAS on her lips as Sable slept the secure sleep that only water lilies know, pristine, protected, in one piece.

46

WHERE SHE WAS

August 1944

"Y ou're awfully quiet, Sabbo! Say your piece. Your bro can take it."

"Have you been talking to Elrod, or Minnie?" Sable's alarmed blue gaze met Freddie's.

"Heavens, no! I just arrived here after spending a jolly good night in town with David. I stopped over to see if you are well enough to escort me to Kettner's Townhouse. I promised you lunch, remember?"

Sable was sitting on the mauve couch, with her legs tucked underneath her, another Agatha Christie balanced on her knee. She seemed to ponder his suggestion, but then shook her head.

"I don't think I'm up to being in a crowded place yet, Freddo. I will. Soon, I promise. But there is something I want to discuss with you."

"Righto. I see that face. Time for a back-to-back?"

A smile broke open on her pinched face. "Yes. And did I recently tell you I love you? You're the only family I've got left."

Freddie jumped on the couch and sat down crossed-legged with his back to her. As always, she marveled at his jaguar-like agility and gracefulness. She locked her back with his.

"It's time to search for Isabella, Freddo, but I'm really shilly-shallying about having a shot at it on my..."

"... just been waiting for you to ask, Sab. Didn't want to touch upon the matter before you were ready. We can pass by the address you have today if you want?" To make the tone of the conversation lighter, he added. "As you intend on screwing me out of a hearty lunch anyway."

"But that's the point," Sable replied in little more than a squeak. "The house on 15 Queen Victoria Street doesn't exist anymore. It was bombed in the Blitz. I asked Minnie to check on it and now... and now I don't know what else to do."

"Buggers!" Freddie shifted his back and gripped her hand, but then added in a more upbeat tone. "But there must be records where people were relocated to after they lost their homes. Maybe the County Hall can help us?"

Sable liked the sound of "us."

"Why didn't I think of that?" Her heart felt pounds lighter.

"You want to try instead of lunch? You know you're doing me a great disfavor, but everything for the Lady!"

"Would you, Freddo? I'd so like to get started on finding Isabella, but I feel weak every time I think about her. It constantly brings back the horrors both before her birth and Von Henkell's awful death."

Freddie let go of her hand and swung his long legs off the couch. "Fancy a drive in the Morris, my dear? It's all ready to ramble around London with you."

A STERN-LOOKING lady with a tight gray bun and dark-rimmed glasses on her narrow nose looked up from the adoption papers with a frown in the yellow-brown eyes. Sable thought she looked like a misplaced great gray owl.

There was rebuff and tartness in her attitude, but Sable was beyond caring what Miss Sycamore might think about her status. Instead, she fixed her eyes on the name plate on the woman's tight-fitting navy uniform and thought she had a befitting name.

"I'm not sure I can help you. If you're not related to Mr. and Mrs. Carter, I'm not entitled to give you their new address."

Freddie stepped in. "Ahh, but there you are mistaken, Miss Sycamore. You see, my sister is related because they have adopted *her* daughter."

The woman looked from Sable to Freddie and seemed much more inclined to listen to the elegant gentleman than to what she clearly considered a loose woman.

"I'd have to consult with my boss first."

"Please do," Sable interjected swiftly before Miss Sycamore might change her mind.

"One moment, please."

The owl-like clerk was gone for what seemed an hour. People were standing in line behind Sable and Freddie waiting for their ration books, muttering among themselves about these well-to-do people holding up the line. Sable felt as if her legs would buckle under her. She still was so weak.

"Here, give me an arm." Freddie suited the action to the word and Sable leaned into him, trying to block the grumbling folk behind them. Finally, Miss Sycamore returned, looking pale around the thin nose. Her bloodless lips pressed together.

"What is it?" Sable already fancied all three of them killed in the bombings. She shuddered as Miss Sycamore spoke the words.

"Mr. Carter was instantly killed in the attack on 11 May 1941. Mrs. Carter died of her wounds in St. Thomas three days later."

"What about Isa... my daughter?" Sable gasped.

"That's the thing we don't know. There is no record of a child having died as well." Now showing some sympathy, Miss Sycamore held up her hands as if in an apology.

"But where can she be? If... if she didn't die?"

"There have been many children orphaned during the war. We don't always know where they are taken. Certainly, during the Blitz there was so much chaos in London that our recordings still aren't up to date. You could try asking at the orphanages?"

"Let's do that, Sab!" Freddie grabbed the adoption document that still lay on the clerk's counter, ready to steer Sable away. The latter was so flabbergasted by this news that she muttered a confused "thank you" and scurried past the grumbling crowds into the street, blinking against the light that reflected on the river Thames.

"Oh Freddie," she yammered, "what if Isabella is hurt or adopted all over? How can we ever find her now?"

"Easy, easy, old girl. One thing at the time." Freddie was still holding her arm and directed her to the green Morris.

"I know nothing about orphanages, but I do remember my father telling me about one in Kent. I guess we could ask Doctor Howe?"

"That's an idea." Freddie was clearly also racking his brain about how to go about the search for Isabella.

"Sure, Sable, the name of the largest orphanage in this part of the country is known as Babies Castle in Hawhurst. I could phone the current director, Dr. Barnardo's son. He's an acquaintance." Doctor Howe, silver-haired and in his late sixties, but youthful as ever, jumped up from his chair and already made his way to the sideboard where the black phone stood.

"Wait, Doctor Howe, I'm not sure I'm ready for this." Sable sat sunken deep into one of her physician's chintz armchairs, feeling small and frightened.

"Let Doctor Howe make the phone call, Sab. It's best you know as soon as possible where your daughter is," Freddie observed, sitting across from her and also half disappearing in one of the enormous, floral-patterned chairs.

The doctor raised one silver eyebrow. "Whatever you wish, Sable, but I agree with Mr. Frinton-Smith that it's best you get a hold on this now. The uncertainty is eroding your health."

"All right." With difficulty Sable got out of the chair and, lighting a cigarette, started pacing the doctor's living room. She had the urge to put her fingers in her ears so she couldn't hear the conversation that Doctor Howe was having, but she caught his answers anyway.

"A your girl, orphaned at age four and a half, during the Blitz. Adoptive parents Mr. and Mrs. Daniel Carter. First name unknown."

Silence.

"Yes, I'll wait. Thank you."

Silence.

"I see. Yes, of course. The biological mother."

Silence.

"Very kind of you. No, that will be all. Goodbye."

"What?" Sable screamed the one word.

"Sit down, Sable." The doctor's voice was full of authority. She immediately did as she was ordered, her knees trembling so hard she couldn't keep them still.

"Are you ready for this, Sable?" The authority was gone, just kindness now.

"I am. Has she been found?" Her voice was almost like a child's.

"Yes, Sable. Your daughter, Belle, is at Dr. Barnardo's Babies Castle in Hawhurst, and you may visit her."

Freddie was at her side in one gigantic leap, hugging and kissing her. "Oh sis, oh my dear sis!" he kept repeating. The elderly doctor was also visibly shaken at the sudden good news.

"I will escort you there, Sable, as well as Mr. Frinton-Smith. I think I want to keep a professional eye on you at one of these most important and emotional moments in your life."

Sable couldn't utter one word. She tried but choked, so she just nodded.

Then she managed through the lump in her throat. "Belle. Isabella."

∼

As Doctor Howe's chauffeur steered the gray Austin 12 HP Saloon onto Cranbrook Road in Hawkhurst, Sable couldn't believe her eyes.

In front of her stood a huge, ivy-covered mansion that almost resembled a castle. Swings and seesaws were scattered over the lawns and children of all ages raced around, chasing each other and throwing balls, playing tennis and riding bikes.

Nurse-like matrons in white aprons and bonnets shepherded the children to stay on the lawns. Older children were sitting under an age-old chestnut tree reading comic books.

"Is this it?"

Sable instantly felt better. She'd imagined a kind of prison where her child had been held in a damp and chilly cellar, not this great out-of-doors where she had plenty of space to play and learn.

"Yes," Doctor Howe replied, "Barnardo's is not just known for its charities but also for looking well after orphans. Your daughter will be fine, Sable."

"And you told them we were coming?"

"Yes, don't worry. Mr. Frinton-Smith and I will give you some time alone with Belle and then, if you need us, we will be there."

Sable met Freddie's gaze next to her in the back seat. He nodded and squeezed her hand.

"You'll both be fine, Sab!"

NOTHING COULD HAVE PREPARED Sable for meeting eye-to-eye with a seven-year-old precocious nymph in blond pigtails and a blue smocked dress, white socks and black shoes. The child ran into the room and then halted her steps. Isabella blonde? She'd been so dark when...

"Who are you?" The blue eyes darkened. "I thought it was Prissy."

Sable managed two steps toward her daughter, but then hesitated.

"No, I'm not Prissy. I'm... uh... Sable."

"Sable?" Belle's pretty, round face adopted a puzzled look. "I don't know a Sable. Have you come to choose one of us?" Belle showed an inclination to run out of the room again. "Not me!"

"No." Sable shook her head, though every nerve in her body

wanted to move close to her daughter and embrace the elf-like, little creature. "I just want to have a little chat with you if that's all right? Maybe you can tell me a little more about Babies Castle?"

Belle pouted her red lips. "Babies Castle is a stupid name. Like everyone is a baby here. I'm seven. Prissy is eighteen now. She was here until she was sixteen. Babies Castle." Belle repeated it as if it was the stupidest name in the world.

"You're certainly not a baby, Belle."

"How do you know my name?" The round eyes scrutinized Sable's face, missing nothing.

"I was told your name by Mr. Barnardo. It is Belle, isn't it? Though you're more an Isabella to me?"

The name thing seemed to need some pondering on Belle's behalf.

"All right," she said, pointing to the two chairs that were put ready in the visitor's parlor. "I think I like you. Let's have that chat."

Sable was glad to sit down. Her legs felt like gummy, and her heart raced. She yearned for a cigarette, but smoking in her daughter's presence seemed like a bad habit.

They sat staring at each other for a while until Belle remarked, "You're pretty. I like the color of your hair. I'm all right with being a blonde, but I think black hair is posher. Prissy has brown hair, curly, which is also nice."

"I love your hair." Sable smiled, taking in the wispy pigtails that reached to the small shoulders.

"So why are you here if it isn't to take me for a try-out?" Belle seemed to think it was time to leave the hair business behind.

Sable kept her daughter's eyes locked with hers, biting her lip. "Do you want to know the truth, Belle?"

"Not if you look so serious. That frightens me." Belle turned her eyes to the window, her upper body very still. Only her legs swished under the chair. Sable took a deep breath.

"You seem like a girl who tells it how it is."

"Prissy always says call a spade a spade, which I think is a funny expression. Nobody would call a spade a rake or something like that."

Belle was buying time, sensing something was amiss. *She's so like me,* Sable reflected, and the thought rubbed raw like the wound on her tummy.

"I would like to meet your friend Prissy." She wouldn't push Belle toward her confession. The round eyes went from the window back to Sable's face.

"Why? Prissy is not *your* friend." But after a brief silence, she added, "I didn't mean to be rude. You may if you really want to. But then you would have to come another time. I can ask Mrs. Higginbottom to organize a tête-à-tête. That's what she calls it. Mrs. Higginbottom arranges the visits."

"That would be great, Belle."

The next thing went in a flash, so fast Sable didn't know how it came to pass. Belle slid from her chair and came to stand against Sable's knee. It was a shy movement, but without knowing what she was doing, she threw her arms around the little girl and held her in a tight embrace.

"I'm your Mummy," she sniffled. "I'm so sorry, Belle, for leaving you, but they took you from me. They took you against my will when you were only three days old."

Belle said nothing, but also didn't leave the embrace. Sable drank in the scent of her child, and it was the sweetest thing she'd ever smelled, fresh apples, hay, and sweet baby skin.

She knew that smell. She'd had it in her nose for three days and forever after. And here it was again, and she couldn't get enough of it. Just couldn't. *That's why I became an alcoholic,* flashed through her, *because I needed to drink in this. Just this.*

It was wise, little Belle who ultimately broke the silence. Still covered by her mother's embrace, the smart mouth declared, "You can be my Mummy if you want to, but then you must call me Isabella. I like that much better than stupid Belle. Belle is a name for a cow." The word "cow" came out with great disgust.

Sable hugged her even tighter. "Oh Isabella, I've lived for this moment for the past seven years. If only you knew."

At that, Isabella wriggled herself free from her mother's embrace and looked at her with the darkened eyes she'd seen before.

"Now that's a lie, Mummy Sable. If you wanted to be with me for seven years, you would have come here earlier. I've been here for years. I don't even remember my parents in London. I was so little when I came here."

It was too difficult to explain to a seven-year-old how her mother's life got in the way from the beginning of her daughter's existence.

"I've only this week found out you were living at Babies Castle, Isabella. If I had known your parents had passed, I would have come earlier. I thought you were still with them in London."

"Well, I wasn't."

Sable changed the subject for now. "Would you like to meet your Uncle Freddie? He's here with me."

"Uncle Freddie?" Isabella repeated. "I have more family?"

"Yes, my dear, you have the funniest and nicest uncle in the world. He'll take you to places so exotic, you didn't know they existed."

"Like a safari in Africa?"

"If you'd like that."

"Oh, I've seen pictures of zebras and giraffes. I would love to see them for real. Prissy promised to take me to the London Zoo when the war is over. But a safari." Isabella held Sable's hand as she skipped into the sunshine and toward the lawns filled with children.

Sable was sure her heart would burst with happiness and pride.

47

THE WAR IS OVER

London, July 1945

"What do you think, Auntie Minnie?" Isabella was pirouetting in front of the housekeeper in her pink dress with a pleated skirt. "Mummy bought it for me at Harrods. It's ex... exclusive."

"It's mighty fine, Isabella." Minnie's hazel eyes shone with equal delight as Isabella's pride in her new garment. But very like young Sable, the little girl's face darkened the next moment.

"Oh," she exclaimed, a podgy, dimpled hand in front of her mouth, "but it's Mummy's event. Mummy's getting medals. Mummy is the star, not me."

"You're always a star to us, little rascal," Minnie added with a big grin.

Ever since Isabella Montgomery had come to live with them in the fall of 1944, the household had undergone a pivotal, exuberant change. The high-pitched voice ringing through all the rooms, the dolls and the miniature pram, the coloring books, and the sweet little dresses on the line.

But most of all, how Sable had risen from the ashes! Nobody

could have fathomed what motherhood would do for a woman like Sable. She'd proved to be a natural mom, strict but fair and always lovingly doing her very best for her child after all the years she'd had to miss out on her development.

Every day was a merry song now in 6 Cavendish Square. Isabella insisted on calling everyone auntie or uncle after having had to do without family for years. So, it was Auntie Minnie and the Uncles Freddie and David and Grandpa Elrod.

In the first months, Isabella had continued to call Sable 'Mummy Sable' but gradually the Sable had dropped off and it was all day long, "Mummy, where are you?" "Mummy, come look, I've baked a cake." "Mummy, I want to go to the park."

Elrod stuck his head around the door and the same ritual was completed for his eyes.

"Look, Grandpa Elrod! Do you like my new dress? Mummy says I'm picture-perfect."

"You're a sight for sore eyes, little madam." Elrod dabbed his watery blue eyes. They seemed to fill way too easily when he caught sight of the apple of his eye.

"Where's Mummy? I want to see what she looks like. She also has a new dress from Harrods. But it's green, not pink!" Isabella pulled a face.

"Do you not like green, my doll?" Minnie was trying to fasten two huge pink ribbons in Isabella's hair.

"I like green all right but not drab green. Mummy says it's what she wore in the war, so that's why she chose it."

"It's not drab green, silly. It's olive, and it looks fabulous on your Mummy." Minnie tried to keep the bouncing Isabella under control, but the ribbons kept slipping from the soft hair.

"At least it's raw silk from China." Isabella was keeping her head sideways, clearly pondering if she'd consent to the olive.

"Rough silk!" Elrod roared with laughter. "One of these days, you'll be the death of me, little Isa."

"Noooo, Grandpa! Don't die, never die!" She raced toward him and into his arms, Minnie standing with the pink ribbon in her hands.

Three mouths uttered "oh" as Sable swished in, wearing an elegant, body-hugging dress, silk stockings and black high heels, her shiny, raven-black hair in a tight bun on top of her head, her makeup modest but perfect. The sapphire necklace that Minnie had put around her slender neck so many years earlier now glittered on her creamy neckline.

But it was her dancing blue gaze that drew all attention. Sable Montgomery was happy for the very first time in her life, and her eyes told it all.

"Mummy's also a sight for sore eyes!" Isabella cheered, escaping from Elrod's embrace to touch the silk of her mother's dress.

"Are you ready, my little bun? Why's one ribbon missing from your hair?" Sable kissed the top of her daughter's head. "The taxi with Uncle Freddie and Uncle David will be here any minute now."

"We're going to Baker Street," Isabella announced to all present, while Minnie quickly took the opportunity to fix her hair. "I'm going to see all the real spies. And then we're going to have cake."

"You'll be all right? You know he could be there too?" Sable felt her brother's gaze rest on her. She and Isabella were sitting in the back of the taxi, opposite Freddie and David, while they swirled through the London streets.

"Who's going to be there?" Isabella was quick to pick up the strain.

"Nobody in particular, little bun. Just some friends from the war."

Sable gave Freddie a warning look, at which he rolled his eyes. Isabella snapped up everything. Her daughter's fine-tuned antennae surprised her every day.

The possibility of William Mitchell being present at the ceremony was the only shadow hanging over a glorious day. The last Minister of Economic Warfare, Roundell Palmer, would decorate the surviving

SOE agents. She looked forward to seeing Wooly and Killer and Lock, even Anna, but her gut clenched at the thought of laying eyes on Bill again. Even after over three years, it was such a tender spot.

"I'll be all right." She nodded, just to reassure Freddie.

David, who usually played a background role when Sable and Freddie were together, added in his gentle giant's voice, "I'll be glad to congratulate Major Mitchell on his promotion. He worked so hard for the new rank." Thus, taking the sting out of Sable's possible meeting with her former beau.

She sent him a grateful smile. Let all thoughts of Bill Mitchell rest. That was the best path forwards.

Though a six-foot-three Hercules with broad shoulders, arms like thick ropes and the head of a wrestler, David Southgate was the kindest and most congenial man she'd ever met. He was the calm eye in the storm that Freddie could whip up, consistent and considerate. A brilliant match for her agile and restless brother.

The taxi pulled up at 64 Baker Street, and the three former agents were silent for a moment, remembering the times they'd been called to the office. Sable also recalled how she'd set her affairs in order in case she wouldn't return. Today, she was here, alive, and better than ever. Though the day certainly would also have a dark edge, as they would finally hear of those who would never be among them again.

"Let's get cracking!" Freddie broke the spell and adding to Isabella, "Or they'll have eaten all the cake."

"No, Uncle Freddie, Mummy says it's going to be a huge cake. Maybe even three layers."

"Let's check it out then." And grabbing Isabella's hand, they were the first to exit the taxi. David paid the driver and Sable stood looking up at the building. There were a handful of people at the front door, but no one she knew. She took a deep breath, straightened her expensive new dress and, giving David an arm, followed her brother and daughter into the office that had played such a major role in her war life.

"Sugar!"

Wooly, bald as a billiard ball but not having aged one bit,

bellowed from the other side of the smoky, crowded room. Holding Isabella tightly by her side, Sable made her way to her former boss.

As they embraced, she smelled his scent of tobacco and Old Bond Street soap, savoring the brawny arms around her. He'd been, he was, like a father to her.

"Wooly!"

"And who's the little urchin?" The gray eyes rested on Isabella, who looked up at him with that particular dark look in her blue eyes.

"What is an urchin, Sir?"

"A lovely young lady." He winked at her.

"I've never heard that word, but I'm Lady Sable Montgomery's daughter," she answered in her most huffy voice.

The old major's eyes went nonplussed from Sable to Isabella, but as an old spy master used to dealing with unforeseen circumstances, he recollected himself within seconds.

"Is that so? Well, let me shake hands with you, Isabella. It's not every day I meet such a well-spoken, beautiful lady."

Isabella gauged if he was mocking her but seemed to decide he was serious. She put her little paw in his. "As you're Mummy's friend, I'll call you Uncle Wooly."

"Uncle Wooly it is!"

Standing close to Wooly, who was immediately engaged in a deep conversation with Isabella about the white-icing cake on the table, Sable studied the people in the room. Her eyes lit up when she discovered Killer and Lock, who came over to greet her and also ask after her little girl.

"Hey, Mascot!" Sable turned to come face-to-face with Captain Hancock and Helmsman Potter. Overcome by emotion, she faltered for a moment on her high heels until the snow-white captain grabbed her elbow.

"We've been invited to the ceremony. Mighty proud of you!"

"Oh, Captain!" His hug was so welcome. And shaking Potter's hand, she added, "We did what Winston told us to do! We set Europe ablaze. We ran out the Nazis."

"You sure did, girl. Your father would've been so proud to be here today. That's why I came. To represent him."

"Thank you." What else could she say?

At that moment, Dorothy Perkins, the Baker Street secretary, made her way through the crowds in the room to hand Sable a telegram.

"More surprises!" Captain Hancock beamed as he peeked over Sable's shoulder.

She tore the flimsy grey-green paper open, and her eyes flew over the capitalized words.

CONGRATULATIONS, RAVEN. HERE'S TO VICTORY. MEET UP SOON. JEGER.

Too baffled to take it all in, she just savored her friend's words, wondering how she'd found out about the event. It didn't matter. Esther was with her here in spirit and Sable's spirit soared, even past all the dead friends, her comrades.

Seconds later Anna, in her WAAF uniform, pushing the dark glasses up her nose, entered the room, a clipboard pressed to her modest bosom. Both the former Minister of Economic Warfare and the Head of SOE were on her heels. They made for a space at the back of the room where the official ceremony was going to be held.

No sign of Bill. Sable let out a long breath, not sure if it was relief or regret. *Relief*, she told herself, but doubted it.

There were very few agents from Section F that she had known, and her heart ached when Maureen, Cecil, and Diana weren't there. Maybe they couldn't make it, but all efforts to find out more about them had run to nothing.

"Hey, Sable." She heard a voice behind her and smiled widely when Violette and Francis, recently engaged, joined them. They usually met up every three months, also with Freddie and David, now that Violette had settled in England to be with her fiancé. It was always such a delight to see her friends and, though they spoke more of the future than the past, their shared experience had forged a bond for life.

"Ladies and gentlemen, may I have your attention, please?"

Anna's foreign-accented voice called over the buzz. Isabella grabbed her mother's hand and looked up at her in high expectation.

They were one by one called to the makeshift stage to receive their decorations and be honored with a brief speech. When it was Sable's turn, she didn't let go of Isabella's hand. She needed her there for support, and the little wisecracker seemed to understand that without words.

Standing close to Anna was a special experience for Sable. Somehow, before going on her mission, she'd been slightly intimidated by the closed-mouthed, enigmatic spy maker, but now she felt liberated. She'd withstood all the tests of the war. She was a survivor. Anna seemed to feel it too and, for that reason, chosen to introduce Sable.

"Sable Montgomery has been an outstanding secret agent who has spent over two years for SOE in France. Ordered to join the CHASSIS Network in the region of Bordeaux, she found on arrival that CHASSIS had been betrayed by the British-French infiltrator, Henri de Bonheur. Sable still managed to salvage some of the network and singlehandedly built it up again to considerable force as the PAPILLON network, before being betrayed and captured by De Bonheur's henchmen together with another agent present, Freddie Frinton-Smith. Both agents managed to escape but instead of fleeing, Sable went back to unmask De Bonheur, who found his subsequently found his death in France.

"Sable then went to Lyon, where she worked and organised the BROUILLARD network together with Maureen Knight, Roger Moulin and Nora Plewman."

Sable swallowed hard. It was the first time she heard the real names of the sporty Canadian and the lovely, devoted courier. It was hard to take in Anna's inevitable words but Isabella, squeezing her hand, held her strong.

"Unfortunately, the Nazis had infiltrated this highly successful network that brought hundreds of downed airmen via the Pyrenees back to England. The three SOE agents of Sable's team were arrested and most likely murdered in Natzweiler-Struthof Concentration camp in August 1944. Wa are still in the process of investigating the events around their disappearance. ”

Sable shuddered, felt suddenly unwell. All three murdered. Swaying on her elegant heels, she forced herself to listen to Anna, letting the die-hard agent take over once again. Anna kept reciting her own distant adventures in France.

“Sable was arrested for a second time in Lyon in the notorious Hôtel Terminus but escaped again brilliantly when her captor, a high-ranking German officer, unfolded his plans to her to desert the German army.”

Unaware she was squeezing Isabella's hand even tighter at the mentioning of Von Henkell, her daughter looked up to her with a question mark on her little face. Sable quickly smiled down at her and tried to focus on the remainder of Anna's speech.

“As the ground had become too hot under Sable's feet, she fled to Paris, where she and Freddie Frinton-Smith set up two networks. Sable headed the ten-thousand-man strong circuit BROADCAST, which was instrumental in preparing the sabotage needed for the Allied invasion of Normandy.

“This is, in a nutshell, all that Sable Montgomery has done for SOE, for her country and for France. I now want to give the floor to Lieutenant Colonel Jock Woolworth to decorate Sable Montgomery.”

It annoyed Sable that she was mentioned just by her name. After all, she was Captain Montgomery. Was this deliberate on Anna's part? Still trying to belittle her? But as Anna stepped aside and Sable saw the familiar face of her beloved mentor and boss heave his thick-set body on stage, she forgot all about it.

The face under the bald scalp was one big grin, and Sable saw the light-green eyes glistened with emotion. The crowd seemed to hold their breath. Then he bowed for her, deep and long. Applause exploded as the Colonel boomed,

“Sugar! It is my greatest honor to announce that you have been promoted to the rank of major. Guests, may I present to you one of the toughest cookies of the British Isles, Major Sable Montgomery, aka Le Corbeau Noire, aka one of Winston Churchill's best secret agents." Sable didn't know where to look but steadied herself under Wooly's reverend gaze.

"Major Montgomery, it pleases His Majesty King George VI to issue to you the George Cross. This is the premier award given for non-operational gallantry, or gallantry not in the presence of an enemy. It is awarded for acts of the greatest heroism or of the most conspicuous courage in circumstances of extreme danger and is the highest military gallantry award of the British Empire." With a wink, he added, "I didn't write that, but it's as true as the dial of the sun."

Sable was too stunned for a reply, mumbled a thank-you, sought Freddie's eyes in the crowd. *Would he, too?* Her brother put up his thumb, signaling *Go for it, sis!*

Wooly pinned the medal with the man on horseback and the words *For Gallantry* around it on her green dress. His fingers trembled slightly. Then he kissed her forehead, whispering, *"Thank you for everything you did, sugar. You're the best."*

Isabella pulled her mother's hand, wanting to be lifted to finger her mother's brand-new decoration. Sable stood with her daughter in her arms, overwhelmed with emotions, the crowd in front of her clapping, a wave of faces and voices until... her gaze focused on the tall, red-haired man in the middle of the room.

Bill.

He was clapping, too. There was... there was so much in those deep-sea eyes. Reverence, pride, understanding... and love. Above all, love. She felt she'd come full circle, but not knowing to what.

As if the Dead Sea parted, the people made space for Major William "Wild Bill" Mitchell to pass through them and reach the stage where Sable stood, clamping Isabella against her chest.

"Congratulations, blue-eyed girl."

"Thank you... uh, Bill."

Sable felt Isabella shift in her arms, taking in the unknown man with great interest.

"My Mummy is a war hero!"

Whatever hold this man had over her mother, Isabella clearly wanted to let him know not to mess with her.

"She sure is, Miss."

"I'm not a miss, I'm Isabella Montgomery. And who are you?"

Sable cringed. Her daughter wasn't having any nonsense.

"Well, hello, Isabella. I know yer mother from our secret agent trainin' and just came up to congratulate her."

"Thank you," Sable said again, giving him a smile just warm enough to show him her daughter's bark wasn't as bad as her bite.

"Now it's my Uncle Freddie's turn," Isabella told him, pointing the red-haired Scot to the fact that more important matters were about to take place. She even grabbed her mother's face with two hands to direct her attention away from Bill and to the stage where Freddie stood quite affected, even by his old boys' network standards.

Sable, still with Bill next to her and very aware of his male nearness, desperately tried to keep her wits about her and failed slightly as she listened to how Freddie was also awarded the George Cross, this time by the head of SOE, Colonel Stanley Gibbins.

An ambivalent feeling took hold of Sable. Though her heart was full of love for her brother, standing there close to the man she knew so intimately twisted that same heart in pain. There was nothing between them anymore. Too much had passed and changed in Sable's life since they had parted in the early spring of 1942. Bill was past tense. He was just here because he needed to be here and had come up to her because of politeness.

He knew nothing about her at all. Unless... unless David had updated his friend. After all, Bill hadn't seemed very surprised at Isabella's presence.

And what had happened in Bill's life? Freddie had told her he lived the life of a recluse, writing poetry in his free time. Sable's mind raced and the old, foggy unhappiness settled on her again. *Why don't you leave me in peace?*

David and Freddie came to stand with them, and kisses and congratulations were exchanged. Then the inspection of each other's medals. David grabbed Bill by the elbow and whisked him out of the room.

"Time for cake!" Freddie took Isabella from Sable's arms and put her back on her own two feet. "Who's going to have the largest slice? Uncle Freddie or Isabella?"

"Me, me, me!"

~

BEFORE SHE KNEW what had happened, Sable found herself in Anna's office with the door closed, alone with Bill in the room. They eyed each other with a degree of suspicion.

He broke the ice. "Cigarette?"

"Please!" His hand shook as he gave her a light. Their eyes met— full of wonderment, pain, hope.

Sable decided the only way forward was clearing the air. "I think we need to talk."

"That's why we are here." His voice was softer, sadder, shrewder.

"Let's sit down then. I'm still not fit as a fiddle."

They sat on two straight chairs, smoking, silent.

"I don't know where to start," Sable confessed, wishing with every fiber of her being she could hold her child close, feel the little body, not be so out of joint.

"Ye don't have to tell me anything, Sable. I know it all. Would ye like me to read ye a poem I wrote for ye yesterday?"

Surprise replaced confusion. She looked up at him, met the deep-sea eyes and melted.

"Please." Her voice was smaller than the point of a small needle.

Bill took a folded paper from his breast pocket, unfolded it, and stared at it for a while, then read.

The Highland Raven
by Wild Bill

Raven, Rebel, Bird of Prey
Skywards ye rise

Wings wide and still
Yer spirit soars
On silent mists
Besiegin' brutal Beinn Chorranach.

Love lifted ye with heavy might
To where yer heart
Hailed only Highlands
Where God's pure hand
Wipes lonesome tears.
Windblows every catastrophe.

I saw yer strength with weary eyes
I loved ye then
I love ye still
Yer soul in me
What choice had I
Fooled only by my witless pride?

Raven, Rebel, Bird of Prey
Skywards ye rise
Wings wide and still
Now yer love soars
Forever more
If only I could fly with ye.

THE AIR in Anna's office became very quiet. The party was still going on in another part of the building with the chatter of voices, peals of laughter, and the clatter of cutlery against porcelain plates.

Sable sat with her hands folded in her lap, looking down at them. Through her eyelashes, she saw how Bill folded his poem and tucked it away. Then he rose from his chair, muttering.

"Sorry, Sable. I'll leave ye now. I shouldn't have. It was inappropriate." He made for the door while she sat frozen.

"Wait!"

The word escaped her lips against her wish.

He turned slowly toward her, the depth of sorrow in his eyes melted into hers. She couldn't hold out any longer. A throb, a yearn, a torment almost delightful in its intensity.

"*Mo Chridhe*," Bill whispered in her hair, *my heart*, as he held her tight, tighter, even tighter. Sable became fluid as his muscular arms surrounded her, inhaling his scent of musk and leather and the Highland brooks, burying her head against the beating heart in his chest. He caressed her hair, kissed the top of her head, repeating, "Ye're home, *Mo Chridhe!*"

She raised her face to his, waiting for his kiss that landed almost trembling on her lips, then sought her with more passion, gluing lips to love, to heart, to soul.

"Mummy, what are you doing?"

Sable shot away from Bill as if hit by a bullet. Isabella stood gazing up at them with big, round eyes.

"Are you my daddy?" The fiery eyes darkened. "Or why are you kissing my mummy?"

"Isabella!" Sable corrected her daughter. "Remember to knock before you enter."

"Sorry!" A little abashed, she took to looking at her shoes, clearly uncomfortable with this new development in her mother's life.

"It's all right, darling. Bill is not your daddy, but he is the man your Mummy has loved for a very long time."

Still with her eyes on her shoes, Isabella piped up, "I don't know who my daddy is."

Bill took Sable's hand and led her to her daughter, then sinking on his haunches to be level with the little girl, he said in a kind voice.

"Is it all right, Isabella, if I share yer Mummy's love with ye?"

The iris blue eyes looked frankly into his. She weighed him, almost like an adult.

"You will have to love me, too, because Mummy and I are one."

"Oh, precious child, I'll love ye as if yer my own flesh."

Tears filled Bill's eyes, and he wiped them away, embarrassed at his show of emotion before a young child. Sable knew he was thinking of Maisie, and she squeezed his shoulder.

"Come," she said, "let's have cake."

"More cake!" Isabella huzzahed.

48

FULL CIRCLE

Two weeks later

It was raining so hard, the windshield wipers of Sable's Bentley could hardly wash away the rain. She was at the steering wheel, with Bill in the passenger seat reading Robert Burns. The road was dancing with fat raindrops, and it looked as if the entire universe was wet. But ahead of her, through the pelting rain loomed up the Arrochar Alps, while Loch Fyne could be glimpsed at her left.

Bill looked up from his reading, scanning the landscape.

"Yer sure you want to continue drivin'? I can take over if ye want a rest."

"I'm fine, Bill. You know I love driving my car. Even in the rain. And certainly now that I'm going home."

"So ye think Alnor Castle will feel more like home now the ghosts have finally left the place?"

She smiled sideways at him. "I'm not sure, but I think so. I loved living there as a child. It was my father's most sacred place in the world. I know how devastated he was when my mother wrung it out of him during the divorce. I've never really understood how that worked. You know, with him being the Baron and this being his constituency."

"She probably had a powerful hold over him. From what ye told me, yer mother was a fierce woman."

Sable hit a large puddle, and the water sprayed in all directions, temporarily blinding her sight.

"She was a fierce hellcat. Give me a cigarette, darling. I feel a bit jittery."

"First time without yer child and in total possession of Wild Bill," he joked, handing her the burning Craven A.

"Yes to both," Sable giggled, "but Isabella will soon come up with Freddie and David. Maybe it's a good thing for the two of us to miss each other like mad for a couple of days."

"And yer jitters have nothin' to do with me?"

"Everything, William Mitchell." She took a large drag on her cigarette, relieved that the rain was finally slowing down. "But I can live with that."

"Would ye ever have imagined this could still have happened between us, Sable?" He put a loving hand on her thigh that made her flesh tingle.

"I've always hoped it would, Bill." Her answer was honest. "All the long years in France, I hoped one day you'd be among the agents that were dropped. It was a disappointment every time when you didn't come."

"I know, my darlin', I wanted to come. It screamed at my soul that I had to protect ye, but I thought ye were adamant ye didn't want anythin' more to do with me. Still, I quizzed that poor Anna about yer whereabouts so often, she didn't pick up the phone anymore when I rang Baker Street. I shouldn't have tried her like that when I knew she couldn't disclose details about agents' missions, but I couldn't help myself."

"Oh, gosh, what must she have thought?" Sable giggled.

"I'm sure she had more requests about female agents in France from lovesick puppies like me," Bill observed with a dry chuckle, "but in the end, it was Freddie who assured me ye were still thinkin' of me as well."

"So, you stayed in Britain all the time?"

"Of course not. I wouldn't have been able to look myself in the eye if ye'd been riskin' yer life in France and I was just trainin' agents at Beaulieu. I did a couple of missions myself but never to France and never longer than two months because they needed me back here. I did two missions in Poland, two in Romania, one in Czechoslovakia and one in Holland. Nothin' compared to ye."

"Do you... have you ever heard what happened to Egbert?"

Bill shifted in his seat, closed the volume of poetry. Sable shot him a quick glance. Bill looked deeply affected. She heard the intake of breath she suddenly remembered.

"He's dead. Killed. That was my Dutch mission. Tryin' to find out more about the Gestapo's England Spiel, the infiltration of the Nazis into the Dutch Section of SOE." Bill's voice was full of rancor. Sable's hands gripped tighter around the wheel. She saw the desert-sand mop of hair, the eyes that had never seen unhappiness before the war. Dead. Gone. Another brilliant, young life wrecked. The man who'd brought Bill and her together. Who'd always and in every way been such a good friend to her.

"I... I don't know what to say." She swallowed with fixed eyes on the wet road ahead.

"We'll one day visit his grave in Amsterdam together and remember the capital fellow he was. That's all we can do for him, *Mo Chridhe*."

Sable nodded in the dark.

"Let's not talk too much about the war. I'm just so glad it's all over. Look, there's Alnor, gleaming in the rain. I hope the steward has lit the fires to get rid of the damp."

"I'm sure he has."

Sable focused on the huge neo-Gothic castle coming into sight, its gray stones even grayer under the rainy conditions. And yet it looked splendid, as if her Dadaigh pushed her forward to finally, finally make peace with her past.

She was surprised to see colored lamps swinging from the trees on both sides along the driveway.

"Donald has really gone out of his way to welcome us. I wonder if his wife Flora has pressured him into this."

"Could be." Bill smirked.

As she drove onto the gravel courtyard, she saw dripping wet carnations decorating the balustrade and a gigantic sign: "Welcome Home, Major Montgomery."

"Goodness," Sable whistled, "have they gone crackers?"

She hadn't even stopped the car when Bill jumped out and raced around, opening a huge umbrella. There was no sight of the steward, Donald Stacey or his wife.

"Milady," Bill bowed and, holding the umbrella over her head, escorted her to the double doors. He opened them with a master key.

Sable became suspicious. "Have you been meddling in this, Mitchell?"

He looked at her with the face of an innocent twelve-year-old. "I do not know what ye're hintin' at."

Sable stepped into the glorious hall with the oil portraits of all her ancestors, both men and women along the high-ceilinged walls. The scent of her father, talcum, tweed, and tobacco, danced around her. It was as if she saw him coming down the stairs, his Browning hunting gun slung over his Macintosh, his loyal pointers Otis and Roy at his heels.

The image gripped at her chest as if it was real and she stopped, missing him with an acuteness she hadn't felt in years.

Dadaigh.

Mo Bhobain.

"What is it, Sable?" Bill put his arm around her shoulder. "Are ye a'rite?"

"Yes, I was thinking of my father."

"I can imagine."

"I wonder where the Staceys are? I'd expected them to welcome us. Certainly, after this long trip."

"Ahh."

"What does that mean?"

"Just follow me, milady. Yer bath is ready and then dinner in the library."

"What are you up to, Bill?"

Sable turned to him, and it began to dawn on her he'd planned all this. The lights, the carnations, the sign, the absence of the steward and his wife.

He stood before her, looking into her eyes.

"Ye must know by now that I'm only a sentimental minstrel. So please trust me. I may not be very accomplished at romance, but I've done some research into the matter, and this is the result. Whether ye like it or not."

"Oh, Bill!" Sable raised on her toes to kiss him. He kissed her back, then took her arm.

Minutes later, she was lying in a lavender-scented bubble bath with candles around her and Sinatra's slow, lustful "Dream" sounding from the record player next door. Bill came in and leaned against the doorpost, his deep eyes resting on her shape in the bath. It made her bashful, the way he looked at her, but also longing for his caress.

"I'm tempted to step into that bath with ye, but I'm a gentleman... with an appetite," he grinned. "It would be such a pity to ignore the Canard aux cérises and the pommes duchesse that Flora prepared for us."

"They can wait." Sable threw all caution overboard. She didn't take her eyes off him as he unbuckled his belt, pulled the white shirt out of his pants, to reveal his powerful chest with the reddish hairs. Divesting himself of his shoes and trouwers, he stepped into the bath and sat behind her, his legs enveloping hers. She leaned against his chest, his arms around her. They sat like that for a long time, almost afraid to move, to feel too much, until she turned in his arms and kissed him.

"I love ye, Wild Bill, with all my heart."

"*Mah luaidh*, ye own my heart and my soul."

"Have you forgiven me for not being able to tell you the truth?" She had to know.

"I didn't understand it at the time, but I do now." His kiss sealed the scar. There was no barrier between them anymore. It was love so sweet, so sweeping, stormy, like the swell in Pentland Firth.

"Close yer eyes."

Wrapped in a paisley dressing gown, her hair still wet and her body still burning with lovemaking, Sable was led over the threshold into Alnor's library. Bill was leading the way until he announced, "A'rite, open yer eyes."

Sable blinked in the light of a hundred candles, placed throughout the room on tables and stools. They threw shadowy flickerings on her father's leather volumes. The curtains were drawn, and on the study table a festive meal was placed. Her throat blocked, tears pricking her eyes. Bill had chosen the one room she'd fled to in her agony after returning from the Elsie Inglis Memorial Maternity Hospital in early January 1938 after Isabella had been stolen from her and all her hopes had been torpedoed.

"Have I made the wrong decision?" Bill looked lost.

Sable was still rooted on the spot, but she slowly shook her head.

"To choose this place of all the rooms in Alnor to celebrate our reunion shows me the depth of your love, William Mitchell. I'm so glad you're a poet because I lack all of that. All of it." Her eyes looked around the room as if she was a forlorn little girl. Which she had been when Freddie had found her here.

Bill pulled out a chair, and she sat down, still taking in everything this room had been to her. How she'd fought the longest battle to be back here, a different person, a mother, a lover.

"I know ye had yer first marriage proposal here, but I wonder if I might be luckier than the first man, who'd managed to be yer brother." The grin was back on Bill's handsome face as he sank on one knee and popped open a small leather box which held a platinum ring with diamonds around a black opal.

"Would ye give me a try, *Mo Chridhe*?"

Sable covered her face with her hands, her heart brimming over. "Oh, Bill, I love you so much."

She sank to the floor next to him as the ring hovered above her finger.

"On one condition."

"Bein'?"

"That Isabella gets the daddy she wants."

The ring slipped around her finger like a drop of quicksilver. Bill kissed the hand that had killed and loved. Now loved for good.

EPILOGUE

E sther attended Sable's and Bill's wedding in the spring of 1946 with her fiancé Tore Helberg and recovering sister Rebecca. The Raven and Jeger remained lifelong friends and were the guardians of each other's children.

Sable managed to find Lili Hamilton, also married to a Scotsman, Iain Brodie and learned the circumstances of Filippo Maltese's death.

Through Esther, Sable also stayed in contact with Océane and visited her in Paris.

Anna Adams asked Sable's help in her post-war search for missing F Section female agents who'd been stationed in France. Sable came to admire Anna's tenacity and though it remained a professional bond, they came to a good understanding of each other's qualities.

Together with Bill, Sable traveled to Amsterdam to pay her respects to Egbert's parents and to visit her former beau's grave in Zorgvlied.

In 1965, Sable also visited the former concentration camp Natzweiler-Struthof, which was then turned into a memorial site and a museum, to pay her respect to the SOE agents who had been detained and gassed there.

Violette and Francis Starr were Sable's go-to friends when the war hit her hard again. Together they also visited every memorial service that was held in remembrance of their fight in France. They were instrumental in helping set up the SOE memorial for fallen agents in Valençay in 1991.

Captain Hancock and Helmsman Norman Potter remained close to Sable for the rest of their lives. Though MS Canterbury, the Missus, didn't survive her attacks during the war, they often spoke of their treacherous trip to Dunkirk.

Colonel Jock Woolworth, Wooly, passed away in 1948 from a sudden heart attack. It was a tremendous loss for Sable, but she would always remember her mentor and boss in loving affection. "Sugar" visited his grave every year.

Cuthbert "Killer" Drake and Johnny "Lock" Clark both had some difficulties after the war settling back into civilian life, as they'd given their heart and soul to training agents. They were frequent visitors to Alnor, and both ended up working on Sable's estate.

Steward Donald Stacey and his wife, Flora, retired when the new men took up their positions at Alnor Castle.

Elrod and Minnie continued to keep the household going at 6 Cavendish Square. To both Sable's and Isabella's great sadness, Elrod passed away at age 74 in 1947. Minnie married Jim Brawley, a Cockney friend of her youth, and together they presided over Sable's London property. They remained childless.

Doctor Howe retired from his doctor's practice in 1948 and lived in good health for another twenty years. He and his wife doted on their own grandchildren and Sable's children.

Freddie and David remained a loving couple until they died at the respective ages of 87 and 89 in the 1990s. With the help of Sable's inheritance, which she insisted upon sharing with her half-brother, Freddie was able to buy back Frinton-Smith Whiskey Distillery and built it out into one of Scotland's best export items. The couple also never gave up their love of flying machines and were known to have at least ten war planes stored in their hangar near Inveraray—much to the delight of Isabella, who loved to be flown around in a private jet by her uncles. The safari to South Africa topped her dreams.

Isabella Montgomery-Mitchell grew into a fine young lady with a quick tongue and a knack for mischief. She spent her childhood between Alnor Castle, London and Paris, but clearly preferred city life to 'boring' Scotland, much to her parents' dismay. After a long spell of not knowing what she wanted to do with her life and intensive globetrotting at her parents' expenses, the Raven's daughter eventually settled for a life as an actress. Isa, as she now called herself — "I'm just Isa"—became great friends with Lili's younger sister, Rosalie Hamilton, who took the wild young thing under her wing. And at that the light went on, and Isa shone in one movie after the other. She could now pay for her own lavish expenses. Under all that bravada beat a warm heart and sparkled a lovely, mesmerizing personality.

Sable and Bill embarked on their great romance with every fiber of their being, and no force could pull them apart but death. Major Sable Montgomery-Mitchell stayed true to her promise to become a Labour MP for the Constituency of London and Westminster and spent the first years after the war in the House of Commons. On the request of Winston himself, she was then asked to become the Ambassador for the UK in France, a position she held for many years.

Bill loved Paris as well and thrived in its intellectual and literary community. He was, by now, a renowned poet and though he always proclaimed he'd never be the stature of a Robert Burns, William "Wild Bill" Mitchell's love poetry was on numerous bedside tables. He won many prizes and awards, but cherished mostly the T.S. Eliot Prize.

Sable and Bill had another daughter together, Morag Mitchell, whom Isabella persisted was called "Baby." Morag remained Baby until she herself was old enough to stand up to her older sister and claim her rightful name back. Morag "Baby" Mitchell was in every way her father. Strong, healthy, red-haired, and with that deep—almost too deep—love for her next of kin.

~

THANK YOU SO MUCH for reading **The Highland Raven**. This was already book 5 in the captivating world of **The Resistance Girl Series**. There are two more!

I'm thrilled you've read the fifth installment. Your enjoyment of my stories about Resistance Women in WW2 means the world to me and I hope you'll continue to read all 7 books.

BUT WAIT, THERE'S MORE!

As a token of my appreciation, I invite you to join my exclusive newsletter community. By becoming a part of my inner circle, you'll gain access to exciting extras, promos, and a FREE novella - **The Partisan Fighter** - an exclusive companion story to **The Resistance Girl Series** you won't want to miss.

DON'T LET THIS OPPORTUNITY SLIP BY – immerse yourself in my WW2 world of resistance, courage, and passion by unlocking

<u>The Partisan Fighter here</u>.

Print: www.hannahbyron.com/newsletter

Warmest regards,

Hannah Byron

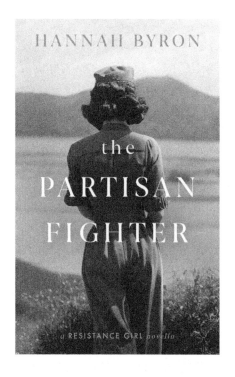

AUTHOR'S NOTE

Dear Reader,

As with every book in *The Resistance Girl Series*, I want to conclude with some notes that I hope you, as a reader, will consider when reading *The Highland Raven*. This is a novel set in a real part of human history (WW2) but built around a set of fictive characters. Real names, dates and places are present, but only if they have become part of our common knowledge about the war—Winston Churchill, Operation Dynamo, Adolf Hitler, SOE, D-Day, to name a few.

All other characters, though sometimes based in parts on heroes and heroines that really lived, are a figment of my imagination.

I have tried—again—to be as accurate as possible, and I do my research, but it is beyond doubt that I make mistakes. I may also deliberately have chosen to divert from actual happenings. In these notes are my most important comments. And feel free to drop me a message at hannah@hannahbyron.com if you have a question or a remark.

Alnor Castle is a fictive castle in Inveraray. The outside is loosely based on Inveraray Castle. The most famous SOE training in Scotland took place at STS21 – Arisaig House, Arisaig, Inverness-shire, which is in the middle of nowhere. It can be visited but is only a basic barracks now.

Lunna House on the Shetlands was the basic training center for the Norwegian Resistance (see also book 4 in the series, *The Norwegian Assassin*). Beaulieu in Hampshire was the so-called "Finishing School" for agents from all nationalities, the place where they got their final instructions and a few days of rest before being sent behind enemy lines.

64 Baker Street in London was where the Headquarters of the Special Operations Executive were established. SOE was Winston Churchill's secret army, which he launched in July 1940 "to set Europe ablaze." Numerous books have been written on this irregular warfare machine, and there is much controversy over what did happen and what didn't happen.

I don't feel it's my place to add more books on the topic, as excellent research material (also from former agents themselves) has been published on SOE. It's just incredibly fascinating and speaks to everyone's imagination.

Personally, I'll dive even deeper into SOE for my final book in *The Resistance Girl Series*, *The London Spymaker*, which has Anna Adams in the leading role. Yes! :-)

Egbert van Eijck's fate is tangled up with what the Germans called "Englandspiel." Fifty-four Dutch SOE agents were killed as the N Section at Baker Street failed to understand the network was infiltrated by the Nazis. This is one of the most gruesome intelligence mistakes made in WW2, but outside the scope of *The Highland Raven*.

And, yes, female agents began to be recruited in 1942 because of the lack of enough males and the ease with which women could blend in in crowds in occupied territory. The fate of F Section female spies has been catalogued intensively and also shows major mistakes being made at Headquarters. I'll go deeper into this in *The London Spymaker*.

As horrific as the stories were of those caught and tortured, there were also many unimaginable escapes that took place. Sable's cruising in the Mercedes with Swastikas upfront through Lyon is loosely based on the story of Robert de La Rochefoucauld, undoubtedly the most daring and flamboyant WW2 spy. He stole a German car. But he did much more. Just reading his Wikipedia page will send your eyebrows to your hairline. It's amazing! *Quel courage!*

The story of Henri de Bonheur, the 'mole' in the system whom Sable kills, is loosely based on the never-convicted double agent Henri Déricourt. If you want to find out more about him, just google his name.

For those familiar with the secret agents' names of those who took part in the guerrilla warfare in France, the names of my characters may have a familiar ring. I have tried to honor the real heroes and heroines by giving them mixed first and last names, the same tactic I used in *The Norwegian Assassin* with Norwegian fighters.

The broadcast of Winston Churchill's announcement of D-Day during Sable's visit to Caen on 6 June is actual. And his full speech can be found here: https://www.nationalchurchillmuseum.org/the-invasion-of-france.html

D-Day was scheduled to take place on 5 June, as Freddie tells Sable, but was postponed by one day due to bad weather.

Further topics of interests for your own research may be:

Or sign up for my Newsletter to be informed when the information booklet on these topics is ready.

I sincerely hope you enjoyed *The Highland Raven*. It's been my absolute pleasure to introduce Major Sable Montgomery to you. May the spirit of the real and illustrious SOE agents live on in this novel.

Sneak Peek Chapter 1 The Crystal Butterfly

49

SNEAK PEEK THE CRYSTAL BUTTERFLY

CHAPTER 1 THE STAGE IS SET

Amsterdam, December 1937

No one can touch the dancer. No one can touch the dancer who may dance till the end. If she may only dance till the end.

In the Royal Theater Carré on the River Amstel in Amsterdam the stage smelled of floor polish, of perfumed roses and pine needles. The scents mingled with the Philharmonic Orchestra strumming their instruments. A piano scale, its highest tones evaporating towards the ceiling; a wailing violin stroke tugging at the heart, the brassy dominance of the trombone drowning in the hum of voices from the audience.

Sounds and smells filled the ringed theatre to the nook and yet, at intervals, there was a moment of silence, as of bated breath. As if more was at stake than a ballet performance at the "Stone Circus of Carré" in the middle of Amsterdam's throbbing heart. As if time itself wondered about the breadth of human capacity, both for the good *and* the bad. On either side of the closed curtains all senses were heightened for the Nutcracker tale to unfold.

In the middle of the stage stood a towering Christmas tree decorated with lights and tinsels. Larry, the floor manager, stood balancing on top of a portable ladder to secure the red tree topper. It was to be his finishing touch. He'd been at it all afternoon, setting up the stage props for a dazzling Christmas Eve at the Stahlbaum house.

As Larry descended from the ladder to take a step back and admire his work, he was smiling to himself. Giving the magnificent tree a last glance, he anticipated the joy his work would bring to the dancers and the audience.

Suddenly, he heard a loud crash, followed by a lull in the voices on the other side of the curtain. The tree had fallen over and was lying on its side. Rather pathetically. Larry rushed over to take stock of the damage and saw to his relief only the red tree topper had come loose. Tiny pieces of glass lay shattered over the stage floor as drops of candescent red blood. He quickly brushed up the pieces, pricking his fingers in his haste. With no time to waste, he worked the tree up to its full height again.

Sweating and cursing under his breath, he secured the floor-to-ceiling pine with rounds of sisal string. It looked amateurish and, without its red topper, unfinished, but time was up.

The falling tree had ruined Larry's premiere night. To him it was a bad omen. Props didn't topple over when Larry De Jonge was in charge. A knock on the wooden doorpost on his way out begged for no further calamities that night, but the ease was gone from the floor manager's mind.

Backstage - in the corridors - dancers and personnel squeezed past him, everyone in a hurry to get the next task done, an eager expression on their faces.

Tonight was the night. The culmination of months of concentrated efforts to bring Tchaikovsky's Nutcracker to the Royal Carré stage. Rumour had it that even Queen Wilhelmina may attend the performance, accompanied by the young Princess Juliana. Everyone had to give it their very best. Now. *Tout de suite!*

Premiere night. It was as much a triumph for the dancers and choreographers, as it was for the floor manager, the ticket sellers, and the girls in the concession stands.

In one of the tiny dressing rooms, her dark hair lit up by a single lightbulb hanging over the oval mirror, Eddaline Van der Valk sat staring at her own reflection. Delicate, ringless fingers rested entwined in her lap. Her posture, straight as Cupid's arrow, was erect, motionless. Not even the long lashes around the smoky black eyes batted once.

Edda was in her head, repeating the first tones of the Miniature Overture over and over, as she rehearsed her stage entrance as Clara. Prepping herself to portray the excitement about the Christmas party, the festive gathering of presents and guests.

All responsibility to set the exact right tone for the opening scene lay on Edda's slender shoulders. The stress sent tumultuous thoughts through her head while not a muscle in her body twitched. How to throw a party when one's riddled by nerves?

How?

By being still.

The dark-brown hair, usually curly and unruly, was bound tightly on top of her well-formed cranium, jutting out the pronounced cheekbones even more. Tight as tight can be. In contrast her makeup was soft and dreamy. Just a light touch of rouge and a dash of eyeshadow to portray young girl Clara.

Edda's bosom, as flat as that of a thirteen-year-old, heaved slightly above the white satin top, exposing the powdered skin of her chest, the elegant collarbones, the swan-like slender neck.

The polish, the poise, the prospect, it revealed nothing of Edda's inner state. Only a trained eye would have spotted the slight clench of the jaw, the tensing of fingers into fists. Edda was eaten by nerves but controlled her inner state as she was used to control her ankle, or the movement of her arm.

Control.

Tonight was *her* night. All she'd dreamed of since the age of five. Tonight she would shine. Despite the nerves. Tonight she would shine.

She took in a deep breath and then slowly puffed out, releasing the air first from her belly, then from her chest. Who controls the breath, controls the body. That was the drill.

After two more full breaths she closed her eyes. It was time to let the music in her head go. Time for the moment of emptiness as Miss Sterling had taught her.

"It's not *your* music, it's not *your* dance. If you hold on too tight, the magic will escape you."

Mystical words Edda wasn't sure she fully grasped. The ballet mistress was a repository of proverbs, like the Delphi oracle, deep and wise, and infinitely puzzling. *Empty yourself of yourself*, was another saying now flitting through Edda's mind. How on earth did one empty oneself from oneself?

Edda couldn't. With her eyes closed, softly breathing, her body was still dancing in her head. The music wrapped around her like a gossamer veil. She was floating, then *en pointe*, then on full feet, with seamless grace and ease. As she closed her solo in a whirl of pirouettes and petticoats, her arms like slender branches reaching for the sky, the crowd erupted in applause. It was done. Her dream fulfilled, flawless and phenomenal. Nerves were now but a distant memory. *Ahhhhh!*

A brief rap on the door shook Edda from her dream. Quickly opening her eyes, she saw in the mirror how the ballet mistress, Marlene Sterling, leaned her elegant frame against the doorpost, a pink cashmere cardigan draped loosely over her shoulders. She was tapping her Cartier tank watch.

"I'm coming."

Leaping from the stool with an apology on her mask-like face, Edda brushed past her teacher into the chilly hall. The sudden cold after sitting close to the electric heater in the dressing room, stirred the goosebumps on her bare arms. Clenching jaws to prevent her teeth from clattering and with a stomach that made uncontrollable somersaults, Edda stumbled forward in the direction of the stage, far less graceful than expected from a prima ballerina. Until the British voice of her teacher called her to an abrupt halt.

"No need to rush, Edda. Always look where you place your feet.

We can't have you injuring yourself now. Come, let's have a little chat before the show begins. In my office."

"Oh?"

Edda turned on her ballet flats, the gauze tutu swirling around her muscled upper legs, the dark eyes filled with confusion. "I'm sorry I misunderstood you, Miss Sterling."

"We're having a sudden attack of the screaming meemies, aren't we?"

Miss Sterling, a recently retired but dyed-in-the-wool ballerina in her forties, seemed to read Edda like the palm of her hand. Edda stood gazing at her mentor, fidgeting fingers knitted together in front of her rebellious belly.

"I guess so. I thought I'd forgotten the time."

Miss Sterling smiled. She always smiled, benign, beguiling, rather byzantine. Edda thought there wasn't a creature more graceful and sophisticated than Miss Marlene Sterling. But also no one as unfathomable. A showgirl exterior with the soul of a mystic.

A mass of lush sandy curls invariably held under control by a colorful bandana, liquid eyes the color of molten honey and clothes that breathed Coco Chanel or Madame Isobel, the famous British designer. Just one of Miss Sterling's many society friends.

She whipped up fear and fascination in Edda, beyond that perpetual smile. Yet Miss Sterling had, without fail, been patient and encouraging towards 'her star pupil'.

Edda followed the ballet mistress's elegant back towards her office that was near the entrance to the stage. The office was another enigmatic thing about Miss Sterling. The 3 by 3 metres square space was hardly bigger than the dancers' dressing room and filled to the brim with theatrical props and a clothes rack. As if Miss Sterling's life could not be contained by a life in an office.

With difficulty it held a tiny desk and three stools crammed in a corner, also laden with attributes for the show. Miss Sterling's expensive mink coat and Chanel handbag hung almost forlorn among the theatrical props but still managed to shine a light of their own. Like their owner.

"My life's on stage, not crammed in this office," was what Edda had heard the ballet mistress retort to Monsieur Grimond. The Carré director had clearly been appalled that the famous Marlene Sterling would be sharing a miniscule dressing room with her dancers when she could have had a spacious office on the ground floor.

"Come on in, Edda." Miss Sterling pushed the door open and cleared a stool for her pupil. "Sit."

She remained standing herself as Edda perched on the edge of the wooden stool. The liquid brown eyes took her in with unusual sternness though the red lips held their invariable smile.

"Are you ready?"

"Are you doubting me, Miss Sterling?"

"Always, my dear. The day I don't have doubts anymore will be the day I die. But that's not it." Not hearing that last sentence, Edda bit her lip.

"But we went through all the moves, over and over. I know all my steps by heart." If her mentor was having doubts now, Edda was in serious trouble. Panic set in, real panic. The ballet mistress waved a beringed hand.

"It's not that. I have no doubts about your preparation, Edda. I don't have any doubt you'll portray a decent Clara, a very decent Clara. Your dance is your forte, my dear."

"Then what is it, Miss Sterling?"

"It's not you. It's her!" Tapered red nails pointed to the door. Edda was surprised to see Maria Petrova saunter into Miss Sterling's office.

Chapter 2
All Life's a Stage

"*Vous m'avez appelée*, Mademoiselle Sterling?"

"Yes, I called for you, Mademoiselle Maria. Come in for a moment. I'll be quick." The voice was terse.

"Mais..."

"No buts. Not this time." Miss Sterling's voice had an unusually sharp ring. Edda wondered what was going on. Maria's presence further unsettled her already tense nerves.

Whenever she could, Edda avoided the tall, willowy dancer with her heavy accented Russian French. She was overbearing and loud, though a sensational dancer. Petrova was said to have fled the Soviet Union because she got in some sort of trouble with the Kremlin. Edda didn't know what that was. It was all rather hush-hush.

What was certain was that Maria Petrova had been one of the Bolshoi Theater's top ballerinas before arriving in Amsterdam through Monsieur Sergevey, Miss Sterling's partner. But La Petrova made it no secret Amsterdam was just a stopover for a career with The London Ballet.

The Russian moved as a flower in full bloom swaying softly in the light breeze, gazelle-like, graceful legs in soft-pink tights. *Pura eleganza. Magnifica!* That's how Miss Sterling typified Maria Petrova's gait, reverting to Italian when she found the English language lacking in superlatives.

So why were they both called to Miss Sterling's office when the ballet mistress clearly thought highly of both her star dancers? There was an uncomfortable moment in the fit-to-burst office in which no one spoke. As if the ballet mistress held them both on a string to see them squirm. But surely, Miss Sterling was anything but a limb of Satan.

"It's something you said to me yesterday, Mademoiselle Petrova." Miss Sterling's upper-class voice had a hesitance that made Edda even more on edge. The ballet mistress didn't do diffidence. Maria looked unperturbed. She just slightly inclined her finely pencilled face with the bronze cropped hair, widening the light-gray eyes just a tad to feign surprise. She said nothing but the concealed smile on her painted lips showed she knew what was to come and that it was to her satisfaction. Miss Sterling turned to Edda.

"I had no time to discuss this with you girls earlier – as I should have. Mademoiselle Petrova deemed it necessary to stay out late in Hotel Americain, and only returned after breakfast, which forces me to give her a warning now, so very close before the show. Sorry Edda but you need to hear this."

Edda straightened her back, alarmed. 'Mademoiselling' Maria meant Miss Sterling was upset, or angry. Which she seldom was. Dancers were called by their first names, or 'my dear.' Flitting the dark eyes from her mentor to the Russian, Edda tried to understand why she acted so strange. Maria's attitude was more on guard now, her nostrils flaring as a horse sensing danger.

Miss Sterling's voice dropped low, little more than a whisper. Everyone in the ballet ensemble knew what this meant. *Better listen up. This will only be said once.* Maria shifted her weight from one slender foot to the other. Edda sat perched on her stool.

Miss Sterling pointed the painted nail first to Edda and then to Maria, saying sotto voce, "*You* are Clara, and *you* are Sugar Plum."

Edda frowned. No news there, unless...

"I only told Monsieur Sergeyev that I *could* dance Clara, Madame. I've danced her many times in St. Petersburg and Moscow. With great success."

Edda held her breath. So, this was what it was about. Maria wanted her part, wasn't satisfied playing second fiddle. Miss Sterling rose to her full length, which was almost as tall as Maria. The red-tipped finger went up, in the direction of the ceiling and then started wagging left to right, like a metronome.

"You are warned, Mademoiselle Petrova. No games. Dance Sugar Plum as if it is your last dance on earth. Now out, as I talk to Edda."

"Don't off bite my head. I meant nothing by it." Maria gave Edda a dirty look, as if she was a pile of unwashed dishes blocking her work-top. Then turned her back on them.

An instinctual reader of bodies – it came with being a dancer - Edda saw how the Russian's shoulders on her proud back just sagged a fragment. Not defeated but spoken to in a way Mademoiselle Petrova didn't approve of. She mumbled an angry "à tantôt" and Miss Sterling replied with a breezy, "yes prepare yourself, Maria. You'll do fine. Please, close the door behind you."

The ballet mistress blew out a long breath through her teeth.

"I think that will do it, Edda. We all know how headstrong, and - let's say – at times bad-tempered Maria Petrova can be but she's the best of the best when it comes to dancing the Nutcracker. I understand she'd preferred to dance Clara to Sugarplum but..." Miss Sterling paused. Edda thought there was that hesitation again in her mentor's eyes and her breath stuck in her throat. *She wasn't first choice for Clara?*

"I wanted this for you." There it was. Not said in so many words but implied. All feathers had been ruffled since the arrival of Maria Petrova two months earlier. She was a league above them all.

"Oh, I see." Tears started pricking behind Edda's eyes. Her shoulders slumped more than a fragment.

"No. I'm not explaining myself here." Miss Sterling tapped her fingers together for a moment, mincing her words, then continued in a rapid voice, "Let me be crystal clear with you, Edda, so you get the full picture. You were to dance Clara from the beginning. We trained you for that and Monsieur Sergeyev and I were in complete agreement about it. You were ready. You *are* ready."

"But Maria's arrival made you reconsider?"

Miss Sterling shook her head. "Not me, Pyo... Monsieur Sergeyev put the suggestion in my head, but I said a firm 'no' right from the start. You see, we'd never expected Maria Petrova to stop over in Amsterdam. Apparently, she has a boyfriend of some sort here, some German count, don't ask me about it. She would dance a lot better and more focused if she wasn't in love."

Edda felt her heart sink further. Monsieur Sergeyev, himself one of the star dancers in his role as Drosselmeyer, had been her other prop and stay within the company. And now he doubted her performance?

Miss Sterling continued as if reading her thoughts, "it's not what you think, my dear, Monsieur Sergeyev has complete confidence in your Clara. He was just worried for our position in the international dance world. That we were giving one of the world's leading ballerinas a secondary role. I told him straight up that it is my goal to give new talent a chance and he agreed wholeheartedly. But Maria must somehow have gotten wind of our conversation, or she just tried her luck, Monsieur Sergeyev being a fellow Russian. That's all there is to it."

"Oh." Edda didn't know whether to be relieved or not.

"I called Maria in here to make sure she understood where she stands. I think she does so now. Let's leave at that and continue to our pep talk. I can see in your eyes that you need a little boost after this hubble-bubble."

Minutes later Edda left Miss Sterling's office with much more confidence. Ten minutes left for the show to start. She had to hurry.

"Hey!" A hand grabbed her wrist from behind. Edda spun on her heels quicker than lightning to look into the eyes of Maria Petrova.

PREORDER *The Crystal Butterfly* now

ABOUT THE AUTHOR

Hannah Byron's crib stood near the Seine in Paris, but she was raised in the south of Holland by Anglo-Dutch parents. In her bestselling WW2 historical fiction series, *The Resistance Girl Series*, Hannah's heroines also traipse from one European country to the next, very much like their creator.

Now a retired university lecturer and translator, the European traveler and avid researcher still regularly crosses borders to learn about new vistas.

What started as curiosity about her family's connection to D-Day grew into an out-of-controlish study into WW2 history. To blame, or thank, must be Uncle Tom Naylor. If he'd not landed on the beaches of Normandy and helped liberate Holland, her British mother would never have met her Dutch Dad after the war.

Strong women are at the core of Byron's clean and wholesome romance novels. Every book is a tribute to the generation that started the women's lib movement, got dirty in overalls, flew planes, and did intelligence work. Today's girl bosses can but stand on the shoulders of these amazons.

Side-by-side with their male counterparts, Byron's heroines fight for freedom, equality and... love.

As **Hannah Ivory,** she writes Historical Mysteries. *The Mrs Imogene Lynch Series* stars the kind but opinionated Victorian widow of Constable Thaddeus Lynch.

ALSO BY HANNAH BYRON
HISTORICAL FICTION

The Resistance Girl Series

In Picardy's Fields

The Diamond Courier

The Parisian Spy

The Norwegian Assassin

The Highland Raven

The Crystal Butterfly (preorder)

The Agnès Duet (spin-off)

Miss Agnes

Doctor Agnes

HANNAH IVORY

Historical Mysteries

The Mrs Imogene Lynch Series

The Unsolved Case of the Secret Christmas Baby

The Peculiar Vanishing Act of Mr Ralph Herriot (preorder)

Printed in Great Britain
by Amazon

57758321R00263